# HOUSE
## OF
# ECLIPSES

## CASEY L. BOND

capture his heart
steal his crown

# PRAİSE FOR HOUSE OF ECLİPSES

"Stunning world-building, a fierce heroine, gorgeous writing, and a storyline unlike anything you've ever read. House of Eclipses will pull you in until the very last page."
*~Celia McMahon, author of The Unspoken Series*

"A gorgeous journey you'll want to take again and again."
*~New York Times bestselling author, Wendy Higgins*

"House of Eclipses is full of compelling characters, beautiful worlds full of whimsy and wonder, an edge-of-your-seat storyline, a love story for the ages, and an ending that packs in incredible punch."
*~Ethan Gregory, One Guy's Guide to Good Reads*

# ALSO BY CASEY L. BOND

When Wishes Bleed
The Omen of Stones
Gravebriar
With Shield and Ink and Bone
Things That Should Stay Buried
Glamour of Midnight

*The Fairy Tales*
Riches to Rags
Savage Beauty
Unlocked
Brutal Curse

*The High Stakes Saga*
High Stakes
High Seas
High Society
High Noon
High Treason

To Melissa Stevens,

A brilliant, beautiful light in the book community, an inspiration, and a dear friend.

# 1

Father's fiery temper was as brutal and constant as the never-setting sun, as was his seething hatred of me, his third born child and the daughter of the only woman to reduce his heart to a cinder.

His dark eyes shone with wrath as he stood fuming in front of me. I wondered if he saw more than just my mother's features when he looked upon my face. Did he see her defiance as well?

I was through watching even the priests fearfully hold him in high esteem. A murderer.

Rage exploded over him.

His face mottled, his lips trembling as he struck me.

The loud crack startled the gentle priests as the back of his hand met my lips. Their chants fell silent for a few heartbeats until their fear urged them to begin again. They raised their voices in unison, singing a particularly pleasant hymn to Sol. Urging her to turn her eye and her great, burning power upon us for a time. As stinging pain burst over my mouth and nose, I wondered what Sol truly thought of her Aten, if *she* might be ashamed of his actions, or if she relished my humiliation as much as he.

Tears flooded my eyes, but I cradled them tightly and refused to let them fall, begging Sol to turn them to vapor before they could spill as Father waited to see which was stronger: the pain he'd inflicted, or my will.

My will would always win our battles, and one day – *one day* – I vowed to win the war raging between us.

Fighting the urge to pinch my lips together to assess the damage, I kept perfectly still. Unwavering, like Sol herself. And like the goddess, I burned too.

Shoulders back, my spine straight as an arrow, I faced him. Even as the taste of blood filled my mouth, as a rivulet slowly slid down my chin and dripped onto the hot stone between my bare feet. I never blinked. Never looked away. Never shrank.

"You are so much like *her*," he hissed. "And if I have my way, you will share her fate."

He raised his hand again as if to strike me a second time. This time I braced myself mentally and physically, turning every muscle in my body, even those in my face, to stone. Like the great statue of Sol rising next to us, her great arms stretched toward the orb of light that warmed us and gave life to our people, powerful enough to cast only the smallest of shadows at her base.

Everything in me screamed to fight back, to finally defend myself, but I knew if I struck the Aten, if I so much as blocked his assault, not even Sol's priests could save me. Their chants would flow over me as my body lay on the altar of incineration next to Joba.

Joba – Father's eighth wife – lay on her back on a slab of glistening marble. Dead like the seven who came before her. Like my mother.

She lay in my periphery, just over Father's shoulder. I had studied her enough in the hours since her departure from this life to know exactly how she looked.

The priests' song was lovely and serene as they continued in their duty, trying their best to ignore, or possibly diffuse, what was transpiring between the Aten and his daughter, their seven voices raising Joba's spirit from its home within her bones as the afternoon sun blistered her once-beautiful skin.

I wondered if she had despised looking in the mirror, for it was her beauty that caught his eye. I wondered if her soul hovered above us all, reveling in the fact that her lovely face was being destroyed.

In death, Joba looked more at peace than I'd ever seen her in life. Long, dark lashes fanned her cheeks. Her silken ebony hair shone on the pillow tucked beneath her head. One of the priests had delicately folded her hands over her stomach.

She was barely older than I am now when she was plucked from the beginning of what promised to be a beautiful life and forced into one she hated. At the time, she was betrothed to a man she loved and who loved her in return. My father was invited to attend the betrothal ceremony. He took one look at the bride-to-be and decided she was a jewel he needed to place in his treasury. He accused her intended of treason and had him put to death, right among the feast and flowers splayed to honor the happy, new wedded couple, before stealing her away as his own.

When her womb lay barren after a year and she had not produced the male heir for whom he had always longed, he found her dead in his bed – just as he had the seven wives before her. Not even the priests dared question the Aten about the marks emblazoned on her throat.

Each of Joba's thin fingers held an intricate golden ring and layers of gilded necklaces were heaped on her unmoving chest. The cuff Father had commissioned for each of his wives was still clamped around her bicep, marking her as his even in death.

But she wasn't his anymore, was she?

Death offered Joba a chance to get away from him, and though she lay burning, she seemed to revel in the distance between them now, a distance even the powerful Aten could not traverse.

Did I imagine the teasing smirk on her lips?

Through my blood, could he see that I wore one to match?

Droplets gathered and built, then fell from my chin.

Splash. Splash-splash. And then the sizzles of steam came as Sol took the water in my lifeblood as her own.

Father's dark eyes narrowed before he slowly lowered his hand, as if he was still considering the second strike or something far worse. Sol's rays glistened off his shaved head. A second later, he turned his back to me, walked to Joba, and hovered over her. He raised his hands high into the air before calling on Sol. The air vibrated with a ripple of arid, brutal heat. He brought her closer and concentrated the sweltering rays onto Joba's body. Her blistered skin began to bubble and boil. Char marks appeared on her clavicles, on the sharp angles of her cheek bones and jaw, just before the first elegant flames appeared.

They slowly danced over her. As the priests' cadence changed and the men rocked back and forth on their knees, all seven crying out to the goddess, the flames followed the harried, feverish rhythm and soon an inferno roared over Joba, consuming her just as Father had. She became brittle, quickly shrinking to nothing more than a nondescript heap of ash and chips of bone.

Sol accepted only the good parts of a person – their heart if it was clean, their soul if it was still made of light, their flesh and the organs that gave the body life if they were undiseased. Only that which she found unacceptable remained for us to scatter over the sand from which she formed us.

I wondered if her flames would accept any part of Father's body when *he* lay dead beneath her, or if we would bury him whole – all of him lacking. All of him foul.

I wondered the same of myself.

Father did not stay to watch the priests scoop and sweep Joba's remains into the sleek golden urn. He would not be the one to spread her ashes in the dunes. His dark eyes met mine as he started toward us, his three daughters.

Zarina, his first born, held her head high and always kept quiet in his presence. Father believed Sol would choose her as her heir. But if she was part of Sol at all, I couldn't feel a hint of warmth from her. She was tall and lithe and beautiful enough, but Zarina was made of pure ice and was as frigid as she was aloof.

Father nodded his approval as he passed her. He then focused on Citali, who stood between Zarina and I, missing the curt bow Zarina thoughtlessly pressed.

Citali hated me almost as much as I hated her. One year my elder, she believed my mother was the reason the Aten had killed hers. Citali was a fool, always blaming the women, never our father, for the constant death in our lives.

Citali was not statuesque like Zarina. She stood almost a head shorter than me and was very thin. Her delicate features shrouded her harsh, greedy heart from most people, but I knew her best. Her eyes often screamed, even when her lips remained sealed. They were the a dark brown with hints of shadowy gray and sharp as shards of glass. They cut to me, a smile playing on her uninjured, perfectly bowed lips.

Father nodded to her and she bowed deeply, lowering herself beyond what custom required. Citali *always* went beyond. From instances like these when she tried desperately to capture Father's attention, to her countless attempts to kill Zarina and me.

*Always beyond…*

Father paused in front of me. My gaze fell on his broad, beaded collar necklace, blue and green and gold. He tipped my chin up, snapping my jaw against my tongue. My eyes darted to his. "Since you interrupted Joba's departure, you will be tasked with carrying her back to the sand," he said, waiting to see if I would react.

Again, my will was stronger than his.

A muscle ticked in his jaw as he took me in, his thin upper lip curling in disgust. He walked away, two of his eldest priests struggling to keep up with his anger-fueled stride. The muscles in his shoulders and back flared with every step and the hot wind blew his pleated white kilt sideways as if to push him off the temple's flat top the way I fantasized doing.

The men disappeared when they descended the great staircase that trickled down to the stone street that led to the House of the Sun – a palace that had once been my home, a safe place where I was loved and wanted, but now was little more than a prison.

Zarina quietly trailed away, her head up and shoulders back. She followed Father's footsteps but wisely kept her distance from him. Citali watched the remaining priests finish the task of sweeping what was left of Joba into the large, golden jar. Then one capped the jar with a lid and hefted the monstrosity as Sol's rays reflected off its perfect, polished surface.

"Enjoy your time in the dunes, sister," Citali taunted. "You'll join the sand soon enough."

I glared. "And what about you? When Zarina is chosen by Sol, what do you think will become of you, Citali? He'll have no use for you then."

She brushed her long, dark hair off her shoulder and crossed her arms. "Father has no reason to kill me. I never provoke him."

"No, perhaps you're right. Perhaps he'll sell you to the highest bidder instead."

She narrowed her shadowy eyes. I was right and she knew it. Father did not love his daughters. Father loved nothing but himself and the power that being the Aten afforded him.

It wouldn't surprise me if he killed all three of us just to keep Sol from choosing one to secede him as Aten. I believed the only thing that had kept him from doing just that was that deep inside, he feared the goddess's wrath.

Citali left me and followed Zarina, their pristine gowns rapping in the fierce wind as they made their way down the temple steps, across the paved stones and into the House. The head of Father's guard lingered at the bottom. He fell into step with Citali with the intention of seeing my sisters home. He knew better than to wait for me to join them.

Father made it seem like the only reason I would carry Joba was because I had earned the punishment today, but there was never any question which of his daughters would be given the task of carrying Joba back to the sand. At seven, I carried my mother's jar into the dunes, and I'd carried every jar since hers. That of his fourth, fifth, sixth, and seventh wives, all dead.

All murdered by his hands.

None able – or perhaps, willing – to produce for him an heir.

Father thought giving me such a macabre chore was a punishment, but I considered it a great privilege and honor to bear the ash and bone of the women who hated him. For they were my kindred.

8

# 2

The sweltering heat that had pressed down upon us slowly lifted. Once nothing remained on the stone where Joba had lain and a quiet prayer to Sol was spoken, all but one of the priests silently disappeared into the temple as Sol lifted herself higher into the sky, reclaiming her place in the heavens.

Perhaps the goddess was offering a reprieve, leaving *him* as the priest chosen to escort me into the sand.

Kiran was my friend.

If anyone knew, even his station and the privileges and rights that came with it couldn't save him from Father's wrath, but Kiran refused to abandon me as he should. And I was too weak to refuse his kindness and support.

His long hair was pulled back and neatly tied at his nape. He stood, carrying the heavy urn, patiently waiting for me as any of the priests would have done. I moved toward him and his eyes tracked mine, but neither of us dared speak. Not here.

The muscle in his jaw clenched as he took in my lip and the now-dried blood on my chin. Other than that tiny tell, he didn't give us away. He pretended to be the benevolent, gentle priest everyone expected.

In truth, Kiran was the only priest I worried might one day rebuke the Aten. The day he did would be his last. I'd told him that many times. I would not be able to survive this life without him. I told him that, too, refusing to hold anything back in the few stolen moments we were able to speak. Moments that were becoming rarer the older my sisters and I became. My obligations as Atena and his as priest kept multiplying, greedily consuming our free hours as we rose into adulthood.

I took the heavy, hot urn from his hands, noting how his palms had blistered from touching it. The heat did not harm the priests for long. He would heal before we reached the bottom step. But Sol did not spare them from the temporary pain and effects of her heat. The priests were chosen by Sol, but I wasn't sure how she indicated them to the others in their order. There were many secrets Kiran could not reveal to me. His oath was to Sol alone.

Down the center of each of the temple's four sides ran a broad staircase. Kiran followed me down the temple's steps opposite the ones my family had taken, ones that drifted away from my home. The staircase we took did not lead to a stone pathway, or into the city. When our feet left the carved stone, they found nothing but burnt orange sand, stretching far into the desert as far as the eye could see. Swells of dunes rose here like charred waves of the seas that used to grace these nearby lands. Seas that only churned in tomes now.

Had Sol hated the oceans so much that she burned them into the red sands upon which we built our home?

I paused as Kiran stopped on the bottom step and deftly wrapped his feet in pale strips of cloth. If he waded into the dunes barefoot, his feet would blister so badly I'd have to carry him back. While I wasn't a waif of a girl, I wasn't strong enough to lift Kiran for any time or distance that would truly help him.

He was a few inches taller than I, his skin the familiar deep olive tone all Helioans shared. His hair was the common shade of dark brown that bordered on black, and his face was cleanly-shaven. His lips pressed into a thin line as he concentrated on his task.

Kiran wore a golden kilt in honor of Sol. All the priests did. And they did not adorn themselves as Father did, and as he insisted we do. The only gold he wore was a cuff on his bicep, forged by Sol herself and given to him when he accepted her call and took his vows. Father had stolen the idea for his brides. I wondered if he thought himself as important as the goddess herself.

I tried to ignore the way his body had changed in the past year or so. The way he'd gone from boy to man. Priests were not to be ogled. But even though I knew that, and even though it was a slippery slope, for just a moment, my thoughts strayed down the path of what might have been if Sol had passed him over and chosen my sister as her Aten...

I quickly reined them in. *It wouldn't have mattered,* I told myself. Kiran was strong. If Sol hadn't chosen him, he would've been sent into the guard and I would never see or hear from him again.

Besides, if Father would kill him or use him against me for being a friend, what would he do if Kiran and I became more? It wasn't worth it. I needed to thank Sol for keeping him in my life in this way and not covet more.

Kiran straightened, satisfied with the way his feet were thickly bound. We didn't speak as I led him into the sand, our feet barely making prints as the grains spread thinly over the bedrock lain for Sol's temple foundation.

Soon, though... it thickened. Our feet sank deep into the orange-red grains and we struggled into the dunes, climbing up their unsteady sides to the tops where it was easier to walk.

Their crests were hardened; our feet punched holes in the crusty layer scorched on top of the towering waves of sand.

The winds that tore at my family's clothes and the priest's kilts as they left the temple, now clawed at us.

When we were far from the temple and wholly swallowed by the desert, Kiran finally spoke. "Are you okay?"

My lip was sore. "Of course I am." I adjusted the urn to hold it with one hand, balancing its weight on my hip as I walked, then pressed a few fingers to my mouth to assess the damage.

"You shouldn't have spoken to him so boldly," he said softly.

I speared him with a glare. He knew better than to blame me for Father's actions. I'd told him enough times what I thought about Citali doing that.

Kiran raised his palms to me. "I'm not defending him, Noor. I'm hoping to protect you, or more importantly, encourage you to protect yourself. I wish there was something I could do to free you of him for good," he lamented.

We both knew there was nothing to be done. The only way I would be free of Father was when he or I departed this world for the next.

"He threatened to kill you today, in front of all of us. He's never done that before. I fear you've pushed him too far this time." Kiran held his hands out as if he wanted to relieve me of the weight of the urn, willing to scorch his palms to help, but I wouldn't have it. He rolled his eyes at my stubbornness. "Noor," he said, staring at the urn. His eyes flicked to mine. "What if he had tried to?"

"If I thought my life was in danger, I would have no choice but to fight back." Father knew I would, too. Perhaps he hoped to provoke me to anger so he could rid himself of me.

"Then I would have no other choice than to fight alongside you," he said resolutely, lifting his eyes to Sol as if apologizing for the truth that left his lips. Sol already knew. She knew our hearts, minds, and souls. The good and the bad.

"I don't want you to ever do that," I told him, meaning every word. "Remember your oath, Kiran. You are a priest and your duty is to Sol alone, not to the Aten, and certainly not to any of his Atenas. You owe me nothing."

"That's not true," he weakly protested before closing his eyes and taking a deep, cleansing breath.

When his eyes refocused on me, the sandstorm in them had settled and relief washed over me. Their hue was so familiar. Sol had scooped up the very orange-red sand beneath our feet and sifted it into Kiran's eyes, along with the warmth the sand held within.

Those red-orange beacons lit with the orneriness I remembered, but rarely saw now. "As you *are* still among the living, I should tell you that the look on his face when you remarked on the burst vessels in Joba's eyes was worth all the gold in Helios."

I tried to smile, but the weight behind that comment settled over me.

The whites of my mother's eyes had burst with red, too. A sight that still haunted me to this day. Some days, they were all I could see when I closed my eyes to sleep.

For years, I wondered why they looked like that. I stopped wondering when I learned what had caused the effect. Once, when I became ill, I asked my healer what would incite such trauma and he, albeit uncomfortably, told me that when a person's breath was cut off and pressure built in the head and face, vessels often burst.

I asked him what else might cause it, but he had no other answer. That was the only one.

Today, I snapped. I couldn't take another departure without uttering the words to insinuate publicly what everyone privately knew, to make sure Sol heard me atop her temple, among her priests, beside her Aten. Every word I'd spoken was retribution for every second he held her throat and refused to let go – until the light bled from her golden eyes. Eyes that matched mine.

I wanted the priests to know that their suspicions were right; the sort of man they bowed to, the man standing before them, was unworthy of Sol's blessing. And I wanted Father to know that I would one day carve out the cinder she'd left behind in him and finish what she started before he ended her life – or die trying.

The latter might be true sooner rather than later. Father would not let this transgression slip from his mighty, crushing hands.

A comfortable warmth settled into my chest as the memory of his surprised, horrified expression resurfaced. Kiran was right. It was a sight worth all the gold in Helios.

I looked to the great burning disc overhead and wondered why she hadn't burned him away with Joba, why she didn't punish him for killing the other women.

*Why?*

Perhaps Sol kept the priests from stripping him of the title and duties of Aten. Perhaps the goddess admired the dark opposite of her flame, the alluring shadow that even she could not penetrate that lay in the bony pit where Father's cinder heart lay.

Surely Father did not hold power over the goddess who chose him.

Without another word, I led Kiran further into the dunes to the place where I had carried all the others. As we drew near, the wind died away. Even Kiran's breathing quieted. He paused and waited for me to complete my task.

Sol's burning corona could almost be heard flaring and calming, only to roar to life again. This was a sacred place. Uniquely undisturbed. The sand was exactly as I'd left it a week ago. Even my footprints remained. I couldn't help but wonder why Sol preserved it for me, when she would not guard me from her Aten. Though I had to thank her for the small mercy of leaving them as I'd arranged them so I could tell my mother apart from the others, so I could sit with her.

No part of Mother was undesirable to me. I had loved her wholly while she was in my life and loved her now just as completely. I missed her with an ache in my heart that even Sol could not assuage or burn away.

Across the highest dune in the sea of sand, my mother's remains led to a line of other women's. Each small pile of ash and bone resembled the vertebrae of a great beast I hoped might one day be resurrected to consume the one who'd cruelly slain it.

I knelt in the grains a respectable distance from Father's seventh wife's remains and removed the lid of Joba's urn, then shook the urn to empty her as Kiran whispered to Sol to commit Joba back to the sand from which she was made.

Kiran was quiet as I walked to my mother and sat beside her in the indented sand that always cradled me. I wondered if she could hear me. If she'd seen what happened and had already moved across the sky to find Joba's light and comfort her, welcoming her into the hereafter.

Kiran fought it, but the burning sand began to hurt his feet. He lifted one foot, then the other, switching back and forth. Before taking up the empty urn, I promised my mother I would be back as soon as I could.

"Let's go before the cloth burns away," I told him.

# 3

Kiran took the golden urn from me at the bottom of the temple steps and dared a whisper, begging me to come to the temple if anything seemed amiss when I returned home. I lied to him just to get him out of the sand. I would never endanger the priests by hiding among them. Besides that, I refused to hide.

It seemed that all that remained of mine and Kiran's friendship was lies I spoke to comfort worries he voiced. Our former relationship, if you could call it that, was preserved like the bits of bone entrenched in the sand.

Pale curtains waved from my window as I approached the House of the Sun, just before ducking inside and walking to my rooms. Servants buzzed about the corridors, ever tending the hive they lived in, careful of the deadly stingers my family brandished.

A petite girl carrying freshly laundered linens stopped and bowed to me as I passed. She kept her eyes averted and folded her spine. I hated it. No person should bow to another.

Our House was cool and inviting and I wanted nothing more than to collapse into a warm pool of water and float for days. The desert heat never drained me, but the heaviness of the day settled into my bones.

That weariness was compounded when I entered my rooms and saw Citali waiting for me on a settee. She'd changed from her pure-white, pleated departure dress into something more her style: a blood-orange skirt and matching top that plumped her small breasts and bared her stomach.

Her legs were crossed and she managed a bored expression, though her impatience simmered below the surface in the way she drummed her fingers on her crossed arms.

Her dark hair lay in waves over her shoulders. She brushed it away when she leaned forward, sending it splaying down her back.

"Father wishes to make an announcement. If you don't hurry and change, you'll be late to the feast he's arranged. After today, you wouldn't want to anger him further." It almost sounded like she cared. Almost… Her eyes slid over me, her lip curling in disgust. "You brought back half the desert on your skin."

*Feast? Why would he arrange for a celebration to directly follow a departure?*

"A new wife?" I asked. He never wasted time filling his bed.

Citali shrugged.

"Why did you wait for me? He could've sent a servant with the request." I narrowed my eyes at her.

"You took forever," she complained.

She wasn't worried about *my* wellbeing, but hers. "You thought Sol had chosen among us?"

"Zarina has not transformed. Neither have I," she admitted with an unapologetic shrug. "I had to be sure."

"I thought you said Sol would never stoop so low as to consider me for the role of Aten."

I moved to the folded screens where someone had hung a pressed gown and stripped out of the departure dress. A basin of fresh water sat on a table beside me. I scrubbed the blood from my chin and cupped water to my lips before wiping down my legs and arms and dragging the ruddy sand away. I dried my face and dove into the mustard yellow gown. It was sleeveless and straight to the ankle, my curved hips stretching the seams a little.

"We are to wear our aureoles."

My eyes locked with hers as I stepped from behind the screens. "You don't know why?"

She shook her head, toying with her aureole lying beside her. I hadn't noticed it before. We only wore the heavy sunburst crowns on occasions of great importance. Not even departures required them. What could Father possibly announce tonight?

Citali could be lying about Zarina. Had Sol chosen her after all? Father expected it at any moment. He had recommended our eldest sister to Sol when she came of age many years ago. When his recommendation was ignored and Zarina seemingly looked over, Father consulted the Sphinx, who warned that Sol would not choose among us until all the Atenas were of age. Citali was eighteen and I would be seventeen in less than two weeks. Perhaps Sol had grown impatient and decided to declare her heir, and the next Aten, now.

Citali stood, plucking her aureole from the settee. I glanced at her shrewdly. "Why did you tell me any of this?"

What was in it for her?

She gave a predatory smile, full of teeth. "Because I am your sister." She lithely moved toward the door, pausing with her hand on the door. "And, because after what you dared say to him earlier, I want to watch when you face him again."

My heart drummed so loudly I wondered if she could hear it and feel the reverberation, but I kept my face stony and my back straight. I would not let her see me squirm. I wouldn't let anyone see my fear.

After a lingering moment, she slid from the room. I locked my door behind her.

Aureole in hand, I made my way down the long corridor, the seamless, polished stone cold underfoot. There was no time to bathe or arrange my hair. I had just enough time to hastily brush it, layer bracelets onto my forearm, slide rings onto my fingers, and clasp chains around my ankles. I raked the pads of my fingers over the sheer fabric layer stretching from breast to stomach, focusing on the faces of the servants bowing as I passed.

*They're emaciated.*

*Their cheekbones are so sharp, I could use them as knives.*

*They're starving, and it's Father's fault.*

*But the Aten and his family never starve. We are lavished upon. We feast.*

The dining hall teemed with people – all finely dressed. How had Father gathered them so quickly after Joba's departure? I paused at the door, watching the wealthy nobility of Helios meander around the room, eating their fill. Watching the servants refill platter after platter, even as their clothing hung from their gaunt frames.

At the Aten's table, my father sat at the head. Zarina sat at his right hand; Citali sat to his left. Their aureoles glistened from the sun rays beaming in from the grand terrace outside. There was an uncommon, pleasantly hot breeze wending through the room, toying with the curtains and the hair of noble women.

Most were draped in gold. Many were giggling from too much drink. Few noticed me, but Father did. His dark eyes fastened on mine the moment I stepped into the room. I raised my chin, placed my aureole onto my head, and strode purposefully into the room.

Many considered me a princess, when I knew I was a queen.

People always noticed the aureole first, then their faces would show surprise. Reverence. Fear. The crowd parted for me as a wave of bows raced across the room. I made my way to the table and took my seat beside Citali, still unsure why we were gathered.

I held my tongue, even as Father smirked in pleasure at the sight of the split in my lip. Servants filled a decadent plate and placed it in front of me along with a goblet of wine. By the rich aroma, it was our finest. My suspicion was confirmed when I swirled the liquid in the golden cup and took a sip.

I sat the goblet down and picked at my plate, never eating a bite nor taking another drink. How could I when my people were starving just outside these polished walls? Not to mention the fact that Father had threatened me. Poisoning me would certainly silence my lips for good.

"This afternoon while you were strolling about in the dunes, Noor, I spoke with the Sphinx," he finally said.

I laid down my fork. The gold clinked against the golden table.

*Strolling around the dunes?*

Gritting my teeth, I struggled to hold my tongue and somehow managed a bored expression. I was curious about his dealings with the Sphinx. "And did she give you a prophecy?"

His brows lifted with his lips. "Indeed she did. A very *fortunate* prophecy."

Father was far too pleased for it to be of anything but my demise.

I looked to Joba's empty chair at the end of the table opposite Father. Yesterday at supper, she'd eaten her last meal with us and none of us were the wiser. I wondered if he planned to kill them, or if a moment of passionate rage consumed him like Sol's fire and his composure broke like the spine of a bird before it was prepared for the dinner table.

The fact that her seat lay empty meant he hadn't taken another wife... I hoped.

The fowl on my plate made my stomach turn. I pushed it away.

"In fact," Father began, "her prophecy was so precise, it began to fall into place the exact moment I stepped out of her lair. Zuul met me with a missive right then."

Zuul, a cold-eyed man built like a stone wall stood behind him. He was head of Father's personal guard for a reason. He was ruthless in the sparring matches Father insisted his men partake in, and fiercely loyal to the Aten. So loyal, he cut out his own brother's tongue when he made a joke about my father. His brother was a laborer now, cutting stone in the oppressive heat until he dragged himself back to his ramshackle shanty each day, or collapsed with exhaustion so that others had to shoulder the burden of dragging him home.

Zuul always hovered near Father, scanning the room for threats I wasn't sure had ever existed. Veins bulged under his shaved scalp and down his forearms; his chest was half as broad as our table.

The crowd, which had gone back to their mingling once I took my seat, parted once more, bowing to Sol's priests as they entered the room single file. The priests were an order, none more important than the rest, as all were valuable to Sol in their own way. With no head or hierarchy, they were equals, each an edge of a connected circle with Sol in its center.

There were no struggles for power within their number; there was no strife or jealousy, envy or hatred. They were a family of servants who wanted nothing more than to please the goddess. As such, when her Aten called for them, they came.

Father stood to greet each priest. They folded themselves in half for him while he barely deigned to incline his head. The priests did not glance upon the Atenas and we did not bow to them. We were to limit all contact with them, per Father's orders.

The last thing he wanted was for the priests to be tempted by one of his daughters. My eyes slid to Citali, then back again. I didn't allow myself even a glance at Kiran.

When all greetings were made, Father asked the priests to seat themselves with us. Kiran took the seat next to Zarina, far enough from me that our eyes would not have to meet. They each accepted plates from our servants, who swarmed in with laden plates of food and drink.

Before any of the men took a bite, they rose their hands and voices, singing a prayer of thanks to Sol for the food. I watched the pinch of Father's mouth when they failed to thank him as well, and instead, began quietly eating their fill.

Beneath the table, Kiran's foot gently pressed down on mine and then withdrew. I sat up straighter, wiped my mouth on a napkin, and sat back to see what would come next. Priests rarely dined with us. They would accept invitations for vital events, so whatever this was, it must be something of great importance.

And if Kiran dared touch me, even if no one else was likely to see... it must be bad.

I examined Zarina, staring until she felt it, and my sister lifted her eyes to mine. Their warm amber hue was unchanged. Her skin was radiant, but it often was. Her golden gown hugged her svelte form even as she sat. As I combed over her features, she studied mine. Zarina didn't know what this was about, either. Sol had not chosen her as Aten – *yet*.

Her eyes narrowed before she looked away to dissect Citali's expression. Both sat up straighter as Father stood.

He struck a fork against his goblet and a sharp ping rang out. "Thank you for coming to the House of the Sun on such a difficult day, a day that was filled with mourning and despair... before Sol intervened on my behalf and on yours."

My fingernails dug into the arms of my chair at the audacity of his words. How quickly he'd finished lamenting Joba's death.

"The Kingdom of Lumina has a new Lumin. He has written to inquire about a negotiation of peace and trade between our people and lands. My personal guard, two of Sol's priests, the two youngest Atenas, and I will travel to the House of Dusk to meet with him. We leave tomorrow, in the first hour."

The room erupted with gasps, lending sound to the feeling crashing through my chest. Some clasped their hands over their chests, whether in worry or hope, I wasn't sure.

When the Great Divide happened, the gods cleaved the earth in two and divided it among their peoples. Sol built Helios in her inherited northern portion, while Lumos created Lumina among his bottom half of the world.

As fiery Sol ruled over our skies, Lumos, god of silver and frost, governed theirs. And like Sol had her Aten, Lumos had his Lumin to represent him. Both Aten and Lumin were endowed with powers, though I'd heard the Lumin's were more fearsome than Father's.

Our kingdoms did not battle one another, but when the Great Divide occurred, contact was severed.

This missive changed everything. I wasn't even sure how the Lumin had managed to deliver it.

The thin strip of dusk lands where neither Sol nor Lumos guarded were uninhabited and considered neutral ground. The people who once lived there had abandoned their homes long ago to move closer to their gods and leaders. But amid the crumbling cities that once lived and thrived stood the House of Dusk, a palace that once was used by both peoples and stood as a house of unity.

According to the history scrolls, before the falling out between Sol and Lumos, there was free trade and travel between our kingdoms and the land was filled with small cities and towns interspersed with countryside and farms. There was comradery between our people. Once, the Aten and Lumin worked together, their gods blissfully sharing the sky. I wondered if such a peace was possible after so much stagnancy, or whether the gods would allow their peoples to strike such a bargain.

Father waited for the initial shock to wear off before continuing.

Zarina fumed because Father was leaving her behind. But why?

Her chest heaved beneath thick, red beads. Zarina preferred the fiery color and only during departures ventured away from the bloody hue. Fury flooded her face until it matched her gown. She glared at Citali, who smiled at her from across the table. Zarina's eyes flashed to mine. I was not smiling.

I suspected what Father was trying to do. If Zarina was left behind, closest to Sol, would the goddess be forced to choose her as heir? Traveling to the dusk lands would take several days, negotiations could take weeks – beyond my seventeenth birthday when all three Atenas would be of age. The Sphinx once told Father that Sol would finally make her choice only when she could choose between us all. That day was fast approaching. But what if Citali and I were removed from Sol, sent to a land where even her light didn't reach?

Citali would not be smirking if she took a moment to consider what Zarina's proximity to the goddess might mean for her.

Then again perhaps I was paranoid, and the Sphinx had instructed Father on who should travel with him to the dusk lands to meet the new Lumin. Perhaps, he had no other choice but to leave one of us behind in his stead. Being the eldest Atena, Zarina would be expected to oversee the city in Father's absence.

He would never leave Citali with such a responsibility, and he would rather die than entrust me with something so vital.

I let my eyes trail over the priests' faces, careful not to stop on any of them. Kiran's expression was pensive – a replica of the others in his order. He was the youngest by many years and the eldest's eyes drifted closed despite the fanfare.

The elderly priest Saric had been charged with escorting me into the sand all those years ago when my mother was taken from me. Once we were free of prying eyes, he carried the heavy urn despite the blistering and pain and advised me to listen to Sol as she led me to the perfect resting place for her. He brushed away my tears before singing over her ash and bones. Then he let me sit with her for a long while, so long his feet were charred when we returned.

I'll never forget his kindness in those terrible moments. It was difficult to see age claim dominion over his bones and body.

Saric's chin drooped; his mouth slowly fell open. His brother gently nudged him awake before Father saw or a snore escaped. The tension filling my ribs eased when he sat up straight and returned his attention to the Aten, who began talking again.

"I cannot make any promises other than to vow to hear what the Lumin might propose for Sol. I will relay the fruits of our negotiations to Sol and the goddess will decide what is acceptable and what *isn't*."

Father's eyes flicked to mine.

Citali beamed hungrily at my side. Zarina still fumed. The priests remained quiet.

"We have much to do to prepare for this journey. Feel free to enjoy the feast as long as you would like or retire early if you're in the traveling party."

The priests wasted little time. Excusing themselves from the table, they bowed to their Aten one by one as they filed away from the table and retraced their steps through the crowd, making their way back to the temple.

I wondered which two priests would go and which priests would stay behind for Sol and to care for her temple, for our people if the need arose. I hoped she wouldn't choose Kiran for the task, and yet, I hoped she did.

If we were traveling together, the temptation to talk to my friend would be too great to bear. He would be safer here.

Father took his seat again, snapping his fingers to indicate that his goblet was empty. A young man swooped in to fill it before reclaiming his place against the wall. Father wore a rare, self-satisfied half-smile, but it fell away when he looked upon Zarina, who still could not hide her rage.

He leaned forward, that unusual smile falling quickly away. "You dare question me, Atena?" he asked, a dangerous taunt in his tone.

"If I am to be Aten, I need to be seen at your side, not left behind," she calmly voiced.

He shook his head. "And what if I tell you that you will not become Aten if you leave Helios for the dusk lands?" He leaned forward, harshly holding her gaze. "I'll hear no more protests about the issue."

"Yes, Father," she quietly answered, her tone still sharp. Her aureole flashed when she turned away from him to face us once more.

Outwardly, the argument was over, but inwardly Zarina's inner fire had not been doused. White hot, it scorched my half-sister. Could everyone sense her disdain, or was it only visible to those who also burned?

# 4

I dressed in a gauzy, royal blue dress embroidered with gold, then tidied my room. There was nothing personal here. Nothing I cared too much to lose or have destroyed. If Father knew I cherished anything, he would have destroyed it already. The bed, wardrobe, and desk might belong to anyone, as might the trunks sitting in the doorway.

At Father's request, servants arrived in pairs to gather the three trunks. One should have been more than enough to suffice, but Father insisted Citali and I bring our best gowns and adornments and to pack heavily, as no one knew how long this diplomatic journey might take.

Glancing out toward the balcony, the red-orange desert stretched as far as I could see, beyond to the rooftops that glistened past the polished temple of Sol. Outside it, my mother lay. I wished I had the luxury to visit her one last time before we left.

Father had positioned guards outside my rooms and Citali's last night as if he thought we might run away. I wouldn't lie and say I didn't consider it. I'd imagined it a thousand times.

A girl no more than twelve came to make sure I didn't need further assistance, bowing as she waited for an answer. "Everything is in order except for the mess beneath my bed. I'd like for *you* to clean it up for me. Do not pass the duty to another," I warned, watching as she withered from my gaze.

She bent lower, averting her eyes. "I'll clean it right away, Atena Noor."

"See that you do."

She hurried to the bedside as I breezed from the room, then made my way through the labyrinthian House.

I'd hidden food from the feast beneath my bed. She could smuggle it outside or hide in my rooms and eat it there, but either way, she would have a good meal for a day. I only wished I could do something about the hunger she would battle tomorrow.

Citali scowled when I joined our traveling party on the riverbank. I was both terrified and relieved to find Kiran waiting with one other priest. Saric, the eldest priest who'd fallen asleep as Father addressed everyone at the feast only hours ago, stood at Kiran's side, patiently waiting. Age had bowed his spine and legs. The graying hair he had when I was a child had thinned through the years. He kept his head shaved now, like Father and many of the men in our kingdom.

Did Sol choose Saric and Kiran for this task or did they volunteer?

Saric's pale brown eyes were as sharp as the wit and wisdom for which he was renowned. He watched as I joined their group.

Kiran did not acknowledge me. He warily looked to the ship bobbing atop the river's surface, his pallor taking on a greenish hue. The last time he sailed, he was sick for days.

Father had gathered far more than the small party he'd mentioned. Half his personal guard were here: fifty men skilled in the art of warfare, protection, and spying. There were servants still moving things onto the ship, but clearly intending to travel with us, as well as a band of entertainers – a group of dancers.

"What is all this?" I asked Citali as I moved to stand with her.

"We are to throw an opening feast. If the river wasn't so shallow, the ship might sink from all the food and wine he's bringing, not to mention the people." She glanced around at the guard, her eyes snagging on some of the men. I wondered if she knew those she targeted, or if new conquests had caught her eye.

Then... her eyes slid to Kiran and she was slow to look away from him.

I gritted my teeth. "The Aten provides a feast. What will the Lumin offer in return?" I asked.

Her eyes reluctantly tore from Kiran and met mine. "They call it a ball. It is a feast the same as ours, per Father."

When the last crate of supplies was carried aboard, Father clapped his hands from the ship's deck and invited everyone on board. Citali and I moved to board the shallow vessel, followed by the eldest priest, Saric, and Kiran. Father's guard spread out to various positions, armed to the teeth with weapons I could see and those I had no doubt were hidden, before the girls he brought to dance and entertain our southern counterparts boarded. Lastly, a small retinue of servants stepped aboard.

The riverfarer awaited Father's command to depart. When he gave it, those in his employ freed the ship from where she was tied at the shore, wound the ropes that bound her, and guided her into the river's middle. The water was disturbingly shallow at the edges, but its middle was more than deep enough to carry us.

I gripped the railing as the ship gathered speed, hot wind catching the white sail overhead as it proudly puffed its chest and dragged us over the blue water.

In the shallows, women washed and wrung clothes while children splashed close by. Here and there the thick, bony

31

armor of crocodiles hovered at the river's surface. They drifted out of the way of the ship, steering with their strong tails.

The banks changed with the receding water, but remnants of the river's past greatness could be seen where the earth had dried like scaled skin. The soil was darker closest to the river's edge, lightening little by little the further away one walked from the life-giving flow.

Sol remained high. Her heat mixed with the moisture in the air and I knew in my bones I would miss her, and Helios.

I took a position at the ship's side next to a few crates, leaning on the rail and watching as we smoothly slipped by our kingdom. I smiled when groups of children ran to the river just to wave at us, some of them racing the ship for a distance. I lifted my hand and happy squeals shrilled from their tiny chests.

Did they recognize us, or would any returned wave excite them?

Citali surrounded herself with the handsomer members of Father's guard. Their eyes fought a battle not to look at her rather revealing dress. She didn't care if any of them were punished for lusting after one of the Atenas, reveling in the power her body had over them. And like fish in the water they gaped, swimming toward her bait. They wouldn't even know they'd been hooked until she lifted them from the water they needed to survive and cast them to the shore to suffocate and die.

Zarina hadn't seen us off. No doubt she was still sour at being left behind. If Sol did choose her while we were away, would she be different when we returned?

I tried to envision Zarina as the Aten.

The Atens of old were depicted on temple walls as having a glow, like that of Sol's corona. Father did not emit light; in stark contrast, darkness flowed from his every word and action. As hard as it was to imagine Zarina as the Aten, it was even harder for me to imagine that she would choose me.

Still… what would it be like to have the goddess's favor? To be the Aten, to have her ear, see her face, and walk with her?

Father never spoke of his dealings with the goddess. I had a feeling it had more to do with greed than secrets he was bound to keep. Other Atens had detailed their meetings with the goddess of gold and fire in such detail, it scorched my fingertips to glide them over their carved depictions.

Father was silent about anything that didn't prominently feature him and hoarded her wisdom and gifts, almost as if he resented Sol for perpetually outshining him.

Saric shuffled toward me. I stood as he stopped and gestured to the wooden crates. "Would you help me sit, Atena?"

His voice was rusted and as weak as his body. He reminded me of reed husks lying at the older edge of the river, bent and broken. A servant girl saw us and brought over two pillows. I gently took hold of his arm and eased him onto one, then positioned the other behind his back. "Are you comfortable enough?" I asked, knowing there was little comfort to be found aboard the rocking vessel. The ship did not offer comfort. It wasn't built to accommodate so many.

"I am well, Atena, thank you," he wheezed.

Beneath the wrinkled, sagging skin on his chest lay his kind heart. Sol dwelled in her priests, they said. Just a spark of her. But I thought that sometimes when Saric looked at me, her proffered spark was visible in his smile.

Saric caught his breath, settling against the pillows. He smiled and thanked me again unnecessarily. Kiran walked over, carrying a cup, and offered his elder a drink of water. The old priest's eyes lit up. "Thank you, brother." Saric took a sip. His withered hands shook as he clutched the golden cup, but the water did not slosh or spill. "There was a time when I was the young lad taking care of *my* elder brothers, you know," he told Kiran in thanks.

Another sip.

Kiran did not look at me when he asked, "Would you like some water, Atena?"

"No, thank you. I'm not thirsty," I replied woodenly.

The old man glanced from Kiran to me, the space between his brows further wrinkling. I should've softened my voice.

"Brother." He patted the crate beside him – the side farthest from me. "Take a seat. The water sickness will pass."

Kiran eased down beside him and let his back thump against the wooden rail. He looked as green as the hair-like algae drifting from the riverbed.

Saric cleared his throat, looking up at me from his makeshift seat. "Atena, Sol has been disturbed of late. Have you noticed a shift in her?"

*Yes.*

Her fire burned hotter. She didn't lift herself far enough into the sky to give us respite as she once had, but instead poured her heat upon us. What had we done to anger her?

"I have," I admitted.

"I raised my concerns to your father, but the Aten does not believe anything is amiss."

It did not surprise me to hear that Father dismissed the worry of Sol's eldest living priest. How predictable. I would not ignore Saric's words. What he spoke was true, even if we did not know the reason.

"Could it be that she's ready to shift her heir?" I asked. "Perhaps she has drawn nearer to better assess the three Atenas?"

He paused to consider my words. "Perhaps, but I have a dark feeling in the pit of my stomach that no amount of Sol's light can banish."

A shiver coursed up my spine at the thought, but I pushed it away. Sol seemed more powerful than ever, not less. Perhaps Saric's days were growing dark as the sands of time in his life's hourglass sifted away. The top was nearly empty. "Sol's light can send away any shadow," I argued, shifting so my hip leaned against the ship rail to better see Saric's face.

The old priest tilted his head to the side and winced. "It *can,* but what if Sol *chose* to allow the darkness to descend, and to remain?"

I couldn't look away from him. Saric knew more than he admitted. I could feel it. "Why would she do that?"

My father's voice boomed from the bow where he stood among his guard, drawing our attention away for a second.

"Why indeed?" Saric quietly asked.

# 5

When everyone settled to rest despite the blazing, hot sun overhead, a young servant boy of no more than nine came to fetch me. "Atena," he greeted with a deep bow. "Your father requests your presence in the riverfarer's quarters."

The dark shadow Saric said he felt? One lived in me, too, and it plumed now in the pit of my stomach. I inclined my head, raking my upper teeth over my healing lower lip. "Did he call for Citali, as well?"

"I can't be certain, Atena Noor. I was only ordered to find you and bring you to him."

Saric was awake on his seat beside me. His pale brown eyes met mine and in them swam a thousand words and warnings.

None of them mattered. I followed the boy to the door of the small room in which the riverfarer lived, and which Father had taken over. Lush pillows and blankets were piled atop the small bed, just large enough to accommodate one person. The desk was covered with food and uncorked bottles of wine. Boxes were stacked all along the walls.

The scent of pipe herbs lingered. I smiled, imagining it clinging to the Aten's pristine things. Father would consider it all soiled, no doubt.

The riverfarer stepped inside, removing his straw hat. He bowed to me, his wiry gray beard bending with the warm breeze streaming in from outside. "Atena, I hope you've managed to make yourself comfortable."

"I have, thank you," I replied, studying the copse of maps behind his desk. They were hand-drawn and so detailed it was hard to look away from them. I moved closer. "How long will the journey to the dusk lands take, exactly?"

The riverfarer folded his hands behind his back and rocked on the balls of his feet. "I've never been farther than two days downriver. The dusk lands are three days away, according to the best map I have. But do not worry, Atena. The river stays smooth for the whole journey. This was drawn and charted by my grandfather, and he made meticulous notes as he sailed the entire river and its tributaries to chart it."

"The river – does it continue into Lumina?"

The riverfarer nodded. "It does, indeed, but the map ends at the Division, Atena."

I looked at the bottom of the map and noted it did not end, but was folded with the back half tucked behind the visible one. The river was an umbilical cord linking our kingdoms. For far too long it had been severed, but if blood in the form of trade flowed its route once more, it might save Helios.

Movement behind us.

I tensed, expecting Father, but relaxed when Citali sauntered in. I never thought I would welcome her presence, but being alone with Father after what transpired yesterday froze me to the core.

The riverfarer greeted my half-sister, then excused himself from the room when Father's strides ate the small space inside his quarters. He closed the door, nodding to Zuul now lurking in the corner, his thick arms folded in front of him.

Father offered a slight grin and even Citali fidgeted with her gown.

I forced myself to remain still and stand tall. No matter what, I would not be broken.

"What I am about to reveal is never to be spoken of again," he began, his cool eyes flicking from Citali's to mine. "The Sphinx gave me a vital prophecy when I spoke to her after Joba's departure. While she admitted that the Lumin genuinely seeks peace, she revealed a way to ensure it for an eternity, and in doing so, ensure that my reign as Aten will never end."

Never end? He wasn't immortal. The goddess could make it so, but why would she choose *him?* Why bind herself to him for an eternity?

Even Citali's brows drew in.

Observing our confusion, Father explained. "Lumos gifted his first heir a crown made of moonlight. The one who holds this relic is endowed with the god's great power."

"Anyone who possesses the crown?" Citali asked, ticking her head to the side in sudden interest.

Father confirmed with a nod. "Anyone."

We were heirs of Sol, but if what he said was true, we could become the Lumin with possession of the crown. Citali's eyes greedily sharpened along with mine.

"I asked Zarina to remain behind to assure that Helios has an heir," Father said. "It is no secret that if Sol *must* choose, I wish for Zarina to become Aten rather than one of you." The words stung. I knew his feelings better than my own features, but hearing him say it managed to pierce something inside my chest anyway.

"In his letter, the newly chosen Lumin alluded to a potential alliance with Helios, forged not only from ink and parchment, but from the blending of our families. He is open to discussing a marriage with one of my daughters."

Citali's lips parted and she flicked a glance to me.

"Such a match would be ideal for Helios. The Lumin and I could begin our work together, while his wife – one of you – secretly seeks the crown. It is in the best interest of Helios, and Sol, to have an Aten endowed with dual powers. And it is Sol's will that *I* be that Aten."

Father paced a few steps, back and forth, rolling his hands as he explained. "Just imagine it. The orbs could chase one another across the sky again. Our land would flourish instead of being forced to wither. This could change everything. *I* could change everything."

*And control it all.*

His excited mood shifted like the wind. He grew serious, but beneath his expression, a fission of harried mania boiled. "We have only until Noor's birthday. If I do not possess the crown by then, as you all will finally be of age and eligibility, Sol will choose Zarina, I will be removed, and our kingdom will continue as it is. The river will dry along with the fertile soil, and slowly, everyone will perish. If we fail, Sol will send the sands to swallow Helios. The priests say there are signs that the dunes have already begun shifting toward our great city."

Father watched me with guarded features. He expected Citali to comply. He expected me to balk. "If you will not do this for me, please think of our people," he tried, his eyes pleading with me for the first time I could remember.

"What benefits can I be assured if I complete this task for you, Father?" Citali dared ask. Father's lips parted. He looked at her as if a stranger stood before him, but this was Citali through and through. My half-sister only ever worried for herself. Citali drummed her fingers on her arms impatiently, feeding off the fact that Father needed *her* for once, and not the other way around. She finally had his attention, though I wondered if she might soon regret it.

Father focused on her. "I expected Noor's defiance, but not yours, Citali. And I believe you know what is at stake if you fail me."

Her sharp eyes sliced him. "I will be putting my life in danger. Risking everything. As such, I will expect something equitable in return."

Father went terribly still and for a moment, I thought she might have gone too far. But then he seemed to settle himself and the tension bled from his shoulders. "Name it, and it will be yours. Land. Riches. A title." He brightened and shook his head, smiling, then promised, "If you bring me the crown of moonlight, there is *nothing* I won't be able to offer you. Nothing will be denied you, Citali."

Citali eagerly hung on his every word, her greedy eyes glittering as she considered the pretty vision he'd painted for her. But she was forgetting something we'd learned time and time again: Father's promises always came with a catch.

She went still. "Father... why are you telling both of us? Which of us will you send to him?"

"In our correspondences, the Lumin asked to spend time with each of you so he could determine the best match."

Doing so would further divide us, pitting sister against sister. It would cause strife within our family, but the Lumin and his people would be whole...

A darker thought emerged. What would Lumina's army be doing while the Atenas were distracted, and while the Aten watched and waited and schemed? While we focused on the Lumin and finding the mysterious crown of moonlight, would they turn their sights on Helios and take it while we weren't paying attention?

This felt like a trap. I wasn't sure whether the Lumin had constructed it or if the Sphinx had, but either way, I had the distinct feeling we were being used as bait.

"You remain quiet, Noor," Father noted.

Citali interrupted again. "Father, with all due respect, did the Sphinx say *why* Sol wishes for you to... shoulder this burden alone?"

*Nice word choice, Citali.*

His chest puffed. "Sol believes that if I hold both powers, I will be able to free her."

From her unchanging position, Sol could lower herself toward Helios and raise herself high into the heavens, but she was otherwise immobile, fixed in a sky so vast and blue. It hurt to see her thus confined.

Citali's eyes released their sharpness. I wondered if she lusted after the possibilities the crown might afford her. She seemed to have swallowed Father's answer but missed his insinuation that *he* would be Sol's savior – that *he* would be the one who set her free.

That wasn't true at all. If Sol was freed, it would be mine or Citali's doing, though Father would take the power and praise and never give us a second thought. Citali was a fool if she thought otherwise.

Could Sol be persuaded to reward the one who *truly* freed her? If it was me, could I ask her to free us from him? If I held the crown, I would never give it to someone as undeserving and cruel and selfish as Father.

My thoughts scattered like sand in the wind.

The Sphinx's prophecies had never been wrong. Sol had formed the lioness after the Great Divide, long before she chose her first Aten from among her people. The Sphinx's wisdom was unrivaled, her guidance unquestionable.

But how could I trust the lioness when I questioned Sol herself? Sol had chosen Father from the first Aten's long lineage when she could've chosen someone – *anyone* – kinder, gentler, and wiser for the task. Perhaps the goddess of gold and fire's mercy had burnt away, leaving nothing but uncontrollable anger, her grace drying like the deserts breaking into tiny grains, mounded like the encroaching sand dunes.

Did she see Father's cinder heart as a mirror of her own?

Or... perhaps Father concocted this bargain to force Sol to give him what his heart truly wanted: power with no constraints. He would use his newly stolen power to free her, *if* she would make him godlike in return.

"Both of you will meet the Lumin at the feast we host to begin the negotiations. You'll need to capture his attention, and keep it," Father advised. "But most importantly, you'll need to search for the crown." He looked to Citali. "You may leave us now. I need to speak privately with Noor."

I inhaled slowly so he didn't see the nervousness fill me. Citali flashed a knowing smile before bowing to him and gliding from the room. The door closed behind her with a soft click, sealing us inside.

The quarters felt remarkably smaller in her absence. Zuul still lingered, but kept his eyes fixed on the wall behind me.

My father dusted his hands as he walked to where I stood, stopping before me and staying silent. Silence often preceded his rage. "You will do your best to bring me the crown, or I will rid myself of you once and for all. Embarrass me or reveal my plans to the Lumin, and I'll bind your soul to the sand where you will *never* rejoin your treasonous mother in the hereafter."

I raised my chin defiantly. "My mother was not a traitor."

He gave a cruel laugh then lunged. Grabbing my throat, he slammed me backward. The back of my skull hit the map the riverfarer's grandfather had painstakingly made. Stars danced in my vision for a moment and the room spun. My feet lifted from the ground as he forced me upward. "You want to know what it felt like to watch the vessels in her eyes burst?" he hissed.

I tried not to kick, but he was crushing my throat. I looked to Zuul, whose flinty eyes found mine, but he made no move to help. Pressure built in my face and head. I gasped for air but found none.

It took everything in me not to claw at his hand and wrist. "You want down?" he asked, his brows raised.

I tried to nod. To speak. My lips moved, but only strangled sounds eeked from my throat.

"You are pathetic," he spat. "A monster, just like her. The only way I'll allow you to leave the dusk lands alive is if you somehow convince the Lumin that *you* are the one he should choose." He slammed me into the wall again just as someone knocked on the door.

I saw the war raging in Father's eyes. He didn't want to let me go. He *wanted* to end me, but two daughters increased the odds that one of us would succeed in the dark task he'd given us.

He dropped me and I slumped, my back raking against the wall and map as I fell to the floor. I inhaled sharply, gasping for air, my lungs aching from the pressure. I pressed a hand on my chest for a moment to stifle the ache. The pressure slowly ebbed from my face.

Father turned to see who'd dared interrupt him and found Saric waiting in the doorway.

"My Aten, I hoped I might have some of your time. I didn't realize you were occupied." The old man's eyes flicked to me, then returned to Father's, acting as if he saw nothing, as if I was unworthy of his worry. The only indication of the opposite was that his arthritic fists were balled at his sides.

"I'm finished with her," Father said with a jovial smile, waving the eldest priest into the room. Zuul grabbed my arm and hauled me up as I coughed and sputtered, still sucking in breaths.

The guard led me out of the room, then closed the door. I hoped Saric had something interesting to say or else Father would see through his interruption.

On shaky knees, I tried to steel my bones and pretend that nothing was amiss. I walked back to my small spot at the ship's side, settling near Kiran and leaving a Saric-sized space between us. My priest friend muttered a curse I was sure hit Sol's ear. My eyes flared at his words.

Dark fury flooded his countenance. The servant girl who'd brought pillows for Saric stared at us from where she sat petting a few lambs nearby. "Could you bring fresh water and a rag, please?" he discreetly asked her.

She gave a quiet nod before scurrying away to get what he'd requested. In a moment, a small bowl and cloth lay in Kiran's youthful hands.

"You can't," I warned.

"It is a priest's duty to care for his Aten – *and* the Atenas."

But how could he do both when the two were constantly at odds?

If Kiran showed me kindness, he'd be repaid in cruelty. I tried to move away, but he stopped me. "Stay."

Kiran dipped the pale cloth in the cool water and scooted into Saric's vacant seat. My vision tilted again and my stomach turned. The cool cloth paused on my neck. "There are marks on your throat," he rasped.

I didn't nod. Didn't speak.

If I moved an inch, I'd be sick.

He pressed the rag to my throat and held it there. The cool water soaked into my skin, but Sol quickly drank the moisture. He wet it again, holding it to my lip. It stung. The split had opened again. I licked it and tasted the tang of copper.

I pressed my eyes closed to keep everything from spinning, gently prodding the back of my head where a goose egg swelled.

"Your head, too?" he asked.

A guard strolled by, one of Zuul's men. He slowed as he glanced between me and Kiran.

I panicked and took the rag from his hand, pressing it on my skull. "Thank you, priest," I said formally. "I fell."

The guard continued his march but kept his steps slow, obviously straining his ears to overhear our conversation.

Kiran moved back to his seat. He could probably sense the fear radiating from my heart, feel the reverberation of it pounding against the wood we both leaned back against.

How many times had I 'fallen' throughout my life? Those words felt hollow, but I didn't. I brimmed with righteous anger.

Father wanted the crown of moonlight more than anything. He was willing to push his own daughters to seduce the Lumin so he would wed one of us, only for that unlucky bride to steal the very source of his power and deliver Lumos and his great, dark power to our father. Sol's fire wasn't enough to satisfy him.

How could Sol allow this? Was she so desperate to move?

My throat throbbed, reminding me that I was as desperate as she. Maybe more. The battle between Father and I had to end, one way or another.

Saric returned to us, settling between Kiran and me. His gentle eyes met mine.

"Thank you," I said so only he could hear.

He inclined his head just a touch.

"Saric?" I paused, searching for the words and strength to ask them. "Is what he said true? Did Sol make this agreement with him?"

The elderly priest pressed his withered lips into a fine line. "I am sorry, Noor, but the Sphinx did deliver him such a prophecy."

I didn't trust Father at all, but I trusted Saric. If he said the bargain was real, it was. And though he didn't elaborate about how it came to be, whether Father had persuaded the goddess to give him a chance to free her, or if Sol truly chose him and wanted him to be her vessel forever, it didn't matter in the end. The outcome would be the same.

A dull throbbing drummed behind my eyes. I would be fine. I just needed to rest and hope my throat didn't mottle too badly, that my lip would somehow heal before I met the new Lumin.

I had no intention of marrying him, but I needed to get close all the same. Not only close, I needed him to want me. To choose me over my sister.

And while I lured him in, I needed to keep Citali from finding the very source of the Lumin's power.

Because I was going to steal the moonlight crown.

Not for Father.

Not even for the power it would afford me.

But to keep him from becoming something unstoppable, something ruinous.

I was through living in his shadow. Through with threats and bruises and fear.

If I could find the crown, I would destroy him. I would win this war.

And when I bested him, I wouldn't hesitate to tear the sun from his damaging grasp.

I would free myself.

Then free Sol.

And hope the goddess's fire didn't incinerate me for putting her second.

# 6

The further we traveled downriver, the more I noticed that Sol, still stuck in the sky, did not move with us. I felt a strange tug from her, as if she held the end of a rope coiled around my chest. The reluctance to leave her light and heat settled uncomfortably in my bones.

In the fifth hour of our third day as we journeyed down the river, the riverfarer's earlier words came to life. I could still see part of Sol's face in the northern sky, but she was almost gone.

A shadow had settled over us. The sky was at war, the vibrant blue losing the battle to a muted gray. An unsettling hue. The temperature had dropped as well, and while most of the people on board marveled at the feel of cooler air on their skin, the feeling sent shivers skittering up my spine.

Sol's fire, lodged in my veins, fought valiantly to chase the frigid feeling away again and again.

Kiran and Saric were walking around the deck, Kiran finally having adjusted to the undulating motion of the ship on water. Saric needed to stretch his back and legs, but as they strolled, they occasionally glanced over at me.

Father hadn't spoken to me since he shared his secret plan, then tried to strangle me. As the ache in my head subsided and the rush of fear from what occurred wore off, I was finally able to relax. Kiran's eyes kept catching onto mine.

"What?" I quietly asked.

He didn't want to tell me, so I rifled through crates until I found a hand mirror. I was horrified to see that a vessel had burst in my right eye, a red bolt surging from my caramel pupil.

I hadn't spoken to him or Saric since. Not because I was angry with them, but because with all the attention they'd given their Atena, it was only a matter of time before Father saw how much they meant to me and decided to hurt them to hurt me. Being silent might not be enough to keep them safe.

When they were on the other side of the ship, I stood and stretched and made my way to the stern, leaning against the railing and watching the ship's wake. Without Sol's powerful rays, the water looked murky and indistinct. I couldn't see the patches of grass and algae that should lay beneath, and unless a fish rose to the surface, even the flicker of their metallic scales eluded me.

Citali came to stand beside me, cocking her hip against the rail and crossing her arms. I considered tossing her overboard; a smile graced my lips at the thought of her flailing in the river and attracting the crocodiles that lurked nearby.

She grew more impatient the longer I ignored her.

"What do you know of him?" she finally asked, relaxing her posture. For the first time since we were girls, Citali looked unsure, almost nervous.

Even though she didn't mention him by name, I knew she was referring to the elusive Lumin. What did I know about the Lumin? In all honesty, I didn't know much and certainly not enough for the plans I needed to make. The Lumin was newly chosen, and while I knew about his power, I knew little else about the man. It was the man I needed to learn. I had to earn his trust, get close, and unravel his shadowed secrets.

"No more than you, I'm sure."

"Some of the guard say he is part beast," she whispered. "That he feeds on blood and flesh instead of food."

I'd heard whispers of the same since silver dusk had fallen over us. Apparently, the shade unsettled the others as much as it did me. Sol was so far away I could barely see her now. In another hour, she would be beyond reach, completely out of sight, and we would trade her warmth for the gray shroud laying over the earth. It felt like we were being buried.

Citali shivered and rubbed her bare arms.

"You should've chosen warmer apparel," I remarked dryly.

She smirked and moved closer to keep our conversation private. "I'll wear far less than *this* in the House of Dusk. If you think I won't do everything possible to win over the Lumin, you're wrong, Noor."

I watched the river eddies disrupt the cool surface, hoping she didn't see that I was equally as desperate to garner his favor and attention, but for a far different reason.

She leaned in to whisper, "I *must have* the crown of moonlight, Noor."

"So you can give it to Father?" I snipped. "Never."

"You have me all figured out, huh? You think you actually know me? Know anything about my life?"

"I don't want to know of it."

Her eyes dropped to my throat and she smiled. I expected her to turn and leave. To go find some male to entertain her. But she surprised me by shoving me backward and pinning me to the rail with her forearm. My back cracked against the rail, bent over it. The river water, placid only moments ago, now roared in my ear. She put her weight onto my chest. I clamped desperate hands onto her wrists to keep from falling. My heels lifted from the planks. My toes. Then… she let go, raising her hands as if she'd thought better of killing me.

"The crocodiles in the dusk lands won't leave a trace of you for Sol. Remember that. I've found a way out, and I won't let you or anyone else stand in my way now."

Citali sauntered away like she hadn't tried to feed me to the crocs, like we'd had a lovely, sisterly chat and now were parting.

My heart thundered.

She could have killed me. Might have come closer than Father did when he tried to strangle me. I just couldn't figure out why she didn't.

I had no idea why she wanted the crown, but now I questioned whether she intended to hand it over to Father, after all.

I gasped when the ship finally dragged me away from Sol. It felt like she'd taken hold of my heart and was tearing it from my chest for a few anguished moments. If it weren't for the ship's rail, I would've fallen into the river and the currents would have drowned me. The riverfarer promised the entire journey to the dusk lands would be smooth, but the water here churned and eddied in ways I'd never seen. Where my heart should be, a cold, darkness took root, desolate and lonely as the shifting sands.

Across the ship, Citali laughed with the guardsmen who still unwisely entertained her. She didn't seem to struggle from the absence of Sol at all. I searched for Father, but he was likely ensconced within the riverfarer's quarters.

Did Saric and Kiran feel this, or was I the only one? Had I upset the goddess so badly she'd abandoned and left me for dead?

A tear fell from one eye, then the other. I stared at the undulating water, my sorrow splashing into and adding to the water pushing me to a fate I might not survive.

# 7

The House of Dusk was enormous. The Lumin and his people were already there by the time the riverfarer and his crew guided the ship to the river's edge and secured her by tying ropes to enormous boulders. We were met with unexpected fanfare by a crowd that was respectful but jubilant, and music unlike any I'd heard from instruments I'd never before seen. But that wasn't the best part.

Father led us from the ship, Saric and Kiran right behind Citali and me. Every person in the crowd held small bags, and reached into theirs at the same time. Father was taken aback, fearing the worst, until they released what their hands had found within: silken petals in every shade of white, pink, red, and even blue.

My heart leapt to watch them fall. I stooped to collect a few, running my thumbs over their softness as a smile blossomed on my lips, unbidden. The petals rained onto our shoulders and caught in our hair.

Citali inched closer to me. "There are so many of them. They outnumber us..."

Of course, Citali thought of war and peril before assuming the Lumin had been sincere in his attempt to garner peace.

Still, she was right. We were outnumbered, but scanning over them, I didn't see one that stood out from the rest. Had the Lumin deigned to come?

Father stopped when our entire party had disembarked and turned to face the delighted crowd. "Thank you, Lumina, for this beautiful and grand gesture. We look forward to hosting a great feast in your honor tomorrow."

The Luminans cheered, moving back to afford us more room. Some hurried back inside the House of Dusk while others lingered, watching our servants unload the ship's cargo. Some voyeurs even offered to help and carried our things inside.

A gentleman wearing silver armor stepped forward. His hair was dark, but the hair at his temples matched the metal guarding his body. Worry lines streaked his serious face. He bowed to Father. "Welcome, Aten. The Lumin has had many rooms prepared to ensure your comfort upon arrival. May I see you to yours?"

Father smiled as a lion might smile. "Of course you may." He followed the silver soldier inside without a glance back at his daughters.

The House of the Sun was three stories tall, whereas the House of Dusk was seven. Built of precisely cut gray stone, it rose from the muted earth and seemed to brush the gloomy, cloud-filled sky with eager fingers.

A woman dressed in a simple, but fine gray dress approached me and my sister. "Atenas," she greeted while bending at the waist. "I'm happy to escort you inside." The woman looked no older than Father, and like him, she clung to the strength youth provided. Silvering hair fell to her shoulders where it had been cut into a blunt line. She was beautiful, her eyes blue and kind.

I inclined my head respectfully and we stepped into the House, leaving the gray dusk outside. I thought it was dark outside until I entered the windowless hall. The woman led us to a stairwell where we climbed to the top floor. Citali was winded when we reached the top. The woman took note.

"The Lumin thought you might appreciate a view of the sky, even though it's different from what you're used to."

Like a fool, Citali muttered something rude and the woman's sweet smile faded.

"I appreciate the gesture," I assured her.

The woman glanced between us and fixed her smile once again before leading us down the hallway.

Citali scanned every door we passed until we arrived at the end of the hall. The woman withdrew a key from the pocket of her dress, unlocked the door, and pushed it open to reveal a spacious room with stark white walls, trimmed in gold. A large bed sat against the far wall with plush white linens draped over the canopy top. A small writing desk was situated in front of one of the three windows, the lamp pouring buttery soft light over the stack of blank parchment resting on its top. A small vat of ink and a quill sat ready beside the paper.

Citali moved to a doorway in the center of the right wall and disappeared inside. "This will do," she said approvingly, her voice echoing from inside. She reappeared in the doorway, bracing her hands on the facing and glancing at me. "It is a private bathing room." She tugged the doors of the pristine armoire open just as the first of her heavy trunks were brought in.

The woman looked to me. "Your rooms are across the hall. Would you like to get situated?"

"I would, thank you," I told her. *I would especially like to put distance between me and my spoiled sister.*

Citali paid no attention as I left her rooms. She was already unlocking her trunk and throwing the lid over the back. The oversized armoire might soon burst with all she planned to stuff into it. Citali brought twice the trunks I had. Her gowns were her armor, and she was prepared for the war that would rage between us over the coming days and weeks.

The woman pulled out another key and unlocked the door to my rooms. Inside, I saw that it was a darker reflection of Citali's. My bathing room was on the left wall, but that wasn't what made my feet halt. It was the beauty of the space. Citali's room was white trimmed in gold, whereas mine was all gold and black. Darkness and warmth. A devastating clash of opposites.

I loved it.

"Is the décor to your liking, Atena?"

I turned to the woman, belatedly remembering she was still with me. "It's the most beautiful room I've ever seen," I replied truthfully.

Her shoulders relaxed a fraction.

My large bed was draped in alternating swaths of gold and black fabric, with sheer matching panels lacing together over the canopy. The wooden bed frame was painted the dark hue while golden vines and leaves had been painstakingly painted onto the posters. The writing desk and armoire were painted in the same manner.

I walked to the bathing room, marveling at the black stone inlaid on the ceiling, walls, and floor. The room was polished and clean, the stones smooth and cold underfoot.

A commotion outside drew me from the room.

Our escort instructed the placement of my three trunks, smiling at the servants as they deposited them and left to fulfill other duties. "I'll have water brought up for you and your sister," she promised.

"Wait! What's your name?" I asked.

"My name is Vada, Atena."

"Mine is Noor."

She stood taller, almost regally. "We were instructed to call you Atena as a sign of respect."

"Atena Noor, then." I smiled. "My sister's name is Citali."

She glanced toward Citali's door before inclining her head. "I'll send for water and bring something for you to eat and drink."

"That would be lovely. Thank you."

She bobbed a quick curtsy, placed my room key on the trunk nearest to her, and closed the door behind her.

I didn't bother unpacking. I walked to the window and let my fingers drift over the cool pane. My room was higher than the platform atop Sol's temple, high enough that the wide river looked more like a small stream. Our shallow-hulled ship looked unimpressive from this height, its hull bobbing in the water where we'd tied her.

The Luminan ship was much like ours: able to sail in shallow water, pale sails precisely tucked away. Their deck was empty now, but they must have brought even more than we did if they managed to provide all these comforts to us. Or had these things always been here, available for either kingdom to use?

Two soft knocks came at the door.

"You may enter."

A host of men and women came in, each carrying a steaming bucket of water. They marched straight into the bathing room, emerging when their buckets were empty. Vada returned carrying a tray of fruits, bread, and a carafe of fresh water.

"Thank you... for everything. I can't tell you how famished I am, and how glorious a long, hot bath will be after spending nearly four days on the river."

She laughed, giving me a knowing nod and pressing a sachet and soap bar into my hands. "I brought some salts for your bath and a bar of freshly made soap."

I almost groaned when I smelled the herbs. Glancing at the gifts in my hands, I saw flecks of herbs were trapped in the bar. I didn't recognize their scents.

"They're from Lumina," she explained, seeing my puzzled expression. "A gift. From me to you."

"Thank you." My heart squeezed. Vada was a complete stranger, but so kind. I never expected to find kindness on this end of the river. "I didn't have the opportunity to arrange for gifts. We left rather abruptly," I admitted.

She pressed her hands together. "Atena, in Lumina, gifts aren't given for the hope or expectation of reciprocation."

She was more gracious than I deserved. "Thank you," I told her again, smelling the deliciously scented soap and salts.

When the final bucket of hot water had been emptied, the last person stepped out of my rooms, leaving me and Vada and the thoughtful gift I held between us.

"Do you require further help, Atena?"

"No, thank you." I looked over at the platter of food. "Tomorrow we will host a feast for your people, and I hope we can come close to the kindness you've shown in the first hour I've known you, Vada."

She smiled warmly and gently took hold of my arm. "This is no feast, but I hope it will satisfy your hunger. Rest well, Atena Noor." She turned to leave.

"Rest well," I told her. She gently closed my door with a motherly smile that left an ache in my chest long after her footsteps trailed down the hall.

I stayed in the tub until my skin was wrinkly and every inch of hair and flesh had been scrubbed with the delicious-smelling soap. The salt eased the ache in my limbs. I saved plenty to give Saric. Once I found him, that is. I wasn't sure where his and Kiran's rooms were.

Someone had placed thick towels on a bench within the bathing room. I wrapped myself in them before finding the key to my trunks and finally unlocking them.

As I hung up the dresses and gowns I'd brought, I popped crisp grapes in my mouth and sipped fresh, cool water from a silver goblet. I noticed a small drawer at the bottom of the armoire. I pulled it out and saw it was empty. There was nothing beneath it; nothing hidden beneath the mattress or behind the headboard. I felt along the walls and tugged on the sconces to be sure, but there were no drafts of air to be felt and no secret passages to be found. I was only fractionally disappointed that my room was just that.

I dressed in the plainest dress I had so I could blend in, choosing a simple, pleated cotton gown the bright color of river grass. I perched on the bed and ate the rest of the grapes, then spread the creamy cheese on the small knotted roll of bread and ate it, too.

My eyes kept returning to the window. The gray outside was as constant as Sol in the sky, but so different, it was hard not to study it. I moved the writing desk over so I could sit in the windowsill, and there I stayed until Citali strode in unannounced and uninvited.

"You should lock your doors."

"What do you want?"

She eyeballed my tray. Given her lack of a reaction, she'd received the same. I ran my hands through my still-damp hair as she surveyed the room with a critical eye. I'd put away all my clothes, situated my sandals beneath the armoire, closed the trunks, and stacked them along the wall as best I could.

"I prefer the white and gold of my rooms," she said haughtily.

"I prefer the black and gold of mine," I retorted.

"What smells so good?" she asked, sniffing the air as she drew near. "It's you!" she decided accusingly. "Was your soap scented?"

I rolled my eyes. It was always something. "Jealousy never looks good on you, Citali."

Her dark gray eyes narrowed and she crossed her arms. "I was *going* to invite you on a little adventure, but if you're too busy pampering yourself..."

My curiosity piqued. "What adventure?"

"Father has opened some wine and the dancing girls are getting dressed. He's invited the Lumin to join him for drinks and to watch them dance."

My mind whirred. I smiled at her and leaped down from my window perch. "Let's go." I paused halfway across the room. "Wait. How did you learn about this, Citali?"

"Gold," she said, giving a toothy grin. "It *always* buys information. You just have to know who has the truth and needs the gold most."

I gestured to her fine gown. "You'll need to dress in something plainer if we're going to blend in."

She scoffed, holding the skirt of her dress out. "This is the plainest dress I brought."

I shook my head and waved a hand to my armoire, where she helped herself to a plain gray dress. "At least I'll match the water, earth, and sky in this forsaken strip of nothing," she pouted, quickly exchanging dresses.

I laid hers on my bed and waited for her to leave so I could lock the door. She was right about that much. I dropped the key into a small pocket hidden along my skirt's seam.

We made our way downstairs, passing the sixth, fifth, fourth, and third floors, exiting onto the second floor where Citali tugged me down a hallway. For a second, her touch felt strange, like we were children again, back when her seething hatred of me vacillated instead of festered. When we were young, balancing with one another on the precipice of innocence and awareness, sometimes we were just sisters.

Sometimes I missed those days, but in my marrow, knew they were long gone. Whatever insignificant remnant of those moments remained would soon be ground to nothing as we faced one another as true foes.

Music and laughter rose from the first floor. Citali and I followed the hallway until it shrank and one wall fell away to reveal ornamental balustrades that overlooked a vast room below. Chandeliers with more candles than I'd seen before poured golden light over those who gathered below.

I spotted Father right away. Zuul was nearby, quiet and looking over the crowd. His gaze pulled upward to where we stood, and I hurriedly ducked back into the hallway to hide.

Citali laughed, clutching her chest. "How does he always see everything?" she asked.

"I'm not sure, but I wish he didn't," I answered, giving a nervous but thrilled laugh.

We crouched and watched as the musicians strummed, drummed, and cajoled their mizmars in a relaxed, winsome song. Wine was readily poured and passed around. There was a light, jovial feel to the room, smiles curling on most lips. Along with Father and his guard were a few of the servants I recognized from the House of the Sun.

Saric and Kiran were not in attendance, but neither was…

"Do you see him?" Citali asked.

No one was seated in the broad seat matching Father's. "Maybe he hasn't arrived yet, or perhaps he will return soon."

"The seat is there for a reason. He'll come," she sighed, clutching two thick, stone balustrades. "I need to get closer." Her eyes flashed as she pushed up to a crouch. "Wait here."

"Where are you going?"

"To get a better vantage point," she snipped.

Of course she was. And she wanted me to remain behind. She retraced her steps and took the stairway that curled to the first floor. A few moments later my sister emerged, her face and head wrapped. She planted herself among the servants and grabbed two wine bottles, weaving among the attendees and refilling cups. No one paid her any attention. I had to give her credit. It was a bold move to walk among them, even as she seemed to go unseen.

I needed to do something equally as bold.

I turned to peer down the hall when tittering giggles filtered down it. Dancing girls streamed from a nearby room into the hall, pausing at the stairwell to glance down. They boasted toned muscles and glistening skin, garbed in revealing ensembles with colorful veils draped over the bottom halves of their faces.

They noticed me and jerked to attention, bowing and lowering their eyes to the floor. The last to leave the room pulled the door closed and took out a key to lock it. The tips of her long, glossy black hair grazed the small of her back. "Stop!" I urgently ordered before she stuck it into the keyhole.

She turned, her eyes wide. "Atena –"

She was older than I thought. Likely in her thirties, but still beautiful. Hers was still the body of a well-trained dancer.

Desperation lanced through my veins. This was foolish and reckless and... I'd never wanted anything more than to not be *me* for just a few minutes. To have fun without having the weight of the title of Atena or her aureole hanging on my head and neck.

"I need your help." I twisted the knob and opened the door, waving her back inside. The woman told the other dancers to wait for her while she eased the door closed behind us.

"What can I possibly help you with, Atena?"

"I need to conceal myself. To look – to dress – like you."

Her full brows kissed. "Atena – I'm not sure that's a wise –"

"My sister and I... we need to see the Lumin. My father would kill me if I strolled brazenly into that room, but disguised as one of you, I could get in and he would be none the wiser."

She huffed a laugh, though it lacked humor. "He would kill me if you were discovered. I can't risk that, Atena. I'm sorry." She turned to leave again. "Come along. There's a small place in the shadows where you can stay and watch."

I shook my head and attempted to convey my desperation. "My father won't kill you if something happens, because I won't make a mistake. I can dance. He'll never know. I'll keep to the rear of the group, near the shadows, and leave at the first sign of trouble – not that there will be any." She shook her head and opened her mouth. I knew another protest would fall off her tongue. "Please," I added, giving her my most beseeching plea.

"Why do you need to see him so badly?"

"One of us may marry him," I told her. The woman's eyes glittered as our secret and all its implications registered. I slipped a gold bangle off my wrist and held it up, remembering Citali's words. "You can't tell anyone."

She snatched her prize, slipping it on and holding her hand out to admire it. "You can dance?" she asked, sizing me up shrewdly.

I nodded.

"How well?"

"Well enough."

"You'd better hope so," she chuckled. Beneath her breath, she added, "For *both* our sakes."

Then, she ordered me to strip.

# 8

Kevi helped me into a dancing costume with silk panels in the deep teal shade I imagined the deepest fathoms of the ocean held, layered with sheer ones over my hips and legs. "The panels allow for movement," she noted, cinching the silver belt a little tighter where small, silver discs hung all over it. "When you roll and shake your hips, you become the musician," she teased.

My stomach was bare, as was most of my back. The small halter pushed my breasts up and together. "It fits you well," she noted, arranging my veil. "Though I'm not sure what dancer could possibly afford sun diamonds."

I quirked a brow at her. "Those, I keep."

They belonged to my mother, and the bracelet and anklet were never leaving my skin. Not that I could take them off if I wanted to. The gold would not break.

Kevi laughed and innocently batted her eyes. "I wasn't implying anything."

*The hell she wasn't.*

"You're ready. I hope you're not clumsy and that you can keep up."

I scoffed inwardly. *Kevi is twice my age! Surely, I can keep up with her. I think...*

She swayed from the room as if she owned the House of Dusk and everything in it, my thick gold bangle unabashedly adorning her wrist. Locking the room behind us, we joined her dancing crew. "Not a word about this or you'll be out on the streets that fast." She snapped her fingers. "Understood?" Kevi asked, her tone leaving no room for argument.

"Yes, Kevi," the girls answered in unison. A few bowed out of habit again.

"Stop that!" Kevi reprimanded. "Act like she's one of us until we return to this room." The question of why swam in their eyes, but Kevi's hand landed on my back reassuringly. "Ignore them. Your explanations are your own."

*Hmm.* Maybe I shouldn't have given up the bangle. I could have merely ordered her to comply. I just hated using my authority to crush others. Kevi, however, would become a boulder if given the chance, crushing without a single thought to those who wound up beneath her.

The lead dancer led the girls down a narrow set of stairs. At the bottom, she nudged me. "Stay near this staircase. If anything looks amiss, you run up it and find someplace to hide. If there's trouble, my girls and I will stay out of it," she warned.

I nodded. "I will."

She winked, playfully clapping my arm. "Then let's see exactly how *well* you dance, Atena Noor." Kevi slid from among the women and sauntered onto an empty area of the floor. She made her way to the musicians and bent to speak with them, a broad, flirtatious smile on her crimson lips. Kevi was the only dancer who didn't bother with a veil. She laughed with them for a few more moments before striding away to bow before her Aten.

He gave her an approving once-over. Bile rose in my throat.

The women swayed into the room, each bowing before him, then spreading out to cover more of the empty space left just for them. I didn't budge from my shadowed hiding place near the stairs. He knew my eyes.

I couldn't get too close or he would know.

I didn't see Zuul lurking anywhere, but knew better than to think he would leave the room or Father's side.

A current of startlingly cool air made the skin on my arms pebble a moment before someone came to stand beside me. He was a head taller than I was, with neatly cropped hair the blue-black shades I imagined the fabled night sky hoarded. "Are you injured?" he asked, his crystalline blue eyes twinkling like I envisioned the stars might.

"I'm sorry?" I asked, already having forgotten his question.

"Are you injured?" he asked again, his lips quirking into a smile. His voice was deep and raspy, unexpected. "Why are you not out there with them?" he asked, nodding to the other dancers.

"I will be. I... I'm new." His presence made me feel off-kilter, like the world had somehow tilted and everything lay sideways. Maybe the earth was fine, and *I* was off-balance.

"Ah, I see." His nose was perfectly straight, and I wondered if he could tell mine had been broken. His jaw was square and strong, his posture rigid and confident as he looked out over the room.

I noticed with a start that the blissful chill... came from him.

Dressed in a dark blue tunic and pants that showcased the muscles beneath the material, I wondered how he managed to produce such frost.

He was distracting me, I realized as Kevi began to speak. I reluctantly tore my eyes away from him as she bowed to the gathered crowd before explaining to the Luminans that the dances we were about to perform were more than just entertainment. In Helios, every dance told a story; its words were movement and strength, flesh and fire.

I glanced to the empty seat beside my father.

"Are you looking for him, too?" the cool stranger asked.

My eyes found his again. "Are you here to see the Lumin? Aren't you from Lumina? Don't you know what he looks like?"

"I do," he said with another smile.

My mouth fell open. "Are you one of his guards?"

"Something like that," he agreed.

"Where is he?"

The dark stranger stood up straighter and looked perfectly uncomfortable. Had he lost his bravado?

"Is he old?" I blurted as the drumbeat began.

"Old?" He chuckled.

"I know nothing about him other than what rumors course through Helios."

"What rumors?"

My face heated. "I don't want to repeat them."

He laughed and folded his arms over his chest. "That's likely wise."

"I should go," I said, looking back to the dancers as the drumbeat began.

He slowly reached for my wrist, his brows furrowing. His fingers were like ice and he took in a sharp breath when my heat flared into him, but he didn't let go. "Are these sun diamonds? The Aten brought some to the Lumin as a gift this afternoon just after he arrived. I thought only the Aten and Atenas could bear to wear them? The Lumin had to wear gloves just to handle them…"

My heart pounded and I hastily pulled my wrist away. "I have to join the others," I stammered, scurrying onto the floor as a sensual rhythm filled the room. My mind spun. I didn't know Father had met with the Lumin this afternoon, or that his guard paid him so much attention. Not that Zuul didn't do the same for Father. Still, this could be troublesome if he saw the stones again.

I couldn't worry about it now. I had to focus and follow the dance and not make another mistake.

The scents of herb smoke and incense combined to form a heady fragrance. The air grew hazy and the dance began slowly... then built. A dam inside me broke and I was nothing more than bone and music, muscle and rhythm. With my body I told the story of our people, the story of Sol. I was veiled and free and danced like I'd never dared before, like each step, sway, and bend might be my last. When the song was done, panting and covered in a sheen of earned sweat, I looked back to the dark little corner, wondering if the Lumin's guard still lingered in the shadows, hoping he might have seen me and had enjoyed watching.

I wouldn't be the first woman to use her form as a weapon.

My hopes were dashed when I found that the corner lay empty. I swiveled my head to find that the seat beside my father, the Lumin's seat, was not.

My stomach dropped and I felt sick when I saw the familiar man who occupied the chair. I clutched my midsection and rushed to the stairwell, tripping over a silken skirt panel as I scurried up it. Kevi noticed and rushed after me.

The music began again without the two of us. My absence might not attract unwanted attention, but Kevi's certainly would. She led the dancers.

"Atena?" she whispered as she caught me in the hall outside her room. She hurriedly unlocked her door and pushed me inside. With shaking hands, I tore off the outfit and shrugged back into my plain dress, stooping to pick the garment pieces off the floor. Kevi stilled my hands. "Are you okay? Are we in danger?"

"No," I choked. "I just thought it wise to leave before our luck ran out. Mine always does."

Her thick brows kissed. "Are you sure?"

"I give you my word, Kevi. Father is none the wiser. My nerves just got the best of me." I tried to laugh. "My heart is beating out of my chest."

She relaxed a fraction, clutching my arms. "I imagine you've not had a true chance to just be a girl."

"No," I admitted. "I haven't. What I did just now was terrifying. It was the most frightening and daring thing I've ever done." And possibly the most foolish.

At that, she chuckled. "If you're sure you're okay, I should return. Someone will come looking for me."

I nodded. "I'll return to my rooms. Thank you, Kevi."

She jangled the bangles on her wrist, mine included, and winked. "The pleasure was all mine."

Citali was waiting at the seventh-floor landing when I emerged. She pushed off the wall she leaned against. "Where did you go?" she asked, her eyes narrowed suspiciously.

"I found a hidden staircase and wanted to get a closer look," I lied. "Not that it worked. The dancing girls blocked my view."

She grinned. "That's too bad."

"Did you see him?"

One perfect brow rose. "Of course I did."

"What did he look like?" My heart drummed like I was still dancing, because I knew exactly what he looked like. Beyond that, I knew the gruff sound of his voice, the strength concealed by his clothing, his cool, clean scent. I knew the frost he radiated, the soft touch of his hand.

"You'll find out soon enough," she teased, striding back to her room and disappearing behind it, but not before tossing a cruel smirk over her shoulder.

I took the key out of my pocket and unlocked my room, letting the dark and gold surround me. It was comforting somehow. Not pristine and white and perfect, but a truer reflection of my heart and all its shadows.

I sank onto the soft bed and tucked my knees into my body, hugging them tightly. The man I thought was the Lumin's guard wasn't that at all. The man with the star-shimmer eyes was the Lumin.

More to the point, he knew who *I* was, and that I'd disguised myself to see him.

He knew my voice and my eyes, the shape of the diamonds my mother clamped onto me as a child and which couldn't be removed. He felt my heat and saw me dance.

My head fell onto my knees.

I wished I could plead to Sol, asking her to intervene and forbid him from telling Father what he knew, but there was too much distance between us. Besides that, I wasn't sure she'd help me even if I held her in my hands.

I just had to hope the Lumin – a perfect stranger – kept my secret.

# 9

A tentative knock came at the door just before Vada's muffled voice announced, "Atena Noor, it's time to wake and dress. The Lumin has asked you to join him this morning to break your fasts."

I sat straight up, kicking through the tangle of blankets binding my legs, and rushed to the door, opening it to let her in. Citali stood in her doorway, scowling, then slammed her door closed with a growl. Vada looked taken aback.

"Don't mind her," I explained. "She gets angry when she's hungry."

"Oh, I can send some food up for her if it would help," she offered kindly, walking with me to the armoire.

"If it would help, I'd let you," I mumbled under my breath.

"Did you say something, dear?"

I smiled. "I was just wondering exactly who'd been invited to dine with the Lumin this morning."

Her eyes glittered. "Only you, Atena Noor."

My heart skipped. I straightened my shoulders. Her eyes caught on my throat and her lips parted. I distracted her, ignoring the question painted on her face.

"What should I wear?"

She gestured to the hanging dresses and gowns. "May I?"

I nodded and watched as she combed through them to see what I'd brought and what might be appropriate for something as simple as breakfast.

"Does my father know about this invitation?"

She winced. "I'm sorry, I'm not sure."

I smiled and shrugged a shoulder. "It's nothing to worry over. I was just curious."

Her eyes slid to my throat and caught for a second, but she didn't ask what happened, thankfully.

Her hands settled on a pale gold dress with a high neckline and long skirt. It was form-fitting, but lovely. "This," was all she said, pushing the others back so I could see it better.

I nodded and took it from the armoire while she rifled through the drawers for a pale corset. "Thank you for your help, Vada."

She gave a motherly smile and set about straightening the mess I'd made of the bed, all the while shooing me into the bathing room to ready myself.

I combed and tamed my sleep-snarled hair, dusted powder onto my throat in a feeble attempt to hide the purple and green bruises making their appearance when I needed them to fade, and raked my teeth over the line of scab traversing my lower lip. There was nothing I could do about any of it, so I finally gave up. I'd have to come up with a lie to cover them, as no amount of powder seemed to do the trick.

From a dainty golden pot, I dusted shimmer onto my cheeks, then quickly dressed. Vada waited in my now-tidy room. It looked as pristine as the moment I walked in yesterday.

She held out a pair of woven gold sandals to me. I strapped them on and stood up straight as she circled me, her eyes shrewder than I would have imagined them capable. "The Lumin is likely waiting. We should go."

I wanted to ask how I looked but didn't want to seem like I was begging for compliments or was worried about what he might think. I followed her from the room. She locked my door behind us and led me down the winding staircase to the first floor. We passed the hall where I danced last night, along with more rooms than I could possibly keep track of.

Eventually, we emerged from the side of the House of Dusk and stepped into a small garden that overlooked the river. The water was silver, reflecting the muted sky. I turned to thank Vada for her help and for showing me the way, but she was already gone.

"Good morning," the Lumin said as he stood to greet me. A small, knowing smile played on his lips.

For several moments, we stood, both studying the other, our eyes locked.

"You're not a guard," I noted, breaking the awkward silence and deciding to confront my discomfort head-on.

"And you're not a dancer."

I moved toward my seat. He rushed over and pushed the chair in for me, dragging a "thank you," from my lips. Then, he took his own and settled across from me.

He hadn't seemed like a cruel man last night, but I knew better than to assume he was good. Good men had no need to lurk in the shadows.

I sipped from my glass of water while he sat perfectly still, watching my every movement. While he still exuded an air of confidence, his muscles were tense. His shoulders were broader than they appeared in the dark last night, and he seemed taller than I remembered. He'd shaved the shadow from his jaw. His dark hair contrasted with the stark white shirt he wore.

He seemed content to sit all day and not speak, but it made me antsy. I didn't know the Lumin well enough to discern his mood.

I severed the silence. "Why did you ask me to breakfast?"

"Why did you disguise yourself last night?"

I folded my hands over my chest. "You know why. I wanted to see you."

"You were simply curious?"

"Yes." A long pause. "Why were you hiding?"

"I needed a moment to gather my thoughts."

"And watch my father when you weren't in his presence?" I volleyed.

He grinned because he'd been caught. "I worry for my people. This negotiation is important to them. I need to see if the Aten is sincere."

"He gave you sun diamonds. Did that not *buy* your loyalty and affection?" I teased, pressing a manicured hand against my chest.

He tilted his head, likely wondering if he imagined the sarcastic tone I'd employed. "It would take far more than a handful of shiny rocks to earn those, I'm afraid."

His eyes slid to my lips, then lower. When they caught on my throat, he went rigid. His brows slowly slanted. "Atena, why are you bruised? Did something happen last night?"

"No," I said, sitting up straighter as two servants emerged carrying plates of steaming bread, fresh fruit, and sizzling strips of cooked meat. They arranged our plates and the platter between us and then left us alone. "Despite my grace on the dance floor, I can be quite clumsy."

His expression softened. "I can see the fingerprints you've tried to cover. The split on your lip can't be hidden, either."

Rage filled me.

For the way Father had marked me.

The fact that the Lumin could see it. The pity in his expression. Pity I did not need or want.

I felt like stabbing the table to prove that I was not weak. My fingers inched toward the dull knife beside my plate. My hands began to tremble as a wave of fury washed over me. I grabbed the table edge to still them even as they thrummed, then began to burn. A tendril of smoke curled from where I gripped the wood.

He noticed, his head bending to the side in curiosity. "What was that?"

I took in a deep breath, calming myself, and removed my hands from the table's edge.

Embarrassed, I realized I'd left marks on the wood. "It was nothing." I eased my napkin over the charred impression of my fingers, clearing my throat. "When you envisioned breakfast, did you fantasize about droning on and on about my imperfections?" I asked breezily as I filled my plate.

His mouth fell open. "Firstly, I haven't seen any yet. And secondly, how do you know I thought about this at all?"

"Because you've obviously put effort into it, and because *I* sit across from you while my sister fumes inside."

He laughed, the sound almost as startling as it was glorious. "You are refreshing, Atena."

I'd never been described as refreshing before. I wondered why he chose that word. I popped a grape in my mouth and chewed. "Thank you, Lumin."

He groaned and scrubbed a hand down his pretty face. "The titles are exhausting, are they not?"

"Do you not enjoy being Lumin?" *I will be* most *happy to remedy that for you and relieve you of the title you find so tiresome.*

"No, I do," he quickly corrected, filling his plate with meat and bread. "It's just... may I be candid?"

"I'd prefer it."

He grinned. "I'm sure your father explained that I'm open to forming an alliance with Helios."

"To picking a Helioan bride, you mean. Specifically me or my sister." Crimson stained his cheeks as he blushed, and I couldn't help but smile.

"Yes, but only if one of you wants such an arrangement, and only if your father is serious about the alliance beyond what the marriage might bring to our kingdoms."

I almost asked him what he might do if my sister and I decided we were both interested in being his blushing bride just to see how he might squirm, but he continued.

"If we are to learn one another, I think we need to get beyond our titles quickly and move on to other more pressing things."

I chewed a bite of bread and took a sip of water, wondering how to proceed, what sorts of pressing things he was referring to, and how to go about garnering the information I needed...

"I'd like for you to call me Caelum. And if you'll allow it, I'd like to call you Noor."

"In front of my father you will need to address me as Atena Noor," I warned. "Father values titles almost as much as sun diamonds."

He nodded. "I'll be careful when we are in mixed company, but when we are together, are you comfortable with you just being Noor and me just being Caelum?"

His eyes sparkled, not like last night, like the stars. This morning, hope gleamed within the silvery hues.

"Very well," I relented.

He'd proposed we get close fast, drop proprietary titles, and try to be ourselves. I was one step ahead of where I thought I might be this soon, and more importantly, one step ahead of Citali. I wondered what the crown of moonlight looked like, then pictured Caelum wearing it, his dark hair silhouetted against a glowing crown of silver and blue to match his eyes. Next, I would envision tearing it off his pretty head and running as fast as I could back toward Helios and Sol.

"Will you see my sister today?"

He looked properly embarrassed. "I've invited her to lunch."

"You certainly waste no time, *Caelum*."

His pupils flared at the sound of his name on my tongue. "Our kingdoms can't afford for more time to be wasted, *Noor*."

When he got to my name his voice deepened and a shiver coursed up my spine at his tone. I was suddenly glad we'd dropped our titles.

"I take it your father doesn't know you snuck down last night?"

I shook my head. "He doesn't, and I hope he will never learn of it," I said pointedly.

Caelum smiled and brushed his fingers over mine where they rested on the table. "Thank you for trusting me with your secret."

I shrugged, moving my hand away. "I have no other option."

He laughed again, shaking his head. I wasn't sure what was so funny.

Slowly, he sobered. "If I keep yours, will you keep mine? I, too, was spying."

"I suppose that's fair."

"Thank you. You—" He stopped himself, flashing an embarrassed smile, his dark lashes fluttering against his cheeks.

"What?"

"You're not how I expected you might be at all. And your skin is so incredibly hot. To the touch, I mean. It's very warm. And soft. And beautiful. You are an intimidating beauty." He groaned. "I'm making it worse with every breath." His cheeks turned pink again as he smiled.

It was my turn to laugh. "My skin is not hot; it's just that *yours* is frozen."

He scoffed, then spent the next few minutes regaling me with the story of his four-day journey upriver, his good humor apparent in his tone and demeanor. Just after they departed, the river began to freeze and he said he wasn't sure they would make it. I couldn't picture ice having the power to sheathe such churning strength. In all honesty, I couldn't envision ice. He described it as frigid and glass-like when I asked, but said it melted to water when warmed.

"If you were to enter my kingdom, Noor, you might melt the mountains." He said it playfully, but I couldn't tell if the idea that I might ruin his kingdom was distasteful, or if he'd enjoy seeing them dissolve.

"Have you considered inviting me there?" I teased.

"I imagined you and Citali there, though I had no idea what you'd be like or look like."

"Even though we might melt your mountains? Are you so easily willing to give them up?"

He laughed again, full-bodied, from his taut stomach. "The mountains themselves are made of hard rock, but they're covered with snow and ice. We wouldn't be risking the mountains, just their blanket of frost."

"And how do you know I *couldn't* melt the mountains, hard rock and all?"

He shook his head good humoredly and grinned. "If anyone was capable, I believe it might be you, Noor."

I wasn't sure what he meant by that, either, but the way his eyes smoldered felt as familiar as flame, and suddenly, I wondered if his temperament was as icy as originally thought. The way he teased and laughed made me think he might be someone I could grow to like.

"I hate to cut our time short, but I have to meet with your father and Sol's priests."

Kiran would meet Caelum. I wondered what he would think and what Saric would intuit from the exchange between Aten and Lumin. I wished I could attend so I could hear both kingdom's needs, demands, and concessions.

"Thank you for breakfast." I pushed away from the table and Caelum was there to tug my chair out, his hand proffered.

I slid mine into it, his cool palm soothing my heated fingers. When my napkin slid onto the ground, he saw the charred impression of my fingers.

He smirked, then laughed, squeezing my hand just before releasing it. He dubbed me, "Noor, melter of mountains. Not even the timber would stand a chance against your brilliant fire."

I tugged my hand away again and tucked them behind me. I wasn't accustomed to being touched.

"Have you walked the grounds? They're quite unusual. The hue here is so somber," he remarked.

Somber. I almost snorted. It was positively dismal. Still, it was something different and a place I might never see again. "I think I'll take a walk, then. I need to see this unique depression for myself. Commit it to memory."

He nodded, raking his teeth over his bottom lip. "I'll see you tonight. Save me a dance?" Mischief twinkled in his crystalline blue eyes. The dull silver light almost drowned the blue, but there it was in the depths.

"Perhaps," I teased, quirking a brow.

He all but had to drag himself away. Last night, we'd met in an unexpected way. It both terrified and thrilled me, and I now knew it had the same effect on Caelum. He'd invited me to dine with him first, then obviously enjoyed the time we spent together. He didn't want to leave.

I offered a sly smile.

He paused at the door and turned back, lifting his hand. I waved back as a warm feeling blossomed in my chest. The sun diamonds on my wrist made a tinkling noise from the gesture. When he disappeared into the House of Dusk, I turned to walk the grounds. I needed to familiarize myself with them, but beyond that, needed time outside.

When the urge came upon me back home, I walked into the dunes to *her* resting place. I sat with her and told her about my life, sharing secrets and thoughts I would never tell anyone. The dunes were quiet, and it was the one place I could be alone. There was no place for anyone to hide and few could withstand the pressing heat, let alone the burning sand. It was safe in the dunes.

Here? There were many places for someone to conceal themselves. It wasn't safe, and I hated the feeling that I had no security and no place to run if I needed it.

It was temperate here. Neither hot nor cold, but an uncomfortable tug-of-war between the two. The strange in-between chilled me and I longed for Sol's comforting, burning heat. If I was being honest, I was homesick.

Perhaps it was just the gray feel of the place. Somber, Caelum had called it. He was right, but also wrong. It *was* somber, but it was more than that. Melancholy fit, but didn't perfectly describe it.

I ambled along the drab gardens full of plants that had thrived at one point but didn't any longer. Walking the bank of the dull gray river, I watched curiously as dingy brown frogs hopped into the flow with my every startling step.

Something occurred to me as I reached the Luminan ship. My first impression of Caelum was a pleasant one. I groaned. *Pleasant* was too mild a term. I couldn't name anything correctly today.

If fire met ice, that might be akin to the first time I locked eyes with him. There was an initial confusion, but it only lasted a second before he seemed to recognize something deep within me. Something only visible to someone who truly looked, something I usually kept safely hidden, but for some reason didn't conceal from him. He saw *me*.

Noor.

Not one of the Atenas. Not the Aten's third born daughter.

Not a thief. Or a liar. Or a million things worse.

And, I think I saw the real him.

Caelum.

Not the Lumin.

Kind and concerned Caelum.

My second impression, which formed during breakfast, was far worse. Caelum was kind and funny and charming. He genuinely cared for and wanted the best for his people, and part of me wished he was the opposite. I wished he was cruel and as serious and sad as the dusk lands. I wished he was repulsive and not handsome.

Because if he truly was what he seemed, my plan would carve away at his kindness, erase his laughter, and kill his charm. If my plans succeeded and I managed to get close to him, I would break his trust. It would feel like an arrow struck his heart at the same time I plunged a dagger into his back. I would hurt him, and if I let myself get too close, I'd hurt myself in the process.

But this wasn't just about Caelum or me. What I did, I did for Helios. For Sol. And for me.

*It would be worth it.*

# 10

I was still meandering along the riverbank when Kiran found me. "Atena," he greeted.

My heart stumbled. No one was with him. No one seemed to be watching us. Was it safe to speak to him? "What are you doing here?" I hissed.

"Looking for you. It seems you're missing."

"Clearly, I'm not."

The corner of his lips turned upward just a fraction. "I'll see you to your rooms. Vada is there. A bath is being filled for you." He swept an arm toward the House of Dusk, the sight of the drab stone pulling a sigh I couldn't stifle.

"You don't like it in the dusk lands?" he asked as we walked.

I glanced across the grounds and through the gardens. I didn't see anyone hiding, but if Kiran had been sent to find me, others were likely looking.

"It's gray and so sullen, I find it hard to feel anything but the same."

"You miss Sol," he rasped. "It's hard being so far from her."

I felt ashamed for my selfish behavior. Kiran and Saric were Sol's priests. She'd chosen them, but her priests also had to choose her. They either accepted her call and gave up their lives, possessions, and dreams to dedicate themselves to the sun goddess, or they rejected such a life to carve out one without such constraints.

Kiran had done exactly that. He'd left his family when they needed his strength in their crop fields. He'd moved away from them into the temple where he joined a new family and a mysterious brotherhood. He loved his chosen life because he loved Sol.

"What did you think of the Lumin?" he asked conversationally, but the way he watched me from the corner of his eye made me wonder how weighty the question was.

I shrugged. "He seems nice."

"Is that all?" he asked.

"He's considerate, clever, attractive... but I've only spoken to him a handful of moments and we both know that's not enough to form a true opinion of someone."

His pinky drifted across mine as we drew near the House. I stiffened at his touch. What if someone saw? I hoped it was only the seed of our friendship and his caring heart that led him to chance it. It couldn't be anything more. He and I knew that. We had to tread lightly even daring to be friends. We could never be more. And if someone had seen what he just did, Kiran could be killed for touching me, even discreetly.

He could not do such things anymore. The sands were the only safe place for us to be friends. And even there, he shouldn't touch me, regardless of the emotion behind the action.

Kiran quietly saw me inside and escorted me to the seventh floor where he deposited me with a very worried Vada. I opened my mouth to tell him I'd see him later before stopping myself. I had to be careful. I'd almost spoken to him irreverently in front of Vada, a stranger who might tell others that the priest and Atena were close friends.

Rumors like that could more than damage reputations, they could kill. They could also ruin my chances of making progress with Caelum.

Vada clutched her chest. "We've looked everywhere for you!"

"I was near the river. I didn't realize it was so late. It's hard to tell without Sol above us."

The worried pinch in her lips smoothed. "I thought Sol did not move."

"She doesn't slide across the sky, but she has a dark spot that rotates. We can tell the hour based on its position."

"Ah." Vada nodded in understanding. "Your bath is ready," she said, urging me toward the bathing room. "We have much work to do before the feast tonight."

"What kind of work?"

She stopped in front of the tub of steaming water and took another of her sachets, emptying divine-smelling salts into it. We quietly watched them dissolve, each lost in our own thoughts. "I know you dined with the Lumin this morning. I won't deign to guess how that meal went, as you disappeared afterward—"

"No," I interrupted. "Vada, breakfast was perfect. It's just that everyone was busy afterward, and I don't like staying in my room all the time. In Helios, I can disappear into the sand, which is actually a vast sea of desert dunes that would entrap even a seasoned traveler, but it's my back yard and I know it like I know my own heart. There, Sol's rays are so hot that the sand burns the feet of even the priests if they don't wrap them well enough."

"But it doesn't bother you?"

I shook my head and closed my eyes, remembering the comfort of Sol's rays. "It feels cool to me. Comforting. I spend my free hours walking in the sand." I swallowed thickly. "It's where my mother's remains are spread. I spend time with her."

Vada turned to me and clasped my upper arm gently. "I'm sorry, Atena Noor."

"You can just call me Noor. And, I promise I'll try not to worry you again."

As the steam fogged the room, Vada gestured to the door. "I'll leave you to bathe, unless you require help."

"I don't, but thank you."

"I knew what the Lumin would wear to breakfast this morning and what dress you brought that would best fit the occasion, but I've no idea what to suggest for tonight." She cleared her throat. "Your sister is already dressed."

I laughed. "From your reaction, I'm guessing she's showing plenty of skin."

"That, my dear, would be an understatement." Her eyes widened as if the shocking memory arose again.

The Luminans, thus far, covered more of their bodies than we did. In the heat, my people had to stay comfortable, so we were not modest. Besides, Citali did not know the meaning of the word.

"My sister is not subtle. She never has been."

Vada flicked a glance at the armoire. "Do you intend to wear something similar?"

"I own nothing similar. My style differs from my sister's. But I'll tell you what I'd prefer if you could find it for me while I bathe. It's red and gold. The top is cropped, but the gown's skirt is full and intricate. The most it will bare is my collar bones and a sliver of stomach."

"Of course."

I closed the door as she strode to the armoire. Undressing, I wondered if Citali's approach would win the Lumin over. Was Caelum the sort of man who was easily manipulated by beautiful things? If so, Sol help him. Citali would eat him alive.

Citali wanted to show him what she would look like on his bed. She would leave nothing to his imagination.

I chose a different path. I wanted him to know how I would look as his queen.

Vada brushed my hair until it was mostly dry. I caked as much powder as I could onto my throat. Again, she noticed the mottling, but didn't pry and for that, I was grateful.

I was grateful to her for other reasons, too. She was kind and helpful. She seemed to intuit what I needed before I was even aware. And she made this strange, gray place a little brighter just by being present.

There was also the fact that Vada wasn't afraid of me. The servants my father employed were scared of us all. One misstep and they knew it might be their last. Father had put many to death for mistakes anyone could've made just because his emotions were severe and untamed.

She watched as I carefully traced coal around my eyes and added shimmer powder to my cheeks and red stain to my lips, covering the scab that Caelum noticed even though it was thinner than ever now.

She weaved the top layer of my hair back in a series of intricate braids, leaving the rest full. "Do you need help dressing?"

I shook my head. "I could do this with my eyes closed. Father enjoys hosting feasts." *Even as our people starve.*

"Noor," she began, but hesitated. She held her back straight and clasped her hands in front of her.

"You can speak freely to me. I hope you know that."

She nodded. "I just want to make an offer, but don't want to offend you in any way."

I smiled. "I won't be offended."

"The Lumin will host a ball which will include another lush meal and dancing. The gowns you have would more than suffice. They're beautiful. More beautiful than anything I've seen, but... would you like me to have a dress made for you in the Luminan style? In the colors of our kingdom?"

*In the colors of Lumina... Hmm.* "Are you doing the same for Citali?"

She tipped up her chin. "No."

I smiled. Vada was on my side. I wondered how well she knew Caelum. "Then, I'd very much appreciate it."

Her eyes glittered. "I just so happen to know the most skilled seamstress in the kingdom, and she just so happens to be here with us. She'll need to get your measurements first thing tomorrow to get started in time to finish by the evening of the ball."

"The ball will take place at the end of negotiations. That will likely take weeks, but if things go well, it could happen much sooner, perhaps within days."

She nodded. "No matter which, it'll be enough time."

I grabbed Vada's hand and squeezed. "Thank you, Vada."

She nodded. There was something about her I couldn't figure out. Servants were treated far greater in Lumina than Helios. That was beyond apparent, but she didn't act like any servant I'd seen. There was a familiar keenness to her; an air about her that made us equals, neither better than the other despite the blood coursing through our veins. We were both born into our stations, helpless to escape them, but Vada still wore a crown.

It was in the gray braid encircling her head, yes, but it was also in her posture and bearing. In the pride she took in her work. In the sharp intellect that lay in her observant eyes.

She rifled through the armoire for sandals while I changed into my favorite, most flattering dress. It fit me better than any other I owned. In fact, it felt like I didn't own the gown at all, but the gown owned me. I was born just to hold it up so others could see her grandness.

Twisting threads of pure, spun gold had been sewn through the red silk. Gold embellished the short sleeves, collar, and coiled around my bare stomach like a gilded serpent.

When Vada found a pair of dark gold sandals, she turned, triumphant. Then she gasped and clutched her chest. "My goodness! You look exactly how I imagine Sol might look if she walked the earth for an evening."

I blushed at her compliment. "Thank you."

"If the Lumin doesn't say the same, I'll be shocked."

"You know him well enough to assume that?" I teased.

She held the sandals out for me to take and I bent to strap them to my feet and ankles. Together, we chose a wide choker collar that would hide most of the bruising on my throat. "Will it be painful to wear?" Vada worried.

Not nearly as painful as the crushing hands had been, or as sore as the bruises were the hours after he left them on me, or as painful as the concealed lump on my head was until it sank back in. "It doesn't hurt," I lied.

It didn't hurt terribly bad, but with every movement of my neck, I was reminded of my father and his hatred. It made me crave the crown of moonlight all the more.

Vada chose a pair of golden earrings to match my choker. They dangled from my lobe to skim my collar bones. I slid a few more bangles onto each wrist. She glanced from the sun diamonds to me. "Would they burn me if I touched them?"

I nodded. "They would."

"Why does Citali not have them?"

"I inherited them from my mother. While Citali and I share the same father, we emerged from different wombs."

"The two of you look somewhat alike, but…"

"Not," I finished with a smile. "I've been told I look like my mother. *Exactly* like her."

A knock came at the door and Zuul stood in the hallway, quietly speaking to Citali. The two were probably plotting my death.

Vada promised to lock my room after she finished tidying up if I wanted to leave with Zuul and Citali, but I told her it was fine and that I would wait for her. She hurried to straighten the mess we'd made and bustled out the door. I followed her and closed my door softly, then locked it and slid the key into my pocket.

Citali glowered when her eyes combed over me. She wore a dress that was little more than scraps of cloth carefully stretched to cover her nipples and backside. The fabric was orange, fading to yellow. She looked like a scantily clad lily.

"You used your best dress this early?" she laughed as if I was stupid.

I shrugged. "You know what they say about first impressions. Not that you aren't making your own."

"Exactly," she said, sashaying down the hall and away from me. Zuul trailed her, not bothering to escort me even though that must have been his order. "And, it's actually our second meeting, not the first," she corrected.

In her mind, it was time to begin the game she and I were playing, and she was prepared to do whatever it took to win.

I made my way down the staircases and paused to look over the crowd of Helioans and Luminans gathered at the landing, waiting to be allowed into the great room where the feast would take place. I smelled the smoked meat and heady spices, reminding me I hadn't eaten since breakfast.

Citali made her way down the steps and Caelum, ever the gentlemen, waited to greet her at the bottom. He smiled at her, took her hand, and placed a soft kiss on the back of it.

He said something that made her laugh, then her smile melted away and she turned to look at me over her shoulder. His eyes followed, catching on me where I stood at the top of the steps. My pulse raced as if my heart wanted to burst from my chest and run the race in which Citali and I were competing, as if she alone wanted to claim him as her prize.

He didn't wear his crown tonight, but he did wear a startling black tunic and matching pants. The fabric was crisp and fit him as well as my gown fit me. His blue-black hair was slicked back, but a few pieces fell into his eyes. He brushed them away and waited, hands folded in front of him.

His crystal blue eyes didn't leave me for even a second.

Citali tried to speak to him and pull his attention away but failed so miserably she pouted like a petulant toddler.

I proceeded down the steps, suppressing a smile.

The sides of Citali's breasts were on full display, as were her tone, trim legs. If he was the sort to care only for appearances, he wouldn't be watching me this way.

His attention never flinched and mine was fixed on him just as eagerly. The apple in his throat bobbed as I drew close, then stopped on the bottom step.

"Are you going to kiss my hand the way you kissed my sister's?" I asked in a low voice only he could hear.

His lips quirked. "Would that please you, Atena Noor?"

"No," I said, raising my chin. "It would not. I am not my sister and she is not me."

"Whatever shall I do?" His words trailed away.

He proffered both hands and I almost rolled my eyes. If the best he could come up with was to kiss the backs of *both* my hands, he needed to work on his creativity. But instead of drawing my hands to his supple lips, he tugged on them so I had to step down, placing my chest almost flush with his. He bent to reach me and leaned in close. The phoenix in my stomach awakened and flapped her fiery wings when his warm breath ghosted over my cheek and those perfect lips found the corner of my jaw.

"Was that acceptable?" he rasped.

"I suppose," I said, desperately trying to tamp down a smile and unable to completely do so.

Citali's glare from over his shoulder could've melted the sun diamonds I wore. In response, I winked. She bared her teeth, faking a smile when he stepped away and remembered her again.

Within the crowd, my father stood. For the first time I can remember since Mother died, he smiled at me.

At first, I thought it might be pride filling his expression, but he'd never been proud of me. What filled his features was greed.

I smiled back, thinking all the while that I would soon be responsible for wiping that greedy grin away for good.

The doors of the great hall opened and people parted to allow the Aten, followed closely by Zuul, then Caelum and the Atenas into the room first.

Helios's best musicians sat in a corner of the room so the sound of their instruments would project to every angle. They began to play as Father observed the artistically arranged, still-steaming food. Long tables stretched most of the length of the room, but one smaller table sat apart, perpendicular to the long ones for the masses.

It was an honor to have been invited here, but Father wouldn't deign to sit and eat with anyone he didn't consider chosen by one of the gods, set apart from the common citizens. Father moved to one of the heads of the table and waited for Caelum to stand in front of the opposite seat.

Saric and Kiran, dressed in their ceremonial golden kilts, their chests bare and wearing the bicep cuffs given to them by Sol, hovered nearby with two priests of Lumos. Their counterparts were dressed in loose, pale blue tunics and matching pants, tied at the waist by a silver braided cord. Their feet were tucked into thick, white boots. I wondered if they were too warm, and Saric and Kiran too cold.

Citali and I waited to see which seat we'd be taking. I prayed mine would be far from Kiran. Today's brush was too much, but I hadn't had the opportunity to tell him so yet. I didn't want him to be encouraged by my silence.

My eyes flicked to Caelum, but he was already looking at me. My heart skipped happily as he smiled.

Father gestured to me and Citali. "Where would you like for them to sit, Lumin?"

He was letting Caelum decide. Deferring to him. Something Father never did at home, but which was a wise move on his part. He was pretending to be kind, acting like a perfect father who genuinely wanted peace and trade to exist between the two kingdoms. He acted like he thought Caelum was worthy of one of our hands.

In reality, he was more than happy to offer us up to him like we meant nothing and had no minds to choose our own husbands.

Caelum smiled and thanked him. "I'd be honored if Noor would sit at my right hand, and Citali at my left."

Father inclined his head. He shot us a permissive look and we moved to the seats he'd indicated. I nearly glowed, forgetting my internal grumblings about unfairness. The right hand was considered a place of reverence. It is where his queen would sit if he had one.

Citali occupied the second most important seat. And it ate away at her.

She fidgeted with her place setting, refusing to meet my taunting eyes.

The Luminan priests, clad in loose, silver tunics and matching wide legged pants, sat beside me and Citali, then Saric and Kiran took the seats at Father's left and right hands.

"Your mother is not joining us tonight?" Father asked Caelum.

"I'm afraid she has a terrible headache. She said she would come down as soon as the herbs she took eases it."

Father nodded. "It's the light."

*What light?* This gray in-between felt so dull, I wouldn't consider it light at all, but in a place where true darkness crept into every crevice, it must seem bright here. I hadn't thought of how different the dusk lands were to those from Lumina.

"I hope she feels better soon," Citali cooed.

Caelum inclined his head and thanked her for her concern.

I noted that his mother came with him. I wondered about his father. Did he have siblings? His eyes met mine as I studied him. He offered a small, quizzical smile, which I returned.

Our table was served fresh food as guests filled the hall and made their way around the luscious buffet. Helioans were excited to have a comforting meal from home, while Luminans seemed eager to try something new and different from what they were accustomed to eating. The atmosphere was light and jovial.

Caelum leaned toward me and whispered, "I'll admit I'm not sure what to try first."

*A Lumin in need; I am lucky indeed.* "I can help you decide."

"I'd love that."

I gestured to his plate and he scooped it up, relinquishing it with a curious smile when I took it from him. I stood to reach a few of my favorites and filled his plate with them. When I sat his plate back in front of him, I realized that the Luminan half of the table had gone still and quiet.

My eyes flicked to his. He coughed to cover a laugh. "What did I do wrong?" I asked, alarmed.

His priests looked down at their half-full plates. They smothered their grins, poorly, might I add, for the pious.

Citali quirked a sharp brow as she sat back and crossed her arms. She smirked, clearly enjoying my evident faux pas and gleefully watching to see exactly what I'd done and what it might mean for her.

Caelum inclined his head. "Thank you, Atena Noor," he said. "I understand that things are different in Helios. It's just that in Lumina, when a woman plates a man's food or a man hand-feeds a woman, it announces their intent to... uh..."

"To?" I stiffened.

"To be intimate with that person," he continued. He put a hand up in defense. "But I know that was not your intent. We all know that."

My face turned to flame. "No," I said, quickly recovering my composure. "I simply provided my favorite foods for you to taste. I wasn't implying anything other than that you should try them."

He gave a gracious nod and thanked me again.

Lumos's priests finally resumed eating and plucking food from the golden platters lining the table's middle. Candlelight flickered overhead. The chandeliers had been lowered to provide more light for our feast, but I wished they still hung high. My cheeks were still hot. I sipped water to cool them, but it seemed nothing would extinguish the flame.

Citali straightened her spine, so pleased with my mistake, she struck up a conversation. "How interesting the differences in our customs, Lumin. Please, tell us more about Luminan culture."

Citali *did not* care about Luminan culture.

Citali was crafty and didn't want to chance a mistake. Unlike me.

She wanted to learn about him and his people, marching each step toward the crown of moonlight, perfect and precise. Citali would not stumble.

The priests exchanged stories of their people's customs and how they'd originated. It was interesting to hear about Lumina and Lumos, so different from Helios and Sol. We could sit for weeks and still not know all there was to tell about one another's kingdoms and ways of life, but this was a start. Maybe my mistake opened the door to communication and something constructive could come from it.

A frigid hand squeezed mine under the table. Unlike Kiran's earlier brush, this cool touch was comforting. It was strong and sure. "It's okay," Caelum whispered.

I nodded and tried to smile but was certain it looked forced. Nervousness shook my hands. "I hope you like the food."

He cut into a piece of cooked pheasant and his eyes widened when he tasted the spices coating its skin. "It's delicious!"

I grinned, the tension easing as he tasted delicacy after delicacy, complimenting all but the raw sunfish eggs. I laughed at his expression when he forced himself to swallow those.

Citali pushed her plate away petulantly and waited for our laughter to end. "Lumin, would you honor me with a dance?"

His lashes fluttered in surprise, but he wiped his mouth with a napkin and accepted her invitation. "Of course, Atena."

I wondered if he had asked her to drop her title in private as well. If when they danced, he would only call her Citali.

He scooted his chair out, his crystal eyes meeting mine before he offered her his hand. The two made their way to the dance floor and every eye in the room fell on them as they swayed to a mild rhythm. Citali might have worn half a dress, but she truly was beautiful. She laughed with him and his hand settled on her back, the other clasped with hers. He held it out in the air, their arms stiff.

Citali looked at him like his face was Sol herself and she'd been away from her rays too long. He seemed at ease and completely comfortable with her. His shoulders were relaxed, as was his smile when it wasn't his turn to speak.

Father noticed them, too. His pleasure was as palpable as his greed. His plan was blossoming. It didn't matter to him whether the Lumin chose Citali or me; he just needed one of us on the inside. But if Caelum chose Citali and Sol chose Zarina, he would have no use for me.

I had to find that crown before my sister did.

They danced for a few more songs. Father quirked a brow at me. A challenge. He'd told me what would happen if I failed. He was reminding me of it now, telling me to rise above if I wanted to live.

The sun diamonds warmed against my wrist and ankle.

# 11

A woman wearing a dress dotted with uniquely-blue moon diamonds strode gracefully into the room. Her hand lay over the forearm of a handsome young man who could almost pass as Caelum's twin.

Almost.

There were subtle differences.

As they reached me, I noted that his eyes weren't the same shade of blue, but a deeper tone. Not only that, but they weren't as sharp, but were lazily taking in the scene despite the fact he seemed to miss nothing.

His nose wasn't as straight and perfect, but it had been broken in the past. The woman leaned in to whisper something in his ear. A dimple popped in his cheek as the two glided to our table. Servants scrambled for two additional chairs and we all slid down to make room for them.

When the woman sat down across from me, I went still and every muscle in my body tensed. Wearing her hair in a sleek gray chignon with a few tendrils purposely untucked and a dress made for a queen, was Vada.

"Good evening, Vada," Father greeted her. "I trust your headache has eased?"

"It has," she noted. "I'm feeling much better now, thank you."

*Vada is Caelum's mother? Why did she act as my attendant? Why did she pretend to be a servant?*

The only truth I could infer was that she wanted to see how we might treat her, to learn how the two women vying for her son's hand might act privately and to those beneath their station.

Vada inclined her head, a promise on her face that she would explain eventually.

She didn't have to. It was like the dancer Kevi told me – she owed me no explanation. Her motives were her own, and if I was being honest, hers weren't nearly as deceitful as mine. She gestured to her other son as they took their seats. "I don't believe you've met Beron, Caelum's younger brother."

Beron glanced from his mother to me and back, then inclined his head to everyone at the table. "Pleased to meet you."

Father urged them to eat and asked for water and wine to be brought out for them. Beron ate with the speed and intent of a starving crocodile, while Vada politely sawed, chewed, and complimented each dish she sampled. Her posture was impeccable. Her motions poised.

I'd noticed some of that queenly grace even in my rooms, but never imagined…

Beron cleared his throat. "Atena Noor, would you permit me to lead you in a dance since my brother seems indisposed at the moment? A woman as beautiful as you should not be left waiting."

Smooth as silk and just as charming. I liked him immediately and wholeheartedly agreed with his opinion. I looked to Father who gave a slight nod, then lay my napkin on the table. "I'd love to."

Vada smiled conspiratorially. Perhaps she still favored me and wanted to allow Beron's attention to provoke jealousy in Caelum's heart. Or maybe she wanted me in her family even if Caelum chose Citali. Either ploy could work in my favor. Either scenario brought me one step closer to the crown of moonlight.

As he likely had noted the differences between me and Citali, I compared Beron and Caelum. Beron wasn't as tall as his older brother, but the two were similarly built with broad shoulders and tapered waists. Beneath Beron's dark blue tunic were lines defining corded muscle. Caelum certainly was well-built, too. When we were far enough away from the table, he smirked. "Time to see where you stand with my brother." I laughed incredulously. He cocked his head to the side the way Caelum sometimes did. "Don't tell me you aren't wondering how he'll react."

"I absolutely am," I admitted.

He glanced all around us. "You and everyone else in the room. It's like they're holding their breath to see what he'll do. I've heard you're a good *dancer*," he punctuated with a wink.

My lips parted.

He continued despite my shock. "These songs, they're a little boring, though. Would you like to stay in this comfort zone, swaying to these boring rhythms, or do you want to put on a show?"

"I'm a born performer. I only worry my dance partner might not be able to keep up," I teased, one brow quirked.

He chuckled. "Oh, I think you'll find that I can. I love a challenge."

He led me to the musicians who slowly stopped playing. I bent to request a few songs I knew would liven things up a bit. While they prepared, Beron led me to where Caelum and Citali stood. Citali's frown was as frosty as Caelum's touch. And Caelum? His gaze burned.

Beron leaned in and whistled. "There's no love lost between you and your sister, I take it? When I nodded, he asked, "Because of my brother, or due to an older wound?"

"Much older," I answered.

He nodded knowingly, then clasped my hand and spun me in a circle as the music began. He jerked me forward, snaking a strong arm around my back, then whispered. "Eyes on me. It'll drive him crazy."

Beron was ornery and apparently loved to see his brother squirm. Or make him angry. Caelum calmly led Citali to the side, then stood at her side watching as Beron led me through several steps. My sister tried to coax him back into a dance, but he held up a hand.

Good. He was intrigued.

"You *are* an impressive dancer. I may finally have met my match," Beron admitted with a teasing grin. In a sweeping motion, he dipped me backward, holding my neck and supporting my weight with his arm. His free hand drifted over my sternum, across my bare stomach. I gasped at his boldness. His hand stopped on my waist, then I was up and spinning again.

I laughed as he moved us along with the bolder shift in the music, then he spun me again and I slammed into a hard chest, glancing up into Caelum's calm but steely face. The Lumin flashed Beron a look that dared him to interrupt and flicked a stern nod toward Citali.

The younger brother moved to ask my sister to dance, but I couldn't focus on them.

Not while Caelum's broad hand splayed the bare sliver of my exposed lower back, his cool touch exactly what I needed to soothe my heated flesh. The Lumin seemed to glow from within, his skin cool and pale, like I imagined ice or snow might look, lit by the moon I'd never seen but desperately wanted to. It controlled the tides, strong enough to pull and tug on bodies of water that were unfathomably deep and wide as the earth herself.

"My brother invited you to dance." It wasn't a question, but it seemed like he wanted an answer.

"He was kind enough to, yes."

"Kind? My brother was *not* being kind. He's part wolf. To him, you were prey. But you quickly reframed his perception. Now, he considers you his equal."

I cocked an eyebrow. "You can tell all that from one dance?"

He nodded. "I know Beron."

I stood tall as he spun me so my back was pressed against his chest. We swayed together, lost in the moment. Citali and Beron danced nearby but her dress and his brazenness made it look almost lewd.

*Is that what we'd looked like?*

Soon, other couples came to the dance floor. Luminan and Helioan joined by music, spurred on by wine and curiosity. I felt myself relax. Caelum's tension bled away, too.

"I'm sorry," he finally said.

My lips parted. *The Lumin apologized to me!* Never in my life had my father uttered those words. "For what?"

"For allowing Citali to take up so much of my time."

"It's only fair that you spend time with her. You barely know either of us."

"You're right. That's something I'd like to remedy, and in time, I hope to know much more about you."

*Both of us, he meant.*

"Is Beron your only brother?"

He nodded. "It's just the two of us. I assume you met my mother."

I opened my mouth but stopped myself from telling him I'd gotten to know her rather well. If he didn't know, it seemed like she didn't want me to tell him. "She's lovely."

He smiled toward the table where Vada raised a golden goblet toward us and drank. He laughed. "She's not bothering to hide which of you she favors."

"She doesn't know me or Citali," I argued.

He pulled me in tighter. "No, but she knows me. She can see I'm drawn to you, Noor."

"Did you tell Citali the same thing just now?" I challenged, walking around him to the drumbeat, letting my hand trail over his chest, arm, back, and his other arm, then returning to face him. His crystal eyes flared, a slight glow emanating from them now.

"No, I didn't," he said. "Our conversations have been as shallow as the river at its edge."

"And ours?"

"We've barely spoken, but it feels like you're a siren and have already dragged me into the depths."

"What's a siren?" I asked, curious. But he only chuckled. "I hate to interrupt your giggling, but I think you should ask your mother to dance."

"You wouldn't mind? You and I haven't danced for long."

"It's obvious her headache still plagues her. She might not stay."

He looked at her just as she discreetly rubbed her temple. "You're right. How did you notice that?"

I shrugged. "I notice many things." I gestured to the musicians. "You should go and get her before it's too late. We can dance afterward. Would you like a softer song for now?"

He nodded gratefully. "That would be perfect. Thank you, Noor."

I spoke with the musicians as he went to coax his mother into a dance. He helped her from her seat and led her to the floor as I moved back to the table and took a sip of water. Saric and Kiran paid me no attention. The priests of Lumos averted their eyes, as they seemed to do when I stood before them. Perhaps that was another of their customs.

Father came to stand beside me and bent to speak so only I could hear. "I can't tell which of you he favors, but how fortuitous that there are *two* brothers..."

He walked on, mingling with some of Caelum's guard, waving over Zuul and a few other of his most trusted warriors. They began exchanging stories, boisterous laughter flooding the room with the music.

Caelum still danced with Vada, and Beron was slowly guiding Citali around the floor. While they were occupied, I made my way from the room and slipped outside into a small garden, stepping into the drenching gray light. A few moments later, the door opened behind me. Music and smoke escaped from the door as Caelum emerged.

"My mother noticed you left," he explained. "She's going to retire for the evening to ease her aching head."

Vada missed nothing. "I hope she'll feel better tomorrow."

"After some rest, I'm sure she will." He put his hands in his pockets. "My mother is amazing. I don't know how much you know of how the Lumin is chosen..."

"I only know how Sol chooses her Aten."

"Sol's choice follows a particular bloodline... a lineage, right?"

"Yes."

"Lumos chooses his Lumin from among the people. Male or female. Old or young. Rich or poor. He doesn't care. He only cares about the person's heart and whether it aligns with his, and whether the person's ambition is strong enough to carry out his will."

My mouth gaped, thinking about how different it was for Sol.

"My mother was a ladies' maid to a wealthy Luminan family when I was chosen. She came from little, but even though she has much now, she helps everyone she can. She's an advocate for those less fortunate. She's seen the best and worst of people. Her opinion is important to me. Not only because she's my mother, but because of her upbringing and experience. Mother's impression of people isn't formed lightly, and under normal circumstances, she wouldn't form one so quickly. Though, our circumstances require swiftness, don't they?"

I could do nothing but agree with him. "Yes, they do."

"She spent the last couple of years searching for anyone she thought might be a good match for me, and for Beron. A moment ago was the first time she's ever mentioned a woman by name." I took in a slow, deep breath. He took my hands in his and brushed his chilly thumbs over the backs of my fingers. "It was *your* name she spoke for me, Noor."

The phoenix in my stomach stirred, lifted her proud head, and let her fire grow. But his expression wasn't one of joy. It was wary.

"Yet you're hesitant," I remarked quietly.

"I am. I've heard rumors…"

"What sort of rumors?"

His eyes glittered in the gray, somehow alive when everything surrounding us was dead and dull. "Play a game with me?"

I tilted my head. "How do you play this game?"

"You tell me a rumor you've heard about me, then I'll do the same, and we'll go back and forth until all the rumors are dispelled or confirmed."

"Citali will be looking for you," I tested.

He squeezed my hands and looked down at them. "I don't want to think about Citali right now. But if you don't want to spend time with me, I–"

"I do!" I interrupted quickly. "I want to. I'm just jealous."

It was hard to admit, but it was the truth. I'd never needed anything more than to play his game and learn why he was reticent to accept his mother's advice. Beyond that, I wanted this for me. Not because of the crown or the expectations or hopes that lay with it.

Kevi had remarked that I hadn't had time to just be a girl. And now... with Caelum in this garden, for the first time, I finally felt like one. What was even better was this time, I didn't need to dance or disguise myself. With him, I could be me for a time.

Perhaps that was why my voice shook, or why my knees felt like they might buckle. Caelum was a balm of sorts, the cool to my warm, and I desperately craved his attention. Maybe that made me more like Citali than I'd like to admit, but I didn't care. When Caelum focused on me and I focused on him, it was like nothing else existed. The gray landscape suddenly burst into colors, some of which I couldn't even name.

He grinned and led me to a bench overlooking a stagnant pond. Someone had tried to add river reeds to it, but they'd died and now laid over the pond's edge like stiff hair.

"Who will begin this game of ours?" he teased.

"I will," I volunteered.

His eyes lit. "Very well. What do they say of me, or of my kingdom, in Helios?"

"One rumor that was dispelled by this trip was that Luminans had difficulty seeing in any sort of light and lived in the ground like moles. You don't seem to have trouble with your vision, so that rumor – in part, at least – was false. I'm not sure about your living arrangements, so I can't verify that portion."

He snorted. "We don't live in the ground." He shook his head. "Moles."

When I was little, I overheard Zarina tell Citali that story and for many years I believed her. I envisioned Caelum as a mole, with a little mole nose, and a laugh bubbled from my chest.

"You're picturing me as a mole, aren't you?"

"Never," I tried to vow, trying desperately to smother my laughter.

"Well, Atena Noor, I was told that the Atenas glowed. That Sol's rays radiated from you at all times."

I held my arm out and shook my head. "Not even a little."

"It's not wholly untrue," he said seriously. "Your eyes have a golden glow to them in certain lights. Citali's don't, though."

"It's probably a trick of the light. The candelabras—"

"No, it's not," he interrupted. "I see it even now."

I blinked rapidly, breaking his stare.

"I thought you knew," he said softly.

"Sol's priests… and even Citali mentioned it on the ship. That was the first time… I'm still not convinced it's not due to the gray light here." I glanced at the sky. "Another rumor I heard when I was a child was that Luminan skin could not survive the sun. That it was so pale, it would flake away like ash."

He half-smiled. "That remains to be seen. I've never felt the sun on my skin. Now my turn. I've heard your priests sacrifice people to Sol." He watched me carefully for my answer.

"Never. Sol loves her subjects. All of them. But I heard something along the same lines about Luminans," I turned the tables on him. "When we were little, my eldest sister told me that you didn't eat food, but instead had fangs and drank blood like bats. She said you lived in caves. Then there were concerns of you only feasting upon raw meat."

He opened his mouth, then snapped it closed like he didn't know which part to address first before his eyes began to twinkle. "Caves?" He smiled. "It's an upgrade from mole hills, I suppose. I'm sorry to disappoint you, but we love cooked food and abhor blood. Did this same sister tell you the story about us being moles as well?"

I nodded.

"How could both be true?"

"Children do not rely on the tenets of logic."

"Ah." He nodded, then his smile fell away. "Someone told me that you and your sister are only entertaining the thought of marrying me to get to the crown of moonlight."

My breath seized. For a second, I wondered how to answer. He valued bluntness and humor... "Of course we are." I let a smile stretch over my lips.

He shook his head. "Do you think marrying me would mean that you would wear its match?"

"Its match in appearance, you mean, not in power."

"What do you know about its power?" he asked, watching me carefully.

"My father can draw Sol close to earth or lift her into the heavens, but he cannot move her across the sky. I've heard that the crown of moonlight allows the wearer to move the moon wherever he likes."

"What else?" His voice wasn't sharp, but it lacked the warmth to which I'd become accustomed.

"The tides. The wearer of the crown can calm or raise the tides."

He nodded. "That's all you've heard?"

"Perhaps it makes blood taste like honey?" I teased.

He grinned. "Seriously?"

"I made that one up. That's all I've heard."

"Do you know where to find the crown you seek?" he asked, half-playfully.

"Do you know where to find sun diamonds?" I volleyed.

He grinned. "I don't."

I sat back a little, satisfied. "Then we both have our secrets."

"You won't find the crown, Noor. If that's what you're after, I should warn you before you waste your time, and mine, searching."

I met his stare. "Nor will you find the source of Sol's tears."

"Sol's tears?" He gently took my hand and lifted it to see my wrist and the tiny diamonds hanging from the bracelet there.

"Sol's tears. That's what Citali says they look like," I told him. "I wear more than Father has in the treasury. The fact that he gave you one is significant."

"He gave you these?"

I shook my head. "My mother had my bracelet and anklet made for me." Sun diamonds, and the knowledge about them was a secret, but I'd given it in exchange for an ounce of his trust.

"Why can only you wear them?"

"When we were girls, Citali said that my mother cursed them before she clasped them on."

He pursed his lips together. "What do you think?"

I smiled. "I think I don't care if she did because I miss her every day and this is how I carry her with me."

He turned my palm up and gently kissed the center of it. Instead of pulling away, I scooted closer. "You've kissed my jaw and palm," I said. "But never my lips. They're jealous."

His eyes hooded, dark lashes fanning as he stared at my mouth. Slowly, he leaned in until his lips hovered just over mine. Our mouths brushed together. I lifted a hand to his jaw and ran my thumb over the stubble there as his hand found the back of my neck and raked up into my hair. He pressed his lips to mine, his tongue sweeping over them, and I forgot myself, every silly rumor I'd ever heard, the crown, and even my father's threats.

There was only Caelum and his perfect, perfect lips.

We parted too soon, and his hand tightened on my nape as if he didn't want to let go. As if he wanted to hold me in the garden for an eternity.

I did, too.

Just then, the door behind us opened.

Citali emerged, wearing an innocent expression I immediately recognized as fake. "Father is looking for you, Noor."

I narrowed my eyes at her.

Caelum stood with me and offered to escort me inside. "It's okay," I told him. "I'll be right back."

"If you're sure."

I nodded and walked around him toward the door where I let my shoulder check Citali's. She huffed and rubbed the spot as I kept walking. She, of course, joined Caelum in the garden. I would've done the same.

I wondered how long she'd been behind the door. If she heard the kiss and the secret I'd given him. If she'd run to Father with it if she had. Would Father care if it meant I got close enough to steal the precious crown of moonlight? Admittedly, a crown Caelum warned I would never find.

Who told him what we were after? It didn't take a genius to come to that conclusion, but neither of us had blatantly mentioned the crown... unless Citali did at lunch or during their dance tonight. Did she prematurely arouse his suspicions?

Back in the great hall, Father was still standing with Zuul and the other men. They parted when I drew close, not bothering to conceal their lustful glances now that the strong wine had turned their eyes to glass. "You wished to see me?"

His mottled face exposed just how much wine he'd imbibed. His dark brows furrowed angrily. "I did not ask for you, Noor." He turned his back and his men waited until I left. I felt their eyes clinging to me as I walked away.

*That lying minx!*

Beron caught up with me in the hallway. "Hey," he greeted.

"Hi," I bit out.

"Where are you going? You look... angry."

"I'm going to kill my sister."

He barked a laugh but stopped when he saw I was serious.

"She lied to get you away from my brother?" His brows rose appreciatively. "Can't say I haven't used that trick before."

"How many women have you and your brother played for fools?" I asked.

Because now I realized that was what this was. Citali and I thought the game board was ours, but they'd laid it down before we stepped off the ship.

"Before we were men, yet worlds away from childhood, one girl caught both our eyes. We came to blows over her before she turned her sights to another."

"You fought over her?"

He nodded with a shrug. "So, I get what you're going through with Citali. My brother gets to choose, but who knows what happens to the one he doesn't ask to marry him?"

"Assuming he likes either of us enough for that," I remarked dryly.

He stopped just outside the door that led to the garden. "Trust me. He does."

"*One* day. He's known us one day, Beron."

"The same length of time you've known him, yet look how worked up you are, Noor." He pushed the door open and I stepped outside, only to see Caelum's lips pressed to Citali's. My heart squeezed uncomfortably. "Oh, shit," Beron muttered.

I pivoted and walked back inside, Beron lingering in the doorway. My ears were thrumming so loudly I couldn't hear if the Lumin said anything more. I just wanted... away.

"Noor?" Caelum's urgent tone called out. Beron stopped him at the door. "It's not what it looked like!" he shouted from the garden.

I stopped and whirled around. "It's only fair, right? Enjoy the rest of your evening, Caelum." Dismissing him, I walked to the grand staircase and made my way upstairs. Seven flights later, I pushed the key into the lock of my door and twisted.

My stomach was in knots as I walked inside, but I didn't get a chance to process everything I was feeling because seated at the desk was Vada.

"I owe you an explanation."

I shook my head slightly, pushing the door closed behind me. "You don't. I understand completely. You wanted to see which of the Atenas would be the best match for your son."

"I wanted to see how you treated *everyone,* even behind closed doors and to those below your station."

"He told me how he was chosen, and that you help a lot of your people now that you have the means," I revealed.

She stood to face me, her dress glittering in the muted gray light filtering in from outside. "Did he also tell you of my suspicions?"

*Ah. It all adds up now.* "About the crown?" I asked.

She nodded.

"He did."

"And *is* that all you're after?" she asked, her lips pursed.

"No." It was true. I wanted that crown, but not the crown alone. If I was being honest with myself, seeing Caelum kissing Citali felt like Sol flung a lava-like rope of fire down and lashed me with it. I wondered if there was a charred scar across my back, and if I only imagined the smell of burnt hair and flesh.

"I'll be honest and blunt. You are much different than your sister, Noor. But there's something about both of you that makes me worry for my son. There's a bitterness to the two of you, and I'm not sure if it comes from the fact that you are second and third born in a family that inherits in succession, or something far worse." She was quiet for a moment, then her brows delicately drew in. "Why did you leave the feast? And why are you upset?"

I looked out the window, away from her. "I'm not."

"Noor. It wasn't so long ago that I was a young woman."

"He kissed my sister," I croaked.

I didn't know if it was the fact that I could feel the crown of moonlight's cool exterior slipping through my fingers or if, for once, I thought someone wanted me for me and not for what I could give him. But Caelum wanted things, too, though not a crown or sun diamonds. He wanted a wife whose familial ties would garner what he wanted: trade, cooperation, and peace.

She looked away from me, crestfallen. "It seems very early to begin such physicalities…"

"He kissed me first. Just before her."

Her brows rose. "Pardon me?"

I made it sound worse than it was. Not that it wasn't horrible, in any event. "He kissed me in the garden. She came to tell me my father wanted to speak to me, but I later learned that was a lie. When I went back outside, he was kissing her."

She shook her head. "That doesn't sound like Caelum. Beron maybe, but not Caelum. He's loyal. Steadfast and true."

"He doesn't have to be right now, I guess. He needs to see with whom he fits best."

"That is the perfect segue to let you know that negotiations today went far better than expected. Your father is most agreeable and has made many concessions. The formation of the peace and trade agreement should be complete in days. Tomorrow, the treaty will be drafted. Of course, revisions might have to be made, but once it's finished and signed, likely later this week, you'll both come to Lumina with us. Do you have any reservations about coming to our kingdom? Any questions?"

This time, my brows rose.

*Go to Lumina? Citali and me?* "What?"

"The treaty… your father and Caelum have already worked many details out together."

"No, not that. What did you say about us going to Lumina?"

"You didn't know?"

116

I shook my head, mouth agape.

"Your father didn't tell you?" Vada turned to face the window. "Life in Helios is much different than life in Lumina. The temperature, the ever-present darkness. There are concerns that it might drive a Helioan into a deep depression."

I couldn't contain my shocked expression. Why hadn't Father told us we would be going to Lumina? Was it a detail just 'worked out' between them like the other points of the treaty, or did he know in advance of our trip? "This certainly is a surprise. Are we both going because he won't have time to decide between us?"

She smoothed her hands down her dress. "Not exactly," she drawled. "I'm guessing your father also failed to mention that my son isn't the only one who must choose his bride. Lumos must accept her. That's why he made it clear that *both* of you must go to Lumina. That way, if one isn't accepted..."

"Perhaps the other will be," I finished for her. I took a long, steady breath. Father left that part out of his great speeches, both public and private. He told us to pack our things to last several weeks, not only for the time we'd spend in the dusk lands, but also because we would be traveling to Lumina and staying there until the matter of who would be Caelum's wife was decided.

"Caelum made everything clear in his correspondences," Vada added, obviously vexed by being the one to reveal the news. "You'll both travel to Lumina after negotiations have concluded. Know that you are welcome to stay for as long as you like, but if you or Citali feel it's not for you, we'll honor your wishes and return you to Helios."

"How exactly does Lumos approve of Caelum's bride?"

She smiled wistfully. "That's up to the god of night. He never does the same thing twice." Vada strode toward the door. "I'm sorry to have deceived you," she said.

I grinned. "You're not, but I accept your false apology."

She laughed. "I'll miss your wit. I'll send someone else to attend you if you require help."

I shook my head. "That won't be necessary."

A knock came at the door, startling both of us. "Noor?" Caelum said from the other side.

Vada cupped my elbow. "Maybe hear him out? I know my son. He doesn't make it a habit to toy with others' feelings."

"I wouldn't accuse him of that, necessarily, but of not knowing his own," I quietly told her.

She pressed her lips together, then let her hand fall away and opened the door.

"Mother?" he asked. "What are you doing in Noor's room?"

"That's my business and Atena Noor's."

"Is she okay?" he asked softly. She stepped into the hallway and closed the door. They spoke for a moment, Vada's voice so quiet I couldn't discern her words, but I heard her tone loud and clear. She wasn't happy with her son.

The cool timbre of his voice resonated through the wooden door, vibrating through my fingers that were pressed against it and worming its way into my bones. I could feel it thrumming through my sternum.

The two went quiet and then soft footsteps trailed away. Another knock.

"Noor, can I have a moment of your time?" Caelum asked again.

I took a deep, quiet breath and schooled my features before twisting the knob.

Caelum stood there, looking anxious. "I know it's improper, but may I step inside for a moment?"

I moved aside and opened the door completely. He stepped inside and I closed the door. He was quiet as he took in my room. "It suits you," he said.

I crossed my arms. "If you wanted to see my rooms, you could have done so before I arrived. I'm not in the mood to provide a tour, especially one of my bed. You should return to Citali if a warm body is what you sought by coming here."

His eyes widened. "That wasn't my intention at all. I came to tell you that what you saw wasn't what it looked like," he said, echoing what he'd shouted from the garden.

"It looked like your lips were pressed against one another," I said drily. "It looked like you were kissing her."

"Well, yes, but I didn't initiate it. We were talking and all of a sudden, she leaned in and kissed me. I don't know where it came from. It certainly wasn't like the kiss I shared with you."

"And how would you describe the kiss *we* shared?" I challenged.

He stepped closer and I moved back. The dance continued until my back was against the wall. "Noor, I would describe your kiss as perfect. Blazing and fiery as the light in your eyes, as warm as the heat in your skin. As perfect as Lumos in the midnight sky and as vital as our ancestors winking at us from their eternal homes in the heavens."

Crisp air wafted from him. Mixed with that comforting scent was something I'd never smelled before. I memorized it quickly, assigning it to him in my mind so that when I came across it again, I would associate it with Caelum.

"The stars are your ancestors?" The notion was beautiful; the thought that one's loved ones could watch over them from above. In the hereafter, Sol took worthy spirits into her. They were what fueled her fire, so perhaps they looked down on us, too.

"They guide us from above," he rasped.

The way he spoke of them with such reverence made me want to see them with my own eyes to see if my view of them matched his. And maybe to see if they looked anything like Sol and the spirits of the dead she'd collected, to see if I was right and that our ancestors might all be looking down to guide and push us toward our destinies.

"Did they tell you to come to my room?" I asked quietly.

"No, but I had to explain what happened. I don't want any deceptions between us, Noor. No secrets. And no lies."

It was a beautiful sentiment, if only it could be true. If there were no secrets or lies between him and me, would things be different? At times, I felt this pull to him. Indescribable. Urgent. Consuming. I felt it now.

"Your eyes are haloed in gold again." I pressed them closed. "Don't hide them from me, please." There was an ache in his tone I felt in the chasm of my heart.

Slowly, I opened them, staring into his crystal blues. "It hurt seeing you kiss her," I told him honestly. "And it would hurt her to see you kiss me. No matter what happens, someone will get their heart broken, won't they?"

Beyond that, someone will lose. The crown, perhaps their life, or at least their life as they knew it.

If he chose Citali, or if Lumos did, I would have to go back to Helios. I could not bear to leave my mother in the sand alone or stay in Lumina and watch as Caelum made Citali his wife. But if I went home, Father would kill me.

What if Caelum chose me, and going with him meant never seeing Mother again? She would remain atop the dune, never weathering away, the sun slowly bleaching but never breaking down what was left.

My heart ached at the thought.

She was all alone now. I'd never gone so long without walking out to visit her.

And Sol. Being so far away from her was almost as agonizing. I missed her heat, her constant watchfulness, the way she shone her light on the good and bad so that nothing could creep through the shadows. The feeling in my chest when she faded from sight is one I would never forget. It was as if she had reached out and taken my hand and the ship dragged our fingers slowly apart until we couldn't hold on any longer.

Maybe Vada was right and one or both of us might decide that living in darkness with only the scant, silver light of Lumos was something we couldn't bear after all.

"I don't want anyone to get hurt," he said. "But I think you might be right."

"Your mother just told me we are to go with you to Lumina when negotiations are ended."

His lips tightened, along with his shoulders. "Your father didn't tell you that before you left Helios?"

I shook my head, angry. He'd intentionally withheld that important detail. "Do you have any idea when we will leave the dusk lands? She said things are going well."

He sighed. "Your father is very accommodating and far more receptive than I imagined he'd be. I expected negotiations would take a lot longer, but he's conceding so much and I'm trying to match his generosity to foster a good relationship, one beneficial for us all. Add to that the fact that he received some sort of missive that he's needed back in Helios soon, and it seems we'll be able to sign the treaty of peace and trade on Wednesday. Lumina will host a ball that night, and we'll depart for Lumina early Thursday morning."

Father was cooperating because he wanted us as far from Sol and as close to the crown as possible. Caelum had questioned mine and Citali's motives regarding the crown of moonlight, but never considered Father's role in seeing our plans come to fruition.

"I'd love to show you my home and spend more time with you. I want..." He struggled for words. "Assuming you're still open to pursuing a relationship with *me*, I want to open up to you, Noor. I've never considered it before. To be honest, I've been too afraid, but you're different. My heart feels different with you. Lighter. Freer, maybe? Maybe it's because you understand the responsibilities I have. You understand the duties that come with the yoke of the Aten. Being Lumin cannot be so different. Then again, it may have nothing to do with you being an Atena, and everything to do with your heart and the glow I see spilling out sometimes." He brushed a thumb near my eye. "I hope you can see that I'm laying my heart bare for you, and I hope you can find it in yours to forgive tonight's misunderstanding and still consider coming home with me. I want to introduce you to my kingdom and see if you could love it the way you love Helios."

Sincerity shone in his eyes, though it didn't ease the ache the image of that traitorous kiss left in my chest. Even so, I felt like Caelum was being honest. Citali would do anything to force herself into his life. I was surprised she hadn't already tucked herself into his bed. My sister was no stranger to a man's body and had been very generous with hers to those who could keep their mouths closed about her 'indiscretions'.

"There are three days between now and Wednesday," I said. "That means there will be more chances for us to speak and for me to decide. I'll either board your ship or I won't."

The sincerity in his eyes changed to hope again, but it wasn't unabashed. Caelum wasn't convinced I would go with him. Not yet.

The balance of power between us had shifted in my favor. Before, he was the one with the choice between me or my sister. Now, he was asking if I'd entertain the idea of going to Lumina with him.

He didn't know that I had no real choice in the matter. Father had already decided Citali and I were going. We were like seeds and Father the great wind that tore us from our plant and sent us flying according to his will.

I took a measured breath. Citali and I would be traveling into the dark to Luminos in only a few days. We would enter a land where even Sol's distant light couldn't touch and make gray. We would be under Lumos's dominion, subject to his rule, and to the laws we didn't even know. I didn't want to consider the danger into which we were being thrust.

If it hurt so badly to be torn from Sol's view, I couldn't imagine the pain that might come with completely leaving behind even the remnants her light left in this silvery void.

Caelum said he truly wanted to open up to me. If his words were truthful, this was better than I could've planned. I just might be able to learn more about the crown I needed.

For a moment, I'd lost sight of the crown and allowed Caelum's pretty face and charm to enchant me. His lips on Citali's reminded me of my target faster than the back of Father's hand had ever put me in my place. It stung worse, truthfully. A blow to one's pride cut far deeper than one to the flesh ever could.

"Well," I said to him, "it's late and I'd rather not have anyone see you leaving my rooms."

The apple bobbed in his throat. "Of course," he answered, offering a polite smile. "Can I see you tomorrow?"

I waited for him to step into the hall. "If there's time, perhaps."

"I'll make time, Noor."

I gave a wan smile. "Prove it."

I shut the door behind him and locked it, then exchanged my gown for a night dress. Mechanically, I washed my face and slipped into bed. For a long while, I stared at the bleak, gray light pouring into the window from outside, wishing it was the bright sun I was used to dozing off to.

It wasn't only the lack of brightness that bothered me. Every time I closed my eyes, it wasn't a crown I imagined, but my sister's lips on Caelum's. I heard Beron's curse and felt a band tightening around my heart and lungs.

It took hours for me to relax enough to drift off.

# 12

When someone knocked at my door the next morning, I ignored them for a solid two minutes, hoping they'd go away. When they steadfastly refused, only knocking harder and louder, I finally threw back the blanket and trudged to the door, unlocking it and looking through the slender crack I made with one eye pinched closed, the other squinting.

Beron chuckled from the other side.

I slammed the door in his face, then stomped back to the bed, fell back into it, and covered my head again.

He pushed the door open and rudely intruded. "Not a morning person, I see."

"Not in the least," I rasped.

"My brother wants to see you before he meets with your father."

"Whatever for?"

"Because he just wants to."

*He just wants to.*

I huffed beneath the blanket when the bed dipped under his weight. "Go away, Beron."

"I just met you last night and you're comfortable enough to order me around already? Perhaps you *will* make a fine queen."

I didn't deign to respond.

He cleared his throat. "Caelum told me what happened and assured me that he'd explained and apologized for as long as you'd allow him in your presence last night. Now that you've had a chance to sleep on it, how do you feel about things this morning?"

I threw the cover off my head to glare at him. "Like my sleep is being disturbed."

"He'll be heartbroken if you don't go and meet him on the ship."

I perked up. "What ship?"

His chest puffed a bit and I bit the inside of my cheek to stop from laughing at him. In that moment, I could almost picture him as a child, proud and believing himself the strongest young man in the world. "The Luminan ship, of course. I understand it'll be your home away from home in a few days, if all goes well."

Should I go? Caelum just wanted to see me. What about what *I* wanted? Did I want to see him, or should I make him wait? Pushing him away might backfire and push him toward my sister. My mind was split. Part of me wanted to go, but the other part wanted to refuse him. I picked at the blanket in my lap, unsure.

"He prepared breakfast."

I *was* hungry. And seeing the ship wouldn't be so bad. I'd studied it the other day from the river, but it was so different from ours. Its bottom was just as shallow, but the riverfarer's quarters were much larger than those on our ship.

"Wait. Did you say *he* prepared breakfast?"

Beron smiled. "That's right. He went all out for you. My brother is quite a chef. You'll see it for yourself if you can drag yourself into the bathing room and get ready in time."

I flicked a glance toward said room. "Get out." Shooing him from the bed, he stood, barely deflecting my swats. I pushed him from the room and locked the door.

"How many hours will you be, Atena Noor?" his muffled voice came from the other side of the door.

"Fifteen minutes!" I yelled, already rifling through my armoire for a simple dress.

"I'll believe *that* when I see it," he grumbled.

I found a deep crimson dress and rushed into the bathing room to tame my hair, scrub my teeth and face, and tug on my clothing, emerging from my room in ten minutes to a gaping Beron.

"You... how?" he stuttered.

"Never underestimate a woman, Beron. We are quite adept at getting ready quickly when properly motivated, but can just as easily drag our feet in procrastination if we aren't."

He shook his head. "I'll never understand any of you."

"The feeling is mutual, I'm sure."

We jogged down the steps quickly. When we reached the first floor and made our way outside, I asked, "Why are you escorting me? I know the way."

"I thought you enjoyed my company," he pouted.

"I'm still debating. You woke me very early."

He grinned. "It'll be worth it."

*It better be.*

Zuul was lurking near a silvery, dead tree, his dark eyes sliding along with our steps. He'd no doubt followed Caelum to see which of the Atenas he was preparing breakfast for. Now he could scurry back to my father and report his findings.

"Your father's guard?" Beron asked beneath his breath.

"In the flesh."

"I don't like him."

I laughed. "Neither do I."

We took a trail that wound through the gray-hued grass to the glassy, still river and then turned south where the

Luminan ship was moored. Even its wood looked somber in this lighting. Beron held my hand as I boarded, steadying me from the river's sudden movement. From inside a set of ornate double doors carved with Lumos's great face, Caelum emerged. Wearing a deep green vest, a pristine white shirt, and dark trousers and boots, he looked well-rested.

"Thank you for coming despite the short notice, Noor."

I didn't respond. While getting ready and walking there, I'd given myself a stern talking to. I had to remember the crown no matter what happened, and never again let myself forget that I was simply playing a game to get it. A game where winning was everything and losing was death.

I wouldn't brush away the fact that he and Citali shared a kiss. I'd use it to stoke the fire it ignited. Another reminder that Caelum was playing a game too, even if he wasn't aware of it.

"Thank you, Beron," he said, flicking a glance to the top floor of the House of Dusk.

"Stop fretting. I'm a good second choice, brother," he teased. Then he winked at me and explained, "I'll be entertaining Citali for a little while."

I grinned. "Good luck. She has a short attention span. You'll have to be diligent to keep her busy."

His cocky brow rose. "I think I know how to entertain a woman."

"If you think she's typical, you know nothing about my sister. She'll eat you alive."

Beron laughed as he retraced the path back to the House. *Can't say I didn't warn him.*

Caelum gestured to the cabin and we walked to the door. He held it open as I stepped inside, then joined me. Two crates and a flat piece of wood had been set up as a makeshift table. Two large, midnight blue pillows lay on the ground, acting as cushioned seats. "If this isn't to your liking..." he began nervously.

To answer his lingering question, I walked to the nearest pillow and sat down.

He brought a tray over and placed it in the middle of the table before sitting on the pillow across from me. On the tray was a carafe of water, crystal glasses, several pieces of fruit I didn't recognize, small loaves of crusted bread, and a small glass tub of some sort of jam.

"Beron said you were a chef and that you made the breakfast."

His eyes widened. "My brother may have exaggerated… a lot."

"He's very good at it," I teased, pouring water into my glass and taking a sip.

"Beron and I have been inseparable since his birth. I've always felt protective of him, and he feels protective of me. Not to say we didn't fight plenty growing up, but at the end of the day and after every argument, we knew we loved each other and never lost sight of that."

"I wish I could say the same," I admitted.

"Would you tell me about your eldest sister? About your family?"

I tore a chunk of bread from a loaf, finding it warm and soft on the inside. While I answered, I spread jam onto the chunk. "Zarina is the Aten's eldest child. She is twenty, born more than three years before me and two before Citali."

He nodded encouragingly, so I continued.

"Her mother was Father's first wife. He married her in an arrangement not unlike the one you might forge with one of us. She was from a very wealthy family in Helios, one with strong ties to the guard. Theirs was a marriage of strength and security, but it did not last long. She was very petite and became pregnant right away. She died while giving birth to Zarina."

Caelum's dark brows drew in. "That had to be difficult for Zarina, growing up without a mother. And difficult for your father to suddenly raise a newborn child alone."

Caelum had the luxury of having a mother who was wonderful, which colored his thoughts.

"Zarina is eldest and has always had more privileges and responsibilities than Citali and I. Her whole life, she's been groomed to become the next Aten. I would tell you more about her, but don't know much beyond my dealings with her when I was very young. The older we got, the more the three of us were separated, and now, Zarina prefers to keep to herself." Not that I minded. Her attitude made it easy not to seek her out unless necessary.

"What one word would you use to describe her?"

"Cold," I answered. "Despite being the Aten's daughter, Zarina is cold. That adjective has always rung through my mind when she's near me."

I chewed my bread, uncomfortable.

"And Citali?" he asked, taking some of the sliced pink fruit. The inside was filled with pulp. He gestured to the dish. "It's very good if you'd like to try it."

I took a slice to taste. "Thank you."

If he asked Citali to describe our mothers, or to describe me, he would get a very different answer than the one I would give him. I could only tell him the truth from my perspective. Citali's perspective differed, and so did her truth.

"Father took a second wife, Citali's mother, after he mourned Zarina's for a full year, as is our custom – or *was* our custom at that time. It's changed a bit over the years." I took a deep breath. "Citali's mother did not die while birthing her, but died a week after Citali was born. She developed an infection and then a fever, and though the healers tried everything they knew, they couldn't save her. She joined Sol in the hereafter." Silence stretched between us for a moment before I continued. "If you ask my sister, she believes her mother's death is my mother's fault. She believes Father met my mother and killed hers to be rid of her."

Caelum stopped chewing, searching my face for something I wasn't sure he wanted to find.

It was evident he cared. About me, and even about Citali, but most of all about his people. He had no idea who he was negotiating with, or that I'd spoken the truth when I told him I was actually after the crown of moonlight.

Something shifted in me just then. Kiran was a friend when he could be, when it was safe. But what would it be like to have a *true* friend, one with whom you could be your real self? A friend you could confide in no matter who was around or watching?

What if confiding in Caelum wasn't dangerous, but freeing? What if it brought him closer to me, and that closeness allowed him to confide in me – things he'd never spoken to anyone else? Perhaps… eventually… even about the crown.

If I wanted it, perhaps I needed to earn it by stepping into the unknown.

"Why would she believe he was capable of such cruelty?"

I tore another piece of bread, focusing on the loaf and battling with myself over what to tell him.

He moved his pillow to sit beside me and tenderly reached out to move my hair away from my neck. "Did he do this?"

If he knew the truth, what would Father do to him?

I didn't answer. In my mind, I cursed the tears that welled for a moment before I urged them back into their cage.

"He loved my mother," I said, my voice cracking. I cleared it to recover, then took a sip of water. "He loved her so much. When I was very small, I remembered he always said she was Sol embodied. That she was his light, always chasing his darkness away."

"What happened to her?"

"She died when I was seven, the night she tried to leave him."

I shut my eyes and saw the burst blood vessels in her eyes. Remembered the heavy, limp weight of her body as I tried to tear her from the altar stone so he couldn't bring Sol down to incinerate her, or maybe so Sol could burn me away with her.

Saric had torn me away and held me as she departed, patting my head and smoothing my hair, singing the soft lullaby that my mother sang to me every night before she tucked me into bed.

Kind, loving Saric with his heart of gold and patience.

"After my mother died, Father took one wife after another. His eighth recently passed into the hereafter. In fact, Father announced we were coming here the evening after her departure."

"Departure?" he softly asked.

"When we die, the Aten uses his power to draw Sol close to the earth. She focuses her heat on the deceased and consumes any good, acceptable part of the dead. What's left is ash, bone, and the things she does not desire. The spirit departs this world and Sol ushers it into the hereafter. The spirits are what fuel Sol's fire."

He sat still and quiet. "Why did you tell me all this? You could have lied."

I glanced down, then met his eyes. "Your heart is good and unspoiled, as far as I can see. Your people love you. Your mother and brother adore you. I just wanted you to know what you'd be marrying into if you went through with the offer extended and chose Citali or me as your wife."

He scrubbed a palm over his mouth and held it there. I'd rendered him speechless with the reality of my family history, not that I hadn't expected it.

"No wonder there's such animosity between you and Citali… and Zarina."

I tried to smile. Sipped. Then spoke. "My sisters and I are pretty glass beads strung together by blood, each chipping and scarring one another. Always chafing. Eventually, the friction will break one of us away entirely."

He bit his lower lip and took a deep breath.

"So, when you ask the same question of Citali and she tells you that my mother is to blame for the death of hers, you'll know my truth. She'd rather blame my mother, and by extension me, than accept what actually happened. There were many healers and priests who attended her mother and tried to save her. None were able. But most are still living – Priest Saric included."

"I believe you, Noor," he said quietly. "I need no further proof."

I bit into the slice of fruit he'd brought for us and found it tart and juicy. Very tart. I felt the sourness twisting my face but couldn't contain the puckered expression it drew from me.

Caelum laughed. "Perhaps it's an acquired taste."

"Very acquired," I teased, coughing and reaching for my water glass.

He grew quiet again and my stomach twisted as I wondered what he was thinking, what he might ask next.

"I'm sure your history has influenced the way you feel about love," he said.

"Love..." I gave a mirthless laugh. The only thing love ever gave me was a dead mother and more bruises and bloody wounds than I could count if I tried. "If love is what *I've* seen, it's like a flame, like Sol's fire. It burns and consumes until all that's left are ashes." I turned my head to him, wrapping my arms around my now-bent knees. "Do you know what I'm most afraid of?"

"What are you most afraid of, Noor?" he asked softly.

"I'm terrified ashes is all I'll become, when I feel destined to be the flame."

Just then, a rumble shook the ship. Alarmed, I braced my hands on the planks and looked to Caelum, who seemed perfectly calm. He tilted his head to the side, completely unaffected by the booming noise. But I'd felt it, heard it. "What was that?" I asked with wide eyes.

Caelum laughed. "You've never heard thunder?"

"Thunder?"

"It's your first trip to the dusk lands," he said, eyes widening with realization. "The riverfarers refer to this gray place by a second name – the storm stretch."

I shook my head. "Sol does not allow the winds to shroud her with clouds."

"You've never seen rain?" he exclaimed.

I started to feel embarrassed. "I mean, I've read about it..."

Caelum rose and took my hand. "Let me show you."

I slid my palm into his and walked outside. Another rumble of thunder rolled over the sky, sounding like the uneven wheels of a wagon drawn along a cobbled road. A drop of water splashed onto the deck near my feet. Followed by another. Then another.

The earth smelled different.

It smelled alive, even as the land looked dead and desolate, colorless.

"I'm surprised we haven't had a storm since we've been here. They're known to be quite severe at times."

"Why do storms form here? Do you have them in Lumina?" I asked, watching water droplets fall onto my outstretched arms and hands, feeling them catch in my hair and on my dress.

"We don't have storms in our kingdom, but we do benefit from the waters that trickle south. Here, the warmth of Helios meets the cool air from Lumina. When they collide, storms often form, some building into beasts."

*Beasts?* I watched the sky and a great boom sounded. I crouched low, holding my ears from the sudden noise.

Caelum caught my elbow. "You're okay. That was much closer than before. We should get off the ship and away from the water now."

"Why? Will the thunder tear us apart if we stand near it?" My heart felt like that thunder. It boomed in my chest, a powerful beating beast.

"Lightning often accompanies thunder," he explained, casting his eyes to the shore. "It's attracted to water, and we don't want it to be drawn to us by standing on a ship."

"What is lightning?"

Caelum smiled, then grabbed my hand as we ran down the small plank and made it onto the earth. Thunder came again, louder this time. "Watch the sky," Caelum instructed.

More and more droplets of rain began to fall. The normally placid gray sky seemed to be filled with churning anger. The pale color had turned dark and foreboding. I couldn't tear my eyes from the spectacular sight! Then, a bolt of fire forked across those dark clouds, lighting them from within as it streaked over the sky. I laughed and clutched my chest.

*Is that you, Sol? Is your power so great that it can reach such a desolate place?*

"We should go inside now!" Caelum shouted.

In my exuberance to experience this new thing called *thunder and lightning,* I hadn't noticed it beginning to pour rain. We were getting soaked. My hair and gown were weighed down with water, but I couldn't stop smiling. I didn't want to leave it. If Sol's fire was here in the dusk lands, she wouldn't hurt me with it. But would she feel the same about the Lumin?

It was better not to tempt her to violence. I took Caelum's hand this time and tugged him toward the House of Dusk. We ran to the nearest door and flung it open, the wind pushing it shut behind us with a loud snap. Caelum and I looked at one another and laughed uproariously.

"Look at you!" I teased.

"Me?" Caelum scoffed, then gestured to me. I glanced at my saturated gown and the puddle forming under my feet as the rain escaped the fibers.

Caelum suddenly went quiet. He glanced over me, then cleared his throat and met my eyes again. My gown wasn't whisper-thin, but the heavy rain made it cling to my body so that I felt like Citali in one of her tight gowns. I grew self-conscious.

"I should go change." I gestured to him. "You should, too."

"I have to meet with your father soon."

I nodded, plucking my dress away from my body.

He bent so his mouth was beside my ear. "Thank you, Noor."

I nodded again, a knot the size of the ship's mooring line filling my throat. He placed a soft kiss at my jaw, slowly pulling away. I felt my body drift with him for the briefest of moments, not wanting to part from him, but to get closer.

"Can I see you later?"

I shrugged noncommittally. "Maybe."

He nodded with a small smile. "Hopefully."

I plodded to my room, leaving small puddles in my wake, where I quickly stripped off the gown and dried my skin. Padding to my wardrobe, I chose a gown that was a purple-red hue with gold stitching at the sleeves and neckline.

I sat in my window and watched the storm. The gray punches and greenish brushes that mottled the sky reminded me of my throat now that it was finally healing. The forked lightning had moved on, but flashes still lit the clouds from behind. And the rain. The glorious rain spattered my window and drenched everything in sight. It fell so hard that everything beyond the House looked hazy.

Last night, I struggled to sleep.

It turned out that all I needed was the calming voice of the rain and the soothing flashes of Sol's fire.

# 13

Saric woke me, the eldest priest pushing my door open and gently saying my name. I blinked, raised my slumped neck and sat up straighter, giving him a smile. "I must have dozed off."

"I'm sorry to have woken you, Atena," he apologized, stopping just inside the room.

"I'm glad you did."

He held something in his hand, a tome, a very old one by the look of it. "I thought you might like to learn a little about the first Atens. It's good for a young person to know their heritage before carving a future for themselves."

I swung my legs down from the window seat and moved to hold the desk chair out, helping him down into it. "These old bones," he sweetly cursed. "Growing old might be the greatest battle I've fought in this life." He panted as he rested in the seat. "I've not seen physical war, but have waged a spiritual one for Sol every day of my life since taking my oath."

He adjusted his position and cracked the book open to the first of many brittle pages, looking over the page as he told me to reclaim my window seat and make myself comfortable, warning me that old men were notorious for their ability to talk for hours.

I hoped that adage was right. I enjoyed his company, and in Helios rarely had the opportunity to enjoy it. Saric's visit warmed my heart.

"Over the years, Sol has chosen Atens. Your father is the seventh." He smiled. "I know what your instructors have told you, and some of what they've said is truth. Some, however, isn't. You were taught that the Great Divide was sudden and unexpected. Lumos and Sol had lived for millennia in peace, sharing the sky and guarding their creations – those who dwelt below on the earth. The first people were formed by the Sculptor, who even made Sol and Lumos. He gave this new race everything they might need to survive. Water for their bodies. Air for their lungs. Nourishment, until the seeds they gave them to plant grew and could be harvested. The list goes on and on. And for centuries, things were good."

I knew this from my studies.

"What your instructors never told you was that Lumos and Sol were lovers, and that when they appeared in the same sky, or the rare eclipse happened when their paths aligned, blessings rained down on the people of earth. No one is sure what drove them apart."

I quietly wondered if that could be true. Her fixed position was burning away our water and food, turning our kingdom to sand and ash.

"You've likely been taught that Sol proposed a truce, encapsulated in a separation unlike any the earth has seen before or since."

"The Great Divide."

He nodded. "The scrolls say that the two gods touched one last time, their hands each holding a great axe with which they cleaved the earth, dividing it between them. Sol drifted into the northern sky and claimed every soul on her lands, while Lumos ventured south. Many centuries afterward, each declared an heir, someone who would act as their representative on earth, a chosen one to carry a tiny amount of the god's power within their hearts."

I looked down, picking at my nails. He said that some of what we'd been taught was true and some wasn't. That part couldn't possibly be true. Father would have to possess a heart for it to be real. His cinder heart wouldn't be able to contain the greatness and power of Sol. Unless Sol herself had incinerated it somehow, leaving the cinder behind to claim my mother, dead and innocent of what he'd accused.

Saric gently eased the book closed. "The first Aten was a woman of great virtue. She was also a meticulous record-keeper, as her father was a scribe and she'd trained to take his place. She kept many journals, and it was she who was responsible for many of the carvings adorning the inside of the temple. As she was first, she felt it was her duty to write her history down. But more than that, she began a tradition. This book," he said, holding it out to me, "has been passed from Aten to Aten. Each has contributed and added his or her own section so the history of the Aten is never forgotten. I think that once you read the *true* history, your view of it might change."

*How so?* I wondered. "I can't accept this. I'm afraid to even touch it."

"It is *yours,* Noor. As Atena, you could be the one Sol chooses."

I shook my head. "Father will recommend Zarina."

He offered a satisfied smile. "I think you'll see that Sol is the decider of all things, and does not always heed what – or who – is recommended."

Saric insisted I take the book and told me to keep it until I read every word, even if that meant taking it to Lumina when we departed the dusk lands. Then he tried to stand. I helped him up and steadied him as he walked across the room.

"Why doesn't Father have this book?"

He pursed his lips. "He added all he wished just after he was chosen, then gave it to us to keep until the next Aten is named. We've had it ever since. I really must go now. I'm afraid my body demands rest."

Concerned, I kept my hand on his arm. "Can I walk you somewhere?"

He shook his head. "I walked up the staircases, Atena. I can walk back down them. I'm just not as spry as I used to be."

At that moment, Kiran jogged up the steps, not even winded, and I couldn't have been more grateful. Saric was unsteady and too stubborn to let me assist him. Fortunately, he didn't mind Kiran assisting him, accepting an arm to cling to and another around his back. Kiran's gaze met mine for a moment before he slowly started down the steps, one at a time.

I turned my back to see Citali there, leaning against the wall, twisting a leg out and in, her arms crossed. "Was it your idea or Caelum's to send Beron to me this morning?"

I ignored her and walked back down the hall. She followed me into my room and noticed the book right away. "Since when do you read?"

"Since always. Haven't you paid attention all these years, sister?" I asked in a nonchalant tone, knowing that if I outwardly placed importance on the book, she would demand to see it.

She rolled her eyes and returned to her earlier tirade, the book forgotten. "What did you and Caelum do this morning?"

My brows rose. "We ate breakfast," I responded as if she were daft.

"You weren't downstairs," she accused.

I thought Beron would be able to distract her. It sounded more like she led him on a great hunt to find us instead. I felt bad for Caelum's brother, but only for a second.

"We ate on the ship."

She put a fist on her hip. "When will *I* get equal time?"

I sighed heavily and trudged back to the table, where I picked up the book before climbing back into the window seat. "I don't know if you've noticed, Citali, but I'm not Caelum. If you want time with him, you'll have to ask him for it. Not me."

"How can I, when you take up his every waking hour?" she seethed.

I grinned. "Then perhaps that should tell you something."

If looks could scorch, I'd lay in ashes.

Tired of our squabble, I rolled my eyes and cracked open the tome Saric *loaned* me, pretending to slowly scan the page. Loaned, because though he said it was mine to read, it was his to protect.

Citali was wrong. I wasn't monopolizing Caelum's time. I would if he'd let me, but I wouldn't push him. He wanted both of us to go to Lumina so he could make his decision based on what he learned from us here – and there – and see which of us, if either, Lumos felt was worthy of his chosen. And in fairness, we needed to get to know him here, as well as there, and see if he met our standards as well.

A thought struck me. Had Caelum informed Citali that she and I were leaving with them in only a few days?

"Have you packed your trunks?" I tested.

"I'm not going home just because you had breakfast together," she snapped. "I'll just have to try harder."

I took a calming breath. "That's not why I suggested it. Caelum asked Father before we even left Helios if we would travel to Lumina to see if we'd like living in the dark kingdom. Father just never mentioned that tidbit to us. And as Father is particularly determined, negotiations are progressing faster than expected."

Her mouth gaped in surprise. "When will we leave?"

"The ball was moved up and will be held Wednesday night. We'll set sail Thursday morning."

Beyond the excitement glittering in her dark eyes, there was cunning. She'd never looked more like Father in that moment. It frightened me to see that familiar hatred flare. I wanted to claw her eyes out just so I didn't have to look at them again. To see *him* reflected in them.

If we'd had any other man as our father, would we behave this way?

She turned and left the room, carelessly slamming the door in her wake.

I read the words of the first Aten, in her own hand, and her story was one of awe, wonderment, and gratefulness. She felt unworthy to have been chosen. She was humble. She was everything my father was not, and I was determined to know why Sol chose him after beginning her legacy with such a perfect choice.

But first, dinner.

Still dressed in the red-purple dress that more aptly resembled a deep, fresh bruise, I made my way downstairs to find that though no formal dinner was being presented, prepared food waited for us in the great hall. I filled a plate and sat down. A servant swiftly placed two goblets in front of me, one holding water and the other wine. I thanked her and she took her position along the wall again, scanning the area nearest her to see if anyone needed anything.

The chandeliers were low again, casting warm light over the space.

Someone sat down across the table from me and I looked up into Beron's smiling, handsome face. "Have you been sent to distract *me* this time?"

He laughed. "No, I was just hungry and sought out the most beautiful girl in the room for company."

I looked around as if searching for something or someone. He glanced over one shoulder, then the other. "Are you looking for Caelum?" he asked, crestfallen.

"No, I'm looking for the creature you described," I teased. "I expect you meant my sister. I've noticed that distracting her is not exactly a chore for you."

His dimple popped and I sipped my wine, satisfied that my barb hit its mark.

"The two of you couldn't be more different," he noted, cutting into steaming, tender meat.

He was right about that. Citali and I were as opposite as Lumos and Sol. I still couldn't grasp that the two gods had once loved one another, but I supposed that perhaps in childhood, Citali and I had, too. Children had innocent hearts and few burdens to fill them.

A clap of thunder made me flinch and my thumb punched into my bread loaf. I eased it out as another chair was dragged to the small table. Caelum grinned. "Still not used to the sound?"

"I didn't know another storm had built." My eyes drifted to the terraces on the other side of the room.

"You want to go outside, don't you?" Caelum asked.

His hair was a little mussed, but it looked so soft. My fingers inched toward him and I tucked my hands under the table. "I do."

Beron grinned. "Citali was frightened by the storm this morning, but you don't seem to be afraid at all."

"I'm not, and neither is she," I told him, then focused on Caelum. "My sister fears nothing but *being* nothing. Our father's rage is far more deadly than light bolting from the sky. She's lying. She's playing you to get sympathy."

Caelum sat back and crossed his arms. "And you aren't?" A teasing smile hung in the corner of his lips, but his crystalline eyes held a challenge.

"No," I said, taking a sip of water. "I most certainly am."

Beron burst out laughing and craned his head back, groaning. "Lumos, save me. She's perfect. If you don't want her, brother, just say the word."

Caelum shook his head, a full smile now stretching over his handsome face. "Noor, you are *dazzlingly* dark to be named for such brilliant, divine light."

My inner phoenix purred, wondering how he knew the meaning of my name.

After finishing the meal, I walked to the terrace, which was partially covered and protected from the rain unless a gust pushed the droplets sideways. Caelum joined me. Things were easier to keep in perspective when others were around. Beron at dinner, for example. A table of people, like at the feast. But the moment Caelum and I were left alone, I forgot what I needed and let my heart ruin what my mind had fastidiously planned.

The private breakfast where I'd spilled our dramatic history, standing with him in the garden where we'd shared an intimate kiss, even dancing with him when it felt like we were the only two in the room was dangerous.

So, I quickly built a mental wall between us and imagined my sister's face and puckered lips chiseled into it.

"Where is Citali?" I asked.

"I'm not sure."

"She didn't know we were going to Lumina. I told her."

He nodded, thrusting his hands in the pockets of his dark trousers.

"I think you should spend time with her this evening," I told him.

His brows furrowed.

"It's only fair, Caelum. To her *and* to you. You have no control over which of us Lumos will approve of. If you get too attached to one of us and Lumos chooses the other, what happens then?" I stared out at the rain, unable to focus on a single drop. Only his frustrated breaths.

"I'd rather stay here with you," he said, trying to take my hand.

I pulled mine away and crossed my arms. "I'd rather be alone." It was a lie. Not my first or last, but the greatest in many ways.

He lingered. "Are you *sure* that's what you want?"

"I'm sure."

A deep, frustrated exhale came from over my shoulder. "Do you want me to fetch Beron?" he asked, concern lancing his pretty features.

"I need no company or watchdog, Caelum."

I'd survived for years alone. I could certainly survive an hour. I could survive years of solitude if I had to. My walks into the sand and the seemingly infinite days and nights I'd spent alone after Mother's death had taught me that.

"It feels like you're intentionally pushing me away, Noor," he rasped.

"I'm not." But I was. I just couldn't bring myself to tell him. "So much has happened in such a short time; I just need time to think about everything."

"Are you still undecided about going home with me?" he asked.

"Caelum..."

He put his hands up. "Your message is perfectly clear, Noor. I won't bother you again this evening."

As his footsteps trailed away, each made an ache resonate through my chest. I'd let him get too close again. I'd given too much and hadn't gotten an inch closer to the crown.

I had to put distance between us for a time. For me.

So, that evening while he spent time with Citali, I spent time with the storm.

Her thunder was my heart. Her lightning, my blood.

# 14

The following day was Tuesday, and Beron didn't wake me to have breakfast with Caelum. Only two more mornings until their ship dragged us south to Lumina.

I rose and quickly washed, dressing in a fuchsia dress that was low cut on top, but draped to the ground beautifully. In the great hall, breakfast was laid out with an array of Luminan foods, declaring it was their turn to host.

I recognized the small bread loaves, the jam Caelum brought to the ship yesterday, even the tart fruit sliced into perfect wedges, but there were still many foods I didn't recognize. Familiar laughter caught my ear and I turned to see Citali and Caelum sitting with Beron in the corner. Beron saw me and waved me over.

I finished taking a sample of a few of the foods that smelled sweet and made my way to them. "Am I interrupting?" I asked.

Caelum and Beron answered "No," at the same time Citali smiled sweetly and said, "Yes."

Citali's hair was sleek and shiny. Her golden gown was fitted under her breasts, flaring around her hips to accentuate their roundness, and falling to her ankles. She wore no sandals. Rings of gold on her toes winked in the candlelight. They matched those she wore on her fingers and the bangles on her wrists.

"Father wishes to see us after breakfast," she said, smirking evilly at me.

I sipped from the water that had magically appeared in front of me, searching for who to thank and finding no one hovering nearby. "Very well."

Caelum looked handsome as ever, cleanly shaven and smelling like the soap Vada had given me. Soap and salts still appeared nightly in my bathing room even though I hadn't seen Vada since the night of the feast. He wore a dark gray vest over trousers today with another crisp, white shirt tucked underneath. Beron was dressed in all black from his collar to the tips of his boots.

"Did you inherit some of Lumos's powers, Beron?" I asked.

He sat up straighter, flicking a glance at Caelum.

I spread jam on my bread. "I only ask because Zarina, Citali, and I have the barest touch from Sol. We can withstand her heat without burning or even feeling flushed. Do you have a similar blessing from Lumos?"

Caelum nodded his okay and Beron cleared his throat. "I do. I can see exceptionally well at night and can withstand cold temperatures."

"And do you have an oracle of sorts in Lumina?"

Caelum used his napkin to wipe his mouth, his attention fixed on me.

"Do you have an oracle in Helios?" Beron returned.

"We do. A Sphinx. A small part of her is woman, human. A greater part is lioness. You don't want to anger the lioness in her," I said with a wink.

Citali stomped my foot, so I jabbed her in the thigh with my fork. She scooted away from the table out of my reach, gaping and rubbing her thigh.

"Is there a problem, Citali?" I asked, one brow quirked.

Caelum glanced between us with his head tilted slightly. Beron sat exactly as his older brother did, tilting his head exactly the same way, and also looked from Citali to me, then back.

"We have no Sphinx. In Lumina, there is a Wolven. Part man, part wolf. Before you ask, he does not live in caves or beneath the ground," Caelum answered with a face of stone. But I saw the shimmer of laughter in his eyes.

"Are your diamonds actually made of Sol's tears?" Beron asked, a friendly smile on his face. He looked pointedly at Citali.

*She told him that? Interesting...*

"Her tears?" I laughed. "Why would a goddess cry?"

Citali's eyes shredded Beron as she sat stiffly at my side.

"Your father said they burn anyone who touches them. He gave one to Caelum."

"They're very rare, and yes, they burn anyone but me."

"Why not you?" Beron pressed.

"I'm not sure. Perhaps it's because I've worn them since I was little. Those who sip a tiny amount of poison over time can become immune to its effects. Perhaps it's the same with these." I rattled my bangle playfully and tucked it under the table, dreading the question I knew would come next.

He nudged Citali. "Why don't *you* have them?"

Citali slowly froze, anger fusing her bones until she was rigid as a corpse.

"My mother gave them to me the evening before she died," I interjected.

Citali's rage bubbled over. "Pray tell, Caelum – is the crown you hide away *actually* made of moonlight?"

Beron's laughter dried up after I answered his question; now there was a drought of humor at the table. Silence, thick as the jam in the jar in front of me, spread between us. "It is," Caelum said. "But, as it is sacred, no one has seen the crown except for me and the Lumins who came before me."

"You mean *you* haven't seen it?" Citali sneered at Beron.

There was no anger in his voice when he answered, "Never."

Citali turned in her chair, snubbing the brothers, and glared at me. "We shouldn't keep Father waiting. Are you finished?"

I stood to leave.

Caelum's eyes flicked to my neck, tracing the fading bruises. "See you after?"

"Maybe."

Citali looked between us sharply and strode away. With a murmured farewell, I followed her to Father's rooms. I couldn't accept Caelum's offer to see him, but frankly, whether I could see him after Father spoke to us would depend greatly on what he wanted, his temper, and whether he directed it at me.

Saric and Kiran were inside Father's rooms, also waiting.

The Aten's rooms were floor-to-ceiling gold with golden furniture. Painted or pure, I couldn't tell. The gray light spilling into the window couldn't diminish the sunny feeling in here. The gold shone. Even my sun diamonds seemed to hum happily, as if they'd seen a friend they hadn't seen in far too long.

You could fit five of my large rooms inside his. In addition to an immense bed and a closed door that I imagined led to his bathing room, there was also a long table with chairs askew around it. It looked almost large enough to seat every person both he and Caelum had brought along with them.

Kiran and Saric quietly sat in two of the seats. Father gestured to the chairs across from Sol's priests. Citali slid into hers, thankfully taking the seat closest to Father, and I took the one beside her.

Her greed for being at his right hand worked in my favor. She became a buffer between us.

Father didn't waste time. "You're going to Lumina."

Citali did not speak up to tell him we knew. I remained quiet, too.

"Who is to go to Lumina, Aten?" Saric gently asked, keeping his eyes averted.

"All four of you. Lumos himself must approve of any union between his Lumin and the one he would like to marry. Not only that, the Lumin fears that you may not acclimate well to the darkness that drenches their kingdom."

I was certain Caelum had not described it *that* way.

Kiran sat quietly but grasped the edge of the table anxiously. If he had my abilities, he would have left char marks. I was sure of it.

"So, even if Caelum chooses Noor," Citali purred, "Lumos might reject her and choose me to marry him instead?" The way she said it made me wonder if she had something planned, a means to exactly that end.

"That's right," Father said. "Once in Lumina, I need the four of you to work together toward our common goal."

"To guide the Atenas to their future paths?" Saric asked, patiently waiting for Father to explain, his weathered hands crossed over his stomach as he sat back in the golden chair. "And remind them of the light?"

Father laughed, though it lacked humor. He glanced at the door, paranoia washing over him like a ship's wake upon the shore. He crossed the room, pulled the door open, and checked the hallway, then locked it again. When he returned, he braced his hands on the table. "What I'm about to say does not leave this room."

Saric and Kiran respectfully inclined their heads. Their duty was to Sol. And as Father was her Aten, their duty also extended to him, then to us.

"My daughters have been ordered to do whatever they must to find the crown of moonlight and bring it back to Helios, and to me."

"What about the marriage arrangement?" Kiran asked, sitting forward. "I imagine it might complicate things for the newly wedded couple if the bride steals something so sacred from her groom."

"Easily dissolved if I possess both crowns," Father smirked.

"What if it puts one of your daughters in danger?" Kiran pressed.

"My *daughters* can fend for themselves, *priest.*" Father's tone shifted into one we all recognized as dangerous.

Saric spoke then, the wisest among us. "Do you not fear Lumos, Aten?"

Father laughed. "No more than I fear Sol."

Her priests gasped, but his admission didn't surprise me. He'd gotten away with multiple murders and had never even been admonished by the goddess. What did surprise me was his lack of respect, especially in front of her priests. That was new. Father had always at least *pretended* to be reverent until now.

Father stood up straight. "If one of you finds the crown first, neither of you will have to marry the Lumin."

Citali squirmed beside me, but she did not tell him what Caelum had said. That no one, not even his brother or Lumos's priests, had ever set eyes on the crown of moonlight.

His dark gaze slid to me and Citali. "Both of you are to meet with the Sphinx tomorrow, early, before the House of Dusk awakens."

"The Sphinx is here?" I breathed. I didn't think she could leave Helios.

Father began to pace in a small space, back and forth. Harried. "She sent word that she would be here in the moments before daybreak, but only for a short time. Prepare yourselves. Be reverent. Listen carefully to her every word and intonation. The Sphinx does not lie, but speaks in riddles."

"Is she to speak to Noor and I together, Father?" Citali asked.

His footsteps halted. "She will see you separately and privately." The cold tone in the last word meant he'd insisted on being there and was denied. *Interesting.*

I'd seen engravings of her image and had seen her fly. Her small shadow drifted over the dunes sometimes when I walked to and from my visits with Mother. I'd heard Father tell of her prophecies but had never seen the Sphinx up close. Beyond that, she'd never asked to speak with me before.

Father looked to Saric and Kiran. "I wanted to let the two of you know so you can prepare for the journey, spiritually as well as physically. You'll need to pack your things, I'm sure."

Saric stared at Father and Father's brows drew together. "Very well, Aten," the elder priest finally relented, his tone far kinder than his expression.

Without a word, Kiran helped Saric from his chair and led him from the room.

Father pinched the bridge of his nose after they left, muttering, "The old priest likely won't survive the journey."

"Why must *they* go?" Citali asked petulantly.

"You are the Atenas. Your persons and spirits must be guarded. Who better to guard you than Sol's chosen priests?"

Citali screwed up her nose. "You should send Zuul and some of his men instead. That old priest is nothing but a bag of skin and bones. He couldn't protect a fly."

I gripped the golden arm rests with fury pulsing through my veins.

*How dare she talk about Saric so callously, so disrespectfully!*

My palms heated and a moment later, the armrests began to soften under my grip. Looking down in shock, I realized the gold I'd gripped had melted, leaving indentations of my hands in the once solid metal.

Citali's mouth hung open at the sight, but it was Father's haunted, almost frightened look that made me release the molten metal in my hand. It hit the floor, cooling quickly into solidified splatters.

"Get. Out," he muttered.

My lips fell open.

"Get out!" he shouted, pointing toward the door.

Citali jumped up at the same time I did. When I didn't move fast enough, he grabbed my hair and flung me across the room, tossing me out into the hallway. Citali ran out a second later and Father's door slammed behind us, followed by a roar of rage bellowing from within.

"What was that?" Citali panted, a shaky hand on her chest.

"I don't know why he –"

"Not *him*, Noor! How did you melt the arms of a chair made of pure gold?"

I shook my head. "I have no idea."

"Is that the first time something like this has happened?" she asked accusingly.

No, it wasn't. I recalled the charred table in the garden from my breakfast with Caelum. With a shake of my head, I started back to my rooms. She stepped in front of me, asking again. I shoved her out of the way. Her back hit the wall. Hard. She shook her head, hatred marring her pretty face.

"I'll find out what secrets you're withholding from him, Noor. Then *I'll* be the only one of us left for Caelum and Lumos to choose."

Deciding not to go back to my rooms, I found the nearest exit and strode outside.

*What is happening to me?*

Kiran met me in the garden where the charred table still sat, mocking me. He froze when he saw me, a war raging over his features. "Are you okay?"

I nodded once, refusing to speak.

He walked closer and stood right behind me, closer than what would ever be appropriate.

"You have to stop this, Kiran," I whispered. "I want you to stop."

I felt, more than heard, him leave.

I raked my hair back away from my face and craned my neck to the sky. My eyes caught on movement on the second floor. Citali lingered in the window at the landing, her eyes fixed on me.

I walked along the meandering garden paths toward the river, then downstream until the looming House of Dusk disappeared, then farther. I didn't think about the distance I walked or that I was alone in an unfamiliar place. I didn't think about the gray sky and grass and water and land. The strange light that wasn't light at all, yet wasn't darkness, smothering me. The atmosphere was so viscous I could taste the stale flavor of it.

Pretending I was in the dunes, I walked without stopping.

There were areas where the river deepened and twisted so much I couldn't follow it. I cut through a wooded area, expecting to find it again, but the river never emerged. The trees surrounded me, dull and dead, seeming to thicken somehow despite their brittle, skinny frames.

I turned around to retrace my steps but couldn't find any impressions in the silvery soil.

I walked in the direction I thought would take me back... and found myself completely lost and utterly hopeless.

Alone.

In the unending, nondescript dunes, I never would have gotten so turned around. I knew each mountain and grain by heart. However, I didn't know the dusk lands and cursed myself and my temper for fueling my steps so far from what I was familiar with, namely the river and House.

I sat on a boulder to rest and think, twisting the bracelet around my wrist. The diamonds warmed under my touch. Were they to blame for me scorching and melting things? Or were they innocent and I was becoming a monster?

Closing my eyes, I imagined the dunes with the House of Dusk perched in the middle of them. From my wrist, a light shone, pointing me straight to the place I needed to find. I opened my eyes, wishing it were that simple, and found that my diamonds were still casting that light through the wood.

I rushed over a knoll and stopped short, fear squeezing my chest. An enormous black wolf was tracking my progress through the forest with rigid ears. It stopped, snapping its head to the side when a branch snapped underfoot. It sniffed the air and I tucked myself behind a tree as best I could, covering the luminescent diamonds on my wrist and bending so my skirt covered the light beaming from my anklet. I remained still, my heart thrumming, wishing Sol could burn my scent away.

The beast let out a loud howl that made my knees tremble and the hair on the back of my neck spike. A moment later, the wolf left, trotting over the next rolling hill and disappearing. I hoped the beast wasn't slyly hunting me and that it wouldn't circle around and snap me from behind.

The light from my bracelet guided me, urging me to follow the dark creature. I listened for a long moment to see if I heard it ahead of me and heard nothing.

The diamond light intensified, as if urging me to move.

I mustered enough courage to weave through the needle-like trees following in the wolf's path until they thinned and I found the winding river again. Then the light disappeared.

Just then, a worried-looking Caelum and a mussed Beron jogged over a small hill. Caelum rushed to me, taking me in his arms and spinning me around, my feet drifting over the gray grasses. "Thank Lumos!" he breathed into my hair. "Where have you been?"

I held tightly to his shoulders, breathed in his familiar scent that I still couldn't name, and let myself *feel* for a moment. "I went walking and got turned around," I admitted. "I just found the river again."

"It's so late. You've been missing for hours."

Chastened, I pulled away and he sat my feet on the ground. "I'm okay. I didn't mean to scare anyone. I just got a little lost."

He finally smiled. "A little?"

I nodded. "Only a little."

Beron coughed and spoke at the same time. "Very lost."

I spun to face him.

His face had the look of wounded innocence. "What? Even Sol's priests are outside, summoning Sol to help you find your way back."

My ribcage tightened. *Is that what happened? Was it her light that poured from the diamonds?*

"I didn't mean to worry anyone."

Caelum threaded his hand through mine and refused to let me pull away. "Not now," he said, nervousness and fear still caught in his voice. "Please."

I clasped his palm and walked with him back upriver as Beron ran ahead to let everyone know I was safe.

"Did you see the wolf?" I asked.

Caelum's hand flinched. "We heard it. I was so afraid for you."

"There are no wolves in Helios. I didn't know they lived in the dusk lands."

"How did you recognize what it was?" he asked.

"I've spent hours poring over books. Reading has always offered an escape, however brief. We have a book with a few stories from before the Great Divide in our collection."

Outside the House of Dusk, a crowd had gathered. Beron had delivered the news, but they still cheered when Caelum and I appeared. He held our clasped hands in the air victoriously. Glancing over the crowd, Citali's calm demeanor set me on edge. Then she smiled. She didn't seem to mind that

Caelum and I were holding hands. She seemed genuinely happy that I had been found. I wasn't foolish to believe that either of those things were true, so I wondered what she was up to.

She rushed to us. "Noor!" she said to me, her dark eyes glittering with unshed tears. "You're okay."

Caelum dropped my hand to comfort her, patting her back and offering a hug.

*Nicely played, Citali.* Her dark eyes flashed my way as she hugged him a final time, winking over his shoulder.

Insufferable bitch.

"I'll have dinner brought to your rooms. And water. You must be famished, sister," she prattled, dragging me away from Caelum, through the crowd and past Father, who looked completely annoyed, and into the House of Dusk.

"Nice acting," I bit at her as we entered.

"Thank you," she said, pursing her lips into a heart. I wanted to peel them off. "Though I should be complimenting *you*. Your little lost sheep routine drew Caelum straight to you."

I tore my arm from her grasp. "You think it was a ploy?"

"Everything is a ploy, Noor. You're more naïve than I thought if you think otherwise."

She left my side to head toward the kitchens. "Caelum will check on you soon. I'd better get that food I promised." She grinned over her shoulder. "Or will the handsome priest beat him there?"

I growled at her and her tinkling laughter trailed down the hall.

Once in my rooms, I changed out of my ruined dress. The hem had been irreparably shredded by the underbrush and thorns, still sharp and thickly twined among the bases of the trees. Citali arrived a few moments later, carrying a tray with a crust of bread, a jelly I didn't recognize, a few pieces of meat left over from the dinner I'd missed, and a glass of water.

"Why didn't you have a servant bring this?" I asked, leery of her poisoning my food.

She scoffed, "Because they're all still outside. Besides, Caelum will be *so excited* to see that I care so much for my sister that I would lower myself to serve her."

I gave a disgusted snort. "He'll see right through you eventually, Citali. You're as sheer and shallow as the dresses you wear to beg for the attention of men in Helios and out of it."

She sat the tray down hard, the jelly knife clattering on the tray. "At least I can *hold* their attention. You can't even keep hold of his hand!"

She was utterly ridiculous. "Get out."

Citali didn't fuss or fight. She held her hands up in supplication, feigning innocence and defeat before turning and leaving my room.

A knock came at the door just before Caelum entered. He left it ajar so that anyone approaching would be able to see in, to keep my integrity and reputation intact. He noticed my destroyed gown lying over the back of a chair, catching onto every rip and tear, as he strode inside. He glanced at the food for a moment, a pleased look sliding over his face. Then his eyes caught on the jam and he stopped short.

"What sort of jam is that?" he asked.

"I thought it was from Lumina. Citali brought it a moment ago."

He strode to the tray and used the knife to scoop out a dollop of the jam. It was bluish-purple with a hint of green. His crystalline eyes flicked to mine. "Did you eat any of this?"

I shook my head, swallowing thickly.

"The nightthorn berry grows wild in Lumina. Someone's made it into a crude jam."

"Is it sweet?" I asked.

"It's poisonous," he answered. I waited for him to smile or laugh. For him to admit he was only teasing. But he didn't.

And I knew in that moment that Citali had once again tried to remove me from this race we were running.

She'd warned me that everything was a ploy. This was no different.

*I'll be the only one of us left for Caelum and Lumos to choose.*

Maybe she decided she didn't care about learning my secrets and had skipped that part of the plan and moved on to eliminate me altogether. If she removed me, she'd have no other obstacle keeping her from Caelum, his secret crown, and ultimately, his kingdom.

"I'm going to go ask her where she got this," he said, taking the glass jar with him as he turned away.

"She'll deny it. She'll say she didn't know what it was."

"But you believe she did?" he asked, turning to face me.

I hugged myself at the waist. "She absolutely did."

He walked back to the tray and sat the jar back down. "I came to tell you the treaty is drafted, ready to sign tomorrow. The ball preparations are underway."

I nodded, unsure of his point. I already knew as much.

"I want you to come to Lumina. Your father insists that Citali and Sol's priests go with you, but what do *you* want, Noor? Do you want me to reject her and send her back to Helios? If what you say is true and she just tried to poison you, how can I even consider marrying her? It's just... very hard to reconcile what I've experienced while spending time with her, and... this." He gestured to the jar.

"Only because you don't know her," I rasped.

"Do I know you? Which of you is lying? Or are both of you? I keep hearing whispers that you and she only want the crown of moonlight. If that's your goal and you're not interested in my heart or hand, I suggest you return home now, because I vow that you will never see it or find it. Never take its power into your hands. Not that you need it. You have fire in your palms, in your spirit – even in your eyes."

I could tell he could see that glow as he spoke.

I pinched my brows and walked to the bathing room where the only mirror in my rooms hung from the black and gold wall. I looked and looked, but never saw the glow of which he spoke. There was no gold in my eyes, aside from the flecks of amber that had always been divided among the chocolate shade.

Cool air slid over my skin as Caelum stepped behind me. He pointed to the reflection. "It's not visible in the mirror," he croaked. I turned to face him. "But when I look you in the eye, it's all I can see. I don't understand."

Neither could I.

"I believe you, even though I can't see it," I told him. I desperately wished he could see Citali for what she truly was. "You asked me what I want. I wish you would believe *me* when I tell you of my sister's true nature. Citali is a snake. If something happens to me, or if I decide not to go with you, remember that."

He tipped up my chin, his cool fingers steady on my skin. "And are you any less serpent?"

"Oh, I am also a viper. The difference between me and Citali is that I don't hide my fangs. I have *never* lied to you, Caelum. *Every word* I've spoken to you has been truth. I would pledge my life that Citali cannot make that same statement without a tick beneath her left eye. It's her tell."

His dark brows kissed. Had he seen her face flinch before? What was he thinking?

"Every word?"

I nodded.

I could almost see him recalling the conversations we'd had. How he'd asked if I was searching for, coveting, the crown of moonlight, and I told him I was. I'd told him the truth and he thought I was teasing.

"What did your father want with the two of you today?"

"He finally told us that we're going to Lumina and instructed our priests to go with us as escorts and protectors.

And... Citali and I are to meet with the Sphinx before we leave. She's coming here for us."

He swallowed thickly. "How well do you know the lioness?"

"I don't."

His hand ghosted over my throat. His eyes dipped to the skin there. "He didn't hurt you?"

"No. I think he was frightened of me."

"What made him fear you?" he asked.

I glanced up to see his reaction. "I melted a golden chair."

He blinked rapidly, then recovered. "That would do it."

I nodded once.

"Do you fear him?"

I didn't want to admit it. Didn't want to be honest. But I had never lied to him and for whatever reason, didn't want to. I couldn't even stomach the thought of it. I'd told countless lies to my father, the Aten. I'd lied to myself. I'd lied to Sol's priests, including Kiran. I'd even lied to Vada, Caelum's mother. But never him. Meeting his eye, I steeled my spine and breathed the truth – something for which I hated myself. "Yes."

Yes, I feared my father.

Yes, I feared one day I would anger him and he wouldn't restrain his fury. Or that he'd kill me for no other reason but that I existed, that I lived and breathed when he wished I didn't.

I feared the vessels in my eyes would spill and spark and that Sol would reject me entirely, even as he pulled her down to burn me out of his life.

"There is such light in you, Noor. And such darkness."

"I know," I rasped as his hand fell away.

"I'm not sure which part of you to believe."

"Both parts are me, Caelum," I admitted softly. "Believe it all."

He swallowed thickly, stepped backward, then turned and left the bathing room. My door closed a moment later.

My heart felt cold as I realized I was torn, stretched between Caelum and his beautiful, kind heart, and what I knew in mine had to be done for the fate of us all.

# 15

That night, I lay awake in bed for hours, unable to quiet my turbulent mind. It was so hard to tell the time here, but somewhere in the middle of restlessness, I rose and walked to the bathing room, smiling when I saw Vada had left more of the aromatic salts there.

I went downstairs to the kitchens and found the embers still warm in the hearth. Like the hide of a fiery beast, they flared from blue to red to yellow and orange, writhing as if they were desperate to hoard the heat and stop it from escaping.

"Noor?" someone said from behind me.

I turned, surprised. "Vada?" She nodded. Caelum's mother wore a thick, silver robe. She'd combed her matching hair that fell straight to her shoulders and didn't dare stretch an inch farther. "What are you doing up so late?"

She held up a cup. "Tea. I'm an early riser. For my entire youth, I woke long before my mistresses. The habit is a difficult one to break. Why are you awake?"

"I was going to heat some water for a bath."

"Are you feeling well?" she asked, sitting her cup down on one of the long, wooden counters that were riddled with slices and scars.

I waved off her concern. "I'm fine. I just have an important meeting this morning."

"How important?"

"How important is the Wolven to Luminans?" Her eyes rounded and I nodded. "Yeah. I'm meeting with Helios's Sphinx."

"No wonder you're too nervous to sleep."

Nervous. Upset. Confused. Distraught. Overwhelmed. Terrified. She could've named any or all and been right.

She moved around the kitchen and found two enormous pots. We each hefted one to the back door where Vada asked a pair of Luminan guards in their stiff, dark blue uniforms to fetch some water for us. They didn't complain or say it was beneath their station. They each inclined their head to Vada respectfully and told her they'd return as quickly as possible. And they did. It only took a few minutes.

"That was fast," I said as they carried the water inside and hung the pots over the fire for us. I thanked them before they went back to their posts. Each gave a slight, deferential bow and left us alone again. Vada gathered wood from a stack along the wall and began throwing split pieces into the fire. "Wait!" I said, bringing my own pile. "Fire needs air. If you stack it so that it can breathe, it will roar to life in no time."

Vada sat back on her haunches and gestured to the hearth. "Queen of flame, please show me."

I offered a wan smile.

"One does not have to wear a crown to be exactly that," Vada offered softly. "My mother was a queen. If she was still alive, she still would be, and she never had two silvers to rub together long. She'd certainly never believe in a million years that my son, her grandson, was chosen as Lumin. Lumos blessed us that day, but I'd like to think he's well-pleased in his choice."

"Caelum is exceptional."

"Yes. He is," she said, meeting my eyes and holding them. She stacked her wood in the pattern I'd showed her and before long, the fires roared the way I promised they would. She sighed. "I don't pretend to know your heart, or your sister's, but as a mother, as Caelum's mother, I hope you don't break *his* heart vying for power or prestige just because you're not likely to inherit the role of Aten."

"Sol can choose any of the Aten's three daughters as her heir," I defended weakly.

She pressed her lips together. "How many third borns have ever served as Aten?"

"None." Most were first borns. One was a second son. Never had there been a third, fourth, fifth born, or beyond in the line of succession. But Sol was a goddess of firsts, I tried to remind myself.

"I don't seek a title," I told her honestly. "I've never truly believed Sol would choose me either, but beyond that, it's not a position or a crown that drives me."

Her eyes sharpened when the word crown fell from my lips. "What does drive you, Noor?"

"Freedom," I rasped, staring at the fire wistfully.

The flames were free. They danced along the wood we'd fed them. Roared and flared. Sparked. I listened as the wood snapped and popped under the fire's attention and wondered...

*If I was part flame, what would I seek to consume?*

Father's face drifted into my mind, overlaid onto the wood in the hearth. The only way I could truly be free was to incinerate him and damn his plans to ruin Caelum and Lumina.

The only tangible way to protect Caelum, Beron, and Vada, the kind guards and their families, their very way of life… was to strip all power away from my father. And to do that, I had to be stronger than him. If Sol did not choose me as her Aten, only a Lumin could stand against him.

She glanced behind her, over each shoulder. "You are more powerful than Citali. You have fire in your hands."

I stiffened. "How do you know that?"

"The table outside. The chair in the Aten's room. Most of all, by the whispers."

"Rumors are often wrong," I volleyed.

"Is this one?"

I blew out a breath, noting that the water was beginning to steam. Silky tendrils danced upward. They dissolved, only to be replaced by more. A cycle of life not unlike our own.

"Are you saying Citali shares your ability?"

"Citali has never melted or burned things, no. But maybe her ability hasn't manifested yet."

Vada was still for a moment as we knelt there on the floor in front of the hearth. "Are you coming with us? Caelum said you're unsure."

"I'm not sure he wants me to. I think I upset him."

She stood. "I'm not sure there's anything you could do to temper his feelings for you."

"How can he feel anything for me? He barely knows me."

She shook her head. "He doesn't care. My son follows his heart – always – and his heart guides him to you. Regardless of his reservations or what it might mean for Lumina, he intends to present you to Lumos."

My lips parted. My heart filled with joy and hope and a million perfect things for which I had no words. And as soon as my heart felt them all, a fissure formed in her side and all those wonderful feelings spilled away. My heart inexplicably, despite my plans, was guiding me to Caelum, but even as she wanted him, she was still willing and determined to break him if it saved him and everyone and everything he loved.

"You really can't feel how much he longs to be near you?" she asked, her face softening.

"I thought he liked Citali just as much."

She shook her head and gestured to the roaring fire. "No. His feelings for her would not kindle a fire, let alone encourage it to burn."

Could Vada be right? I wasn't sure what to think or say, so I kept quiet.

"I'll have these carried to your rooms if you'd like to go let them in."

I nodded and turned to leave, then stopped. "Vada?" I asked over my shoulder.

"Yes?"

"Thank you."

"For what?" she asked, a confused smile on her lips.

"My mother was taken from me when I was only seven, but for the past few days, you've reminded me of her."

Vada clutched her chest and tears crept into her eyes. "Thank you."

I fought to give her a grateful smile, my chin wobbling and my eyes welling to match hers. I nodded once and walked out of the kitchens.

On the staircase, I allowed my tears to fall. I couldn't hold them in any longer. I stifled them as soon as I could muster the strength, but it took three flights of stairs before I got myself under control again and reined in all the feelings trying to pour out.

This place was weakening me. I hadn't cried since the day I carried Mother into the sand.

I unlocked my room and waited for the hot water to arrive. My trembling fingers pressed against my lips. Before I left Helios, I thought this would be easy. I told myself to pretend and sneak and steal this crown. The one who wore it would never matter to me.

Then I met Caelum and everything changed.

An insatiable ache formed in my chest and I hated myself for what I still had to do.

The two guards who'd fetched the water for Vada arrived at my room a few minutes later. I held the door wide open and waved them inside. They emptied the heavy pots into the small bathing tub, worried it wasn't full enough, and offered to get me more water. I promised them it would more than suffice for my needs and thanked them for helping me in the middle of the night. They told me it was their pleasure and that the nights could grow monotonous with so little to keep them busy, then left to take up their positions again.

The salts quickly dissolved when I poured them into the hot water; their heady aroma filled the small bathing room. The water was not boiling, but it was deliciously hot. I scrubbed my hair with a sliver of remaining soap, scoured my skin until it felt raw, and sat back in the not-nearly-full tub.

The first time I saw the Sphinx's shadow was the day I carried my mother into the sand. She didn't appear until Saric and I were far into the dunes, but her shadow darted over our heads and I remembered Saric falling to his knees, bowing his head and holding Mother's urn in his hands, muttering prayers to Sol. I knelt with him, unsure what to do, shielding my eyes from Sol's face while trying to catch a glimpse of the lioness.

I wondered what she looked like. She was called a lioness but was said to be part human, though one who could fly. Some claimed she was terrible to look upon. Others swore she was the most beautiful thing anyone would see in their lifetime. Could both descriptions be true?

I toweled off and sat in the steamy, warm air until the vapor dissipated and the room cooled. I padded to the armoire and opened the door, observing the interior filled with clothing. Father thought we would be here for weeks while the negotiations took place. We'd packed with those expectations in mind, but it had only been days. *Days.*

After less than a week, Father managed to convince Caelum that he truly wanted peace and an alliance between our kingdoms who'd been separated since the Great Divide, even when no Aten before him would dare make such a deal. He made promises he had no intention of keeping. His nefarious plans had nothing to do with the treaty the two men would sign later today, and everything to do with Citali or I infiltrating Lumina to find that crown.

For a brief moment, I wondered if any of this truly mattered or if we were just fooling ourselves into thinking we could possibly control or manipulate one of the gods.

I selected a gauzy black dress. It would expose my back from the dimples at my hips to the wide collar encircling my neck but would hide the lingering bruises too stubborn to fade completely away. I dressed quickly and didn't bother with sandals. If we were to meet her early, I didn't want anyone hearing me leave my rooms or walking the hallways and ask questions as to where I was going. How would we know when to go to her or where to find her?

Combing my hair, I waited in the windowsill for it to dry, still unsure of the hour and crawling with nervousness and fear.

My hair was still damp when a knock came at the door, but when I opened it, no one was there. Movement caught my eye, not from a person, but from a broad shadow that swept down the wall. I followed it, somehow knowing the knock came from the dark figure, and also to whom the shadow belonged.

Instead of walking down the staircase, the shadow continued past it, down the opposite side of the hallway, and disappeared up a small flight of steps I never would have known were there.

The narrow steps ended when I came to a door. I pushed it open and emerged on the roof of the House of Dusk.

Heights had never scared me, until I turned to find the Sphinx waiting. She was enormous, the size of a giant with golden fur covering her body. Her legs and abdomen were muscled beneath shorter fur. Her mane was a shade darker and served as hair, drifting down her back and cascading down to cover her breasts. Her feline tail was tufted at its end, the same dark gold of her mane. She flared her wings and a gasp flew from my chest.

They were magnificent. I couldn't tell if they were solid or soft, but unlike her fur which looked animalistic, her wings were something other... They were iridescent, then turned translucent as she flexed and then tucked them into her back.

A thin coat of fur covered her face, which looked nothing at all like a lion's, but looked like the most ferocious woman I've ever clamped eyes on. She sat on her haunches, large front paws bolstering her proud chest. Her solid black, fathomless eyes had no whites or pupils. As she watched me, she tilted her head.

She opened her lips. "Atena Noor."

I swallowed a knot of fear at the sound. It would have frightened me less if she'd let out a thunderous roar, or at the very least, if a deep, fearsome tone had resonated from her chest to chill my bones, but the Sphinx did not roar and her voice did not strike fear because it was dangerous. My body began to quake because the Sphinx sounded like a small child.

Kneeling before her, I inclined my head respectfully and waited.

"Rise, Atena. We don't have much time," she chirped.

I raised my head and met her eye.

"You are clothed in indignation and bravery, where your sister wears fear. It is her weakness."

"Which sister are you speaking of?"

The Sphinx grinned. "Clever girl. Do you enjoy riddles?"

"No," I answered honestly, afraid to lie.

My legs quivered uncontrollably. I had never wanted to run in fear from anything so much in my life, yet I was completely transfixed and didn't want to turn away. The rumors were right. She was a terrible beauty.

The Sphinx's black eyes twinkled. "I love them. I gave your sister a riddle. I wonder if she'll unfurl it before it's too late."

"You came all the way here for word games?"

She readjusted her front paws, muscles flexing beneath her fur. "I flew here to see *you*. I only met with her to conceal *this* conversation, and to warn her that if she ever tries anything as foolish as to try and poison you again, I'll carry her into the sky, use my claws to spill her guts, and let them rain over Helios. She'll never reach the hereafter if she kills you. Sol will reject her entirely."

"Why does Sol care what happens to me?"

The Sphinx slowly blinked. "I came to provide answers to exactly three questions. Choose them quickly and wisely. While I'm here, Helios is unguarded."

My stomach plummeted. "Is my kingdom in danger?"

She smiled. "The answer to your first question is yes. Helios is in danger. But dear Noor, is the threat from within, without, or both?"

I winced and mentally cursed myself for not thinking before I spoke. Father had tried for years to teach me that habit. Perhaps the Sphinx would finally succeed...

"Ask from your heart, Noor. Not your head," she advised.

*My heart?* "Does Caelum truly want to present me to Lumos as his choice?"

Vada had said so, but he was so spent the last time we talked privately. So torn.

"That is his intention right now, but... many decisions and paths lay between intention and actuality."

*So, it could change.*

A question roared through my mind and I spoke it before I could decide if it was the right final thing to ask her. "How can I defeat my father?"

She gave a feral smile. "There you go." She prowled forward, then circled me. I should've felt like prey, but my heart thundered that we were both predators in our own right, that I was her equal at the very least. That the fire in my veins would scorch her before she could extend her claws. Finally satisfied, and with that same wicked grin, she stopped in front of me.

"That was three questions, Noor. The sands of time have run out."

"You haven't answered my final question." I reached out to her, stopping when she growled.

"Don't touch me, Atena," she warned, her childlike voice deepening into something that struck terror in my heart. If lightning and thunder could speak, it would've been less frightening.

I tucked my hands behind me, bowing low. "I meant no disrespect, Sphinx. I hold a firm belief that my father *is* the threat to Helios. I need something more specific than the answer you gave. Something tangible. I'm terrible with riddles, remember?" I asked, keeping my eyes on her as she seemed to loom taller, larger.

"You *have* courage and humility, Noor, a powerful combined weapon if you brandish it well against your father. But you are distracted because you *seek* the thing you do not need." She paused, seeming to consider me, my question, and its answer all at the same time. But many more blew through my mind, like sand scooped and scattered in a gust of wind.

I didn't have time for this. A riddle. She said she'd given Citali one and now she'd given one to me. One I didn't want to waste my time attempting to unfurl. She said that I was distracted yet offered another, worse distraction. If she could only speak plainly, this conversation would be meaningful.

*Where is the crown of moonlight hidden, and is there any chance Citali or I will find it? Would stealing it truly make me the Lumin? What will happen if Citali gets her claws on it first? Has Sol already made Zarina her Aten? Can Father be both Aten and Lumin? Would Sol and Lumos allow it?*

I pressed my eyes closed.

*Will Caelum hate me if I take his power and crown away? Would being Lumin allow me to end Father's reign? And, is that what Sol wants? What does the goddess truly want? Freedom? Is she truly a hostage in her own sky, or did she choose stillness over movement?*

The Sphinx shrank away, wincing, a great paw raking over her forehead. "Calm your thoughts, Atena."

"You can hear them?" I asked.

The Sphinx laughed in her tinkling, childlike voice. "Sol will guide you, Noor, in light *and* in darkness." She flapped her translucent, golden wings once, twice, then pushed off the roof with her muscular legs, launching high into the sky. This time, I didn't need to guard my eyes from Sol's face. In the moody, clouded sky, I watched until the Sphinx flew too far to see.

Her voice filled my mind. "Here is something more meaningful, Noor."

And then... I wasn't on the roof at all, but seated in my father's room at the long, golden table, in the chair with melted arms. I shrank against the chair back as he strode through wearing his finest kilt, gold held up with a thick, golden belt. His head and face were freshly shaved. Golden laces vined up his legs to his knee. It was what he would wear to a great event...

A ball.

I tensed, waiting for him to see me, for him to scream and rant and tell me to leave, but he didn't notice I was there. In his hands was a small book no bigger than his palm.

The dark binding was worn thin. The leather was cracked in places. Part of me separated from my body and a translucent version of me rose and walked to him. When a knock came at the door, he tucked it into a hidden pocket on his right hip. See-through me grinned over her shoulder, then walked up behind him and eased a ghostly version of the book from the pocket where he'd hidden it.

I swallowed thickly and clutched at the chair arms to find they were melted away.

Heat pressed down upon me from overhead and I breathed deeply and calmly. *Sol.* I was standing now, feet punching through crusted sand as I made my way to the sacred place I knew by heart. The white bones I'd carried shone in white mounds atop the red-orange dune. Sol flared above, and comforting waves of heat poured over me.

I sat with my mother and told her everything that had happened since I left – my worries, my fear that I would be gone longer than expected, and how I missed her so badly it hurt.

Grief and the loneliness it left behind were a well that never seemed to run dry.

No amount of Sol's fire could burn it away.

I stared at her bones beside me as a shadow passed over them. I shielded my eyes and saw her there... the Sphinx. She smiled at me, flapped her great wings, and launched into the sky. Her shadow circled me for a moment before streaking over the dunes, carving a path I knew led straight to Helios.

And suddenly, I was back on the rooftop, surrounded by gray once more. I clutched my chest, feeling the distance between Mother and me, between Sol and me, once again tearing at my heart. The warmth from Sol slowly faded from my skin as I considered what the Sphinx showed me and the kindness she'd done in letting me see the one I needed most.

I needed that book. I needed to steal it and take it with me, and that meant it had to be done tonight, during the ball. After Father woke, he would know it was gone.

I needed help.

Pinching my lip, a thought struck me. *I think I know where to find it.*

# 16

I closed the door to the roof, shouldering it until it fell into place, then rushed to the staircase, down to the second floor. Knocking on Kevi's door was a gamble. She'd helped me once. Would she put her neck out again for the third daughter of the Aten?

Would she take offense at what I was about to ask her?

She cracked the door open, already awake and alert. "Atena?"

"I need your help. Again."

Kevi opened the door and pulled me in quickly. We stood in a room that contained all the dancers' costumes, mirrors, and make-up. Beyond it was a smaller room with a mussed bed drenched in purple with matching furniture against bone-white walls, the barest hint of gray in their hue.

She crossed her arms and propped her hip against the desk piled with slips of fabric, veils made to match, or dripping with golden coins. "I'm listening."

I didn't miss that her gaze drifted first to the sun diamonds glittering against my wrist before dropping to my ankle. I inwardly cringed. The diamonds couldn't be removed, so if that was Kevi's price, I couldn't afford her help.

"I need help stealing something from my father. Something he keeps on his person."

She went completely rigid. Even her breathing stilled. Then she laughed. "You can't be serious."

"I am."

"And you assume I'm a thief because I dance? Because your father insists we entertain his guests?" she spat, holding herself tighter.

"I make no assumptions about you, but I think you can distract him long enough that another dancer could ease it from him without him noticing." I swallowed. The Sphinx had frightened me on a primal level. Kevi's anger frightened me because I thought for sure she'd say no and throw me from her rooms.

"What is it?" she asked instead.

"A small book. He will have it in his kilt's hidden pocket, on his right side."

Kevi shook her head, letting her hands flop to her sides. "What you ask is impossible. And I'm not willing to die, or for any of my dancers to die, trying to extract this book from him. Because that's what will happen if we attempt to steal it. This... this is lunacy. I'm sorry, but I can't be part of it."

"There has to be a way! I leave for Lumina tomorrow and that book must leave with me."

She ticked her chin up. "What's in it?"

"I'm not sure."

She laughed mirthlessly. "You don't know what's written inside, but you want us to risk our lives for it?"

"The Sphinx came to me this morning, Kevi. She showed me where the book is and told me I must have it."

Kevi placed a hand over her heart and breathed, "The Sphinx?"

I nodded.

She sobered instantly. "I wish the Sphinx had clawed it from his pocket herself." She pressed her eyes closed and pinched the bridge of her nose. "I think I might know a way," she said warily. Hope mingled with the fire in my veins. "But it'll come with a hefty price."

I raised my wrist. "I can't remove the sun diamonds, Kevi. Father has tried. He's had his best goldsmith try to smelt the metal, had it chiseled, had his strongest guardsmen try to break the chain – nothing works."

She shook her head and smirked. "Keep your diamonds, Atena. I want you to arrange safe passage to Lumina – and the promise of the Lumin's protection – for me and all my girls. Your father is no fool, Noor. I have a sleeping draught I can add to his wine, but he will wake with a ferocious headache and know he's been drugged. He will come after us all. If his body doesn't burn it away before dawn…"

I nodded, noting the fear in her eyes. I understood it well. "How many girls?"

"Seven in total, including me."

"I have to ask Caelum first. I can't make any guarantees or promises on his behalf."

She inclined her head. "I'll bring the draught tonight, but I won't use it until I know we'll be taken care of and kept safe."

*Kevi will have time to think and reconsider until tonight, when we need to put the plan in motion,* I thought as I went in search of Caelum.

In the great hall, I found him seated across from Father. Beron was at his left hand, while the seat at his right was empty. My heart skipped, wondering if he'd saved it for me.

Citali chose that moment to slide into the seat at Father's right hand, ruining my happy moment.

Caelum's eyes found me as I made my way to them, a suppressed heat in them flaring as he took me in from face to foot. He gestured to the empty chair and I gratefully took it.

As I sat amongst them, Citali frowned, studying me like I was as much a riddle as the one the Sphinx gave her this morning.

"Citali," I greeted. "You almost look surprised to see me." I gave her a smile, promising retribution.

Beron choked on the water he sipped, taking a moment to calm his breathing. So... Caelum had confided in his brother that Citali had given me poisoned jam.

Father's countenance was calm, but I noticed the way his hands tightly clutched his utensils, then the table when he laid them down. He would try to corner me once the meal was over. I couldn't let that happen.

I turned to Caelum. "Lumin, I was hoping you might like to take a walk after breakfast."

When our eyes met, I hoped Caelum could see my plea.

His brows slanted, but he graciously accepted my offer. "I'd love to, Atena." He gestured to Father, deferring. "Assuming there is time before we meet to sign the treaty."

Father chuckled, but his smile did not reach his sharp eyes. "Haven't you had enough excursions, Noor? You got lost the last time you wandered," he reminded everyone.

"Caelum would be with me, Father."

He gave a heavy nod and dread filled my stomach. "Very well. I'm sure there is time enough for a *short* walk."

We ate from platters of meat and fruit and bread, though the sweet dates were my favorite. I froze when Caelum placed a few on my plate when I finished the last one and glanced to see if there was more.

Beron glanced between us, one of his dark brows raised.

We all knew what hand feeding or placing food on the plate of another meant to a Luminan now, but I wasn't sure if Caelum was overlooking his custom to accommodate me, or if he meant it. If my cheeks could glow red-orange, they would have.

I quietly thanked him and ate what he'd proffered.

Caelum was different this morning. I hadn't seen him since he left my rooms and me behind. Since he poured out his soul to tell me that I was darkness and light and nothing he could trust. I just hoped Vada was right about his feelings and that he hadn't written me off entirely. Today he was quieter, but his attention was honed. He was a blade sheathed in steel and I couldn't see how sharp his edges were.

Beron cleared his throat and excused himself, saying he'd promised Vada that he would help with a few things for tonight's ball. Citali turned to watch as he strode out of the room. When her gaze returned to us, I tilted my head in question. She answered with a scowl.

Did my callous sister covet Caelum's brother? Or was he a contingency plan she hadn't discarded just yet? Could it be that to her, he might be both?

Caelum scooted his seat back as he stood, then offered me his hand. I took it and walked out of the great hall by his side. I thought for sure once we were outside he would release it, but he kept his hold as we walked toward the river, toward his ship.

*Is he going to ask me not to go?* The thought refused to budge from my mind as we boarded the ship and slipped into the quarters below decks. "Our conversation will be private here," he said, his voice gravelly.

I kept distance between the two of us when I was able. If I cozied up to him tonight, he would know something was amiss. I hated that I was about to ask him for such a heavy thing, but what choice did I have? I needed that book and Kevi and her girls were the only ones who might have a chance at pulling off the theft. If I tried, I would fail. Just as I was about to open my mouth, he spoke.

"Noor – I owe you an apology about last night. I shouldn't have left your rooms, or you, like that."

"You shouldn't apologize. You're not sure whether you can trust me."

He opened his mouth, but quickly shut it again, knowing he couldn't refute it without lying. "I want to," he finally said.

"I want you to, also. So, I'm going to tell you a great secret and will trust *you* to keep it safe. I met with the Sphinx this morning."

He nodded.

"I want you to know what she said and what I saw. And then I need to ask you for help."

"Name it," he said.

"You don't even know what it is I'm asking," I chastised, trying to keep my tone playful and failing miserably. The fear melting over my bones made it difficult to feel anything else in light of Sol's instructions. Instructions that couldn't have been clearer. "You might decide not to invite me to Lumina after you hear what she revealed."

He swallowed thickly. "There's nothing you can say that would make such a chasm stretch between us, Noor."

I wasn't so sure about that. I bit my lip and tried to pull my hand away. "Stop," he breathed. "Stop running from me."

"I don't run…"

His dark brows kissed. "Yes, Noor. You do."

I held his hands despite mine sweating, despite wanting anything to happen to keep me from asking him for such a ponderous thing.

"The Sphinx let me visit my mother in the dunes."

He tilted his head. "What do you mean?"

"I mean, I was *there*. I felt Sol's heat and saw her bright face. Her light was radiant, brilliant, and the sands were hot beneath my feet. I saw my mother's bones and sat with her for a time. I know it sounds crazy, but I know she heard me."

Caelum's eyes were kind. "It's not crazy. I speak to my father as well. I visit his grave when time allows. He's buried in a field with many, many others from our town. He died before Lumos chose me," he said. The pain and vulnerability on his face, the way his thumb brushed over mine, reflected everything I felt inside and the invisible, golden urn I carried wherever I walked. "I'd like to introduce you some day," he said quietly.

"I'd love to meet him."

Caelum pulled me close and wrapped his strong arms around my back. I threaded mine around his neck.

"The Sphinx also revealed a task I have to complete before I can leave with you tomorrow," I said as my cheek rested against his chest.

His shoulders tensed. "What sort of task?"

"Dangerous."

He pulled back enough to see me. "Tell me."

So, I did. I told him that the lioness gave me a prophetic vision of Father dressed for tonight's ball, and then revealed what she wanted me to do. And that Kevi would help us if he would promise her and the other dancers asylum in Lumina.

He closed his eyes and cursed. "What you're asking could shred the peace treaty I'm prepared to sign."

"I can't get close enough to him to steal it, but I must have that book or see what's in it, Caelum. If it's nothing, I could put it back in his pocket and he'll be none the wiser."

He breathed a heavy sigh and held me tighter. "But if it's something, you would have to take it from him."

I nodded.

"I will grant them safe passage and asylum." His clear blue eyes were steady, not filled with fear or regret – yet. "But I insist we leave as soon as he's unconscious. I've seen how his fire burns away even the strongest of spirits. I imagine it would do the same to a sleeping draught. When he wakes, he'll be angry enough to burn our ship to embers. If we can slip into Lumina before he wakes, that'll be all the better."

He grazed a thumb over my neck, where the dark collar hid the remnants of my bruises. "If there was a way to end him, I would've done it the moment I learned he'd put his hands on you. I haven't figured out how yet, but I won't stop trying, Noor. In the meantime, I offer you a home in Lumina for as long as you'd like it, whether or not Lumos accepts you as my wife."

"*If* you make the decision to present me to him..." I led.

His hands tightened on my waist. "Citali has been kind and accommodating. And while I am sure she will make a man happy one day, I am not he. I wouldn't place her before Lumos even if he turns you away."

I wanted to rejoice at his words. My heart did for a second. Then the doubt and fear swelled.

Would the god of night reject me? I feared Sol wouldn't find me acceptable in death and I'd loved her my entire life. Would Lumos want his Lumin to share even a second of my life? Would he immediately know what I sought and what darkness truly lay among the light in my chest? I pressed my eyes closed. Sol spoke with me through her Sphinx. She needed my help and the book Father kept so close must have some sort of secret inside. Would it contain knowledge that would change everything? What if I didn't need to steal Caelum's crown or become the Lumin at all to thwart my father's plans?

I didn't believe Father when he said Sol wanted him to be her power on earth forever, or that she wanted him to rule both kingdoms. She wouldn't be asking me to steal something from Father if she favored him. She would protect her Aten at all costs if her will and his were the same.

There were too many unknown variables and questions without answers, but I was certain that the contents in that book would change everything.

"I need to meet with your father soon. I'm surprised he gave his blessing for this time alone," he offered apologetically, just before his eyes sparked with blue flame. "I would offer to escort you to the ball from your room, but I think I'd prefer to watch you descend the steps. It's a magnificent thing to behold."

# 17

I spent hours on the roof where Father wouldn't know to look for me and read every word of the book Saric had given me. The first thing that took me aback was that Sol didn't become fixed in the sky until Father became Aten. Before then, the Atens wrote that she traveled her kingdom in a predictable pattern, rising and setting, leaving the land in complete darkness, only to reappear and bring the hope of a new day with her. It was how they measured time. No dark blemish was mentioned on her face.

In those days, the soil rested and did not burn.

Why did she stop? Or what stopped her? The feeling growing inside me that she was trapped, desperately burning to be free again, solidified with every word I read.

The Sphinx hadn't given me a riddle, Saric had. Perhaps the lioness gave me the answer to the questions tumbling through my mind.

The second thing that stood out among their writings were that the Atens, from the first to my grandmother, who was Aten before Father was chosen, all added similar descriptions of their relationship with Sol. They were all meek, gentle, and kind. I immediately knew why Sol had chosen them.

And then I came to Father's section.

What he added was as unexpected as it was heartbreaking.

*My Sol, I am broken and unworthy of your blessing. Of serving you. Of your light and of your love. Please reconsider. Please choose another. I cannot be your Aten.*

It was written by his hand. I recognized the sharp angles and shallow swoops. The last sentence was blurred as if his tears had fallen on the ink before it dried, spreading it across the parchment.

Why had Saric shown me this?

I read it again and again, unable to recognize my father in any word, yet knowing he'd penned them and plucked them from his heart.

Which meant that at some point, he was a different man. Sol knew that. She chose him because of the heart he had back then. *What happened to him?*

The only thing I could think was that my mother was somehow responsible. I'd often said to myself that she'd reduced his heart to a cinder. She was why he had grown to hate me.

I wiped a tear, remembering a few flashes of his smile as he picked me up and tossed me into the air, as I rode atop his shoulders eating a sweet treat, as he smiled at her.

My mother's face was fading from my memory. The passage of every day, every year, erased her a little more. I could no longer hear her laughter. I couldn't remember the color of her eyes. Did she give me the chocolate shade, or did I inherit her amber hue?

Father had written that he was broken. I wasn't sure if he still was, or if he might have healed back wrong and the pieces of him no longer fit where they did before.

Was Sol leading me to the book that would finish his story, or would what it contained within the pages be the beginning of mine?

When I snuck back down to my rooms, Vada was there, hanging a gown on the hook inside my armoire. My mouth dropped and the only word I could formulate or breathe was, "How?"

She smiled, holding out one of the sleeves. "My sister is a very skilled seamstress. She came with me. I snuck out one of your gowns so she could fashion one that would fit as well."

She was incredibly talented, and luckily for me, she also happened to travel with fabric, every inch of which was covered in moon diamonds. The gown glistened, even in the drab light that drenched the room. It glittered and shone, the cool blue equivalent to the warm, golden diamonds adorning my wrist and ankle.

"I might have mentioned to Caelum that I wished to have a gown made for you. He insisted on the best fabric – fabric fit for a queen. *His* queen, Noor."

The phoenix in my stomach cried out for him, flapping her fiery wings and flying in circles, desperate for him.

His mother walked to me and cupped my elbow. "Please don't hurt my son."

I shook my head, my brows pinched. "Never."

There had to be a way to stop Father without hurting Caelum. I just had to find it. I hoped Sol had paved such a path with the vision she granted me and the mission on which she was sending me.

Vada leaned in and gently hugged me.

Lumos had chosen his Lumin well. He'd chosen one with a heart of gold, passed down by a woman who was both wise and kind.

"Do you need help dressing?" she asked as she pulled away.

I shook my head, unable to speak for a moment because of the Sphinx-sized knot sitting in my throat.

She nodded. "I'll see you tonight, Noor."

She let herself out and I locked the door behind her.

I braided my hair down my back, lined my eyes with dark kohl, applied shimmer dust to my cheeks, and currant to my lips. Then I went to dress. The gown was exquisite. I undressed and slid it off its hanger, surprised that it wasn't as heavy as I imagined. The fabric whispered as I stepped into it and slid my arms into the sleeves.

The neckline was straight, grazing the tops of my breasts, and the back dipped in a deep square as well. I tugged the zipper up and held the broad skirt out to watch the fabric catch the muted light. Tucked inside the armoire was an unfamiliar black box.

I took it out and lifted a small hinge, opening it to find a necklace of pure silver. The metal felt cool against my fingers. I clasped it onto my neck and walked into the bathing room to look in the mirror.

I'd never worn anything in the blue crystalline color of Caelum's eyes.

My fingers drifted over the fabric on my stomach. I took a moment to breathe, because I wasn't sure when I might have the chance again. Tonight, Kevi and her girls had to execute her plan flawlessly or we would all be executed.

I breathed out.

I hoped Beron would keep Citali occupied so she didn't notice what was happening or ruin the ball for me the way she was likely planning.

Drew another breath in.

Tonight, I would walk down the staircase and hope that Caelum was waiting at the bottom, that he would drink in the sight of me the way he had the night of the feast.

I pushed the air out again and turned on my heel. Golden sandals were all I had brought, so I slipped my feet into them and tied them on. When I stood, the gown's skirts draped to conceal them. I strode from the room, locking it behind me.

A gasp came from over my shoulder. I turned my head to see Citali standing in her doorway.

Citali looked stricken. "Where did you get *that?*" she bit, hurt lacing her tone.

"It was a gift."

"From Caelum?"

I didn't respond. It was from him, but also from Vada, and from her sister who made it. "You look beautiful, Citali," I responded instead.

She did. She wore a dress that was sleeveless and fitted at the top, with intricate golden beads strung over the bodice. Those beads gave way to golden feathers that cascaded from her hips to the floor. Her earrings were feathers, too, and the beaded collar necklace she wore matched her dress's bodice.

"I look like I belong in Helios, but you… You look like you already belong to Lumos himself," she said disgustedly. "How quickly you forsook Sol for her enemy."

"I'm not forsaking Sol," I growled, my bracelet warming against my wrist.

"I take it that this means Caelum chose you?" she said, looking down and worrying her hands. They were trembling as she wrung them.

"Don't worry, Citali. I'm sure there are poisons in Lumina you've not yet considered."

Her eyes widened a fraction.

I took a step toward her. She shrank away. "Don't think I won't figure out who helped you with that jam." She was insufferable. "We are on the same side, Citali. We share a common goal."

"We share *nothing*, and we never will." With her poisonous words ringing in the air, she strode away, golden feathers fluttering in her wake.

I straightened my back and made my way downstairs.

There was no crowd waiting at the bottom of the landing. The great hall was open. The ball had begun.

There was only him, and her.

Caelum stood talking with Citali. She grabbed his elbow and gestured to the door with a wide smile, but he shook his head. "I'm going to wait for Noor," he gently explained, extracting his arm from her claws.

"Then your wait is over," I announced, starting down the final flight.

If Citali had only waited, she would have had the perfect opportunity to push me down them instead of embarrassing herself by showing how desperate and pathetic she truly was. She'd made it perfectly clear how she felt about me. Though I wasn't sure I loved her as one sister should love another, I didn't harbor hatred for her in my heart.

If anything, I pitied her.

But after those scathing words on what should've been a happy evening to celebrate peace, she made my heart feel more like warring with her.

She bared her teeth as I appeared. Pouting, she whirled around and left Caelum to enter the great hall, disappearing into the ball.

Caelum was dressed in deep blue from neck to toe. His tunic was fitted and didn't hide the planes of his muscles. His trousers were tucked into polished, matching boots. He waited patiently at the bottom of the steps, dark hair sleeked back, pale skin contrasting his clothing like foam sitting upon the fathomless seas I hoped still existed.

His eyes tracked my every step, taking in the gown his aunt made for me, then fastened on mine and held.

When I reached the bottom, he blinked rapidly as if emerging from a spell. "Lumos, help me," he whispered. His cool air calmed my burning skin. His cold hands ghosted down my back as mine found his chest and explored those ill-concealed planes. He leaned in and his lips found my temple, my cheek, my jaw – his favorite spot, and mine. His hands found my waist and clamped down on it like he was holding me to the ground, or perhaps using me to hold his own feet there. "I know we should go inside, but I can't help but want a moment with you without the noise," he said.

So we stayed there, remaining quiet and just holding one another. Until Vada came looking for us, smiling proudly when we parted and Caelum took my hand. "Your father is asking about you," she said to me.

We joined her and Vada led us through the large double doors. The crowd seemed to part, Helioan and Luminan alike whispering over the sight of me and Caelum entering hand-in-hand. The division led straight to Father. He stood with Citali with a mixture of guardsmen from both kingdoms, Zuul hovering close by. I hadn't seen him as often lately. I knew he never strayed far from my father's side, so he must have become more adept at concealing himself.

Father's dark coal eyes raked over my gown. A muscle ticked in his jaw and his fist clenched. The dress was suddenly too tight around my ribs for me to catch a breath.

"A word, Noor?" he asked with a smile, ticking his head toward a dark corner of the room.

Caelum's hand tightened on mine, but I tugged away and straightened my back, following Father beyond that shadow and into the hall. He stopped and turned to face me, staring at me wordlessly with his chilling gaze locked onto mine. "What are you wearing?"

I tipped my chin. "It was a gift."

"From whom?"

"Caelum's mother, Vada."

"You haven't forgotten your kingdom in chasing his crown, have you?"

I tightened my heating fists. "I could never forget Helios."

"Citali says otherwise," he said, stepping closer. He pointed his finger in my face. "Do not disgrace me."

Though my stomach churned in knots, I stood my ground. "I wore it to please him. Citali is only envious because I caught Caelum's attention and he pays her so little."

Father's eyes narrowed. Quick as a viper, his hand clamped around my wrist, squeezing until I thought my bones might crack. "Do not betray me, Noor. What did the Sphinx tell you this morning? I want every word."

"Don't ever put your hands on me again," I growled, something low and deep rumbling from my chest; a voice I didn't recognize but knew so intimately it shook me. The fire in my chest flowed through my veins like water in a riverbed. I focused it to his hand, his crushing, terrible hand.

He cried out when the heat hit him, jerking his hand away with wide eyes, looking at me like I was a monster.

His lips gaped when he saw something in my face. "Your... your eyes."

"If you lay your hand on me again, it won't be Sol incinerating your corpse. It will be *me*."

Father stumbled backward, his shoulder blades hitting the wall behind him. I left him in the hall and waded back into the celebration of peace.

Caelum stood in the darkness, waiting just inside the door. I wasn't sure if he'd heard Father's harsh words, accusing me of forgetting my kingdom while chasing the crown of moonlight. He rushed to me the moment I appeared at the doorway. "Are you okay?"

I gave a harsh word, still hot from losing my temper.

If Citali had shown up in the same gown, Father would have applauded her cleverness in stealing the heart of the Lumin. He would have said *well done*. He would have rewarded her with praise and the attention she so desperately craved.

But Citali meant nothing to Caelum. She not only tried to poison me but had succeeded in poisoning Father's already-spoiled opinion of me.

I shook my head, eager to dispel my gloomy thoughts. I hadn't had a chance to fully take in the room when we'd walked in with Vada. Fear had crept in and blinded me, as it always did. But as Caelum led me back into the room, my steps slowed.

Dark curtains severed the bland light from the terrace and draped elegantly over the few windows built into the wall. The chandeliers held silver candles whose flames weren't warm like the fire I knew, but were also silver, painting the room with cool, white light. Someone had cut intricate shapes from parchment and hung them from the ceiling and chandeliers.

"Snowflakes," Caelum explained. "You could catch and look at a million of them and never see the same shape twice."

I gaped. "Are they made of ice?"

"Of a sort," he said, looking wistfully at the glittering flakes. "It's soft, where ice is hard and sometimes sharp."

"I read that snow was like rain, but these flakes are so large! Do you get large snow in Lumina?"

He barked a laugh and my heart fluttered at the sound, followed by the sight of his genuine smile. The worries he normally carried were gone, at least for now. "No. This is just for decoration. Snowflakes are tiny, for the most part."

"Are you homesick?"

He took my other hand. "Not right now." The look he gave me was indecipherable. "Dance with me?"

"Okay."

We carved a path to the area where others swayed to an elegant rhythm. The Luminan musicians played instruments I'd never seen. Their strings sang such a haunting and beautiful melody, I couldn't look away from them.

Then, Caelum's hand brushed my back. His hand clasped mine and he began to sway as the beautiful music carried us away. He looked at my wrist, at the sun diamonds twinkling there. "You need moon diamonds to match," he noted.

"I have them. Just look at my dress."

He smiled. "I can't stop. You're so…" He seemed at a loss for words. "I've seen waterfalls and the great, vast sea, rolling hills and snow-capped mountains, and millions of stars in the inky sky. But you, Noor, are the most beautiful thing I've ever seen." He bent his head and leaned in. "May I?"

I craned my neck, pushing myself taller with my toes and pressed my lips almost to his. "You may."

His lips were soft and cool and he tasted faintly of mint. His scent, that unnamed fragrance, wrapped around me and made my eyes flutter closed as we kissed and swayed, allowing the world and all its machinations to fade into the background where it belonged.

For a moment, there was only me and Caelum. His hand pressed against my back so that our chests met, the other curling my hand against his chest.

Then he pulled away and I realized that the beautiful music had stopped and the entire room was watching the two of us. A woman nearby clutched her chest, her eyes swimming with warmth. Beron and Citali walked over.

"Brother," Beron said. "The Aten would like to steal you away for a moment for the announcement."

Caelum glanced at me; an apology written on his face. "Go to him. I'm fine," I promised.

"I'll hurry," he promised. He reluctantly let go of my hands and strode to where my father stood near his men. Fear crept into my throat. I didn't like Caelum being anywhere near those cruel, crushing hands, or around so many of Father's loyal guards...

*I will reduce this house to dust if Father hurts him.*

The thought rang true, ricocheting through my chest with surprising vigor. At some point along this twisted journey, I'd developed real feelings for Caelum. The logical part of me said they were far too strong to have only known him a handful of days, arguing that they couldn't be real. That I was merely being foolish. After all, he was the first man I had been given permission to pursue and who showed an interest in return.

Kiran and Saric moved to stand with Father as two of Lumos's priests rose and went to Caelum's side. Kiran glanced at me, swallowed thickly, and thankfully looked away. I missed his friendship, but no longer wondered what things might have been like if he hadn't been called to the priesthood. Caelum had erased such thoughts.

And hopefully my chastising words had stopped his actions.

My heart shone for Caelum now; like it was a sun diamond and I'd been lost, she pointed straight to him.

Kevi slid up to me. "Atena," she said in her sultry voice, "are things in place?"

I nodded once.

"Then we will proceed."

"Good," I answered, not looking toward her before she slunk away.

Citali and Beron watched Caelum and Father address our peoples and announce that today, they had signed a treaty for peace, trade, and a better future for both kingdoms. They declared that tomorrow would be a day for goodbyes – for now. The Aten and Lumin would put their agreed-upon plans into motion once arriving at their respective homes.

Citali and I clapped as Beron put his pinkies in his mouth and let out a shrill whistle. The entire room celebrated the announcement. Word traveled fast, and everyone probably already knew what Father and Caelum were announcing publicly, but that it was being presented as a unified message was significant. Historic.

Change was on the horizon for both Helios and Lumina, and these attendees were the ones gathered to bear witness to its conception. It was a beautiful thing.

If only it were real. If only Father meant the lovely, venomous words pouring from his mouth.

Carrying a bottle of expensive wine, Kevi made her way to Father's table as the two men bowed to one another and told everyone to eat, drink their fill, and dance until their feet were sore. Caelum knew the plan. He knew not to drink down what he pretended to sip when Father proposed a toast. Kevi filled both goblets, Father drinking from Luminan silver and Caelum from Helioan gold.

Caelum winked at me as he eased his glass down.

Some of Kevi's girls brought more bottles and began pouring it for all Father's guards.

Citali kept stealing glances at Beron when he was watching his brother. Caelum waved him and their mother over and hugged each of them, then both together, the two squashing Vada in the middle, who playfully swatted each of her sons as she laughed at their antics.

I didn't miss what Father and Caelum *failed to* announce – that Citali and I, along with priests Saric and Kiran, would be traveling to Lumina with Caelum. That our kingdoms might be united in a more intimate way, by family, and one day if the union was blessed with children, by blood.

I smoothed my sweaty palms along the diamonds on my stomach. It was probably best they hadn't shared that yet. If Lumos rejected one or both of the Aten's daughters, it would spare Father the embarrassment of telling people we were found unworthy by the moon god.

Besides, it would soon be made clear when we boarded the ship to Luminos, and to our brethren when we were missing from the Helioan ship.

Caelum strode to me and whisked me into another dance, holding me close. "Has it begun?"

I nodded.

Caelum, steadfast Caelum, held me tight and told me, "All is ready on our end. Yours and Citali's rooms are cleared and your trunks are already aboard our ship. We leave as soon as possible."

I glanced to Citali, dancing with Beron, then sought out our priests. "Did anyone tell Saric and Kiran we were leaving so soon?"

His brows kissed.

"Our priests. They're supposed to escort us."

"You should probably tell them, Noor. I can send someone to load their things." He cleared his throat. "My mother and two of Lumos's priests are going to sail to Helios with your father."

*Vada?* My body stopped swaying. "No, Caelum. That is not wise."

"The peace we've forged is tentative. Your father is sending his daughters *and* two priests into Lumina. He would not agree to allow you to come without some assurance, a show of good faith, if you will."

"You should leave us here, then. Get your mother and priests and sail south with all haste," I breathed, pressing a hand to my abdomen. "She won't be safe there."

"She will be, as long as you and Citali communicate that you're being treated well. He won't harm her."

"You have no idea what he's capable of. And the sun... Sol is harsh to those who are not hers."

I expected no warmth from Lumos for the daughters of the Aten. He would expect us to adjust to his cool light and biting frost.

He tipped my chin. "Believe me when I tell you that my mother is more than capable of handling herself. She has been trained by the guard."

My mouth fell open in shock.

He grinned. "She's one of the best swordswomen I've seen. People make assumptions based on her position and age, but she's nimble and more agile than Beron or I, and what she lacks in brute strength, she makes up for with cunning and speed. Mother will take her blades and won't hesitate to stick anyone who threatens her or Lumos's priests."

"If she defended herself against my father, it would be her last act in this life."

He shook his head resolutely. "Lumos guides her. Just last night, he told her to go. He promised her safe passage."

"How did she speak to him?"

"He sent a message to the Wolven. Lumos will see her through this journey." He took a deep breath and coaxed me to relax, swaying with me once again. "I know you don't know our ways or our god, but he is more than capable of ensuring her safely to – and from – Helios."

If Sol wasn't stuck, would she also be with me? Was she with me despite the distance between us? I thought back to the light that streamed through my diamonds in that thick maze of wood, then of the Sphinx who flew here just to speak to me, and how I knew it was Sol working through her to allow me time with my mother. I could still almost feel her heat when the memory surfaced. A sense of calm washed over me.

"It will be okay, Noor. I wouldn't have agreed otherwise. I wouldn't knowingly put my mother in danger."

"I know. I just…"

His thumb drifted over my jaw. "You fear for her."

I did. So much.

Despite the fact that I didn't know Lumos, and Sol seemed so incredibly distant even when she was close enough to blister and burn anyone without the Aten's blood in her veins, I knew my father, along with his cruelties and deceptions, far too well to feel at peace with this arrangement.

Citali slithered closer, dragging Beron with her. "You've stolen enough of the Lumin's attention, Noor. Stop being so greedy." She said it teasingly, pushing between us and moving to dance with Caelum.

Beron shrugged good-naturedly. "Waltz with the second-best option?"

I hoped he didn't truly feel that way, but then again, I was third born. Would I feel the same if I couldn't find the crown and returned home to find Zarina chosen as our new Aten? "Only if you're okay dancing with the third born, and therefore, third-best."

He bowed deeply with a flourish, then rose with a teasing glint in his eye. "I would be honored, third-born. But more importantly, as we are amazing dance partners, I was hoping you'd consider showing them up for a dance or two."

"I'd like nothing more." I smiled and placed my hand in his.

With an ornery expression, he clamped a hand on my waist, jerked me against his chest, and whirled me away. "Our proximity will drive my brother to the deepest pits of insanity," he confided.

Inwardly, I wasn't sure he would even notice. When I told Citali she was beautiful, I wasn't understating the fact. She shone this evening, like a beam of light arcing from Sol's unearthly face.

I wished I could've enjoyed the dance as much as Beron seemed to, but I could only think of Vada's fate, then of Kevi and her girls, who still hovered around Father's table, making sure the glasses were filled. Father was getting drunker by the minute. His face was flushed. His movements were exaggerated and sloppy. His eyelids drooped.

"My brother looks miserable," he chortled.

I searched for them and found the gold of Citali's feathered gown. It reminded me of a mortal's attempt to mimic the Sphinx's wings. After seeing them in the flesh, I knew no one could possibly capture their translucence, but her dress properly paid homage to Sol's lioness.

I didn't think Caelum looked miserable at all. He talked to her as they danced. He smiled and grinned and seemed to be enjoying himself. Perhaps Beron was trying to ease the sting of seeing them together. Happy.

"Are you poking fun at my sister?" I faked offense.

"Absolutely. Although, she *is* interesting. I'll give her that much."

"Interesting how?"

We swung around and around in broad circles, whirling around other couples and turning around the room to more of the heart-rending music. He finally answered. "She would make an incredible actress."

"Actress?"

"We have players who pretend to be characters. Citali is a master of acting and pretending to be something she isn't and never will be," he mused. "My brother favors you. She knows that. But she's convinced that with enough time, coaxing, and acting like she's a far superior choice than you, he might change his mind."

"She told you that?" I asked.

"She has and she hasn't. A lot of what Citali doesn't say with her lips, she says with her eyes. They burn, though differently than yours. Yours glow a rich, bright gold sometimes. Hers is a dark fire. A flame sealed in shadow."

I'd never heard anything truer, and despite the gold haloing my eyes at times, I couldn't help but wonder if she and I carried the same shadow flame. Maybe we inherited it from our father.

Beron had certainly spent ample time studying my sister. Interesting. And dangerous –

for him...

He glanced at something over my shoulder and then moved me to a different area of the floor. "Would you care for a drink?" he asked.

I agreed, realizing my throat was parched. "I'd love one, but first, I need to deliver a message."

Beron walked with me to Kiran, where I whispered a quick, urgent message into his ear. Confused as he was, he nodded once and replaced his curious expression with a bland one. I left him behind and Beron and I strolled to a table where bottles of wine had been uncorked and sat ready to be poured. Beron gestured to the spread. "I'll admit, I'm not sure what's best or what you might like."

"Then let me choose for both of us."

He playfully quirked a brow. "You think you know what I'd like?"

My cheeks flushed. He was such a flirt. The table was trimmed in shiny silver fabric that was cool to the touch when my fingers brushed it. I chose my favorite from among the others and poured two glasses, handing one to Beron.

We moved aside and found a place to stand along the wall, watching the dancing couples glide across the floor. "Are you hungry?" he asked.

"Not really." I was too nervous to think about eating. Nervous about the plan. Nervous to leave this dull place for a kingdom I knew so little about.

Watching how the silver candlelight flickered and cast cool light over the space, I wondered what it would be like in Lumina, to see the face of Lumos in his half of the earth. To see darkness and wonder if it felt the way I did inside sometimes.

Caelum and Citali still seemed to be enjoying themselves.

"Do you think you'll be happy in Lumina?" Beron asked quietly. He looked from snowflake to snowflake, then turned to me, waiting for my answer.

I wanted to say I could be happy anywhere under the right circumstances, but I wasn't sure that was true. "I'm not sure. I've never been happy," I hedged.

"You're still unsure of my brother," he observed.

"I didn't say that."

"Citali is the one who told him you were only pretending to want him because you wanted power and a crown to match his."

My fingers tightened on my glass. "Citali is a liar. But a very good one, unfortunately." I shook my head. "Does he believe her?"

"I'm not sure," he said, taking a sip. "This is delicious. You chose well."

"Do *you* believe my sister?"

He pursed his lips for a moment. "I'm not sure we can trust either of you just yet. I'm reserving judgment." He sipped from his glass. "But if you *are* just after his title, know that you don't deserve him. My brother is actually a very good man. As rare as those diamonds on your wrist."

"Lumos would not accept me if the only thing in my heart was greed and a hunger for power and status."

He shrugged. "He hasn't accepted you yet, though, has he?"

No, he hadn't. He wouldn't. But I couldn't let him know that.

"What do you think lays inside what you seek tonight?" he asked cryptically. His mood had shifted from jovial to questioning.

"I'm not sure, but as Lumos guides your mother, Sol guides me, and she pointed me directly to it."

He sucked in a breath. Took a drink. Remained quiet for a long moment. "Sometimes, it's difficult being chosen by the gods who war among themselves and drag us into their fights."

Beron spoke as if he wasn't only speaking about his brother. I supposed he wasn't. Lumos guided his mother. Perhaps he also guided him.

He glanced to me. "Your father is leaving the room."

I stood up straighter from where I'd slumped against the wall, watching as two of his men supported his weight, his arms stretched over their shoulders. Kevi shot me a knowing look and followed behind them.

My heart thundered.

"What will he do when he finds that what you seek is missing?"

"I may not need to take it. I just need to see it."

Beron's dark brows slanted just the way Caelum's did when he was confused and concerned.

"I want to ensure your mother's safety, as well as that of your priests. I just need time to look through it."

"A book, then?"

"Caelum didn't tell you?"

"He said the less I knew, the better regarding this."

"He shielded you," I told him.

Beron straightened. "He shields me when that's the last thing I want or need. Thank you for considering our mother and Lumos's priests. Caelum was concerned that the draught they gave him wouldn't last long."

"I'll figure something out," I promised. I would also figure out a way to shield Kevi and her dancers as they fled.

"Will you keep watch for me?" I asked. "Caelum has to stay here. Besides, he's busy."

He was still laughing with my sister, swaying slowly with her. He even tucked her hand against his chest like he had mine.

"He doesn't harbor the same feelings for her," Beron said, sincerity in his tone.

"Neither does he feel nothing for her," I replied wistfully.

When he gave me an apologetic look, I knew I was right in my assumption. Citali might be his second choice, but it wouldn't break his heart if Lumos chose her over me.

Was he doing as I suggested and keeping us both at arm's length until he knew which, if either, of us Lumos would choose? It made sense. It meant he was shielding his heart against breaking over one of us.

I sat my glass down on a nearby table and glided from the room. Beron fell in behind me. Caelum didn't notice.

"We have to be careful of the men who brought him inside," Beron warned as we strode through the shadows.

"This gown is like a glittering blue beacon," I worried.

He shook his head, voice crumbled to gravel. "That gown was meant to be worn by you."

I glanced at him, but he never returned the look. Did such a sentiment come from Lumos or was it a personal opinion?

Two male voices came from Father's room just as we drew near. "The guards!" I whispered, frozen.

"Dance with me." Beron asked, tugging one of my wrists and spinning me close to the wall. My shoulder blades hit the cool stone. He pressed his cool body flush with mine and bent his head. He leaned closer, his warm breath striking my lips.

My heart thundered as the guards drew near, their sandals slapping the stone. The two noticed us. "Is that the Atena?" one asked the other.

Beron's lips dove toward mine. Our noses touched. His sweet, wine-soaked breath fanned my cheek as his lips moved. One of his hands braced against the wall, the other slid up my waist. His kiss wasn't soft. It was like he'd decided that if this was happening, he was making it convincing. It certainly *felt* convincing. His tongue swept out to part my lips and I gasped, my eyes widening as they met his.

He kissed me, watching my reaction, until their footsteps trailed away. When they did, I pushed at his chest and he took a step back. "What was that?" I hissed, so low I wondered if he would hear it.

"That was me providing them a reason why the Atena was lingering outside her father's door."

"They'll think we're lovers!"

He grinned. "You're welcome."

I shook my head, upset, though not just at the kiss. The kiss was unexpected, but I'd never been kissed before Caelum, and he had never kissed me like that. "Is this some sort of game you and your brother concocted? Play Citali and me against one another to see who's loyal and who isn't?"

"It was exactly what I said it was," he said patiently. "I was protecting you and protecting my family. I want to know what you learn in there." He pointed to Father's room.

Kevi cracked the door and peeked out, waving me inside.

"You're supposed to keep watch. Out. Here," I told him, leaving no room for argument.

I slipped in with Kevi and she handed me a small book bound in black leather.

"You must hurry!" She hovered near Father, gesturing urgently.

Cracking the book open, I fanned the pages and my heart sank. "It's empty! There's nothing written in this."

Kevi hurried over and glanced over the parchment. Beron knocked at the door, then slipped in. "What is taking so long?"

"It's empty," I told him, holding it up to show him the blank pages. "Why would Sol want me to have an empty book?"

He shook his head. "In Lumina, we have ink that only reveals itself by Lumos's light. Could Sol have done the same?"

"I wanted to read it and leave it with him to keep your mother safe," I gasped.

He shook his head. "Mother knows the risks. Beyond that, she can keep herself safe, as will Lumos. Take the book."

Father's breathing changed.

Kevi looked stricken.

With wide eyes, I asked, "Do you have any more of the draught? His body is burning it away."

She tugged a vial out of her skirts and dropped to her knees beside him, tipping the last of the sleeping draught into his mouth. It would buy some time, but how much?

Beron peeked outside. "It's still clear."

Kevi ran to Father's trunks and found a small book. It wasn't the same size as the one she'd pulled from his pocket, but it was close enough that it might fool him for a time if we switched them.

I took up Father's quill and scrawled inside the tome.

*Father,*

*You wanted to know what the Sphinx showed me? She gave me a vision of the book you keep in your kilt pocket, always so close. She told me to take it from you. That it belonged to me.*
*She also showed me where to find the crown...*
*If you harm Vada or either of Lumos's priests, you'll never see the book again and I'll keep the crown for myself.*
*-Noor*

"We have to go," I told them.

I tucked the small book into my pocket, stretching it to its limit.

Outside Father's room, I hooked my arm through Kevi's. Beron escorted us down the hall and somehow, we didn't encounter a soul. He slipped into the ball room and whispered into Caelum's ear.

Few Luminans remained. Vada stood near the front, flanked by two priests. She caught my eye and waved to me, inclining her head with a ferocious glint in her eye. She was strong. I whispered a request to Sol to keep her safe in our kingdom and safe from Father, hoping that just this once, she'd join Lumos in this effort.

In the short expanse of time that we'd been gone, the Luminan musicians were replaced by Helioans, who now played one of our livelier songs. Father's guards were asleep at the table where he'd left them, most believing them passed out from imbibing too much wine.

Caelum took Citali's hand and followed Beron. Kevi waved her girls toward the doors and they slithered from the room using different doors, all meeting us outside. Saric and Kiran stood outside the doors. They walked with me away from the House of Dusk and into the dull gray. A dreadful weight was in my pocket, but it wasn't as heavy as the feeling inside my chest.

Within minutes, everyone who should have been was aboard the Luminian ship. I stood in the stern's back corner to keep everything and everyone in sight as the ship was unmoored. The sails snapped as the wind filled them and dragged us southward.

Vada walked outside, waving to her sons.

# 18

It was no slight breeze that pushed the shallow, long Luminan ship through the placid water, but the breath of Sol. It was warm and urgent, and it filled me with dread.

Beron sat down with me as Caelum spoke with the river-farer near his quarters. Citali had situated herself at the bow, as far away from me as possible. She talked for a moment with Saric and Kiran, her hip jutting out and her arms crossed, likely bossing them around. She probably thought they were here to serve us now instead of Sol. Disgust washed through me.

"Tell me your worries, Atena, and I'll tell you mine," Beron said softly.

I snorted. "You first. I insist."

"Fine," he relented. "I worry that your book will only be that, and Lumos's face will reveal nothing."

I didn't fear that at all. Father wouldn't guard something unless he knew it was important, or damning.

He gestured to me. My turn.

"I worry that only *Sol's* light will reveal it and that we're sailing the wrong direction," I admitted. When Caelum left the riverfarer to speak with my sister, I couldn't stomach watching them any longer. Beron said she believed that she could steal Caelum's favor. It seemed that Citali's plan had worked.

I glanced at the land we traveled through. There were no people settled here. No gardens would grow. They couldn't sustain themselves. There weren't even crocodiles in the land of perpetual dusk.

Beron leaned on the rail with me. I ticked my chin at him. "Your turn."

He grinned and leaned far over to drag a hand through the water. He startled when I pretended to push him in, all the while pressing the small of his back so he wouldn't tumble in. "That was evil..." he said appreciatively. He turned his back to the water, arms folded over his lean stomach beside my head. "I worry you'll tell him what I did in the hall."

"It meant nothing to you, and I don't think it would mean anything to Caelum."

His cool eyes held mine for a moment, then he turned away. "Well, I wholeheartedly disagree and claim superior judgment because I've known him my entire life, so if you wouldn't mind keeping that moment secret so my brother doesn't kill me, I'd appreciate it."

"He wouldn't kill you regardless. Your brother loves you."

I turned and crossed my arms, watching Caelum and Citali.

"Citali told me about your mothers..." he said.

"A lie she foolishly believes in, I'm afraid. I think it makes it easier for her to hate me, and to keep me at arm's length."

"Why would she want to?"

"To protect herself from our father." The river swiftly dragged us along. The sky faded from the pale gray that drenched everything it touched, to a darker shade as the river flowed faster and Sol's breath intensified. "How long until we reach Lumina?"

"We're approaching the division. Rather quickly, too." He studied the sails as if they were a puzzle he couldn't figure out. "It won't take four days to sail to Lumina at this unusual speed."

"It's Sol. Do you feel her warmth?"

He huffed a laugh. "I think I do."

Caelum made his way around the deck, making sure all was well with everyone.

The Luminan guards lingered here and there, several standing close to me and Beron. They weren't close enough to overhear our conversation, but close enough to keep their eye on me.

"Do they think I'm dangerous?" I teased Beron, nodding toward them.

"They're protective of us."

"As they should be."

He tugged on his collar. "They've also been ordered to protect you."

I frowned. "From what threat?"

"Any and all."

"Including Citali?"

His gaze snapped to mine. "Did she truly try to poison you?"

"She served me jam made from nightthorn berries. From what Caelum told me, they only grow in Lumina, which means someone from Lumina must have brought some along. Is it commonplace to bring poisons to a peace negotiation?"

He shook his head and blew out a tense breath. "I'll find out who supplied her, or if she somehow stole it."

I waved him off. "She wouldn't have known what she was stealing. This was deliberate."

He looked uneasy. Did he think no one among his people was capable of treachery? If anything, the circumstances of my life had taught me that those who should love you the most tended to be capable of the most horrific things imaginable.

"And if you find the person who aided her, then what?"

He cocked his head. "Do you really want to know?"

No, I didn't. It couldn't be any worse than what Father did to traitors, but that knowledge could elicit nightmares. It was best to be kept in the dark about some things.

Caelum strode down the deck and nodded to the soldiers closest to us. "Noor," he greeted, leaning in to place a chaste kiss on my jaw. "Brother," he said, raising to his full height. "The riverfarer has never seen anything like this strong, warm wind. He thinks that if it holds, it will have us home before the end of the day."

*It will hold,* my eyes told Beron.

He turned away and smiled at his brother, clapping him on the shoulder. "I'm sure we'll make record time."

The sky was darkening by the minute now. We were drifting out of the dusk lands. Farther from Sol.

Father must have awakened by now. He knew we were gone, and realized he'd been drugged so we could escape. He would find the substitute book left in place of his and read my note.

I meant *every* word.

Not that I'd hand any moonlight crown over to him anyway.

Caelum looked tired. Dark circles had formed under his eyes. "You and Beron are getting along well."

I smiled. "As are you and my sister."

"She was torn about leaving," he explained.

I laughed at how she'd twisted his opinion of her. Beron was right. She was acting a part and had convinced Caelum she wasn't the conniving, venomous scorpion she truly was. Wait until he felt her sting... "I can assure you that she wasn't."

He stiffened beside me. "You know, Noor, she's as adamant about you lying as you are about her."

"Then perhaps you should throw us both overboard."

I looked at the sky. Darker. A hue so dark it was surprising how vibrantly blue it was. And overhead... a flicker of tiny, distant light.

My lips parted as I pointed to the sky. "Is that...?"

He looked to where I pointed. "Our ancestors. Soon, as we drift into darker skies, you'll see millions more. The brightest few are those who were closest to Lumos during their lives."

"The former Lumins?" I breathed, searching the endless blue for more freckles of light.

Caelum nodded encouragingly. "More will appear. The closer we get to home, the more the sky will fill with them."

Another. Just there. I rushed across the ship to the other corner of the stern and caught myself on the rail. This one was far brighter than the first that appeared. It sparkled. Caelum, wearing a warm smile, moved to my side.

I didn't look at him, fixing my eyes on the former Lumins who watched over us, shining a light, however small, in the darkness. It was like they were reminding their heirs they weren't alone.

Sol shone down upon us in Helios, but it was only her. If our ancestors were there, we couldn't see them. Her light was all we needed.

I wondered if the former Lumins cast into the midnight skies were curious about the Helioans aboard their ship; if they couldn't believe the Atenas were crossing into their kingdom after so long. Sol had chosen her vessels for seven generations, including ours. Of course, one of us would only get the chance to succeed him if he failed to ensure his reign.

As if Caelum had summoned them, more and more of his ancestors looked down upon us. Lumos had plucked each spirit and given it a distinct place in the sky.

Caelum's hand drifted down my glittering sleeve. "Wearing this, you look like you belong among them," he said softly.

Vada knew what she was doing in having such a garment made, but I was no Luminan spirit. I was nothing icy and everything scorching flame, no matter what I wore. "I'd like to thank your aunt for making it for me."

"She's sleeping, but when she wakes, I'll tell her you'd like to speak with her," he promised.

Someone at the front of his ship called out his title and he apologetically cringed, then left me again.

"Noor," a familiar voice found me.

I turned to see Kiran helping Saric across the deck. I ran to them, surprised when the old man let go of Kiran's arm and shooed him toward me. Kiran didn't hesitate, taking advantage of our distance from Father and capturing me in a hug. He was taller and stronger than I realized. "I'm so glad you're okay... and that we can finally speak."

Saric waited behind him and pulled me in for a much gentler hug. "Daughter of Sol," he cooed, patting my hand after he'd released me.

My heart swelled with love for the old priest. "I have your book in my trunks. I'll return it when we reach Lumina. I read all of it."

A meaningful look passed between us before he shook his head. "It belongs with you."

"Aren't you supposed to protect it?" I asked, helping him to a nearby bench. The Luminan guard who'd been standing and watching us from there, one leg propped on the seat, kindly moved to let Saric have plenty of room.

The trip had exhausted and aged him.

I glanced at Kiran, worried.

The smile he returned did not reach his burnt orange eyes.

Saric tried to catch his breath. "A glass of water?" he croaked to Kiran. Reluctantly, Kiran went in search of what the old priest had asked for. "Sit with me, Noor," he said, his voice suddenly clear.

I sat beside him, waiting for him to go on.

"The Sphinx guided you to this moment?"

I nodded.

"I, too, have seen your journey's beginning. I dreamt of it last night." He patted my hand. "It will not be an easy one."

"You've seen only the beginning, Saric? What of the middle and ending?"

He smiled, still calming his breathing. "Those depend on the choices you make right now, Atena."

"I'm not sure what to do. Sol seems to be leading me one place, yet..." I lowered my voice, "you know why Father sent us."

He nodded gravely, leaning in close and squeezing my hand in his weathered one, a shade darker than my olive and mottled with age spots. "I don't know what the book in your pocket holds, but you must trust Sol. Trust *this*." He jabbed a thumb toward his heart. "Do not trust your father, Noor. Or your sister. She is scheming, and I fear what she might have planned."

"She tried to poison me, with the help of someone from Lumina."

He searched for her at the bow but Citali had moved someplace else. "With what?"

"Nightthorn berries."

"Watch the youngest brother," he warned.

*Beron?* Could he have supplied to berries to Citali as a way to test both her and me?

"He is very protective of the Lumin, protective enough to test the women who fight for his hand." He patted my hand. "We know that this is much bigger than a simple union, but he does not. He wants the best for his brother."

Is that why he kissed me? More than a diversion, but rather a test to see if I would respond and go beyond what was necessary to sate the guards' curiosity. Is that why he asked me not to tell Caelum, or was it because he was truly afraid his elder brother would be angry?

"You have feelings for the eldest," he observed. I neither confirmed nor denied; I remained quiet and listened. "You want to know if what you feel is reciprocal."

He waited for me to speak, to do something. All I could manage was a single, sharp nod.

He gave a grandfatherly smile. "What does your heart tell you?"

I snorted, "My *eyes* tell me that he likes Citali just as much."

He nodded. "It's good to use your other senses, too, but not to the point where you become deaf to that which should guide you." He tapped his chest again.

"Does it matter how we feel? With different gods in charge, we may be getting led in different directions."

He patted my hand again. Pat, pat, pat. "Listen here. Read the book that is in your pocket when Lumos can help you. Then you will have the knowledge you need to make the decision cleaving your thoughts."

"The ink is truly there?" I whispered.

He nodded. "When you were young, there was still trade among our peoples, however limited it might be. Your mother was kind and giving. People always gave her extravagant gifts and knew where to find anything at market – even the forbidden. Including inks designed to only appear in certain light." *I had no idea.* "Despite what your father has led you to believe, there is still trade among our kingdoms for those who dare travel back and forth."

The riverfarer and his map came to mind. The river was mapped far beyond the division. The truth lurked under the fold. I'd stake my sun diamonds on that if I could.

Kiran reappeared and Saric slumped a little more for his benefit. He gave me a sly wink before Kiran reached us, then took the water with shaky hands as the younger priest knelt before him. His skin was pebbled and in only a kilt, he was cold. I held my hand out and he looked quizzically at it.

"To warm you," I explained.

My friend slipped his palm into mine and immediately let out a breath, relaxing. "That's remarkable."

"We need to find a tunic or blanket for Saric," I added. "I can go look."

He took my seat when I strode away. In truth, they both needed warmer clothing. I hadn't noticed the shift in cooler air, as enamored as I was with the stars.

I made my way around the deck, two men following at a close distance. Caelum's men. Or were they Beron's?

I understood Beron's motives. He loved his brother. But I didn't appreciate his little trials and wondered if he might need a taste of his own poison. I couldn't believe the theory that he was the one who gave Citali nightthorn berries, especially after promising to find who did it and insinuating the perpetrator would be put to death.

The ship's large cabin overflowed with trunks, supplies, and Luminan guards. The riverfarer stood among them, pointing at a map. I'd seen him in passing but hadn't spoken to him directly, even though Caelum seemed to like using his ship for private moments.

His grizzled voice boomed, "This is where we are. I've never seen a wind this fast and sure!"

I cleared my throat and the eyes of all who were assembled snapped to me. "Pardon me for interrupting, but I was hoping someone could help me. Sol's priests are in need of garments or blankets to keep them warm. They did not know they would be traveling to Lumina until we were in the dusk lands and didn't bring warmer attire for the trip."

The riverfarer chuffed a laugh, bracing large, weathered hands on the table. "Atena, *this* isn't cold. Just you wait."

I smiled. "Neither is it the least bit warm by Sol's standards."

He stood up straight and grinned. "Well?" he said to the guards loitering about. "Don't just stand there; someone go fetch tunics, breeches, and two blankets! Give the Atena and I a moment to speak."

I shouted after them that they could find Sol's priests near the stern.

"This is such a large ship, compared to the one we sailed," I told him, folding my hands behind my back and peering around his room now that he'd reclaimed it. "It looks a lot like the cabin of the riverfarer who brought us south."

"Maps," he mused. "They're a riverfarer's obsession. You can never have too many, and should always use coin to buy new ones. The river changes, you know. She can be steady in places and fickle in others. Typical woman," he teased, his green eyes glittering with mischief as he waited for my reaction.

I shrugged. "Fickle or not, you chase her all the same."

He wagged a finger toward me. "Clever."

"There is a divide at the edge of each kingdom, a boundary the other does not typically pass. The dusk lands that lay between... are they considered neutral ground?"

His smile sharpened. "That's right."

*That* was how trade occurred. A Luminan ship could bring wares into the dusk land waters, meet up with a Helioan ship, and transfer goods. Neither would break the accords... and no one would be the wiser.

"The dusk lands are dreadfully dull. I much prefer brightness or darkness to sullen gray," I told him, returning our conversation to a safer ground for him.

He inclined his head. "I couldn't agree more." He crossed his arms and glanced at me shrewdly. "The wind that propels us is warmer, despite the cool Luminan air. Is this great gust Sol's doing?"

I nodded and confirmed, "Her breath fills your sails."

"She must love you and your sister very much to help you along in such a bold way. I've sailed the river my whole life – I was born and raised on a ship! – and I've never reached Lumina from the dusk lands in a single day."

I shrugged again.

Whether it was love for us that drove Sol or the purpose that lay hidden in Father's secret book, I wasn't sure. I was grateful for the speed and secretly hoped she hadn't granted Father the same kindness.

"I enjoyed the dusk land storms, though," I admitted.

He wistfully stared out the door. "The storms are what riverfarers live for."

"I can see why. They're the embodiment of the sky's feelings, and she seems so angry and sad here."

The riverfarer crossed his arms. "I've never thought of it that way, but I can see that, Atena. Thank you."

"How much farther must we sail before seeing Lumos?"

He tilted his head and waved me closer to his desk where an orb sat. Taking it in his hand, he held it out to me. It was made of wood, smoothed by hands and time. Etched into the top of the orb was the name *Helios*. It spanned the entire top half of the sphere. But there were seas I'd never heard of, rivers that must have run dry over time, because they were nothing but pebble beds now. "When was this made?" I asked.

"About twenty years or so ago, give or take," he answered.

There was a small city engraved near a tiny section of dunes. I smiled. "Whomever made it didn't carve these proportionally. The desert sand is as big as the great oceans of Lumina," I told him.

"It wasn't always so," he said, taking a smaller glass ball from the drawer of his desk. He extended his hand for the wooden globe. I gave it to him, and he held it out between two fingers. The smaller ball, he held over my kingdom, specifically our city, the only one left... "Sol stopped moving eighteen years ago. Her constant fire quickly burnt and shriveled the land. The sands weren't always so vast."

He didn't say it, but Sol's damage was swift and decisive, punishing to Helios. But why?

He moved the smaller orb toward Lumina on the bottom of the wooden sphere, making the smaller sphere orbit the lower half of the larger wooden one.

"Lumos doesn't leave his kingdom; it's just so vast that when he circles us, we lose sight of him, but only for a time."

I knew that Helios was fixed and that Lumos still moved, but it was different seeing how desperate Sol's situation was. How desperate we, her people, were. Our kingdom was truly dying, being burned away by the goddess who built it.

In my heart, I knew she didn't intend to harm us. "Why did Sol stop orbiting like Lumos?"

He sat the greater and lesser spheres back on his desk. "That's the great mystery, isn't it? No one knows."

Footsteps came at the door. The last person I wanted to see appeared.

Beron looked between us. "Atena, we've provided for Sol's priests as requested. They seem much more comfortable."

I smiled sweetly, but it seemed to make him fidget. "Thank you."

I turned back to the riverfarer. "Thank you for sharing this with me," I told him.

He shook his head. "Thanks be to Sol. For if that *is* her breath, she's making my task a lot easier."

Outside, the sky was deep blue, nearly black now, and far more stars winked from on high. Beron waited as I exited the cabin, then walked with me toward the bow. Citali had moved from her spot, though she couldn't have gone far. "You're quiet," Beron noted.

The tipped bow of the ship was empty, so I settled into it. Beron settled behind me, to my right, lounging at a respectable distance. I placed my hands on the boards that met at a V in front of me and tried to calm my temper.

"Did Caelum ask you to poison me?" I asked, waiting for his reply.

To his credit, he didn't bother denying his role in it. "How did you figure it out?"

"Did he?" I pressed.

"No."

"Why did you do it?"

"I didn't poison you, Noor," he said, standing up straighter. The stars were innumerable. Millions of his ancestors heard us speaking. I wondered if they were proud or disappointed of his role in the near poisoning of an Atena.

"Did you tell Citali the berries were poisonous?"

He had the decency to look ashamed, at least. "I didn't think she'd give it to you," he admitted. "It was a test for her."

I rolled my eyes. "Which she failed, because *you* failed to see how deep her hatred for me ran."

He folded his hands in front of him. "You're right."

I raised my chin. "And the kiss? Cover, or another test?"

"Can't it be both?" he asked, finally relaxing against the rail. "I fear for my brother. Through the years, we've heard rumors of how cruel the Aten can be to his own people. I feared that cruelty might have been passed down or taught to you both."

"And what have you learned?"

"That both of you are hiding something; I just haven't figured out what. And I fear Citali is loyal only to herself. Is that the case with you, too, Noor?"

I narrowed my eyes.

"Have you kissed my sister?" I asked, turning to prop my hip on the rail to face him directly.

"We came close once..." he admitted. "But no." This younger version of Caelum was devious. Cunning. Infuriating.

"These little tests of yours... Aren't they proof that *you're* loyal to nothing but *your*self, too?"

Beron stood straighter, tugging on his tunic.

"Do you know what I think?" I asked.

He waited.

"I think you watch Citali and she watches you awfully closely for you to only be tempting her fidelity to Caelum. I think you're intrigued by my sister, Beron. But you should be careful. Lumos could still choose her for your brother."

Beron roughly wiped his hands over his lips. The truth was a great silencer.

"Don't kiss her again. No more of these trials for her. Test *me* if you must, but you will ruin both our names if you keep pushing. The only limits Citali knows are the ones she imposes on herself, and those are rarely applied. And no taking advantage if she propositions you. She may do just that if she thinks she's losing Caelum."

"Second-best?" he rasped.

"I don't think that's how she sees you at all, Beron, but rather how you see yourself."

Beron inclined his head fractionally. "Very well, Atena."

"You should know, Beron, that if I would've died from that poison, I would've dragged your spirit into the burning sky with me and you'd never smile down upon your descendants as they do," I told him quietly, returning my gaze to the stars.

"I understand why you're angry, Noor," he said quietly, sliding closer. "But tell me, if you loved your sister and she was in Caelum's position, would you not have done the same?"

I leveled him with a scorching glare. "I wouldn't have been caught."

# 19

I passed Kevi and her girls huddled together along the side of the ship, framed by crates. The wood boxes provided the separation I knew Kevi appreciated. All of them were fast asleep except for their leader. She tipped her chin as I passed. I let my fingers drift in hello. Kevi's sharp eyes missed nothing, but something about her had shifted. She was more relaxed than I'd seen her since we met.

She'd kept her bargain and I'd kept mine. Twice. I wouldn't forget it. She'd earned my trust and I had earned hers.

Citali had taken my seat. She was speaking with Saric and Kiran when I returned to the stern, but severed her words when she caught sight of me.

"We'll be in Lumina in just over an hour at this pace," I told them.

She watched me, that shadowy fire ablaze just under her skin. She sucked in a breath and then stood abruptly. "What is *wrong* with you?"

My brow furrowed. "What do you mean?"

"Your eyes," Kiran interceded.

"Do mine glow like that?" she asked the priests, clearly not trusting me to give her the truth.

"No, Atena Citali," Saric said softly.

"Why are *hers* glowing?" she demanded, waving an angry hand toward me.

"You have different parentage," Kiran offered, slowly standing.

Citali clicked her tongue. "Mothers, yes. But that little trick *must* have come from the Aten."

"Then perhaps yours glow as well, but aren't right now," I offered, trying to diffuse her rising anger.

The ship rocked and she caught my arm to steady herself, jerking her hand away with a hiss. "You're scorching hot!"

"No hotter than you, Citali."

"Noor – you are a living flame. I am nowhere near that hot. I can't even withstand it."

Something *was* happening to me. Something I didn't understand and couldn't explain. I looked to Saric, who sagely and gently answered, "The Atena is coming of age."

"Didn't this happen to you?" I asked Citali. She was older and had already come of age. Surely the same transformation had been forged in her.

A bitter laugh escaped her as she shook her head. "No. It didn't." She ground her teeth, then balled her fists and stormed away.

Saric and Kiran watched her stride away, the eldest offering a kind piece of advice: "Don't let her ire dim the fire that lives within you."

"I won't," I vowed. A promise I would keep.

*My self-worth isn't dependent upon anyone else's opinion. Least of all hers.*

Kiran adjusted his borrowed, much warmer clothes. Trousers peeked from beneath the priests' kilts and thick tunics covered their torsos. A wool blanket lay over Saric's legs. His breathing was labored, and I wondered how he'd been so calm and collected earlier. A rattling sound came from his chest.

I knelt in front of him, holding my hands out for his. His thin, dry fingers slid into my palms. "My hands were once supple." He smiled sweetly. "Though perhaps not as soft as yours."

"Are you ill?"

He shook his head. "If our lives are like that of a candle, Noor, my wick and wax still burn, but only barely. Soon, there won't be anything left for the flame of my life to cling to. But do not worry. I eagerly welcome the hereafter. I wish to see the goddess and fuel *her* flame."

Saric was dying and he knew it. He was far away from his home, his brothers, and his temple. Everything he loved lay in Helios, miles and miles behind us now. "I'm sorry to have dragged you here."

He laughed, then coughed. "Dragged me? I volunteered to see you through the beginning. Remember what I said about that?"

I nodded, tears clogging my throat.

He leaned in and whispered, "Choose wisely. And when I'm gone, I'll watch you from the hereafter."

"I hope I don't let you down."

He shook his head. "You couldn't if you tried." He tapped on his chest, over his heart.

I nodded, understanding what he meant by the gesture.

"I will see you through your beginning, Noor, and I would be honored if you would see me through my end."

I clung to his hands, a silent promise to do exactly that.

Footsteps came from behind us and I swiveled my head to find Caelum approaching. He stopped. "Am I interrupting?"

"Not at all, Lumin," Saric insisted. "Just an old priest talking to his Atena."

"Favorite Atena," I teased.

Saric winked. Another cough rattled from his chest and Caelum's easy smile fell away. "When we reach Lumina, I'll have someone bring some hot tea with healing herbs," he promised.

"I would appreciate that very much," Saric replied, inclining his head. Kiran sat at his side, in the seat Citali had occupied before I arrived.

I turned to Caelum, who rocked back on his heels. "I'd love to introduce you to someone very important to me," he said.

I stood, then bent to place a kiss on top of Saric's head. He patted my hand and told me to go with the Lumin, shooing me away. Kiran's amber eyes followed us as Caelum led me to the ship's bow. "Who am I to meet?"

"Lumos."

Ahead of us, the river water wended. As Lumos's cool white light peeked over the horizon, his brightness pulsating with gray-blue splotches of power, the god of night whitewashed his kingdom with the hand of a brilliant painter. Silver highlighted the trees on either side of us, glistening off their dappled leaves. But it was the water that served as Lumos's mirror. The river turned to glass, mirroring his light as it weaved over the land.

Slowly, he rose.

Caelum did not raise his hands or rush him, but patiently enjoyed the god emerging from the other half of his journey. Then he turned to me, seeming to forget Lumos as he gazed upon me. "Your dress..."

I looked down to see that every moon diamond sparkled, casting pale moonlight onto the ship's planks all around me.

Caelum raked a hand through his dark hair. His eyes caught Lumos's light and I realized his eyes weren't pale blue crystals at all, but held every one of his god's colors and glinting light within them. If my eyes shone with golden light, his were their pale match.

Suddenly, my heart squeezed. I looked away from him to Lumos again, stretching himself higher. Soon, he would fully emerge from the water and claim his rightful place in the sky.

The river looked like it poured directly from his mouth. Sol pushed us faster, as if she knew we could see him and wanted to see him, too.

Lumos and Sol were once lovers. They'd harshly severed that reverence many years ago and completely removed themselves from one another's lives, but could enough time have passed to settle their hearts so they could at least be civil now? Did Sol's heart still ache for him?

I pressed a hand to my chest. A brilliant flash flew from my sun diamonds and pointed directly to Lumos.

*Sol, guide me,* I begged.

"I would like to see Sol someday," Caelum admitted.

I smiled at him. "Then I shall introduce you."

A warm light appeared in the distance near the shore. Then another. And another. I realized the lights came from the flickering flames of candles placed in windows. "Lumina?" I guessed.

Caelum nodded. "This is the home of my people."

I smelled something distinct on the air and recognized it as the scent I associated with Caelum but couldn't quite place. "What is that scent?"

He laughed. "The brine? It's the sea."

I ticked my head back in surprise. "Lumina is situated on the sea?"

"One of them, yes."

"I want to see it."

He winked. "Then I shall introduce you."

I didn't tell him that he smelled of salt. I watched for the flames, and more and more appeared just as the stars above had, drawn to the heat and fire and the desire to see the House of the Moon. The temple of Lumos. So many things I'd read about, but never thought I'd see.

The Luminan homes thickened like the trees in a dense forest; they grew taller the closer we sailed to the land's heart. Tiny flames flickered as far as I could see. How vast *was* this city? How great was the sea it abutted?

While our kingdom was being scorched, drying and becoming brittle, we huddled together in a city that shrank instead of expanded. Under Lumos and the cooler air and light, the Luminans thrived.

*They should just wait us out,* I thought bitterly. Once we were all dead and Sol had no one left, she might burn away, too, and Lumos could claim the entire sky.

"Noor, I had an ulterior motive in inquiring about a potential union between us, and I..." he began.

"You mean between you and either me or my sister," I interrupted.

He shook his head. "I inquired about *you*. Your father was the one who insisted on presenting you both."

Surprise nestled in my chest. "Why me?"

"That's a longer story, and one for another time," he evaded.

I narrowed my eyes shrewdly. "What is your motive?"

"My kingdom needs help. *I* need your help."

I gestured to the flickering lights, to the angular homes stretching as far as I could see. "How could I possibly help you? Lumina is—"

"Bound for the same fate as Helios if nothing changes. Lumina's decline may be slower, but it's dying, Noor. The earth demands a balance. She needs both Sol *and* Lumos. She needs to rest and cool, but her plants need light and warmth. She needs rain and storms and seasons. I believe our existence, and the future of Helios, depends on whether you and I can convince our gods to form a truce."

"What makes you think they would hear us out? What makes you think they would deem us worthy enough to save?"

I looked over his kingdom as the wind from Sol eased and the sail went flat. The riverfarer used the wheel to guide the ship to the left where in the darkness, an enormous structure emerged. "We're home," Caelum said, sounding tired. "We should eat and sleep and talk more about this once we're rested and thinking more clearly."

But I wasn't finished with this gut-punching, eye-opening conversation. "Am I to assume that all the interactions we've had thus far were you pretending to be enamored just to get me here?" I asked.

His brow furrowed. "I've only ever been honest with you, Noor," he echoed my words.

"And would you say the same to Citali?"

"Your father wouldn't agree to let you travel here without her being with you. I tried to be fair to her while in the dusk lands, but in doing so, I'm afraid I've given her false hope. I'll set things right and make it clear to her that I don't harbor romantic feelings for her first thing tomorrow."

Citali wouldn't be deterred regardless of what he told her. She would stay and seek the crown. And if Caelum removed himself as her potential future husband, she would latch herself to Beron like a leech to bare skin.

"I'm sorry if I handled this poorly. It was the only way..." He looked truly stricken. "I'll explain everything, I swear. Tomorrow."

"Tomorrow," I agreed.

The ship slowly edged toward the dock, and when it was close, a few guard members bounded off the ship's deck and began tying the mooring lines to keep her from drifting. Caelum offered me his arm. "Allow me to welcome you, Noor, to the House of the Moon. I sincerely hope that you will make yourself at home here."

*Temporarily, I could.*

The phoenix in my stomach stirred and I envisioned her escaping my throat and mouth and flying through this darkened sky to see Lumos and the stars more closely, reveling in the feeling of Luminans watching her aerial dance.

Caelum and I walked to the side of the ship where a short ramp was extended to the dock. I looked at the churning water beneath us and noticed a shift in the color. "This is an estuary. The river empties into the sea, just there," he explained, pointing his finger downriver. "Fresh water and sea water mix here."

A bright blue streak filled the water, then dissipated again.

I thought I imagined it, until another appeared. Caelum smiled. "Algae. It produces its own light. We have many stubborn forms of life in Lumina that refused to die when Sol left our skies. They learned to produce the light they needed."

"It's beautiful."

He nodded. "It is. Sometimes, the entire tide line flares blue. Sometimes the sea carries in creatures called jellyfish that glow like this, great swarms of them. You can't touch them, though. Their sting can be deadly to humans."

"Jellyfish and nightthorn berries. What else is deadly here? I'm at a marked disadvantage."

He smiled. "I'll warn you if you encounter anything dangerous."

"You can't be with me all the time." Besides, it wasn't *him* I was worried about. Beron might stick something venomous in my bedsheets just to get rid of me at this point, or give one to Citali so she could...

Caelum escorted me to the bottom steps of the House of the Moon. I thought the House of Dusk was impressive with its seven floors, but Caelum's home had ten. I craned my neck to see them all, counting them a second time to be sure.

Caelum brushed the side of my hand with a finger. "Before I left, I arranged for you to have a private suite on the top floor, with a balcony that will provide privacy and plenty of moonlight," he said pointedly.

The book in my pocket suddenly felt heavier. "Thank you."

I wouldn't be able to rest or relax until I spent time reading it.

"Your suite is next to mine."

I nodded once. That was fine.

He cleared his throat. "Per Luminan custom, the proximity of our rooms will send a message."

"What sort of message?"

"The sort that says we are engaged to be married."

I scoffed. "You're quite detailed with the pretenses you've woven."

"Noor, I know my admission might lead you to think that my suggestion of a union was a false ploy, but it wasn't. I sincerely think it is in the best interest of both our kingdoms."

I quirked a brow. "Was that supposed to be your idea of a marriage proposal?"

"I know you need time to consider it," he defended, looking almost hurt.

"This is absurd. We barely know each other!" Add to that the fact that things might change very quickly depending on a number of factors, beginning with the contents of the mysterious book I hoped Lumos could help me read, and ending with the safety of his mother and Lumos's priests.

"You're right. We barely know each other. Yet it doesn't *feel* that way, does it?" he asked, gently taking hold of my upper arms, his eyes searching mine. "Tell me it's not just me."

It wasn't, but I couldn't allow the words past my lips.

Those who disembarked from the ship made their way toward us as two guards rushed around us to open a pair of enormous, ornately carved double doors, waiting until we walked inside. It was darker inside than it was out in Lumos's light. My eyes slowly adjusted to the dimness. I barely got a look at the columns and arches, the shining white floors and artful walls before a locust-like swarm of people surrounded us, all smiling and welcoming Caelum home.

They used his name, not his title. They were young and old, pale-skinned like him and Beron. Like Vada. I wondered where she was and how long she'd be on board. When she reached Helios, would someone greet her the way she'd greeted me at the ship? Would my people make her feel equally as welcome? Would she be able to keep herself safe?

Caelum smiled at me when a heavy-set woman grinned cheekily and asked who I might be. "Someone very special," he answered cryptically. That suggestive comment drew everyone's attention. Their gazes crawled over me and comments flew from all around.

"She's Helioan! Look at her beautiful brown skin."

"She looks like a princess!"

"Like Lumos cast her from the sky just for Caelum."

"A wedding!" someone said, punctuating their swoon with a dreamy noise.

Sensing my unease, Caelum interceded. "Atena Noor and I are very tired from our journey. I'd like to see her to her room so she can rest."

The crowd playfully pouted but slowly dispersed, everyone returning to the tasks we'd interrupted with our arrival. Caelum gestured to a wide staircase, but just before reaching the bottom step I remembered my priest friend and his terrible cough, the way he struggled to walk and labored to breathe even as he sat.

"Saric will not be able to climb far. Would you send him the tea and herbs as soon as possible?"

Caelum caught the attention of a woman passing us on the steps and asked her to personally find Sol's priests. He explained that the eldest had a cough and would appreciate some herbs to ease the tightness in his chest, then asked that Saric and Kiran be placed in a first-floor room.

The woman curtseyed. "I'll see to it, Caelum."

She rushed across the floor and guilt swarmed me. I paused and pivoted to run after her. "I should go see about him."

"Saric will be well cared for, Noor. I promise. He actually pulled me aside on board and insisted that I take you to the moon as soon as the ship docked."

Of course he did. "Then I'll go to him after."

Caelum nodded. "He'll be settled in by then. He needs a warm bed and some rest more than anything."

"Warm?"

"His room will have a hearth."

"Thank you, Caelum. He... he means a lot to me. More than most know."

He glanced at me questioningly, but I didn't elaborate. The heft of the book in my pocket seemed even heavier with every step I ascended.

The tenth-floor landing was paved with the same shining tile that ran along all the floors in the House of the Moon, reflecting Lumos's pale light throughout the interior. There were only two doors on this floor, one to the left and one to the right. He gestured to the one on the right. "This is my suite."

He opened the opposite door and waved me inside.

There was an ornate silver and marble table at the entry, but the space opened to reveal an enormous bath and basin area to the left, all built from the same glassy tile. There were no doors, walls, or separations, only a spacious room sectioned into discrete areas for bathing, sleep, and work. The balcony spanned the length of the space on three sides. Pale curtains, not unlike those in my rooms at home, fluttered on the cool breeze that wafted and swirled throughout the space.

The bed, draped in cool, silvery blue silk, was large enough to sleep ten. It sat alone on the farthest outer wall. An armoire in a matching pale wood had been placed nearby, large enough to hold the clothes of the ten who could fit into the bed.

To our right were tall shelves filled with books, along with a matching desk with quill, parchment, and ink already set out on its smooth surface.

"Is it to your liking?" Caelum asked.

My brows shot up. "It's beautiful." It *was* beautiful and perfect and so much more than both of those combined.

His shoulders relaxed just before a commotion came from the landing. "Your trunks," he explained, waving in those toting the trio of heavy boxes.

While Caelum instructed the placement of the trunks near the armoire, I drifted toward the balcony. Outside, Lumos had risen higher into the sky. It felt like we were at eye-level, staring at one another. Each curious and cautious about the other. The striations of his darker and lighter features were easier to see now, as were his scars.

*What happened to you that you have so many?*

Footsteps came from behind. I turned to the side, keeping Lumos in view as I looked up at Caelum. He hooked his thumb back toward my room. "I'll give you some space, but I'll be next door if you need me."

"Thank you, Caelum," I told him. "For everything."

He and I needed to talk, and we would, but not yet.

I needed to see what was so important in this book that it had to be hidden away. What was so important that Father kept it on his person when he could've left it in Helios or left it in his rooms in the dusk lands. I needed to know what was important enough in it for me to steal, risking his wrath and the lives of everyone who'd helped me.

The Lumin's hand ghosted down my arm. Goosebumps rose in the wake of his touch.

My phoenix's wing extended toward him, brushing the inside of my stomach as Caelum walked away.

When I heard the door to my suite close, I took a seat on the edge of a plush, padded chaise and eased the book from my pocket, the weight now filling my hands and pressing upon my shoulders.

# 20

"Lumos," I said quietly, looking at the god of night. "Sol sent me to steal this from my father. I understand that only you can reveal the ink with which she penned it. I beg of you to show me what she wrote on the pages."

Swallowing thickly, I peeled the leather binding back and waited as Lumos shone down on the first piece of parchment. In the dusk lands, the pages looked blank, but under Lumos's light, portions of pale blue words shone. They ebbed and flowed until the swoops and whorls connected.

Tears pricked at my eyes as I realized this was not penned by my father.

I gripped the leather tighter, my heart racing. Burning. "My mother wrote this?" I gasped.

Did she come to Lumina to write it, or would Sol's light also expose the ink?

I took a deep breath and began to read.

*When the Sculptor chiseled Sol from the creation rock, he took one look at her heart and saw it was one of fire and flame, warmth and wrath. He set her ablaze and hung her in the great darkness. Her purpose was to shine light on the dark world he had envisioned but hadn't yet carved.*

*Her purpose was to burn.*

*He chiseled her equal and opposite, Lumos, whose heart was cold and calm, frost and frigidness, to rule the night. Lumos did not burn. The Sculptor placed in his heart a serene light, bright enough to temper the darkness. Lumos was peaceful, dependable, and sure.*

*His purpose was to soothe.*

*Lastly, from the creation rock, the Sculptor finally chiseled the dark world that haunted his thoughts. He set Sol into motion, spinning around this world, and her purpose was revised. She was still meant to burn, but for those to whom the Sculptor would gift the dark world. She was to burn for them, and to guard, guide, and love them.*

*Lumos was then set into motion. He orbited the dark world opposite Sol. As she was to burn for them, his revised purpose was to soothe these beings. To encourage rest and peace as he guarded, guided, and loved them.*

*The Sculptor breathed onto the dark world and from the fog of his breath, spirits poured onto the sand. From it, humans rose. Half, the Sculptor gave to Lumos to reign over. Half was given to Sol.*

*Lumos loved his people. He shone so they could enjoy rest and quiet.*

*Sol loved her people. She shone so they could thrive and mingle.*

*For millennia, there was peace. A pleasant monotony. Until one day, Lumos grew bored and sped his trek across the sky. The god of night caught sight of Sol, goddess of day, and immediately fell deeply in love with her. He chased her in earnest, then.*

*The moment Sol caught sight of Lumos's pale face, she was enamored with his temperance, his dogged determination, and his cool beauty, so different from her fire. But the two were not made for one another. Their purpose was to serve their people, the sculpted spirits cloaked in sand and flesh below them.*

*The Sculptor noticed an imbalance in the two great lights he'd set into motion around the dark world to chase the darkness away. He rebuked the two gods and punished them by cleaving Sol from Lumos. In the Great Division, the earth, the gods, and their people were also divided. Lumos was set in a new orbit. He spun around the southern half of the dark world, where his people were taken and established again.*

*Sol was set in motion around the northern hemisphere, where her people bathed in her light and feared the darkness when they could not see her face and Lumos was nowhere to calm them.*

*Sol ached for Lumos, too, but knew he was safe. The Sculptor could have crushed them both for avoiding their purposes. As it was, Lumos lived.*

*She could feel his pull, and she was certain he could feel hers.*

*But the knowledge of his presence wasn't enough to remove the pain lancing her heart, or take away the longing she felt for him every moment of every day.*

*She mourned his absence in her life, however fleeting it had been.*

*For generations, she lamented, her heart burning for Lumos.*

*She needed companionship. She was lonely. So, she chose from among her people a special person set aside from the others; someone with whom she would speak and who would reveal her will for the spirits cloaked in flesh. Her people.*

My eyes widened at what was being revealed. Lumin did the same. Had the Sculptor somehow influenced each of them to choose among the people to distract them from their pain?

*She chose Aten after Aten, six in succession, all descendants of the first she deemed worthy. Then came her seventh, who was stronger than the others. Smarter. And like her, something in him burned. Perhaps that was what intrigued her.*

*But beyond the flame kindled in his chest, something in his heart lay empty and unfulfilled. Her chosen was dissatisfied, restless. Sol thought he needed a companion as well. So, she sent a wife to fill the void.*

*Her Aten loved his wife. He was true and faithful. And it didn't take long before his beloved carried his child. But her body was weak, and her lifeblood drained away as his daughter was born.*

My eyes widened. *Zarina.*

*Sol's seventh Aten was distraught, and the corner of his heart that had been empty and then filled with happiness for a time, emptied once more.*

*She sent another wife for him, one whose spirit was stronger than the last. He fell in love with her slowly, fearfully. But soon, the void filled once more and his wife became pregnant with his second daughter. But though the woman's spirit was stronger than the last, her flesh was weak. She succumbed to death only weeks after her daughter was born.*

Citali.

*At her death, Sol's seventh Aten came undone. He begged her for death, for anything but the pain from which he could not escape. Sol searched for another wife, someone strong in spirit. She found plenty who would have sufficed in that respect, but none whose bodies would not eventually relent to cold death.*

*Something in her shifted as she heard his lamentations, as she counted his tears and heard his dreadful thoughts. It was as if his heart was a mirror of her own, a distant echo. The pain she felt, he felt, too. The loneliness pouring through him rushed through her as well. The empty sadness, the ache that would not go away... also lived in her Aten's heart.*

*She fixed herself in the sky, determined to become what he needed for a time and to take from him what she desperately craved and missed from Lumos, and to see if anyone else could fill the void Lumos's absence left in her.*

*Her spirit descended into the sand and she called on it to clothe her. The grains formed her flesh and she walked from the dunes and found him in the House of the Sun. Her House.*

My heart pounded. This must be a made-up story... but my heart... I clutched my chest. My heart demanded more.

*He knew who she was the moment his eyes met hers. He fell to his knees, but she bade him stand. He loved her instantly, and she loved him.*

*The flesh she wore distracted her from the ache in her heart. Months passed. Then years.*

*She did not miss her home in the sky at all as her daughter was born. Her body did not falter, for she strengthened it as she strengthened her babe. She loved the child so much. Much more, she realized, than she did him.*

*Sol spent much time with her babe, forgetting her seventh Aten's heart, his pain. Her Aten grew jealous of the child.*

*An anxious feeling filled the goddess, a feeling of constant prickling. She knew it was the Sculptor because she'd prickled once before, right before he divided her from Lumos. He'd allowed her to follow her heart for a time, but she knew that she must leave the human life she'd constructed, along with her daughter, behind.*

*She tried to convince the Sculptor to release her from her purpose. To fill the great sun with a goddess far stronger than she. But he refused. He had made her specifically to burn... for this purpose and none other.*

*She took her daughter to the sands and explained to the girl that she had to leave. She let her fingers rake through the grains, bringing up sun diamonds and nuggets of gold, then pressed them in her palm and opened it back up. A gift for her daughter lay on her skin. She wanted her to have a piece of her on earth, even if she was in the sky.*

*Sol told the Aten that the Sculptor demanded she return to the skies to fulfill her duty to her people, to burn, but he did not understand. The darkness she once saw in the empty place inside him, spread and consumed him. He grew frantic. His worry turned to fear, his fear sparked anger, and his anger turned to an inferno of rage.*

*For days, he begged her to stay. He did not understand that the decision was not hers to make. For days, he sought a way to bind her to the earth. He found no acceptable solution.*

*In the end, rage consumed him.*

*He took out his overwhelming anger on her fleshly body, wrapping his hands around her throat and squeezing. She let him.*

*Because she had to shed her mortal coil one way or another. She had to go back so she could burn for her daughter. Because that was her purpose now. The Sculptor could drag her back to the sky, but he could not erase the babe from her heart.*

*As her flesh suffocated, she thought only of her daughter. Of her soft, dark hair. Of her baby scent. Of her first steps, first words, the day she first called her mother. Her love for the sun and her laughter. The way her face changed and thinned as she grew older. Seven years. She'd had seven years with the daughter she bore with her seventh Aten.*

*And before her spirit returned to the sky, as he killed her fleshly body, he uttered words of pure evil. "If you leave the sky over Helios, I will kill her. I will kill our daughter, and you will watch."*

*Insanity had claimed him. She fought him then, but it was too late. The flesh she wore perished and her spirit was cast back into the sky.*

*The Sculptor wishes for her to move, but he doesn't insist. He heard the threat. He knows Sol's heart and that it belongs to her daughter. He knows for whom she truly burns.*

*So, she waits over Helios.*

*She will wait... until the girl is of age.*

*Until she can bear her great and terrible inheritance.*

*She will wait. And burn.*

*For her.*

*For Noor.*

Tears spilling down my cheeks, I flipped page after page, waiting to see if she'd penned anything else. "How did you write this?" I asked out loud, desperate. It was obviously penned after her death. "Did you know the ending before he killed you? Did you leave this for me?" I cried.

The rest of the book was empty.

Lumos watched as I crumbled. The girl who thought she was stone broke into nothing but sand. Weak and weathered. My eyes caught on my bracelet and my hand found the matching anklet. I alone could wear them because I was hers. The fire in the stones burned through me, too, because it was her fire.

I still couldn't wrap my mind around it.

I was Sol's daughter?

I raged and stared forlornly at the placid face of Lumos. Now I realized my father was holding my mother hostage.

What would happen when I came of age? My seventeenth birthday was fast approaching; a handful of days remained before I would find out. If Sol moved, if she left Helios to come for me, what would happen to Vada and Lumos's priests?

I needed her to stay.

I slid the book into my pocket, then stood and walked to the balcony's edge. In the distance was sand, and the thunderous roar of the ocean filled my ears. Lumos's light glistened off every facet of the rolling sea and each uncurling wave beckoned me.

*Come.*

Turning to heed that call, I started off the balcony and came face to face with my sister.

My ribs tightened protectively, and my phoenix shrieked. How long had she been lurking in the shadows of my room?

"I just spoke to Caelum," she said calmly, too calmly, leaning against a column.

"About what?"

"The two of you. He has feelings for you, you know. Did you know this very room is an indication to everyone in this kingdom that he intends to marry you? We've skipped the hand-feeding and gone straight to nuptials, apparently."

I stared at her.

"He wanted to tell me before I figured it out. At least he was considerate enough to spare me the humiliation," she spat. "Then I ran into Beron, who admitted to the little game he was playing with both of us," she gritted. "I could've been the perfect embodiment of a Luminan queen, and he would have looked over me because you were there."

"You knew he could only choose one of us, and it isn't entirely up to him. Lumos will have the final say if we go forward."

"*If* we go forward?" she reared back. "Of course *you* will. I know what it is you truly seek. Stealing Caelum's crown and kingdom is the only way you will *ever* garner an ounce of Father's approval!"

I shook my head at the foolishness of my sister. "I don't want his approval, Citali, and you and I both know that even if I tossed the crown at his feet, he would still hate me."

The dark fire in her eyes blazed as she smiled. "So, you seek it for yourself, then?"

"No," I told her. "I don't."

I didn't need it. If Sol was my mother and I'd inherited her fire, I knew who she would choose as her Aten. As soon as I came of age, I would ascend. Mother would be free, and Father would be nothing. I only had to wait until that day, and then make my way back home to claim my rightful place in Helios. But I would never tell Citali such a thing.

Citali's eyes glittered. "I must have that crown. I will find it, Noor. I will find it and I will no longer be threatened," she vowed.

My brows kissed. "Threatened? By whom, Father?"

Instead of answering my question, she asked one of her own. "Why did you bring Kevi and her dancing girls to Lumina?" she asked, her eyes sharpening.

"I'm surprised you noticed," I snapped.

"They've claimed the attention of half the Luminan guard." *Oh, what a tragedy.* She pushed off the column and walked toward me. "I want to know why your eyes glow."

I rolled them. "This again? I don't know, Citali. I don't make them glow, if that's what you're wondering. They simply do."

Her eyes caught on my cheeks, then searched my face. Lumos's light was brighter than I had hoped, and at the same time wasn't warm enough to comfort me. "You've been crying."

"That should make you happy."

"It won't if you don't tell me why."

I refused to answer. She wasn't entitled to my tears or what caused them.

Another step forward, then tears sprang into *her* eyes and her upper lip trembled. "You take everything from me."

"I've taken nothing."

But she wasn't listening. "I cannot lose this time... I can't... I hope you can understand."

She suddenly lunged forward with a screech.

I caught her, but she clawed at me, thrashing and punching and flailing as she backed me toward the balustrades that ringed the balcony. My lower back hit the rail and I bent over its edge. I grabbed hold of her hair, wrapping it around my fist. "You're going to kill us both! If you push me over, I'm dragging you with me!" I screamed.

A bone-chilling howl filled the air from somewhere on the ground. She paused her assault but quickly resumed, even more determined. She tried to wrench her hair out of my grasp. I let my knees buckle to keep her from pushing me off the railing, and she tackled me to the stones and straddled my hips. I held her hair tight. I couldn't buck her off, though she was much smaller than me.

That dark fire blazed in her eyes. "Why *you?* What is different about *you?* What makes *you* so special? I cannot let you best me."

I bucked, finally knocking her off balance. She fell onto her hip and I released her hair. Standing up, I put distance between us, this time backing toward my room.

A wicked gleam entered her eyes before a tear slid down her cheek. "I should've done it. I should've pushed you into the river."

She started toward me again and that angry fire tore from my chest, filling my hands. "Citali, this is your last warning."

"Or what?" she laughed. Then, she lunged.

A low growl stilled her hands before she could reach me. I'd planted my feet, ready to take the hit, but also ready to scorch her the moment her skin met mine. We both watched in astonishment as an enormous black wolf crept onto the balcony from between the fluttering, pale curtains, snarling and snapping at Citali. Her frightened eyes jerked to mine. She backed away from me and the beast as it moved to stand between us, posturing protectively in front of me.

The wolf howled again so loudly my ear drum vibrated. I clapped my hands over my ears. So did Citali.

"Noor!" Caelum cried from inside my rooms. He rushed to the balcony, taking in the beast that had planted himself in front of me. He relaxed and loosed a pent-up breath.

"What is happening?" I shrilled while trying not to startle the wolf. As fantastical as it was, I knew this creature. I remembered him from when I was lost in the woods.

But what became more apparent, and somehow equally as disturbing, was that Caelum knew him, too.

"Thank you. It's okay now," he said to it.

The wolf shook its fur, looked at me, and… before I could begin to comprehend what I'd seen, turned into Caelum's brother. Beron, naked as the day he was born and seemingly proud of his bare body, stood in the beast's place.

My mouth hung open. Citali's did, too. "What just happened?" she breathed, panicked.

He shot her a toothy grin, making the dimple in his cheek deepen, and winked at her.

If her teeth weren't sharper than his, I'd say they might make a good match.

I clamped my lips closed. Breathed in, out. Caelum stepped inside the doorway and jerked down one of my curtains and flung it at Beron, who only laughed and quickly tied it around his waist. Not that the pale gauze hid much.

I was just glad I had the backside view of him.

I finally found my voice. "It was *you* in the woods! You found me."

A look passed between him and Caelum, a permission granted. Beron nodded. "It was me."

I hadn't needed him to find me. I had the bracelet, the light, and my mother. But he didn't know it. He came to help me.

"How?" I squeaked.

"I'm the Wolven. I changed the instant Lumos chose Caelum. I am his protector."

I braced a hand on my stomach. It made so much sense...

"This doesn't mean I forgive you," I told him.

He shot a pouty look over his shoulder, looking at least a tiny bit humbler now.

"Forgive you for what?" Caelum said slowly, carefully.

I swallowed thickly, mentally chastising myself for blurting before thinking. Again.

I was about to deftly change the subject in favor of throwing shade upon my treacherous, murderous sister once again, but Beron winced and admitted, "Noor and I kissed."

It rushed out of him like he'd been itching to tell his older brother but hadn't had the guts to. But still, he got the details of that encounter a bit confused. He and I did *not* kiss. *He* kissed *me*.

Citali maliciously stared me down, the dark fire she held within building back into an inferno. It was one thing for me to take Caelum's attention away, but quite another to kiss Beron. She liked him, whether she would admit it to herself or anyone else.

I suspected it before, but now... Now, I knew. If Beron hadn't turned into a wolf to keep us from killing one another, she would have pounced again.

"*He* kissed *me;* not the other way around. I didn't want to kiss him," I said for her benefit. My reframing did nothing to assuage Caelum, who stood there fuming. I winced as Caelum stalked to Beron and grabbed him by the scruff of hair on his neck. Then the Lumin turned and shouted at my sister, pointing toward the door that led to my rooms. "Citali. *Out.*"

Shocked that he'd raised his voice and likely still terrified from Beron's revelation, she didn't talk or look back, but scurried behind the brothers obediently. I walked after her, watching Caelum drag his younger brother through my room.

"Caelum, stop. You don't understand what happened," I tried to soothe.

He shot me a scathing look that promised we certainly would talk, as soon as he took care of the immediate problem.

As he struggled to keep Caelum's hurried pace bent over as he was, Beron pled for him to listen to reason. "I did it to protect her! I can explain everything," he assured his Lumin.

For his sake, I was glad the Lumin's touch did not burn.

Then a strangled scream slash howl tore from Beron's throat and I wasn't so sure he didn't have fire. Caelum released his brother's hair and a layer of shimmering coldness coated Beron's skin and hair where the Lumin had touched him.

"Ouch!" Beron yelled. "You know I hate that."

Caelum shoved Beron out, waited for Citali to follow him, then locked the door behind them. Then he fumed and paced my room silently for several long minutes. I'd never seen him so upset.

I folded my hands regally in front of me. "Was that snow?" I asked, trying to diffuse the situation.

His feet stopped and I regretted speaking and drawing his attention to me as he stalked over. I stood tall, just as I did when Father's temper flared. "If you're going to strike me, don't think I'll shrink away. But know that if you touch me," my fire flared and I knew it was reflected in my eyes, "I'll burn your hand off. Your snow isn't powerful enough to quench my flame."

I had power now... A defense against such abuse.

His face and anger relaxed, replaced with the steadfast, faithfully strong face he made when he promised something. "Noor, I would *never* raise my hand to you."

I relaxed fractionally but kept my fire close. Not so that it skated my surface, but lay beneath it, easy to draw from if I needed it.

He closed his eyes. "I just... I keep picturing him kissing you. His lips on yours."

"Then you know how I felt after seeing Citali kissing you in the garden."

"It's not the same!" he growled.

"It absolutely is," I insisted hotly. "You begged me to listen to you then. You said *she* kissed *you* and I misunderstood what I saw. I'm telling you the same thing happened with Beron and me. The question is whether you'll trust *my* word the way I trusted yours."

"Will you tell me what happened?" The gravel in his voice resonated through my bones, lighting a different kind of fire in me.

I took hold of his hand. "Let me show you."

Tugging him to the wall behind us, I put my back against it. "After Kevi and her girls served Father the sleeping draught, two of his guards helped him to his rooms. Kevi followed. Beron and I waited a moment, then made our way there. We had almost reached his door when the guards came out."

Caelum braced his hands against the wall, caging me in, then bent low and let his lips hover over mine.

"So, he kissed me so they wouldn't ask why we were there. I panicked and did nothing. If Beron hadn't thought so fast, I might not have been able to steal the book. He truly was protecting me, and more importantly, our plan. And to be honest, if I hadn't panicked, I might have had the same idea." A rumble resonated from his chest. "It meant nothing. I promise."

He kissed me then, my lips dragging my head from where it lay against the wall, following him even after he'd pulled away.

He licked his bottom lip. "Is that the *only* thing Beron has to apologize for?"

I froze.

"Noor…" he warned.

"I don't want to tell you. I'd rather kiss you instead."

"This conversation isn't over," he said sternly.

*Is that so?* I smiled, then threaded my hands around his neck and smothered his serious face, kissing him long enough to erase all thoughts of Beron from his mind.

"Wicked flame," he called me. His lips found the corner of my jaw and neck before returning to my mouth. His hands drifted down, hooked onto the backs of my thighs, and lifted me up. He pinned me to the wall and kissed me like it was the only thing he wanted, the only thing he needed.

My ankles locked around his waist. As we kissed, his hands roamed the moon diamond dress, ignoring the tiny, dazzling stones to memorize the feel of the curves beneath. Mine roved over every muscular plane of his chest, shoulders, and back. They sought out his soft, midnight hair.

He groaned and tore away from me.

I slid to the floor with a pounding heart and swollen lips.

He smoothed my hair. "Did that properly erase my brother's pathetic kiss from your memory?

"Whose?" I teased, my blood boiling.

Caelum finally laughed, but the sound and moment were fleeting. Somberness fell over us once more.

"Did you get a chance to look at it?" he asked, gesturing to my pocket.

"I did, and I'll tell you what I learned, but first, I need to see Saric."

# 21

The priest was the only one who likely had the answers to the questions churning through my mind.

"Of course," Caelum said.

"I'd like to change first. Then would you see me to his room?"

Caelum nodded. "I'll wait outside."

He stepped outside and I trudged to my trunks to find a less conspicuous dress, settling on a deep teal gown that tied at the back of my neck and back and had deep pockets. The book safely ensconced within, I tested the ties to make sure they were tight. The pleated fabric fell to my ankles. Shedding my sandals, I walked barefoot from the room.

Caelum's gaze traveled over me and my phoenix smiled. He handed me a key. "So you don't get any other uninvited guests."

"You mean, so my sister can't slip in and kill me as I sleep."

"I will ask Beron to keep a close eye on her."

*Beron.* I still had so many questions, but they'd have to wait for another time.

Caelum and I walked the flights to the bottom floor where we walked down a long hallway, passing a room large enough to hold three of the great halls of the House of Dusk, a library with more books than I could read in a lifetime, small dining rooms, sitting rooms, and finally, a few bedrooms at the end near the kitchens.

"Each of these rooms have fireplaces. I hated to ask him to walk so far," Caelum explained, "but I thought he would be more comfortable here."

"Thank you."

I knew which room I would find him in when a harsh cough sounded from within. Easing the door open, I peeked inside. Warmth from a popping fire filled the air and cast a soft orange light over the room.

There were two twin beds, one empty and undisturbed. Saric lay in the other.

Kiran sat in a comfortable-looking chair by Saric's side. He straightened when he noticed me, then Caelum. Saric looked incredibly weak. Tired. The type of tired that couldn't be cured with rest or herbs, but only by the solace that the hereafter provided the aged. His body was deteriorating rapidly.

Several blankets were tucked around his frail frame. A bout of coughing overwhelmed him even as he tried to wave me in, barely able to lift the hand he'd stuck out of the pile of blankets.

"I'll see that you aren't disturbed," Caelum said quietly.

"Thank you," I whispered, then eased the door closed behind me.

Kiran rose. "Atena. Please, take my seat."

I shook my head, then padded to the bed and eased onto the edge, careful not to disturb the elder priest. "I want to sit closer," I told him.

Saric extended his hand from the blanket's edge and I took it in mine. "I waited for you," he said. "To say goodbye."

His skin was so brittle and cold. Tears sprang into my eyes. "Do not cry, Noor," he rasped.

I couldn't help it, much less stop them from flowing. "Did you know what was in the book I stole from him?" I asked.

Saric nodded. "Not the words, but the content. Yes."

I looked to Kiran. Had he known?

"I just told him," Saric said, squeezing my hand. "You're so warm. Like her."

More tears fell. They splashed onto my dress and his blanket, spotting the fabric.

"I knew Sol well. When she walked the earth, she often came to the temple and spent time with her priests. Seeing her wearing flesh was something I never expected when I pledged my life to her, but it was a gift I'll never forget. Her presence was indescribable. Overwhelming. Awe-inspiring. And she loved you. She loved you so much, Noor. She did not want to leave you behind, but taking you with her meant that you would die. She couldn't bring herself to snuff out the life she wanted you to have. She wanted this destiny for you, even if it meant leaving you with him and subject to his undeniable anger. She knew you were strong enough to withstand his fury."

"Does he know what I'll become when I turn seventeen?"

"He sent you to the dusk lands, and to Lumina, with the hope that if Sol can't reach you, she cannot transform you… Or so I led him to believe."

My mouth fell open. "You lied to him?"

"I lied for you," he wheezed. "Your mother made me promise to watch over you. To do what I could to fend him off and divert his attention elsewhere. For years, I managed it, but his anger grew despite my best efforts. The morning of Joba's departure… I thought he might kill you before your birthday. There was murder in his eyes."

I remembered how he'd interrupted Father while we were in the riverfarer's cabin.

"Why does she have to wait for my seventeenth birthday? It's an arbitrary day." And so close now. What did it matter?

He shook his head. "Your transformation began when you drew your first breath, Noor. Her blood runs through your veins, but when you come of age, she will replace it with her fire. At birth, you were lit. Now, you are kindling. Soon, you will know what it is to burn. Your body must be ready to contain it."

"Will I survive the blaze?"

Saric gave a weak smile. "Of course you will."

He stared at me as if remembering the day he walked with me into the sand, carrying her ash and bones. Surely if I could survive that, nothing would break me. Every time Father tried to beat me down, he built me into something stronger and more indestructible. A vessel worthy enough to carry not only my mother's blood, but her incendiary power.

I clutched my chest as a feeling of dread drenched the phoenix inside. She shrieked from the dousing, steam wafting from her wings. "He knows you lied, Saric. I burned him. At the House of Dusk, the night of the ball, Father grabbed my wrist. I thought he would snap my bones. The fire bubbled up and I used it against him. He knows I have a fraction of her power, even away from her."

My stomach turned. Even before the night I burned him, he saw the fire in my eyes and the melted chair arms. *He knew.* He'd always known.

Saric nodded his head weakly. "He did know. That's why he came to me for guidance. That's when I told him that the greater distance you were from Sol, the more it would stifle what you are to inherit. I told him you wouldn't be as great a threat if you came of age in Lumina." Saric squeezed my hand. "It doesn't matter that he knows of my lie. I won't live long enough to see him again, and Sol will make it clear that his attempt to stifle you was in vain. I only wish I could live to see the moment she strips him of all his powers. She couldn't do it before because he had you. He used you to manipulate Sol, because he knew how much she loved you. Sol wouldn't have survived if he had hurt or killed you. She would have exploded, and the entire earth would have died from her fire."

"I'm worried for Vada and Lumos's priests," I admitted. "If she strips his power while they're there..."

Kiran glanced at me. "He won't kill them. He'll use them against you, first. Then he will try to use them to sway Caelum from your side."

*Not if the riverfarer smuggles them out of Helios and we send a ship to the dusk lands to carry them back to their home...*

I looked at my friend, holding his rusty eyes. "If I write a letter, can you take it to Caelum? I trust only you, Kiran."

He nodded. "Of course, Atena."

The Luminans had outfitted their desk the same as they had the one in my room. I took a piece of parchment and gripped the quill in my hand. I thrust the nib into a dark pot of ink and let my warning flow in whorls and swoops. Saric fell asleep as the ink dried.

I could tell Kiran did not want to leave him, but I also knew I had to be here when he passed. "I'll stay with him," I whispered.

"I'll hurry," he promised, taking the folded parchment. He eased the door closed behind us and Saric's eyes fluttered back open.

"Will you guide me to Sol, Noor?"

"How?"

The hand Kiran had held rose and he pointed at his chest. "Let it guide you. Always. You are connected to your mother by far more than blood and fire."

Kiran returned, worried eyes scanning his brother. Saric gave him a tired smile, his breaths too shallow as he told him, "I have to go now, Kiran. Noor will see me home."

A storm of sorrow built over the younger priest's features, but he nodded, unable to speak.

I clasped Saric's hand tightly as his breathing became labored and the length between his breaths stretched, until a soft gasp escaped his chest and it went still.

Kiran's tear-filled eyes met mine. "Go with him, Noor."

I closed my eyes, listened to my heart, and envisioned the sand.

A rush of heat fell over me as Saric and I walked into the dunes. He was as young as the day he'd helped carry my greatest burden, but I was no longer a child. He held my hand, walking in companionable silence up and over the hardened crests. Until we came to the sacred hill that I'd chosen that day…

I guided him to his place in the sand and he laid down, staring at Sol above us. I knelt beside him. "I'm ready, Noor," he said with a voice so strong, it tore my heart in two. "Bring her near."

When Joba was burned, she was dead. But this was different because in my mind, Saric was still alive.

"Send me to Sol. Send me to the hereafter, where I will fuel her fire for you, and for the many generations to come."

I shook my head. "Not until you draw your last breath."

It wasn't long then. He accepted my terms. His breathing slowed, then stopped. I watched for his chest to move for many long moments and only when I was certain he was gone, I called for Sol.

Tears falling, I raised my hands to the sky, clutching at Mother's face. I drew her closer, closer… until all of Saric burned away. None of him was deemed unacceptable to my mother.

Though I wasn't actually touching her, it felt like it. In her brightness, my face shone back at me. Father had scarred her face the way he'd scarred me, but we not only survived, we would use that fire to incinerate him.

I felt her fire echo through me, and I knew in that moment, I would revel in my inheritance. This was my destiny. Saric was right.

*That* was why Father hated me and why, deep in his cinder heart, he feared me.

I released her and watched her rise.

Her bones, as well as the bones of the seven other women, shone white in the red-orange sand. That color stayed with me even as the vision faded. It was the same shade in Kiran's worried eyes as he stood beside me. I was still curled on the edge of Saric's bed, but he was gone. His blankets lay flat on the mattress.

"Noor?"

"I'm fine."

He held me to his chest, clutched my head like it was a lifeline, and gently rocked side to side, crying.

I slid my hands around his lower back and held him while he mourned his friend, his mentor. His brother.

"Where did you take him?" he finally managed, slowly releasing his hold on me. He sank beside me, the mattress lifting me when his weight hit it.

"He is with Sol."

"You took his body, Noor. Not only his spirit."

I nodded. Somehow flesh and spirit had combined in the sand and I knew he was real, but spirit as well. A strange, beautiful mesh of the two. "I know."

"I didn't expect that," he quietly said.

"I didn't either."

He scrubbed hands down his face.

"No part of him was found unacceptable, Kiran. Sol took him away from the sands. Through her, he burns for us now."

"We can't let him down," he said. "Tell me what you need, and I will see that it's done. I want to help you as you become what you were always meant to be."

I took his hand and brushed my thumb over the back of it. "Thank you, friend."

He swallowed thickly and inclined his head.

A soft knock came at the door. "Come in," I said.

Caelum entered, his eyes darting to Kiran's hand clasped in mine. "Is he gone?" he asked.

"How did you know?"

He cleared his throat. "Lumos felt Sol – as if she were here."

"No, he didn't," Kiran croaked. "He felt Noor."

Caelum looked over our shoulders, his brows pinching when he realized Saric was nowhere to be found.

"I took him home."

His lips parted, but he didn't press. The wound was too fresh, and Caelum kindly respected it. Something else I loved about him.

Kiran released my hand. "You should get some rest, Noor."

I was incredibly tired. Exhausted, to be honest. "I don't want to leave you alone like this," I told my friend.

"But alone is what I need right now," he gently told me.

My throat knotted again. "If you're sure."

"I'm sure," he said, standing from Saric's bed and waiting as I stood.

Caelum looked to Kiran. "I'm sorry for your loss."

"We're supposed to rejoice," Kiran answered, shaking his head. "But I can't seem to muster the strength to be happy when my heart feels so heavy."

"Then don't be," I chided. "You loved him. You have every right to mourn him."

"You loved him, too," he quietly replied.

I offered a small smile. "I did, and I do, and always will. Saric's memory will live on through me, through the priesthood, and Sol, and through you, Kiran."

He scrubbed a hand over his mouth. "Thank you."

Caelum and I left him alone. I hoped he meant it when he said he needed time and space and wasn't just saying it for my benefit or Caelum's, but I had no other choice but to trust him.

My feet felt like stone as they carried me to the tenth floor, Caelum resolute beside me. I stopped outside my door. "We need to talk, but tomorrow, please," I said.

He nodded. "Rest well, sweet Noor." He brushed a strand of my hair out of my face and placed a soft kiss on my lips.

It made my heart ache desperately, even though it felt like a balm to my fresh emotional wound.

# 22

I went to sleep in total darkness. Lumos was gone and his light left with him. I hadn't lit a candle, but knew where one waited on the desk. When I woke, the moon god still hadn't returned. I felt my way to the taper and struck the match, feeling comforted by the warm flame that caught on the waxy wick.

My hair was snarled, and I wasn't sure anything but washing it would help. My things –including my comb – were still packed, but beyond that, I needed water. And soap. I suddenly wished I hadn't used the last of Vada's salts.

A soft knock came at the door.

I walked to it and waited. Citali's stunt had set me thoroughly on edge. "Who's there?"

"It's me," Caelum answered. "The moon will rise soon. I wondered if you might want to watch it from the beach." He paused. "I have a blanket and packed breakfast."

Him and his breakfasts. I loved it.

"I look hideous," I warned. "All my things are still packed away. I don't even know where my brush is."

"You could never look hideous, Noor."

More pressing than my vanity, I didn't know what to do with the book. I was afraid to take it near the water, but couldn't leave it in the room.

"Can I see you?"

I cracked the door open.

"What's wrong?"

"I need to hide it," I whispered. "I don't want it to be ruined by the brine or water."

He nodded. "Can I step inside for a moment to show you something?

I eased the door open and let him in.

A basket draped in a blanket lay near his feet. He strode in and closed the door. Beside the armoire where the wall looked smooth like glass, he touched one of the tiles and it gave way, revealing a hinged door that opened into a small, hidden compartment. "It'll be safe here. Beron and I are the only ones who know it exists."

"Can I trust him?"

Caelum sighed. "We had a lengthy discussion this morning and he told me about his role with the poisoned jam. I know it probably doesn't seem like it after what he did, but I'm convinced he had my best interests at heart. I swear you can trust him."

"How long have you been awake?"

He smiled. "Awhile."

I took the book from my pocket and slid it into the sleek compartment, closing the tile again. It blended seamlessly.

"One minute?" I asked.

He nodded once. "We have a little time before he rises."

I rushed to my trunks and flung open each lid, rifling through them until I found my toothbrush and the mint and sand water with which to clean them. I rejoiced when I found my comb, then ran with the items to the bathing room, where pitch darkness met me. Caelum's footsteps approached and I turned to see him holding the candle. "You'll need this."

I thanked him and he waited outside while I freshened up as best I could.

My dress snapped in the cool wind as we walked through the Luminan sand, so different from that of Helios. It was cold and soft, powdery but thick. The sky was filled with so many stars, it was startling. Their light did little for my vision as I picked my way across the beach, holding uneasily to Caelum's arm. "How can you see?"

"I was born to it," he said smoothly. "I'm as used to the darkness as you are to Sol's light and heat. I think if you stayed here for a time, you would adapt and adjust to it."

Where the waves had swept the shore overnight, the sand had hardened. Caelum found a flat spot and spread the blanket, then we quickly sat on it to keep it from blowing away.

Caelum whispered to the sky and the wind died away. Over the water, the sky lightened, leeching from black to deep blue. I could see Caelum a little better, unsure if the sky's alteration was a trick of the eye and mine were becoming accustomed to the darkness, or if Lumos was closer than I thought.

"That was a neat trick."

"Lumos is helpful, and he's curious about you. He could sense your mother through you last night."

"He loves her," I told him as he arranged the spread of food. "And she still loves him."

"I know," he said. "His feelings for her are very loud."

"Do you hear him?"

He shook his head. "It's more of a feeling. Here." His hand landed on his taut stomach. "But somehow, what he gives me is never unclear."

There were small plates holding an unusual yellow fruit and I laughed. "Is this as sour as the last one you fed me?"

He flashed a smile and shook his head. "It's sweet." I quirked a brow. "I promise!" he chuckled. "Try a piece."

I took a sliver of the slimy, cool fruit and bit into it. A sweet taste burst over my tongue, exploding with citrus, with a hint of something bitter hidden in the sugary flesh. "It's good," I admitted.

"Told you." He took up his own piece, smiling triumphantly before chewing. He prepared a piece of bread as I tried to focus through the darkness. "Jam?" he asked.

"You're preparing my food." My ribs tightened.

"I am." His tone was completely unapologetic.

"Don't you know what that would imply?" I tried to tease, my mouth going dry.

He tilted his head. "I think I've made my feelings clear. Do you want jam, Noor?"

"Is it nightthorn jam?"

He snorted. "It's the kind you liberally smeared all over everything while we were in the dusk lands. Morning fruit. It's orange in color."

Mmmm. I loved that kind. I raised my chin. "Very well. You can prepare it for me, since I cannot see to do it myself without spreading it all over my dress."

Through the darkness, I heard him grin.

Heard him smear.

Felt him scoot closer.

"Open your mouth," he said in a gravelly tone. It wasn't necessary that he feed me, but he wanted to. Caelum said his feelings for me were clear. Now, he was weighing mine.

My phoenix did as he instructed, parting her beak and flapping her fiery wings.

My lips parted, too. I waited until the soft bread, smeared perfectly with the orange morning fruit, touched them. With my teeth, I tore a piece away.

He watched me as I chewed.

Suddenly, I realized I could see him. My head swiveled toward the sea where the very top of Lumos's face peeked over the horizon. I gasped, turning to tell Caelum how magnificent the moon god's soothing light was as it struck every facet of the sea, when my nose brushed Caelum's and his lips captured mine. When he pulled away, there was an emotion on his face I didn't recognize.

It wasn't worry, but one of longing. "I don't know what the book said, and I don't want to discuss it this morning. But I want you to know that whatever you need from me, I will provide. Whatever decision you make, I will honor. Whatever time I have with you, I will cherish – whether it be a handful of days, or the rest of my days, Noor."

I swallowed thickly. "What if I *can't* stay?"

His lashes fluttered. "I think that if you and I want this, Sol and Lumos will *make a path* so we can meet in the middle. Or we can stubbornly make one ourselves."

I hoped he was right.

"Did you send for the riverfarer and launch the falcon with my note?"

"I did. Is your falconer loyal to your father?"

I snorted. "He is loyal to whomever rewards him better. In my letter, I vowed it would be me. He will give the message to your mother and tell the riverfarer the fare I will pay to take her and Lumos's priests back to the dusk lands."

"A ship is already sailing north."

I nodded. Good. I hoped Lumos filled their sails and saw them safely there.

"Thank you for your concern for them. For *making a path* to ensure their safety," he said pointedly.

Sometimes, I got a flicker of an image of what it might be if such a path could be made from Helios to Lumina, from my heart to his. It was beautiful, golden and pale blue, woven in fire and frost. But it seemed that when I reached out and tried to touch that scene, it dissipated like smoke and I couldn't ever catch hold of it.

"We'd like to host a quiet dinner tonight in honor of your arrival, but if it's too soon after Saric's passing, we can wait."

"If Saric was here and I told him that I could ask you to wait and hold the banquet another day, he'd scold me and say something like, 'Life is meant to be lived; waiting only eats away at the time you've got left.' He would hate it if anything was postponed because of him."

With his thumb, he smoothed the worry line between my brows. "Are you sure?"

I nodded. "I am."

"Do you want Citali there?" he asked.

I knew he'd lock her in her rooms if I asked. I tried not to bristle at his concern for my sister. My anger lay with her. "She and I need to have a talk. I'll decide after that."

He nodded. "More than fair."

I knew he said he didn't want to talk about the book, but I needed to tell him, to prepare him, for what was about to happen. "Caelum –"

He stiffened at my tone. "The book?"

I nodded. "My seventeenth birthday is in a few days. Something will happen then. It's already begun."

"To you?"

"Yes."

He swallowed thickly. "What will happen to you, Noor?"

"I will become Aten."

Caelum's beautiful lips parted.

"I know what Father told you, but Sol will not accept Zarina. Neither will she accept Citali."

He was quiet for a long moment, his chest rising and falling like the soft waves curling onto the shore. "How can you be sure? Was it written in the book?"

I swallowed and took hold of his hand, nervous about telling him what I knew I must. "I am Sol's daughter and heir. She came to the earth for a time in physical form, and she married my father and gave birth to me. Then she was forced to leave it, and me, behind."

He turned my wrist so the bracelet sparkled against the moonlight. "The diamonds."

I nodded. "It's why I can wear them when they burn anything else." Their constant warmth encircled my ankle, reassuring and comforting me.

"And also why you have them when your sisters do not. And why there is fire in your touch when you're angry. The glow in your eyes. You have her light, too," he said reverently.

"Just a touch," I confirmed.

"A touch now, but how much when you come of age?"

I shrugged. "I'm not sure what to expect, but I know that I will burn as she burns. I'm meant to."

Lumos was almost completely above the horizon, only his chin leaking into the sea now. "I have his frost in my blood," he croaked.

I nodded. "I noticed when you tossed Beron from my rooms. When did he give it to you?"

"On my seventeenth birthday. I'm nineteen now. I won't lie and say it wasn't painful," he added wryly. "Our bodies think they're too frail to contain the power of a god, but as Lumin, I only have a touch. How much will Sol bestow upon you?"

"I'm not sure." But I was almost certain it would be more than a touch. Saric had eluded to as much.

"Will you let me be there with you? *For* you?"

I clutched his hands tighter. "I was about to ask if you would stay with me until it was finished."

I was afraid. Scared that despite the assurances of Saric and Sol, my flesh would be weak and unable to contain the power she shed to me. I was as mortal as she when the light of her humanity was extinguished and she was sent back to the sky. I didn't want to die now that I had hope that living would be worth it all. Every bruise. Every hateful word, scathing look, and humiliating moment.

Every lonely hour without her. All the walls I put up between myself and those I cared for to keep them safe. Every burst vessel and golden urn. All the trips to the sand.

He stood up and offered his hand, walking backward to the water. I was afraid to feel it. "It's okay," he said gently. He wrapped his arms around me and held me as a cold wave rushed to cover our feet. His chin rested on top of my head. "You'll get through this."

"What if I boil away this beautiful sea?" I asked, worried it might be possible but trying to cling to any levity I could find in the situation.

"Then we'll walk together on seas of sand."

# 23

Beron seethed as Caelum calmly folded the blanket he'd brought for us and we tucked what was left of breakfast into the basket. The Wolven was still brooding. Anger sizzled beneath his surface.

I snorted. "Let me guess. Citali?"

"How?" he barked, throwing a frustrated hand in the air.

"How what?"

"How can you *possibly* be related to her?" he asked, waiting for an answer.

I shrugged. "She takes after our father. *I* favor my mother." I flicked a glance to Caelum, who bit back a knowing grin. "What could she have *possibly* done to get you so riled up this early?" I asked.

"She snuck out of her room and slipped right by me. Twice!" He held up two rigid fingers.

I pinched my lips together to keep from laughing.

Beron saw my face and I lost the fight. He growled and shook his head. "You could have warned me about her."

"I have! On several occasions, I might add. And if my warnings did not suffice, why didn't her actions tell you exactly who she was? She wears a beautiful face, Beron, but don't let her fool you. And don't let her get under your skin. I promise you'll regret it."

"Under my skin?"

I peered at him earnestly, all trace of laughter gone. "Don't fall for her. Don't give her your heart. She'll shred it. She might even eat it."

"Never."

*Never say never...*

Caelum quirked a brow. Beron growled. "I didn't come to speak about Citali. I came to fetch you."

I burst out laughing. They sent a wolf to *fetch* the Lumin?

Beron wagged a finger at me, a warning flashing in his eyes. "I didn't mean it like that. I'm no trained dog."

"I know. I know how completely terrifying you are, Beron." I bit the inside corner of my lips to stifle the smile he'd dragged from them.

Caelum looked to me regretfully. "I have a few things to do..."

"Go," I told him. "I'm fine."

He glanced at Beron, who also waved him away. "Go, Lumin. Do your Lumin-ly duties and leave Noor and me alone."

Caelum took the basket and blanket, then leaned in and kissed me on the lips, tucking a strand of hair behind my ear. "I'll try not to take too long."

Beron groaned. "Go. I'll look after her."

My hackles raised as if I were a Wolven, too. I narrowed my eyes. "I don't need looking after."

Beron smirked at me, content to have riled my temper.

My hands heated. I flexed my palms, trying to cool them off.

Caelum chuckled as he walked away. "Good luck!" he called over his shoulder.

I wasn't sure if he was speaking to me or the Wolven.

Beron watched his brother's retreating back until he disappeared into the House of the Moon. I watched the sea. Foam drifted on top of the churning surface. I wondered what it would look like during a storm, when the sky roiled and rumbled and lightning struck the waves.

"So, Beron... you turn into a rather large wolf. Do you have any other neat tricks?"

"Other than prophesying for the Lumin, no." He shrugged. Besides being a shapeshifter, I'd almost forgotten he was the Luminan equivalent of our Sphinx. Thank Sol he didn't speak in riddles as she did.

"Where is my sister now?" I asked.

"My second watches her."

"Your second?" I asked, dragging my toes through the sand to draw a line.

"One of the only people I trust with my life – besides my brother and mother." He jerked his head toward the sea. "Do you swim?"

"I've never tried," I admitted. "In Helios, there are crocodiles in the river. People still go down to it to swim, wash, and collect water, but my sisters and I were never permitted to."

He offered a toothy grin. "Do you want to learn?"

Did I trust him enough to teach me? "Do you promise not to drown me?"

He rolled his eyes. "A fellow makes *one* mistake and he'll never live it down. Sheesh."

"You made more than one, and they were huge," I corrected, crossing my arms over my chest.

In the moonlight, the differences between him and Caelum were much more obvious than they were in the dusk lands. Caelum's brows were thick and dark, but not as thick or dark as Beron's. I noticed one of Beron's brows was split with a thin scar.

"Are you immortal?" I asked.

He ticked his head back, a smile finally emerging. "I wish."

"I don't," I told him. "I want one amazing life, but I don't want to live forever when everything I loved would perish. I want to go to the hereafter with my loved ones to fuel Sol's fire."

He nodded slowly. "So... swimming?" His dimple flashed hopefully.

"In the shallows? That's where you seem to want to keep our conversation."

He grinned. "Absolutely not. If we're wading in, we're going until we can barely touch the bottom. But you can't swim in that dress. You'll get tangled and drown."

"I have nothing else to swim in."

He waved me toward the House. "I can fix that."

"I'm not sure your clothes would fit me, Beron."

The Wolven chuckled. "Kevi has something you can borrow."

"You know Kevi?" I asked, hurrying after him.

"I do now. Citali was with her this morning when I finally tracked her down by scent."

Citali had asked why Kevi and her girls came with us. She suspected there was more of a reason than just to escort us or to dance for the Lumin, and since I'd refused to tell her anything, she went straight to the source. I wondered what she thought when she realized Kevi had a power all her own and wouldn't allow Citali to walk all over her.

I also wondered if Citali would be short a bangle or two the next time I saw her...

Would Kevi tell my sister the truth in exchange for gold? She was in a new land, and while Caelum promised to keep her and the girls safe and I'd vowed to provide them enough gold to live comfortably on, Kevi had taken my bribe once. Would she take Citali's now?

Kevi and her girls were in a cluster of rooms on the second floor. Beron knocked on the wooden door and waited until Kevi answered. Her eyes lit when she saw him standing there, then caught on me. "Atena! Beron," she purred. "What a lovely surprise." She waved us inside.

"Did my sister come to see you?" I asked once the door was closed.

Kevi's easy smile fell away. "She asked why we came to Lumina."

"What did she offer you?" I asked, watching Kevi as she sauntered further into the room and sat in a plush chair.

"What makes you think she offered me anything?"

"Kevi."

She rolled her eyes. "Fine. She offered me gold." She jangled bangles on her wrist, some of them I knew belonged to Citali – or had before this morning.

My stomach dropped. "Did you tell her the truth?"

Kevi scoffed. "Do you take me for a fool?"

A feeling of relief washed over me.

"We are simply here to dance for the Luminans at the celebration when one of you joins with Caelum, uniting the kingdoms. That's all," she said, fluttering her eyes at Beron.

He tugged at the collar of his tunic and shifted his weight, then cleared his throat. "As you and your friends went swimming last night, I was wondering if you might have something Noor could borrow to wear in the ocean."

"And you know this, how?" she asked, standing and walking toward him. Beron was a Wolven when he needed to be, but Kevi was like Citali in some ways, like me in others. She'd eat him alive or roast him. I wasn't sure which. But he would learn it the hard way if he kept poking that lioness.

"I saw you from one of the balconies."

"In the dark? We could barely see. One of the guards was kind enough to set candles out in the sand for us."

He nodded. He knew that, too.

"Did you like watching us, Beron?" she asked, running a finger down the center of his chest.

"No. I probably *would have* enjoyed it if I wasn't focused on trying to keep tabs on Citali," he grumbled.

"She's clever, that one. Sneaky, too. I bet you had your hands full."

He laughed and shook his head. "You have no idea."

"Kevi," I finally interrupted. "Do you have something I could borrow to swim in?"

She left Beron to clasp my hand, drawing my wrist close to her face. "No bangles to offer?"

"I plan to offer far more than that. With what you did to help me at the House of Dusk, I owe you more than a bangle, Kevi. I'll see that you and your dancers are cared for."

Kevi's sly smirk fell away. She nodded and tugged me behind a folding screen. "You should wait outside, Beron," she snipped. "If your brother knew you lingered to watch the Atena's silhouette, he'd snap your pretty neck."

The door closed a moment later.

She and I giggled together. "I'm not wrong, though, am I, Noor? The Lumin is smitten with you."

"I think so," I told her, admitting it to someone else aloud.

"I *know* so. I know men," she said. "I've known plenty of women, too, but let me tell you – the Lumin doesn't even know others are in the room when you're with him. It's like the two of you are on a separate plane of existence."

I let my dress fall and cringed when I saw the dark blue scraps of fabric she brought over. "What are those?"

"For you to swim in. You don't want a lot of fabric, Noor. The water will weigh it down and pull you under."

"Those are mere scraps, though."

She laughed. "Wait and see. Arms up."

Kevi waited until I stretched my arms and then folded the fabric over itself, thickening it. She bound it around my breasts, tying it tightly at my back. She folded a slightly larger scrap in two again and tied it around my waist.

"It barely covers my backside!" I gasped, scandalized, bending to see if it even did.

"It does," she playfully defended. "You look divine, Atena. The Lumin will enjoy it. I promise you that."

"Caelum might kill Beron if I go swimming with him in this."

Kevi shrugged. "Invite him along."

"He's busy."

She grinned knowingly. "He won't be if he sees you in that."

"I want to invite Caelum along," I told Beron as we walked out of Kevi's room and down the hall. He quickly thanked my friend and jogged to catch up.

He took one look at what I was wearing and groaned. "You can't saunter through the halls wearing only that. He'll kill me!" he lamented.

"*You* were the one who wanted me to swim. *You* took me to Kevi to be outfitted properly. I don't see what all the fuss is about." I had nothing covering me but the skimpy swimming garment, but I didn't see a problem with it. I wasn't ashamed of my body in the least.

He pinched the broken bridge of his nose.

"Take me to him, Beron, or I'll smile at the next guard I see, flutter my lashes, and ask him instead. *Then* he would kill you."

Beron gave a soft curse. "Fine. Follow me."

He led me back to the first floor to a set of double doors engraved with Lumos rising over the water, the likeness from what I'd witnessed this morning uncanny. Then he knocked. As we waited, I let my fingers drift over the bumps and ridges and dips until the door was jerked open. Caelum stood there, his face surprised when he saw me standing there. Then his eyes raked down me and back up.

I had read once that ice could be so cold, it would burn the skin of someone who held it long enough. Burning ice was such a paradox I never dreamed could be true, until I saw Caelum's icy blue eyes catch with silver flame and felt cool air rush off him like snow being dragged off the mountains he thought I could not melt. I felt confident I could melt them now...

I straightened my spine. "I wanted to invite you to go swimming with me and Beron."

His eyes flicked to his brother as if he only just realized he was present. "She's going swimming. In the ocean."

Beron cleared his throat. "Yes."

"With you?"

Again, Beron answered, "Yes."

"Wearing that?"

I crossed my arms and his eyes were drawn to my plumped breasts. "What, exactly, is wrong with my ensemble?"

Two men, identical twins, approached from behind Caelum. Both waved to me. "Hello, Atena," one said, grinning. Their eyes slid down me appreciatively and I stood straighter. Perhaps Kevi was right and these scraps were more weapon than apparel.

I waved back to him.

"You..." Caelum started.

I put my hand up. I'd heard enough. I wanted to swim and so I would. If he was too busy and couldn't go, that was fine, too.

"Beron is going to teach me to swim. If you're too busy, I'll see you later."

I walked away from the room with the pretty door and Beron fell into step behind me. "Do you have any idea what you just did?" he hissed.

"What?"

"You dismissed the Lumin. In front of his council."

My steps slowed. "What council?"

"Caelum has collected a group of men and women from varying regions and walks of life. He consults them for their opinions on matters that affect them."

"Why?" My father never asked for anyone's opinion. He didn't care about anyone's but his own. He was the ruler. As was Caelum. He didn't need anyone else.

"Because he cares about Lumos's people. He carries their pleas to the god of night and asks for his judgment. Caelum might not be able to do everything they want, but he tries his very best for them. He's good and fair, but he couldn't be that if he didn't know the problems his people face. Lumina has regions. Some are far south in the colder climates where the mountains are. I know Helios is a sole city, but Lumina is vast and there are many cities and towns to consider, not to mention those who choose to live outside them."

We walked out of the House of the Moon and into the pale sand again. I wondered if it was white or blue. I couldn't tell in Lumos's light.

I bit my thumb. Worry made the phoenix claw the inside of my stomach. "I didn't mean to embarrass him."

He opened his mouth to speak when I heard Caelum call my name. I whirled around to see him step out the door and jog down the steps, tugging his tunic over his head. "Wait for me."

I tried not to stare as the moonlight slid over him like pale blue silk, but the muscles his tunics never quite hid looked much better uncovered. My eyes roved over his toned chest, sculpted stomach, and the V that dipped at his hips. As he jogged his body flexed and flared, carrying him swiftly across the powdery sand.

Beron hooked a thumb toward his brother with disbelieving eyes. "He's not even upset! I don't know what you've done to him, but I like it."

Caelum smiled as he caught up. "Hey."

I steeled my spine and held my head high as his gaze slid over me. Somewhere in my periphery, I heard Beron doing something. Then splashes came from the water. Beron trudged through the waves, letting them break on him, then dove beneath one. I gestured toward him and shook my head. "I can't do that."

"Walk in with me," Caelum said, holding out a hand. "I've got you." I clasped his cool palm and he tugged me into the water. "We'll go as slow as you like," he promised.

I walked in a few feet, letting a wave hit my calves, then deeper still. One rolled over my knees. "Where's Beron?" I asked. He'd been submerged far longer than I thought was advisable.

"Don't worry about him. He would live in the water if he could."

I took another step as a wave hit my thighs, splashing up my stomach. It was cold, but steam rose from my skin.

Caelum laughed in wonder. "Your heat is remarkable."

Blushing, I turned to the sea again. "He's been under the waves a very long time, Caelum."

Just then, something grabbed my ankle and I shrieked and climbed Caelum like a palm tree, hooking my ankles around his back like I had when he pressed me to the wall.

Beron emerged, howling with laughter and smacking the surface of the water with his palms. "That was hilarious!"

I didn't respond. Caelum held me, his hands just beneath my bottom. I was fastened to him, unable to see anything but his eyes sparkling in the moonlight, the gleam of it hitting his teeth as he smiled. His dark hair dripped from the splash I must have delivered in my panic to get out of the water and away from the creature who'd grabbed my ankle.

"I thought you wanted to learn to swim," he pouted. "If my brother is going to teach you… other things, I think I should go back inside," Beron said, watching the ocean and waiting for a reply.

I pressed a kiss on Caelum's lips and unhooked my ankles, falling back into the water. His hands trailed away as I turned to face Beron and kicked the next briny wave, delivering a blow of saltwater straight into his teasing face.

Not that it bothered him. Laughing, he floated on his back. "I deserved that."

"Yes, you did."

Caelum walked in a little further, waving for me to come with him. The waves gobbled him to the waist.

Something brushed against my leg, and this time I knew it wasn't Beron. I could see him where he floated on top of the waves far deeper than where I was standing. "Um, Caelum?" I whispered in a shrill tone, my body shaking.

He turned. "What's the matter?"

"Is there a swarm of jellyfish or sirens in the water?"

He tilted his head. "I don't see any jellies, and I was only teasing about the sirens."

"What exactly would a siren feel like if it touched you?"

Caelum looked to Beron, who stood up to laugh at me this time. "Sirens are in the deep ocean, if they exist at all. Some sailors insist they do, but they're half woman, half fish. A woman with a tail. They have beautiful voices and delight in luring men into the water to their death."

"Do they touch the bare legs of those who wade in?" I squeaked, trying to peer into the dark, foaming water for a sign of a hand, or perhaps the scales of a human-sized tail.

"When the men dive in, the sirens take their hands and drag them into the depths, drowning them."

My eyes widened. "Something just touched my leg!"

Caelum waded to me. "There are fish in the sea; that's all it likely was. Beron is right. We've never encountered a siren. They are legend, not fact."

"Every legend is grounded in fact," I argued, unable to peel my eyes from the water.

"Hey," he said gently. I finally looked up into his face. "If you aren't comfortable in the deeper waters, we'll go back to the shallows."

I was pretty sure waist-deep was considered shallow but decided to bite my tongue. "I want to stay." *For now.*

Beron patted the water's surface like he was in a padded chair. "Sink down."

I slowly lowered into it, laughing as plumes of steam rose again from the skin that hadn't yet been cooled by the cold waves and splashes. Knees bent, I tried to bob on the waves like he was doing.

Caelum moved to stand next to me. "I'm glad I ended the council meeting early."

"I didn't mean to embarrass you, Caelum."

His brows twitched. "You didn't." I glanced to Beron, who shrugged. "She didn't," Caelum reiterated for his brother's benefit.

Beron motioned to the water. "You should learn to float, Noor."

He demonstrated, looking like a piece of wood being carried by the waves. I leaned back and attempted to mimic his serene pose, then quickly went under the surface. I inhaled a lungful of saltwater as I panicked and tried to resurface. When my feet finally found the sand, I emerged, coughing and sputtering. I noticed Beron and Caelum each had an arm and I realized they must have pulled me up. Apparently, floating was not as easy as it seemed.

"I don't like floating," I told him between hacks, then I laughed.

The brothers relaxed and laughed with me.

I was content to bob in the shallows under the Lumin's watchful eye, and thankfully I didn't feel another creature slither past my skin. For hours, the Lumin, the Wolven, and the future Aten were merely Caelum, Beron, and Noor, laughing about nothing and chatting about ironies like how the moon had once loved the sun.

Caelum described the eclipses he'd read about, how Lumos would shield Sol from harm for a time. It was a beautiful sentiment, two beings who were sculpted for another purpose, finding one in each other.

It was reminiscent of Caelum and me.

And just as I felt a measure of contentment, I received a vision...

I was home. In Helios. I felt Sol's heat. Felt her fire on my skin. In my bones. In my blood.

And I was filled with a sense of what had to be done as I watched myself walk toward the sun and my destiny.

# 24

When we left the beach, I walked to my rooms to change and found a steaming bath waiting for me. I almost melted into the hot water. The salt and sand fell to the bath's bottom and I washed my hair in soap that smelled of intoxicating flowers. The floral scent filled the room.

Once I washed the brine off my skin and hair, I stepped out of the bath and dried off with a thick towel, squeezing the water from my hair. I combed the snarls from my hair and dressed in one of the remaining gowns I hadn't worn before, a deep brown, trimmed in gold, of course. My sister and I needed to have a little chat, but not before I checked on Kiran.

My eyes were slowly adjusting to the low light and I found the descent and path to Kiran's room much easier to make now. Lumos was high and his light filtered through every window – of which there were many, covered in glass so clear it made me wonder if it was actually ice.

Everyone wore more clothing here than we did in Helios. I always felt warm, if not hot, so I had no idea if the air was cold enough to freeze water like Caelum had described.

There was no ice in the sea… or on the river now. Sol's warm breath could've thawed it when she pushed us here, though. I knocked on Kiran's door.

"Come in."

I eased the door open and stepped inside to see him sitting on the floor beside the hearth. The fire crackled and popped, the embers flexing red to black. "Hi."

He tried to smile. "Hi."

"I hope I'm not interrupting…"

"No," he said, a pained expression contorting his face. "I was just thinking about you, actually."

"Uh, oh," I teased.

He grinned then. "About the revelations we've learned."

"I'd like to keep them between us."

"Us and Caelum, you mean," he corrected.

"I did tell him, yes."

"Do Beron or Citali know?" he asked, moving his forearms to his knees.

"No."

I walked closer, then sat across from him and waited. I thought he might scold me for not allowing him to whisper prayers over Saric's body before I took him away, or for going on with life in the hours since he'd passed. Sol knew I felt guilty about it, yet I knew it was what Saric would have wanted. Not just want, but expect.

The grains in my hourglass were steadily funneling away, counting down the moments until I fully came of age. I wondered if inheriting the full powers Sol would grant meant they would wash over me like a great wave, or whether she would begin with the seed she'd planted, watching it sprout and blossom and grow steadily as I made my way back to Helios.

"I was sitting in the sea when I saw a vision, Kiran."

He sat up straighter. "What did you see?"

"It was only a flash, but I was in Helios, walking through the sand toward the temple. My father was waiting for me on top of it."

"What happened?"

"It ended there. Just a few seconds of a glimpse was all I was given."

Kiran shook his head, his eyes wide. "We have to go back. You have to set things right, Noor. Even if in your heart you want to stay here with him."

I nodded. "I was hoping you'd still go with me. I know I handled Saric's death wrong. I know you have prayers and rituals you're supposed to do before…" I choked on the last word.

He shook his head, leaning toward me and putting a hand on my upper arm. "You did exactly as you should have. We are not in Helios, and Saric took your hand and asked for your help. He knew, Noor. He knew what would happen when he did that. You took him directly to Sol. There's no prayer I could whisper or oil I could rub on his skin that could possibly compete with that."

I nodded, tears welling again.

"You loved him," he said softly. I nodded. "He loved you, too, Noor."

I knew that. He'd done so much for me. Saric was so kind and patient. He'd put himself at risk many times trying to protect me through the years. His wisdom and guidance had been priceless along this journey. And if I was being honest and selfish, I was afraid to keep going without it and him.

"You alone have to guide me now, Priest Kiran."

He gave a tender smile. "Noor, I will gladly walk into Helios at your side as you reclaim what is rightfully yours, but you don't need guidance. You were born for this. You were born to burn. You only have to focus your flame."

My father's face entered my mind, the vision of his sneer as clear as if he sat in front of me. I pictured him burning.

"He's planning something. He won't give up his position and power without a fight."

Kiran nodded. "I'm sure he is, Noor, but with Sol's fire in you, there's nothing he can do to stop you."

I hoped he was right. The scared child who huddled in my heart pushed further into my heart's wall, wondering what blow he would deal next and if it might be the one that killed her.

"Caelum was hoping to have a quiet dinner tonight to welcome us to Lumina, but he said he could postpone it in light of Saric's death if we wished."

Kiran leaned his head against the glassy wall behind him. "Saric would absolutely refuse to allow us to postpone anything."

I smiled. "That's what I told him. I wanted to make sure it was okay with you, though."

He blinked toward the ceiling. "I miss him, but it was time for him to go. He told me he would die in Lumina before we left Helios. I watched his health decline but didn't want to accept the truth. He knew, and he was ready."

"It doesn't ease the pain of missing him, though," I told him.

"No. No, it doesn't."

We were quiet for a few minutes. The only noise came from the popping fire. "A quiet dinner sounds nice," he said, tired. He probably wanted to be anywhere but at the dinner, but I truly needed him there. I wouldn't have asked otherwise. I was running out of time.

"I'll come find you at moonset."

He nodded. "You'll have to. I'll never find you in all this darkness."

I laughed. "It is terribly dark when Lumos leaves this place."

I tried to envision Helios swathed in darkness, but it wasn't easy.

Beron stood outside Citali's door. He looked almost giddy when I approached. He unlocked it, then bent to whisper, pinching his fingers together, a tiny space left between. "Scorch her just a little. For me?"

I didn't make any promises but didn't refuse before I pushed the door open and barged inside.

Citali sat up from where she lay on her bed, her eyes sharpening. "What are *you* doing here?"

"We need to talk."

She fell back onto the mattress. "You're the last person I want to see."

"I can make it so you don't have to see me again," I offered, making myself comfortable in her windowsill. Lumos peeked in the window. His cool light fell over me, spilling onto the floor and reflecting off the glass tile walls, lighting the darkened space.

Citali's lips began to tremble. Tears spilled from her eyes onto her cheeks and left glistening trails down her skin. "I can't... I can't do this anymore!"

I narrowed my eyes at her, unmoved by her outburst.

She tucked a pillow against her chest like she used to do as a child when she was upset. For many long moments, we stared at each other, something urgent passing between us. What could possibly upset her so thoroughly? My unshakeable sister.

She slipped off the bed. I left the windowsill, unsure what she was doing or if she'd lash out. She crept closer and her eyes flicked to the door. She grabbed a piece of parchment, dipped her unstained quill into the vat of ink, and scrawled: *Have you seen it?*

My brows kissed.

*The crown,* she wrote.

We were back to this again? I shook my head.

*I need it, Noor. Please.*

I glared at her, struck a match, and lit the candle on the desktop. Flame caught the wick and climbed, then steadied. I jerked the parchment from her hand and held it to the lit candle on the desk's edge. The parchment's uneven edge burned, then fire spread across in hungry flickers. I walked my hands around the edge to avoid the fire, then dropped the parchment when most had been consumed.

"I can't go home without it," she whispered, a plea on her brow.

"Why? Why is it so important to you?"

She clamped her lips together.

"If you don't tell me, Citali, how am I to ever understand you?"

More tears fell as she looked to the ceiling, as if Sol shone above and she was imploring the goddess of fire for help.

What could Father have threatened her with to turn her into a nervous, stumbling, sad version of the young woman she once was? What could he be holding over her head? What did Citali value? What did she love?

And how was he manipulating and using it to brandish against my sister as a weapon?

Anger flooded my veins. I hated him. His every breath was a dishonor to my mother.

She grabbed my forearm and my fire surged to meet her touch. She shrieked and released me, stumbling backward in shock. Her hip bumped into the bed. Beron heard the commotion and burst in, glancing darkly between us.

Citali held her hand to her chest, panting. "What was that?" she said, her words as ragged as her soul.

"You have your secrets, Citali. And I have mine." I streaked across the room, shoved Beron out, and slammed the door behind me.

"So," he drawled, "does this mean she doesn't get an invitation for dinner tonight?"

"Have hers delivered to her room," I snapped. "And I want her watched at all times."

He nodded, still on edge. "Want to tell me what's really going on?" I flashed him a warning glare. He raised his hands, grinning at my anger. "Or not." I stormed down the hall. "If you and my brother don't work out, Noor, I *love* fiery women."

My feet didn't stop or falter. I didn't want Beron and he knew it. He just liked to poke the lioness when she roared. He wouldn't feel the same way if I bit.

Back in my room, the book was where I'd hidden it.

# 25

Garbed in a fitted dress that was royal blue bordering on purple, I locked my room and stepped across the hall to knock on Caelum's door. He'd intercepted me on the way back from Citali's and asked if I would come and get him after I was finished dressing.

He yelled for me to come in, so I did, leaving the door open behind me for propriety's sake. Caelum was in the bathing room. "I'll be right out."

"Take your time."

I took the opportunity to wander around his room, quickly realizing it was outfitted much like my suite with the same colors and glassy walls. His bed was enormous and far too large for its single intended occupant. His armoire was similar to mine, and where my furniture was pale wood, his had been painted white. At the window, Lumos's light waned. It was almost moonset.

"What could you possibly be doing?" I asked with a chuckle, trying to determine how much longer he would be.

I was curious if our rooms were *exactly* the same, down to the secret hiding place tucked in the wall. Could that be where he kept the crown? I didn't want or need it now, but Citali did. If I knew it was here, I could ask Beron to place a guard at Caelum's rooms after we left.

I drifted across to the wall, feeling along the tiles until one came unhinged. Reaching my hand inside, I discovered the space was bare.

I closed it just as I heard his footsteps, then rushed back toward the entry door. My heart thundered and fire forked like lightning through my veins.

If he would have caught me, he would think I meant to steal it. While that was why I initially came, it wasn't what I wanted or needed now. Now, I needed to keep Citali at bay until I dragged her back to Helios with me.

Caelum finally emerged from the bathing room with his dark hair sleeked back, wearing a black tunic, pants, and boots, looking like a dark king.

Ironically, the only thing missing was his crown.

I smiled as I drank him in, watching the muscles I had memorized earlier flex as he walked. He carried a rectangular box. "I was hoping you'd wear this." Flipping it open, he revealed a silver chain dripping with moon diamonds shaped like tears, the mirror to my sun diamonds.

I gasped. "I can't accept such an extravagant gift from you, Caelum. I appreciate the gesture and I'm touched that you went out of your way, but this is too much!"

"Then accept it from my mother. She had this made for you."

"How did she commission it? She's not here."

He looked down, looking almost shy. "She had it made years ago, before I even wrote to your father. Beron saw it in a dream and my mother wanted me to give it to the woman who captured my heart."

The phoenix in my stomach flew circles. "I haven't agreed to marry you. I'm not even sure I can."

His lashes fluttered. "I know that, but I want you to have this... regardless what happens. It, and my heart, belong to you." He removed the necklace from its blue velvet nest. "Please?" he asked, holding an end in each hand.

I couldn't speak. A knot the size of one of the tear-shaped diamonds filled my throat. Matching tears filled my eyes. I turned so he wouldn't see, lifted my hair, and presented the slender column of my neck.

He fastened it and brushed his cool fingers over my skin. "Thank you."

I turned around to face him. "It's I who should thank you."

He shook his head and took my hands in his. "My heart is yours, Noor. I can't help but feel even closer to Lumos after knowing you, because I now know what it's like to love and want something you might be forbidden from having. I want a life with you. I want nothing more than that."

But we had responsibilities and duties greater than our wants and needs. We were servants, vessels of the gods, subject to their wills and not ours.

Lumos's light disappeared from the room and we were plunged into darkness.

Dinner was held in one of the smaller dining rooms. Caelum and I stopped to pluck Kiran from his room before the three of us made our way down the hall. The room held a simple table, long enough to comfortably accommodate twenty or so people. Pale wood chairs were tucked in all around it. None of them were occupied, though a few people stood conversing in the room. A tall candelabra stood in the table's middle with at least a dozen lit candles, casting golden light over the room. Beron strode in behind us, merging with our small group.

"Thank you for coming," Caelum said confidently as he strode to the table's head, guiding me to the seat at his right hand. He held it out for me and waited until I sat, then pushed it in and took his own. Kiran sat on my right and Beron settled across from me. The others, whom I did not know yet, took their seats on either side of the table.

The room was quiet until water and wine were served, along with steaming plates of food – some of which I recognized from the platters served at the ball Lumina had hosted in the dusk lands, not that I had the time or a stomach solid enough to hold any on *that* particular evening. I'd been a bundle of nerves, worried that the plan to drug Father would go awry.

Kiran was quiet beside me.

Caelum cleared his throat and looked out over the table. "I'd like to introduce you to Atena Noor and one of Sol's priests, Kiran."

I glanced at the occupants who sat at the table. I recognized two men who looked identical with gray beards and hair, broad noses and kind eyes. They were sitting beside Beron, and had greeted me when I asked Caelum to come swimming with me. Beside them was a woman with hair the color of fresh blood. She wore furs around her neck and feathers in her hair. Beside Kiran sat an older woman, more matronly than the redhead across the table. She wore a woolen dress and shawl, and her darker hair was pulled tightly back into a bun at the base of her neck. A man sat beside her in a woolen coat. His hair was light, almost the color of dried reeds. He nodded toward me. "Atena."

"This is my council," Caelum explained, introducing each person by name. "They come from different regions and represent the people who live there and their needs, as I can't be everywhere at once. The twins, Malcolm and Halstrom, come from the eastern villages." The men dipped their chins. "Greta hails from the southlands – the coldest in Lumina."

The redheaded Greta nodded. "And the rowdy couple beside Kiran is Jenna and Landon, from the western plains." The two waved at me and Kiran good naturedly.

"Do you have the opportunity to travel to the other regions?" I asked.

He nodded, a graceful smile blossoming across his handsome face. "I make a trip to each of them yearly."

That was nice. My father never deigned to leave his palace.

"I'd like to see the snow-covered mountains one day," I told them, nudging Caelum's knee with mine and biting back a knowing grin. "If it's safe, that is. Caelum believes my warmth might threaten them."

The table erupted in laughter. "I can feel the heat wafting from you," Halstrom, one of the ruddy-cheeked twins said with a jovial wink. "He might be right!"

Caelum grinned as we filled our plates and smaller conversations erupted up and down the table. This group of people was obviously comfortable with each other. Almost familial.

Beron pointed to a dish. "You should try it, Noor. It's so spicy it makes me sweat."

"I've never sweated," I deadpanned.

His lips parted. "Seriously?"

I rolled my eyes. "No, not seriously. Of course I've sweated. Never from spicy food, but certainly from exertion."

"But not heat?" he clarified.

I shook my head. "Never heat."

Kiran was quiet beside me and I worried this was too much activity too soon after Saric's passing. Then he reached out and selected some of what Beron suggested, scooped a bite of the peppered meat, and chewed. In seconds, his eyes widened as he reached for his water and gulped it down. "Wow," was all he could muster once the water tempered the spicy flavors. Then he laughed.

I was glad to hear the sound.

Not to be outdone, I took a bit for my plate and chewed slowly while Beron watched with narrowed eyes, waiting for a reaction just as severe as Kiran's or for sweat to bead on my skin. "You call this spicy?" I asked after primly swallowing it down.

The twins cackled and Malcolm slapped Beron on the back. He wagged a finger in my direction. "Don't mess with this one!"

I glanced at Caelum to see him already smiling.

After that, everyone seemed to settle into comfortable, companionable conversation and dinner passed quickly. Caelum's council members each told me it was nice to meet me and excused themselves until only the four of us remained: me, Beron, Caelum, and Kiran.

Kiran nodded to the door. "I think I'll go to my rooms now if you don't need anything, Atena," he said quietly.

With his usage of my title, I knew he was erecting a wall between us. I'd built enough between me and those I cared for to recognize the distance he was placing between us with formalities. But this one, at least, was a necessary one for which I would gladly provide the mortar.

"Good night, Priest."

He stood and bent in a respectful bow before leaving the dining room.

Moments later, footsteps pounded down the hallway. An enormous man filled the doorframe, catching himself on it and breathing heavily. "Pardon the interruption, Lumin." He bowed, then turned his attention to Beron. "Beron, sir. We have a situation."

"*What* situation?" the Wolven asked frostily.

"The girl has escaped," the behemoth panted, both from anger and exhaustion. His face was red and sweat poured from his brow.

"How could she possibly escape?" The legs of Beron's chair scraped the glassy tile as he stood. He strode around the table and out the door.

Caelum released a weary sigh. "They'll find her."

I had no doubt. No matter how determined Citali was to defy the rules, or how desperate she was to claim the crown so she wouldn't return home empty-handed, Beron's anger fueled his wolfish senses. As if I'd predicted the future, I heard his howl from outside the House of the Moon.

Caelum and I jogged to the door, down the grand staircase, and stepped into the sand. Beron was still in wolf form, slowly circling Citali, who had the nerve to hiss at the enormous canine snarling and snapping his teeth at her. "*I will not be caged!*" she shouted, turning in a circle along with him. It was a dangerous dance she stepped.

"Citali!" I snapped, my eyes quickly adjusting to the darkness surrounding us.

"Your *eyes,*" she said disgustedly.

The fire in me must have ignited them. "You are a guest here, Citali. Show some respect."

Her laugh was harried. "I no longer wish to be."

I shook my head disbelievingly. "You want to return to Helios?"

She began to cry again, slapping a hand over her chest. It heaved beneath her palm. "I can't."

"Can't what?"

"I can't go back to Helios yet! I. Can't!" she shrieked, completely losing control. "I can't and you *know* why."

"Citali, I can arrange for a ship to carry you home," Caelum offered kindly.

Her laugh was pitiful. She shook her head. "I can't leave without it. Right, Noor?"

"What's she talking about?" Caelum asked.

Beron calmed, wading into the waves where he turned from Wolven to man again. Caelum stripped off his tunic and tossed it to his brother, who tied it around his waist as he waded naked from the sea. Beron joined his brother, pooled droplets of brine dripping from his skin. "I'm curious to know what she's talking about, too."

He shook the water from his hair and gave Citali, then me, a lazy look that was far scarier than Caelum's concerned one. It was like he was trying to hide how angry he was with Citali, and I knew soon, he would be angry with me. So would Caelum.

Citali was breaking. She was going to tell them about our directive for the crown.

I steeled my spine, hoping they could understand, and gambling that delivering the information myself would lessen the blow. "Your suspicions were right. Father asked us to bring him the crown of moonlight. That's the real reason why he accepted your proposal – for one of us – and why negotiations went so quickly and smoothly in the dusk lands."

Citali angrily swiped her tears away. She would regain control of her emotions eventually, then hate me for telling them. She'd say I ruined everything, that she hadn't completely lost control, that she never would have told them. All lies she would have made herself believe.

"He wants Lumina," Beron said, pinching his once-broken nose.

"He wants everything," I corrected.

Citali seethed even as she cried, even as she struggled to catch a steady breath. She inched toward the sea. Her teeth chattered as if she was slowly freezing.

Caelum stepped closer. "I asked you – in the dusk lands, I asked you if you were after my crown."

I stood up straighter as his chest bumped mine. "I told you that I was."

"I thought you were teasing me," he said softly. He rubbed his hands down my bare arms, his cool touch soothing the flame.

Citali stopped crying and flung a hand toward us. "You're not even angry at her!"

He wasn't, which she couldn't understand. I'd told him the truth about who and what I was, just as I was telling him the truth now, and she still didn't know about me, my heritage, or that in two days, I would become the new Aten.

She shook her head, disgusted. "I can't believe this *or* stomach the pair of you."

She took up her skirts and trudged back to the House of the Moon. Despite her frazzled state, I knew she wouldn't leave and wouldn't stop looking for the crown she wanted so badly. Citali was a great many things, but she didn't quit once she set her eyes on something. She might pause to catch her breath. She might cry. Panic. Rage. But she would not stop.

Panicked sobs tore from her frail form and I couldn't help but watch as she fled.

I had no idea how to help her. That was the most devastating thing of all. Citali was terrified to tell me what she needed to rush home for, but she knew she needed to go back – crown in hand. The thought of Father hurting her or even Zarina like he had me soured my stomach. For as wretched as my sisters could be, we three were chiseled by our father's cruelty, and all subject to it, I realized.

Caelum's fingers trailed up and down, up and down my arms. "Walk with me?"

I nodded.

"Beron." Something passed between the brothers and the Wolven angrily rushed after my sister.

Caelum guided us away from the House and we made twin tracks in the dampened sand as the waves reached out for our feet, never quite overtaking them.

"Truthfully, I suspected that you and Citali wanted the crown, or that your father did, or both," he admitted when we were so far from the House, I could no longer make it out in the darkness. "That's why I asked you then, and why I warned you that you wouldn't find it."

"Are you saying it doesn't exist?" I asked.

"No, it does, but it isn't displayed often. It was given to me the day he made me Lumin." He paused as if collecting his thoughts. "Lumos doesn't want people to feel that they should bow to me or that I rule over them. I'm a bridge to him, not an impediment. I don't stand in his way; I foster communication between him and his people."

"Beron didn't see it that day?"

He shook his head. "My mother did. It was the only way I could convince her to go with me to the House of the Moon. I showed it to her and to the priests the day I was chosen, but Beron wasn't home. He came home a couple days afterward. He had left to go on a hunt to find food for us and turned into the Wolven while he was in the woods. He came back from the forest and was terrified because he didn't understand what was going on. He said the change was excruciating the first time. He thought the pain would happen every time he needed to shift, but it didn't hurt after that."

"Does he like being the Wolven?"

"Most days, he revels in it. But there is the occasional difficult day where the duty seems to be more burden than honor."

My sister was making this one of the difficult days. Caelum stopped in a secluded section of shoreline where a few boulders lay on the sand, slowly weathering away by the pounding surf at high tide. I wondered how large they'd once been and where they came from. I saw no mountains here.

He placed a soft kiss on my forehead. "She won't find the crown. Let her look all she likes. As long as she doesn't attempt to hurt or kill you again, she can search to her heart's content." His eyes held mine for a moment and suddenly a cool glow circled his forehead. A white-blue, scarred crown lay in his skin, not over it. It wasn't made of metal, but moonlight. It was part of Caelum as much as the wolf was part of Beron.

I raised my hand and he lowered his head as I brushed a thumb over the crown of moonlight, feeling only his silken skin beneath. Smiling with wonder, I pulled his face to mine and pressed my lips to his. "It's beautiful," I told him.

"You don't need my crown, Noor," he said.

"I don't want it." Somehow, the thing I came here to find turned out to be the last thing I needed.

"The question is, do you want me, Noor?" he rasped.

I pressed my lips to his again, letting them slowly peel away. "Yes."

With the stars glittering in the darkness all around us as innumerable as the grains of sand beneath us, the secrets between us fell away, leaving only caresses of flesh and his lips on mine when we gave ourselves to one another completely.

When Lumos reappeared and we walked out of our secluded, rocky place, back to the House of the Moon, I wondered if Sol had ever burned as hot as I had in those passionate moments. If Lumos had coveted her touch as much as Caelum coveted mine. If, like the gods who wanted nothing more than each other, we might be forced apart tomorrow. I only had today to spend with him – the way I was now - before I was transformed.

Tomorrow was my seventeenth birthday.

# 26

Caelum refused to leave my side, afraid the change would begin any moment and I'd need his help; namely his frost to cool me and keep me from bursting into a flame so incendiary no one could put it out.

He was afraid for me, but afraid for Lumina, too.

I lay with him while he napped in my room, raking my fingers through his hair as his head lay on my chest, his arms around my waist as I reclined on a mound of pillows. The cadence of his breathing was calming and rhythmic.

Beron knocked lightly and let himself into my rooms. He tipped his chin up. "Didn't he get enough sleep last night?" he whispered.

I shook my head, heat flooding my cheeks.

The dimple in his cheek popped as he smiled and raised his brows, likely drawing his own conclusions... which weren't wrong. "He told me to let your sister do whatever she wanted."

"What's she doing?"

Beron smirked. "Sticking her nose in every nook and cranny it doesn't belong in. She thinks we don't know, but we can hear every move she makes. Every swish of her ridiculous skirts, every drawer she pulls out and pushes back in, every door handle she turns."

"Your hearing is impressive."

"That's the least powerful of my senses."

I smiled, mindlessly playing with Caelum's hair and inhaling his scent. He smelled of alpine freshness mixed with saltwater and something distinctly his... Frost, I thought.

Caelum shifted, then blinked once, twice. His crystal blues settled on my face. "I didn't mean to fall asleep."

"It's okay. You needed to rest."

"I need you more," he said.

Beron lamented, "You two are ridiculously sappy."

Caelum lifted his head and groaned at the sight of his brother in my room.

"Good afternoon to you, too, brother."

Caelum's arm tensed around my back. "Afternoon?"

I nodded.

He sat up, scrubbed his eyes, blinked them, and yawned.

"I came to let you know that everything has been arranged as you requested," Beron said, sitting up straighter.

"What has been arranged?" I asked.

Caelum shook his head once, preventing his brother from answering. "Thank you, Beron." He tipped his head toward the door and Beron took the unsubtle hint and left us alone again.

"What is arranged?" I asked.

"I was hoping you'd have dinner with me."

I relaxed. "Of course."

He sat up and leaned in for a kiss. "I was also hoping to show you something before. But... tonight, you should wear something formal."

"Formal?"

He nodded. "I want dinner to be special."

"Okayyyyy." I drew out the word, unsure of what exactly he had planned.

"Would you like for me to have water brought up for you?" he asked.

"That would be perfect."

He kissed my lips once. Then kissed me again, holding the back of my head and staying that way for a long moment. I memorized the sweep of his dark lashes before he opened his eyes and pulled away.

"Meet me in a couple of hours?" he asked, standing up. I stood, too. "Kiran will be there, as will Beron. Do you want Citali to come?"

"You can leave it up to her." She likely wouldn't come now that her leash had been cut and she was given the freedom to snoop. I'd have to drag her home to stop her obsession with finding the crown.

He left my room, stopping to wave goodbye. I waved back, but the moment the door was closed, I pressed a hand against my stomach. He showed me the crown when his own brother hadn't seen it.

He was frost and I was fire. He was moonlight and I was the daughter of the burning sun. I knew what she was capable of. I'd seen her heat ignite flesh and burn it to nothing.

Would the transition change my heart? My mind? Would I still be me?

I panicked in silence until it came time for my bath to be filled. Then, when I was left with only steaming water and my racing thoughts, I panicked some more.

My hair was still wet when I braided it and pinned it at the base of my head. I'd chosen a canary yellow gown made in the style of the one I'd worn to the Helioan feast in the dusk lands. The top was cropped and its skirt clung to my hips, then fell to the ground in airy layers. The fabric was silky and seemed to float as I moved. I wore my sun diamonds, of course, on my wrist and ankle. But on my neck, the tear-drop-shaped moon diamonds hung.

Caelum knocked just as I finished lacing my sandals. His eyes lazily raked down me before his hands slid around my waist and eased me forward where he met me with a fervent kiss. He wore a thick, pale blue tunic tonight, with dark blue trousers tucked into glossy black boots that shone like the tile floors. "I wanted to take you to meet my father. It's a bit of a walk, though."

"Walking sounds perfect." I was abuzz with nervousness.

We left the House of the Moon, skirted the river as it wended north, then cut across town through a gridwork of small, cobbled streets. People lived so tightly packed together here, their laundry was hung on lines strung across windows, close enough that they shouted back and forth to neighbors. Children scurried, dirty, through the streets, laughing and throwing discs to one another.

In the middle of the busy neighborhood was a large, fenced-in field where long slabs of stone lay over the ground in neat rows. Caelum opened the gate and led me through the rows to his father's inscribed name. He knelt beside it and placed a hand on the cool rock. "This is my father's grave."

I knelt and placed my hand beside his. My fingers drifted over the nearest corner, engraved with a wide thatched pattern.

"His name was Darak. He wove nets for the fishermen. It wasn't a high-paying job, but he loved it. He took pride in his work. And he loved me and Beron. Beron doesn't remember him as well as I do. He was very young when he died."

"What happened to him?"

"He collapsed one day and Mother couldn't rouse him. He died before a healer could reach him. There was nothing to be done, anyway. It was just time for him to take his place." Caelum glanced at the sky.

"Do you know which one is him?" I asked, regarding the starry sky.

He shook his head. "I'm not sure, but I don't know that it matters. He's there someplace, guiding, watching, waiting... I feel his presence even though he's physically absent."

"Is all of his body beneath this rock?" I asked.

His dark brows pinched.

"In Helios, when someone dies, Sol's fire is focused on the dead. She burns away every part of a body she finds acceptable and good. What she doesn't take is carried into the sand from which we were made. It's mostly ash and chips of bone. The priests are responsible for carrying most of the people into the dunes, but I was charged with carrying some of the most important remains."

He shook his head. "We bury our dead. The body he shed rests beneath the stone. All of it."

"Did the stone come from your mountains?"

"Yes."

The slab sparkled. It wasn't polished like glass, but I recognized it as the same whitish color of the rock that built the House of the Moon.

He stood and offered me a hand. "Thank you for coming here. We should head back so we're not late to dinner."

Caelum and I retraced our steps through the quaint, busy part of Lumina. Lumos had almost set when we walked up the front steps. Caelum lingered, facing him. I wondered if the two were talking and stayed quiet until he pivoted and opened the door.

Inside, things were quiet, eerily so. Where had everyone gone? It was evening, but I'd never seen the House so still or empty. My ears searched for the slightest noise but could not find anything to hone in on.

Our footsteps echoed down the hall as Caelum took my hand. Someone had already prepared the House for moonset. Candles were lit over every thin table and perched on every sturdy surface in the rooms we passed. They flared in sconces.

We approached the Great Hall, whose doors had been wedged open. It was the only room that hadn't been lit.

And then suddenly, flames appeared all over the space as hundreds of matches were struck and wicks lit at once. The firelight glowed to reveal many faces – the most familiar and beloved waiting just inside the door: Kiran, Kevi and her dancers, and Beron, who stood with Caelum's council. Citali was there, dressed in a wispy, yellow-orange gown. Even the riverfarer who'd shown me the spheres nodded toward me.

*Was he back so soon?* I searched the crowd for Vada's face, but didn't see her. Perhaps Caelum had sent a different ship.

I slid my arms around Caelum's waist as he pulled me close, his cool hands ghosting up my spine. "Surprise!"

"Is this for me?"

He smiled. Hugging me to his side, he gestured to the crowd. "Thank you for coming to celebrate Noor of Helios. Please, set your candles down and fill your plates and cups. Enjoy the music and evening as we celebrate Noor's birthday."

He hadn't called me Atena.

Everyone cheered at his exclamation, but my sister and Kiran stiffened. I ignored them, instead smiling and waving to everyone.

Long tables draped with golden silk stretched through the room, laden with food. Those attending placed their tapers in the candelabras arranged atop them. Beron pulled Caelum aside to whisper in his ear and Kiran took advantage of the separation. He stepped forward, a flash of gold in the darkness near his hands. "I hope you don't mind. Caelum let me into your rooms for a moment to retrieve this. I didn't disturb the rest of your things…"

He handed me my aureole. It had been packed away in my trunks and I hadn't worn it in Lumina yet. I placed it on my head, knowing in my heart it would be the last night I would wear it.

Caelum rejoined us, studying the golden spires and the gilded roses at its base. "It's beautiful. *You're* beautiful," he quietly said, his knuckles drifting over my hair.

The headdress's familiar weight was comforting. Nostalgic. It drew the eye of many of Caelum's Luminan friends.

And yet, it felt strange wearing it. Like I hadn't worn it hundreds of times. The gold didn't sing as mine anymore. The aureole wasn't different; the girl who wore it was. I wasn't just the daughter of the Aten anymore. Third born. Destined to be nothing more than a pretty party decoration.

Saric had said the transition began at birth, but now more than ever I felt just how different I was. I wasn't the Atena anymore, yet I was so much more than Aten.

I was born the heir of Sol, the sun, and fire.

I was born flame.

I was born to burn.

I wasn't born to stand in anyone's shadow, but to cast them.

Citali did not wear her aureole and didn't bother to hide her distaste for the entire gathering. She handed her candle to someone who offered to take it from her and stood silently and alone, looking me over as if she was looking at a stranger. Not at her sister with whom at one point she ran and jumped and played. Not even at the person she'd grown to blame and loathe.

What would she see in me tomorrow when I was completely different?

The change would be severe.

An energy pulsed beneath my skin. I was jittery. Ready.

A line had been drawn in gilded blood between Citali and me.

A brush of Caelum's thumb on my back drew my attention back where it belonged. "I hope this is okay with you."

I gave an indulgent smile. "It's perfect. I'm honored, Caelum."

No one had celebrated my birth since my mother crossed into the hereafter.

Great platters of delicious-smelling foods were brought to the tables. Clusters of vine fruit, a variety of cheeses, hot and cold meats, and my favorite – sliced bread with a seemingly endless assortment of jams.

Beron watched Citali closely, and it set me on edge. If she moved, he wasn't far behind. When she joined Caelum's council as they made their way to a smaller table at the front of the room, she glanced back to see if he was close, narrowing her eyes when she found that she hadn't shaken his attention.

Caelum hesitated near the door. He looked over the room, decorated in honor of my heritage, and for me. "It's a tradition in Lumina to celebrate our years and thank Lumos for as many as he's given us, while wishing for more to come. I certainly am grateful to Sol for your years, Noor."

My phoenix wrapped her smoldering wings around herself, warming my stomach from within.

He handed me a palm-sized, rectangular box. "What's this?" I asked in surprise.

"A gift to celebrate your seventeenth year. And... a promise from me."

I slid a silver ribbon from the box's corners and lifted the lid. On a bed of matching silk lay a silver cuff bracelet, much too large for my wrist. It looked similar to the cuffs Sol gave her priests when they pledged themselves to her. Like the wedding cuff Father had presented every one of his wives since my mother died...

"I heard it was the custom in Helios for bicep cuffs to be worn to show others you are committed. That is one tradition our kingdoms share." He smiled. "Lumos, like Sol, gives a cuff to his priests when they make their vow to him. They're covered by their robes, so you might not have seen them. But, it is our custom that when one wishes to pledge their life and fidelity to another, he offers a cuff of his own."

Engraved in the silver was the face of Lumos. Even his scars lay within the impression. "It's beautiful."

"You don't have to wear it now or... ever." He gently took the cuff from my fingers.

I could barely breathe.

He nodded. Turning the cuff around and around, he met my eyes. "When you're ready, if you want me... that's when you put it on. And I will know the moment you do. Take as much time as you need in Helios."

"What if I can never leave my kingdom for Lumina?"

He smiled. "I've been thinking a lot about that. The solution is obvious, but it will be difficult. Together, you and I can forge a new path. The past does not have to be our future. What if there doesn't have to be two separate kingdoms? What if we combine them to make our own?"

He tucked the cuff back into the silk lined box and eased the lid on, replacing the ribbon. "Does your dress have pockets?"

I nodded. "I insist upon them."

He handed the box to me, his crystalline blue eyes glittering with hope. I felt a glimmer of it in my heart, but the worries I couldn't melt soon snuffed it out. He made me a promise, telling me he wanted only me. I only wanted him, too; I just wasn't sure I could have him yet.

As we walked to the table, the cuff safely tucked into my pocket, I told him, "In Helios, we give Sol a gift for having allowed us another year."

"What will you give her tomorrow?" he asked softly.

I smiled, hoping I could truly manage the gift I wanted so badly to give her. "You'll see."

We ate the beautiful dinner, enjoyed the music that flowed over the room like silken banners of sound, and danced and laughed. For a brief moment in time, I forgot that the moon would soon rise and I would soon burn.

# 27

Before the celebration was over and while we could slip out together, people assuming we coveted privacy, Caelum and I made plans to abscond to our secluded spot on the beach, where we would spend the dark hours together. Where I would be far enough from the House of the Moon to ensure my secret and make sure those who lived in and near Lumina were safe.

Every moment this evening felt like it might be our last, and I couldn't help but again feel like we were a living reflection of Sol and Lumos, separated, yet almost close enough to touch. Stuck in a perpetual cycle of longing for something we could never have.

We made our way out of the crowd, pressing toward the doors that would free us. "Will you find Kiran? I need him with me," I told Caelum, pressing my lips to his once more. I couldn't stop kissing him. Couldn't get enough of his touch, the feel of his hand in mine, on the small of my back, brushing my cheek and jaw, pushing strands of hair from my face.

Time felt urgent. And that harried energy frenetically sizzling beneath my skin intensified with every passing second.

"Of course. Should we meet you at your room, or on the beach?"

"I just have to run and get a few things. I'll meet you on the beach."

He hesitated. "Should I send Beron with you?"

I shook my head. "He's busy watching Citali like he knows she's up to something."

"Is she?"

Sighing, I replied, "Yes. I just don't know what." I spotted Kevi in the crowd. "I just need a few moments," I promised.

He kissed me again and nodded, then located Kiran in the crowd and carved a path toward the priest of Sol, who appeared as a startling burst of warmth – ruddy flesh, gold kilt, and gilded cuff – against the mass of silver, blue, and paleness.

"Kevi!" I called out, tugging off my aureole. A few strands of my hair tangled in the spires.

She pulled me in for a hug with a wide smile. "Oh, to be seventeen again…"

"I want you to have this," I said, holding my headdress out to her.

She coughed a laugh. "Atena, I cannot accept this. Someone will assume I stole it and have my head!"

I insisted. "I'll make sure Caelum and Beron know it was freely given."

"It's too much," she argued, shaking her head, refusing to touch it at all.

"I promised I would see that you and your girls are taken care of."

Kevi quirked a perfectly arched brow. "Caelum is doing exactly that, and without using the sacred Atena's aureole as collateral. He's a good man, Atena Noor. A rare jewel, indeed." She pushed my hand away. "Perhaps one day you will have a daughter. Save this for her. Please."

"If you refuse, I'll have no choice but to leave my other gold jewelry in my armoire with a note that says you and your girls are to inherit it."

"Inherit?" she asked. "Are you unwell, Atena?"

I froze. "I'm leaving."

A fire lit in her eyes. "Are you going after him?"

I nodded once.

A devilish smile spread over her lips. Kevi leaned in and spoke against my ear. "Make him pay for every bruise and every drop of blood spilled. Then collect *our* debts as well."

I nodded, a promise in my eyes that I would do exactly that. "I have to go."

She hugged me again. "I believe in you, Noor."

I rushed to my room and unlocked the door. Hurrying to the desk, I lit the candle and scrawled a note to leave with my jewelry like I'd promised Kevi. Then, I slid my sandals off, tucked my aureole into one of my trunks, and removed the box from my pocket.

I changed into a gauzy dress that was a pale mixture of blue and green, slid Caelum's cuff into the pocket, and took a deep breath to steady myself. I had to hurry. But was everything ready? I only needed Mother's book...

I'd just raised a hand toward the secret compartment when Citali pushed the door open. She crossed her arms and leaned against the facing. "Why did you try to give that harlot your aureole?"

She'd been watching.

"Stop making assumptions, Citali. It makes you look like a fool. I took it off because it was heavy. I asked her to take it back to my room."

She shook her head, her dark eyes flaring. "You are a liar. I *heard* you, Noor. Did you find it?" she pressed. "Are you

319

going to take it to Father, or do you plan to claim this kingdom as your own?"

"Forget the crown of moonlight, Citali."

"Give. It. To. Me. Noor." She stepped inside, a dark flame in her eyes.

"I know you don't understand, but I have to have the crown, Noor."

"For what? Do you *actually* think Father will keep whatever promise he made you? If he has something you love, he will never set it or you free. You know that. You cannot give it to him."

"What will *you* use it for, then?" she asked.

She moved closer and I looked her over, not finding any weapons. "I don't have the damned crown, but rest assured that I would *never* have given it to Father!" I snapped. "*I* would have used it to destroy *him*. I would have moved the moon to forever block the sun if it meant he suffered."

She growled in response. "I wouldn't see it in his hands either, but I would pry from his clutches the thing I love most in this forsaken, wasted world."

"What's that? What do you love more than yourself, Citali?"

She seethed, but kept her secret, if she even had one.

"If you attempt to harm me again, I will take you from this world, and from whatever it is that is so important that you would try to take my life, take Caelum's crown and kingdom when you know… you *know* his heart and that Lumina was meant to be his."

Just then, Beron's large shape loomed in the space behind her. He jutted his chin at me in hello. "They're waiting for you on the beach. My brother gets antsy when he has to wait too long."

"Who is waiting? Who's with Caelum?" Citali demanded. "Tell me what's going on, Noor."

"Beron?" I said, ignoring her.

"Yes, Noor?" He left my former title behind just as his brother had downstairs, but couldn't disguise the grin I heard in his voice. He loved needling my sister.

"He's presenting you to Lumos, isn't he?" Citali whispered. "Isn't he?" she shouted.

I didn't have time for Citali's speculation or hysterics, nor did I have time for her envy or anger. My energy was building to a boil. I needed to get out of here. Fast.

My hands began to glow as I reached for the secret door built into the wall, sliding Mother's book from the shadows and tucking it into my pocket.

I took slow, deep breaths, willing the fire to settle. The light leeched from my skin and melted back into my middle.

"I'm going to need you to restrain my sister until Caelum or I instruct you to set her free."

A rumbling mixture of laughter and a growl tore from his chest. "With pleasure."

Citali scrambled into my room. "Don't lay a finger on me, mutt!" she seethed.

I slid out of the room and locked them inside. Citali would not shake Beron this time. He was far too keen on her tricks now.

Caelum and Kiran stood on the beach. Caelum's shoulders relaxed when he saw me walking toward them. Lumos's wind was cold and urgent. It pushed at my back, urging me away from the House of the Moon, toward his Lumin.

I hurried down the steps and made my way to them, pushing through the powdery, soft sand. Caelum's ancestors winked overhead, each one watching us closely. I could almost feel their concern... and their hope.

A strange, warm hum began to resonate throughout my bones. The ocean roared. Angry waves rushed relentlessly toward our feet. "Citali was asking about you when I found Kiran among the crowd. Beron is watching her closely."

I glanced at him. "She found me, but she won't be a problem."

"Why?" he asked carefully.

I smirked. "She's a little *tied up* at the moment. Courtesy of Beron."

Kiran and Caelum laughed.

I tried to join in, but – couldn't. I planted my feet in the sand, panicking. Choking. I clawed at my throat until Caelum's arms clamped on mine. I shoved him away, frightened because even though I stood on his beach, I could smell the dunes of my homeland. Waves of heat rushed over me. Caelum reached out to me again and a wall of heat pushed him backward. He crashed into the sand, but quickly sprang up again.

Kiran planted himself between me and the Lumin. "Let me help her. I can withstand the heat, Lumin. I swear I won't harm her." Kiran approached, singing loudly to Sol, his voice seeking to comfort me.

The choking sensation worsened until whatever was filling me finally demanded to be unleashed. I opened my mouth and spilled a ribbon of light – warm, beautiful light – into the sky.

In my periphery was the House of the Moon. *I'm too close!* A tear leaked from my eye. Anyone could see me out here, a beacon in the dark.

"She's too close to the House," Kiran said. "We need to move her away. Quickly!" With a steely arm around my back, the priest swept my feet out from under me and began to run.

"Beron!" Caelum cupped his hands and shouted through them.

Over the wind and waves, I thought there was no way his brother could hear him. But I was wrong. Moments later, I heard the pounding of paws on sand.

I closed my eyes, listening. I could hear every grain flying through the air, only to hit the earth again. I could hear Beron's claws digging in to propel him, hear the flexion of his muscled haunches, the way his ears rose to find us in the dark.

"Kiran, can you hold her steady on his back?" Caelum asked.

I was deposited on something warm and soft. Beron's back supported my weight and Kiran's. The priest wrapped one arm around me and clung to Beron's fur with the other. I reached out for Caelum. I needed to feel his frost. I needed him.

"Go!" Caelum shouted.

I started to scrabble at Kiran's arm, my eyes wide in panic, when my friend soothed, "We're just getting you to a secluded spot, Noor. Please calm down. All will be well soon."

I didn't think priests were supposed to lie.

Tears streamed down my face. I didn't want to leave Caelum, but as Beron raced down the shoreline, the light vanished in a flash and the tension in my throat eased. I gasped for air, trying vainly to suck it in, and coughed until I was sure my lungs would collapse.

"We're almost there, Noor," Kiran said, trying to calm me.

I boiled and churned, feeling the urge to scream as he whispered prayers to Sol. The words were steady and rhythmic, settling over me like a warm blanket. I began to feel calmer, like the worst of the transition had come and gone and I'd survived it.

Then, the fingers that were fisted in Beron's dark fur emitted a golden light, the same light that began in my rooms when I was arguing with Citali. It raced up my forearms, to my shoulders, up my throat and down my chest, back, hips, and legs. Even my toes warmed. My face filled with light, reflecting off the churning seawater like a sun rising in the darkness.

"Beron, stop!" Kiran yelled.

Beron dug his paws into the sand and ground to a halt, grains spraying all around us. We were at the place where Caelum had given himself to me, and I to him. We waited for many agonizing minutes for Caelum to catch up and when he appeared in the night, his crown glowed on the skin of his forehead; pale blue, gray, and white all mixing in that intoxicating beauty only Lumos possessed. Beron, still in wolf form, bent and kneeled before his brother when he drew near. A whimper emerged from the great beast.

It wasn't from physical pain. Beron wasn't hurt. This was something deeper. Something far more emotional.

Caelum's steady hands lifted me from his brother's back and held me, watching my face with an awed expression. "Are you in pain?"

"No," I breathed, holding my arm out to see it better.

Kiran slid off Beron's back, inclining his head to Caelum respectfully.

Beron shifted from Wolven to brother in an instant and I saw tears glistening in his eyes. "I didn't expect to see the crown, or the sun, within my lifetime," he said, emotions washing over him. "To see both at once is... I'm honored."

And overwhelmed. I understood the feeling well, but had no time to dwell on it.

Suddenly, a familiar scene appeared before me. I slowly peeled away from Caelum and walked toward the heat I knew by heart, leaving the cold, powdery beach sand for the hot desert of which I knew every inch, crest, and fall. The oppressive heat watered the air, but in the far distance, someone was making their way toward me.

I couldn't make out who it was.

The hot wind tore my skirts to the side. They were golden now, pleated, ceremonial...

So were hers, I noticed as she drew closer. We were mirror images of one another and I wondered if this mirage was a hallucination or if I hadn't survived the transition to Aten and was entering the hereafter. I looked behind me to the darkness where a small, blue-white light shone.

*Caelum.*

I didn't want to leave him.

But I had to know... *Is it her?*

I turned back to the woman to find her much closer. I was thrilled to see she wasn't a reflection of me at all, though we shared the same gait, build, and deep brown hair and olive skin.

*Mother?*

"Noor!" she cried, breaking into a run. I ran, too. I struggled through the sand and tears until I crashed into her. She held me tightly to her chest and Sol, goddess of the sun, cried with me.

Happiness and relief mixed with sorrow and anger, then gratefulness washed over us both. "Are you finally free?" I croaked.

"I will never be free as long as you and Helios are not free, Noor," she answered sadly. "I will shine on you as you claim what is rightfully yours – not only by blood, but by virtue. Your heart is as pure as the flame, as beautiful as gold itself. You know what you must do, and I will look over you as you do it. I will see you through this."

She waved a hand and a scene appeared over the heat-soaked air, rippling then settling. I saw Father in his golden kilt, standing atop the temple of Sol with Zarina standing beside him. She knelt on the stone, surrounded by prostrate priests. He was lying to them all, presenting her as the newly chosen Aten.

Which meant *his* powers were gone now.

Vada and her priests stood to the side, encircled by guards. I gritted my teeth at the sight wondering what had happened to the Luminan ship sent to sneak them out of Helios had gone. Had it disappeared with the falconer's message?

It didn't matter. They were still in Helios. Still in Father's crushing hands and subject to his power. He would use them as a bargaining chip.

The scene expanded so I could see it unfold from above. Father's guard surrounded the temple, strategically positioned throughout the palace and spread over Helios. He anticipated my arrival and obviously expected to fight a battle he could not win.

I needed to go home to set things right and release Sol, my mother. Now.

Father had no power over me, or her, anymore. And he never would again.

"I have to go, Noor. I await you in Helios," she said, drawing away. "Bring the Lumin. And if he will agree, ask him to beseech Lumos to guard you both."

Bring Caelum to Helios? Bring Lumos from the south to the sun kingdom? My heart raced at the thought of the two gods occupying the same sliver of sky once again. If we tried this, would the Sculptor allow it, or would he use his great hammer to smash us all to dust?

I didn't want to let her go. Now that her face was so clear, my faded memories of her sharpened. "I will come for you," I promised. "I'll fight for you."

She smiled, her lips so much like mine, right down to the bow. "Come home, daughter." She placed a hand over my heart and power unlike anything I'd felt poured from her palm into me. It was sharp and searing, but not uncomfortable in the least, because her fire was mine now.

In an instant, the heat and sand were gone, as was Mother. Cold air wrapped around me, the chilled gusts tearing at my now-golden ceremonial gown.

My heart raced from the journey.

Caelum, Kiran, and Beron, wearing only Caelum's pale blue tunic hastily knotted around his waist, were searching for something... shouting, running along the shore. Beron splashed into the waves and called out my name. Caelum tore at his hair.

"Caelum?" I said, my voice as loud as thunder.

He whipped his head toward the sound and his mouth fell open. "Noor," he breathed.

Beron and Kiran must have heard me, too, because they sprinted toward me. "You disappeared," Caelum said, pulling me into his arms. "We felt a blast of heat and saw… I think I saw the red sand you've told me about, and then you stepped onto it and were gone."

"She was there. Sol was there!" I croaked. "I have to go to Helios. Now. I can take us there. She wants you to come with me." I bit my lip. "She asked if you thought Lumos might guard us as well."

His eyes met mine and held. "I can only ask and hope."

"Your mother and Lumos's priests are there under heavy guard. Either they didn't get the missive, or it was ignored."

Beron cursed vividly. "He'll use them against us."

"Caelum, Kiran… We need to go."

Beron snarled a savage laugh. "You three aren't having all the fun without me. I'm going, too."

Lumos's face peeked above the horizon. From the depths, he watched us, spilling light over the water to the shore. "I need a moment," Caelum said. He held out his arms, absorbing the light of his god onto his bare chest. His crown reappeared and he began to speak in a language I did not recognize.

He sank to his knees in the sand, in the surf. Waves surged toward him, crashing over his thighs, soaking and spraying his skin.

Though everything in me wanted to race to Helios now, I waited.

For Caelum. And for Lumos.

# 28

Lumos did not slowly drift into the sky as usual. He dragged himself from the sea and cast himself high into the dark, powerfully planting himself among the ancestors. Caelum rose from his knees, drenched but ready. His crown faded slowly away.

Beron shifted again, becoming Wolven. The waves swallowed Caelum's tunic, tumbling it into deeper water. "You'll roast in Helios in that form," I told him, scratching behind his ear. He leaned into me.

"He's more powerful this way," Caelum told me.

I glanced over his shoulder at Kiran. He gave a nod.

It was time.

I waved my hand in front of me the way Mother had and the air shifted and rippled. Heat poured from the sand and stone streets. We were going to waltz down the main road, pass the House of the Sun, then climb the steps of Sol's temple where they would all be waiting.

Citali appeared behind us, tearing through the sand like a storm. "Wait!"

Beron growled in her direction, snapping his teeth as his hackles rose.

"Noor?" she said, slowing her steps. She looked from me to Helios painted in heat before us. "*You've* become Aten?"

I lifted my chin proudly.

Her chest heaved.

"Thank Sol. Please, take me to Helios with you. I want to go home." There was defeat in her tone. Desperation. "I promise I won't try anything again. I just... I need to go home before it's too late."

"Before *what* is too late, Citali?" I asked.

She shook her head, spent.

"How did you escape your bindings?" Caelum asked. "Beron wants to know."

Citali observed that the two could communicate when Beron was in Wolven form. Her eyes flicked from them to me. *Please,* she mouthed. *I'm sorry.*

Sorry? Citali knew the word?

"Citali," Caelum repeated in a sterner tone. "How did you break free?"

"There's nothing that can bind my will, mutt," she snarled, taking careful steps toward us. "I just want to go home, sister, please."

*Sister?* I quirked a brow at the word.

"Please. I am begging you, Noor."

"And what will you do there? Join Father's fight against us?"

She shook her head as her eyes raced over me. "If he fights this battle against you, Father will lose. He'll finally lose, Noor." Her shoulders sagged, defeated. "He... In addition to finding the crown, I was supposed to find a way to kill you, Noor. Now I know why, I guess, although he would never say. He didn't trust me enough to tell me the truth."

I swallowed thickly.

"I just wanted it to be over. The demands. The consequences. The constant threats." She looked broken and overwhelmed. "And I can't tell you everything yet. Not until I'm sure all is well. All is safe. There's still time for him to..." She choked on the words. "Bind my hands. My feet. Anything. Just take me with you." She held out her wrists. "Please."

Caelum removed his belt and deftly bound her, handing the excess leather to Kiran.

I clasped his hand and he curled his fingers into Beron's fur. Kiran's hand fell on my shoulder and Citali jogged to keep up as we walked into Helios, into the desert, the dunes rippling over the land.

The moment we stepped through the portal from Lumina to Helios, Caelum gasped, the heat overwhelming him. Sweat beaded on his forehead as he lifted one sweltering boot, then the other. Beron alternated lifting his paws uncomfortably. We had to get out of the sand. We weren't far from Sol's temple.

"It's not far, but we should hurry. Your boots and feet will scorch," I warned.

My golden dress rapped like a pennant in the heated wind, announcing our arrival. As we approached her temple, Sol brightened overhead.

Just then, Beron barked toward the southern sky. I turned my head and was overjoyed when I saw Lumos. *He came!*

The crown of moonlight appeared on Caelum's brow as he guided Lumos toward us, toward Sol burning directly overhead. She burned hotter and more ferociously as he approached. I could almost feel her ache to reach him, but knew she would stand with me first.

We crested a dune and the temple came into view below us. I heard Father's voice echoing from atop the temple, the steady cadence of the priests' song, the uncomfortable shuffle of a thousand feet, and the rushing breaths of every Helioan gathered at the temple's base.

Kiran began to sing a mournful melody to Sol – for Saric. He honored his friend and brother as we made our way out of the sand to the base of the temple's steps. The crowd cheered on the other side of the temple in response to something Father said.

Beron leaped several steps at a time as we strode up, up, up the goddess's stone hewn mountain. Overhead, a large shadow passed over us. Caelum paused to shield his eyes and look.

"The Sphinx guards us," I told him.

A look passed between us. One filled with mettle and faith and fervor. Strength.

"You have no need for an aureole now," he said, climbing farther. "Sol's light is pouring from your skin."

Kiran nodded to affirm his words. "There is no denying who you are, Noor. The people will see you and know."

I hoped that was true and that Father's poisonous words hadn't blinded them to the truth. When I stopped and glanced at our small party, everyone else paused, too. Caelum was drenched in sweat.

"At the top, Father is presenting Zarina as the new Aten." I glanced at the brothers. "Your mother and Lumos's priests are surrounded. They'll be standing to our left."

"Are there steps on every side of the temple to the top?"

"Yes."

Caelum looked at Beron. "Circle around and come at them from behind."

Beron growled and loped back down the staircase, taking off around the temple to do as his Lumin commanded. To protect his Mother and Lumos's priests.

Citali tugged on the belt and almost made Kiran fall. "What's your problem?" I asked, pushing toward her.

"Leave me here!" she frantically begged, trying to break loose of her bindings. "Please. I swear I'll go straight to the House. I'll gather my things and will never bother you again."

I narrowed my eyes, suspicious of her motives. "Why are you so eager to leave?"

She put her hands out protectively. "I don't want to be caught in the middle of your fight with Father."

I took the belt from Kiran and loosened the strap. The leather had left red indentations in her skin but hadn't broken it. "You put yourself in the middle of our fight when you agreed to kill me for him."

She stepped down one step, her eyes tracking my movements to see what I would do. Her chest heaved. "Please, Noor." She dropped to her knees. "Don't make me go up there. I don't think I can face him."

I grabbed her wrist and pulled her up off the stone. "Believe me when I tell you that he will not hurt you. I won't allow it."

She sobbed, her face contorting in anguish, terrified and torn. For the first time, I realized Citali and I weren't as different as I'd thought.

I knelt in front of her. Gently cupped her elbows. "You have to decide who you trust, sister. Me or Father. I know he's been stronger than us for as long as we can remember, but he's not now. Whatever hatred and differences lay between us... they are *his* doing. We can put an end to this animosity here and now. Together, we can take the next step and face him. And you can believe me when I tell you that I will protect and keep you safe. Just as I will protect whatever it is you're trying your damnedest to shield from him."

Citali glanced upward at the next stone step. Her dark eyes, still brimming with tears, cut to me.

"Set right your wrongs, Citali."

Sniffling, she he nodded once. "Together," she rasped. She took a moment to compose herself and nodded when she was ready. "I trust you, Noor," she finally said. I stood and held out a hand, pulling her up when she allowed it.

Walking side by side, we led the others up the staircase.

When we reached the stone top, it was just as Sol had shown me. To our left, Vada and her priests were surrounded by guards. Father and Zarina startled as Citali and I crested the temple's top. He took in Caelum and Kiran flanking me. He still didn't know about Beron...

Above us, Sol's great statue loomed. Her arms stretched toward the sky where she watched and waited.

"What is the meaning of this?" Father demanded imperiously.

The priests silenced their song and sat back on their haunches. Kiran gestured to the southern sky where Lumos dragged himself through the heat toward us.

The priests of the god of night bowed, ignoring the protests of those guarding them. They were overjoyed to be in the presence of their god.

Sol's priests were taken aback. One went as far as to stand and point in awe. The crowd at the temple's base turned to see Lumos and gasps rang out, tears falling in fear and jubilation. People weren't sure what his presence meant, whether it was a threat or blessing.

Zarina's face was stony and cold as she carefully inched behind Father. "Guard your Aten!" he shouted.

I laughed at his command, walking around Citali, who'd ground to a stop, still careful to keep her distance. I held out my arms and turned in a circle so they could all see Sol's light pouring from my skin. Even her brightness couldn't dull what lay in my heart and beneath my skin. "By all means, guard me," I taunted to the men and women of the Helioan guard. "I am your new Aten. Aren't I, Father?"

Zuul, father's personal guard stepped toward him. "If you choose to stand with him, Zuul, when he burns, so will you."

Father raised a hand, stopping Zuul's approach.

Caelum stood beside me, his crown of moonlight shining a vivid, cool, white-blue despite the sunlight. He raised his hands and asked Lumos to come closer.

I could feel Sol's joy. She was as incandescent as her light, yet what poured from her was so much more than joy, so much deeper than I could feel or describe. She hadn't seen Lumos in millennia, but her heart had never forgotten him. She burned white-hot, eager to see him. The tendrils of her fire flared toward him as if her fiery arms spread for him. He rushed to her.

As he reached her, shadow spread like a blanket over the land of the sun as the two eclipsed. Another moment, and the kingdom was bathed in an eerie, ruddy darkness.

Father seized the opportunity to try and ruin me. "See? She brought Lumos here to kill our goddess!"

The light within me flared and poured brighter and hotter over my skin. I strode purposefully toward my father. When I reached him, he tried to use Zarina as a shield, roughly tugging her in front of him. She struggled against his strength and her shrieks echoed over the land. The people watched, aghast.

"Father, no!" she cried, struggling.

He shoved her toward me and tried to run like the coward he was. He only made it two steps before grinding to a halt and backing up onto the platform again. A familiar growl, a snarling nose, and bared, sharp teeth stalked up the steps toward him.

*Beron.*

I gave him an approving nod, reveling in Father's discomfort. He knew he'd lost before trying to flee, but realized he couldn't run from his destiny, or from me, anymore.

Father looked to Caelum, whose crown shone so brightly it bit at the eye. "She only wants your crown and kingdom," he sneered. "*She* seeks to ruin you, not I."

To my surprise, Caelum laughed. "So she's said."

Father gestured to Vada. "My guards will kill your mother if I am harmed," he threatened Caelum.

But he found that the guards surrounding her had relaxed their stances. They held their spears toward him now.

His mouth gaped. "You disloyal—"

"The guard *is* loyal, Father. They serve the Aten. They serve *me*."

Father's eyes searched the murky darkness for a way out. I opened the air between us and stepped through the divide of time and distance to position myself right in front of him. I clamped onto his throat and lifted, Sol's fury strengthening my arm. Fury and indignation trembled his upper lip. His hands clamped onto my wrist, squeezing tightly, but I would not buckle or break.

I remembered every time he'd struck me. A blood vessel burst in his left eye. Then two in the right.

I remembered every cruel word.

More vessels burst.

Every time he told me I would die by his hand. When he said I'd never see my mother's bones again. When I carried wife after wife into the scorching dunes for him.

Red overtook the white.

Anger and fear and so much hatred surged through me with Sol's fire. I let out a scream that scattered every dove in the city, their wings flapping so loudly, I could hear the wind rake against their feathers.

Father slumped, his final breath escaping in a heavy sigh.

I opened my eyes and realized he was gone. His eyelids sank, covering the vivid explosions that marked his last moments.

Twin tears fell from my eyes, carving cool paths over my cheeks. Steam wafted from my face. They splashed onto the stone with two distinct plinking noises. I looked down to see two tear-shaped sun diamonds settled near my feet.

A warmth spread across my forehead and Caelum inhaled sharply, then brazenly smiled. I reached up to feel flame dancing over my skin, burning but not harming me in the least. I realized I now wore a crown of fire on my brow, announcing to everyone who I truly was.

Heir of Sol. Heir of the sun.

The nearest priest raised his head, focused on the two yellow rocks. His eyes rose to me in wonder. "Sol?" he whispered.

"I am not Sol," I told him – raising my voice to tell them all. "I am her daughter, her heir, and your new Aten. And I will *right* what my father ruined."

I threw Father's body away from me. Sol's fire had burned through me and found every part of him unacceptable. A ponderous weight was lifted from my chest.

Citali came to stand with me. A strange turn of the tides had developed between us, but one that gave me hope.

I found Zarina glancing across the rest of those gathered, bewildered.

"If you hold any allegiance to him, I warn you to leave Helios now. If you make any attempts to harm me or anyone I love, I'll drag you into the sand and you will never escape it," I warned.

No one moved or even flinched… except for the goddess. A sliver of Sol appeared, peeking bright around Lumos. She shone upon her temple, upon her people, and upon me – her daughter.

A roar came from the people gathered at the temple's base. They rejoiced in seeing her light return. Celebrated her freedom.

The priests of both gods began to sing again, and the assembled guards bowed low. I swiveled to Caelum and held out a hand. He slipped his cooling palm into mine and I was awash in calmness, his peaceful touch tempering my molten fire.

Citali stared at Father's limp form blankly. She shed no tears for him. I wasn't sure if she was relieved or completely numb. Sometimes in the middle of trauma, it felt like the difficulties weren't truly happening. That the truth couldn't possibly be real.

Zarina shot me a frigid look, quietly gathered her skirts, turned, and walked away, trailing down the steps of the temple. Always the first to leave. Always regal. Always cold.

The gathered crowd waited for her to reach them, then parted, unsure what to do next.

Caelum was there at my side. He wrapped an arm around my back, sliding his hand to my hip and pulling me to his side. "She could freeze Lumos himself."

I tried to smile and so did he, but the pressure of what came next settled over us. I realized that being Aten and accepting the crown of flame was a heavier burden to bear than the aureole of the Atena. My people – starved, abused, and hurt – depended on me now. I had to heal the wounds Father left on them and our land.

We'd barely begun, and I had no idea what to do once we left the temple platform.

Beron trotted to his mother, who thanked him and hugged his neck. He nuzzled her and nudged Lumos's priests as Lumos peeled away from Sol once more. I could feel both her joy and sorrow at letting him go. She didn't know how long it would be before she could see him again.

Sol's heart ached as she slowly tore away from Lumos.

I knew the feeling. I wasn't sure what would happen with Caelum now. The weight of his cuff drew down my pocket.

When the eclipse ended, the priests finally stood and watched the remarkable sky. The eldest of Sol's priests, now that Saric had departed, was a kind man named Dex, known for his gentleness. He strode toward us, humbly bowing as he approached. "My Aten," he said, pressing his hands together and bowing again. "Lumin." He dipped toward Caelum. "Please instruct us according to the will of the gods."

Kiran joined his brothers' song, the lovely lilt climbing into the heavens like building thunderhead.

I lifted my chin. "Beginning now, I need the priests of Sol to serve her people in ways they haven't been able to until now. Can you let them know it is safe and all is well, then ensure that the people have enough food to eat tonight?"

"Yes, Aten. I'll see that they are calmed, comforted, and fed."

"Open the food stores. No more hoarding what's desperately needed."

He nodded and promised to do so.

"I could use a few moments of privacy within the temple," I told him. "And someone to carry my father's body into the sand." I refused to perform the task. He didn't deserve another moment of my time or thought.

The priest inclined his head. "I'll see that you have quiet and that he is taken him away. Those of us who aren't needed for the task will await you here, Aten."

I thanked him.

Vada rushed to us, flinging an arm around Caelum's neck and mine. "I'm so proud of you both!" she said, kissing his cheek, then mine.

Beron refused to shift back until we were sure there would be no resistance from anyone who might remain loyal to my father's treacherous whims. Zuul lingered, and he was certainly one of the ones I didn't trust. Beron could sense my unease.

Caelum ticked his chin toward his Wolven brother. "He'll stay here with our mother and the priests to keep watch over them."

I petted his head. "Thank you, Beron."

He nuzzled my hand to show me he understood. He was with us.

Sol's temple was empty. Caelum's and my footsteps echoed through the cavernous space. Great, carved-stone pillars of varying heights held the walls and roof overhead. Painted carvings commissioned by the prior Atens, especially of the first who loved Sol with her entire heart, decorated the walls.

There were likenesses of the goddess everywhere, her gilded face high above the desert sands watching over Helios. People had been carved bowing to her and offering their most precious belongings.

The scent of precious incense slid over my skin and embedded into my hair.

It felt like we were walking into Sol's heart.

She was here. I could feel her all around us.

A great, golden mirror took up much of the wall in the very back of the temple room. Caelum and I paused in front of it, watching how the distortions in the gold also distorted our reflections. Until suddenly, a gust of heat filled the space and the gold mirror sharpened our image, replacing it with hers...

Sol.

*Mother.*

"You are free," I told her. "But I still need your help. Yours and Lumos's."

Caelum took hold of my hand. Sol regarded our clasped palms.

"We have heard from the Sculptor," she said, sounding far away. "He will set us on a new path where we will do what is best for the earth and all the flesh-clad spirits who walk the sands beneath us."

"Will you never see Lumos again?" I asked. My heart ached for her. She'd spent a few blessed moments with him. How long would it be until they brushed so close they could touch?

She smiled. "At times, he will allow us a glimpse of one another in passing. But the most sacred of days – like today – will be days of eclipses."

"I hope for your sake and Lumos's that there is a torrent of sacred days in the years to come," I offered.

She smiled. "I hope so, too. I am proud of you, Noor."

She began to fade, the mirror dulling again.

"Mother, one more moment, please?"

I turned to Caelum. "Would you wait just outside for me? I need to ask her a question privately."

He inclined his head. "Of course."

As he strode away, I watched, knowing Mother watched, too. When he was gone, I turned to her. "I love him."

The goddess of fire nodded. "I know your heart."

"I want him in my life."

She nodded. "Then do as he suggested and forge a new path."

"You accept him, then?"

"I more than approve, daughter. He burns for you." She placed a hand over her heart, patting the spot. I knew what she meant because my heart burned for Caelum, too.

She lifted her hand and breathed into her palm. It stretched, golden, from the mirror. On her gilded skin lay a golden cuff shaped like licking flames, large enough to span his bicep. It was still warm from her fire and her blessing.

"Thank you."

"I wish the two of you a lifetime of eclipses, Noor. A lifetime of happiness and smiles, and more children than you can keep track of. Your unified kingdom will thrive. Your reign as Aten began today. People everywhere will know your name and your power. I will shine a light on Lumina for the first time in many, many years, and I will shine in your honor, Noor," she promised before her image blurred and my distorted one was all I could see in the golden mirror.

A great gust of warm wind tore the flames in the oil trenches sideways. It urged me out of the temple. It urged me to him. I tucked the golden cuff into my pocket with the silver one he'd given me to wear if, and when, I chose.

Caelum was waiting outside, as he promised. His eyes tracked Sol as she moved slowly south. We climbed the temple steps together and watched the path she carved across the sky. With her priests' voices blending into a sweet melody, Sol glided toward Lumina, while Lumos hovered over Helios, finally visible to the people who'd heard about his beautiful face but had never seen it.

"My people will be startled," he said.

"You'll need to go to them." I took his hand in mine.

He swallowed thickly, his thumb brushing the back of my hand. "I don't want to be parted from you."

I didn't want that, either. "Then we work toward building the path that leads between your kingdom and mine."

He nodded resolutely. "Yes, we will."

# 29

Lumos shone over Sol's temple while the sun set to the south, Sol's face softening into a less severe shade of gentle orange. I watched her from the top of the temple steps, the last of her light flowing over me like the comforting brush of a mother's hand on her precious child's brow.

Caelum went back to Lumina. I'd made a portal for Caelum to leave through. The cool air of Lumina had poured from it as he faced his duties. Before he stepped through, I'd promised him that the door between our kingdoms was and would always be open now. He had agreed and sealed the vow with a kiss that made my toes curl and made me want to close the door I told him I would never again lock.

He'd taken Vada and Lumos's priests home.

Beron, however, stayed.

I wondered if Caelum had ordered him to, or if he decided to remain on his own. Beron jogged up the steps wearing one of my father's kilts, holding a large waterskin in his hand. He took several gulps when he sat next to me, stretching out his long legs. He tugged at the pleated fabric stretching to his knees before wagging his brows. "These are strangely comfortable in this heat. They... breathe."

I laughed. They certainly did. "It's not even hot now that she moved."

He quirked a brow. "I stayed the Wolven, in thick, black fur, as your mother poured her heat over us. I'll be hot for weeks!"

"Is Citali still in her rooms?"

He nodded. "For now."

"And Zarina?"

"Same."

"I don't trust them yet."

He shuddered. "I don't blame you. Whomever said to keep your enemies close didn't know your sisters."

Something large rattled the stone behind us and Beron's eyes widened as he looked over his shoulder at the Sphinx. Every muscle on his frame tightened. His eyes raked over her fur, her muscles, mane, and those powerful, beautiful translucent wings as she tucked them behind her. "I think I should go now," he said, his words drifting off into nothing.

The Sphinx tilted her great head, sniffed the air, and zeroed in on Beron. Her solid black eyes blinked. A roar rattled the temple stone and echoed over the land. Her muscles tensed and she postured to pounce. "What manner of creature are you?" she asked him, the child-like voice startling even Beron.

I scuttled in front of him as a barely-still-human growl rumbled from his chest. He would shift if I didn't diffuse this. "He is the Wolven, and a friend of mine. He's Lumos's chosen, just as you are Sol's. You are equals," I told her.

The Sphinx scoffed, "I am no one's equal, and no one is mine." She looked at Beron again, her fathomless obsidian eyes still, but filled with indignation instead of fury.

I swiveled my head to the Wolven. "Beron, I need to speak to her alone."

He made his way back down the steps, keeping her within reach of his senses even as his back was turned. I just hoped he went back to the House instead of circling around. The Sphinx might carry him into the desert just to see if he could scent himself home, if he wasn't careful.

I didn't know what about Beron had angered her so quickly, but perhaps she sensed his power, that he was 'other,' too. Perhaps she saw him as a threat. I didn't want to dwell on it now that she seemed calmer with his departure.

She knelt low and bowed her head, powerful muscles limiting her movement. "Well done, Aten," she said in her child-like voice. "Sol is happy once more."

She rose and looked at Lumos, then at Sol as she finally disappeared and shadows blanketed the earth. Even in her absence, the kingdom of the sun was not cast into total darkness. Lumos poured his restorative light, pale and bright and beautiful, over Helios.

"The land just sighed in relief," the lioness quietly observed. "This is what it needed. *You* are what your people need, Noor." She gave a feline smile, having read my thoughts. "You want me to give insight into what comes next with Caelum? No, Aten. I think this is a riddle you and he must solve together. I will enjoy watching." She looked to Lumos and flared her wings, the feathers stretching. "Goodnight, Aten."

I sat on the temple platform as close to the god of night as I could climb and asked him if he would approve of me if Caelum presented me to him – knowing what he knew of me now. He'd seen me take my father's life, and the darkest part of my heart.

The silver cuff was cool when I pulled it from my pocket, studying Lumos's impression. Then, as if in answer to my question, the cuff began to glow. A cuff of moonlight. *A tiny crown,* I mused, laughing to myself.

I looked to Lumos. "Thank you."

Then I clamped it onto my bicep and hoped Caelum felt it and knew.

A moment later, the portal door that I'd made turned cool. I waved my hand over the air to open it and Caelum stepped through. He settled beside me, beaming his handsome smile. His crown shone in the darkness, matching the pale hues of his god.

"You came."

He pulled me into his lap, my legs straddling his, and kissed me like he hadn't seen me in millennia. His fingers tangled into my hair and raked down and up my spine, stealing my breath and heart and mind. When he pulled away, he breathed, "How could I not?"

I reached into my pocket and withdrew the golden cuff. In my hands, it sparked, lit, and burned. The gold turned to flame, warm but not burning, flickering but not faltering. "I want you to wear mine as well."

He captured my lips before tugging his tunic over his head. "Always."

I fastened it onto his arm and watched the fire dance over his skin. A cuff of fire to match my crown of flame.

"I think we should establish a new House for a newly combined kingdom. And I know what we should call it, Caelum."

He smiled, his eyes glittering. "What's that?"

I kissed him, closed my eyes, and felt nothing but him. Flame and frost. Sun and moon. And knew that I needed an infinite number of blessed days with him. "The House of Eclipses."

His lips pulled into a smile against mine. "It's perfect."

# 30

We kissed and danced, a slow sway to a rhythm that wasn't played but both of us heard with our hearts. And it felt like eternity caught between our lips. Eternity, and hope. And amazing just as wonderful and weighty things.

We kissed until Caelum froze, gasped, then abruptly pulled away. His eyes unfocused as if he was looking beyond me. His dark brows furrowed.

He took hold of my hand, tugging me toward the temple steps and down. "We have to hurry!"

"What's the matter?" I managed as we ran.

"It's Citali," he panted. "Beron says she's dying."

I opened a portal and demanded it take me to my sister, dragging Caelum through with me.

To be continued…

# HOUSE OF WOLVES

# 1

Like a strong perfume too liberally applied, Zarina's bitterness wafted into my rooms before her. I'd never seen my eldest sister look anything but harsh and poised, a façade she'd honed to perfection and one I had always envied. But as she approached, that careful mask chipped away. By the time she drew near, my stony sister was nearly molten.

The soles of her sandals slapping the stone floor were the only sound in The House of the Sun, which lay eerily empty. All the servants had abandoned their positions to watch Noor claim her place atop her mother's temple.

Zarina's pleated gold dress had been tailored to match Father's ceremonial kilt. Her hair was sleek, tied at the nape of her neck. Around it lay an ornate, red collar necklace that draped to the swells of her breasts, its colors alternating in shades of dried and fresh blood.

The affronted look she wore made me wonder whether she felt as if she'd been stabbed in the back, or if she felt Noor had taken a dagger straight to her heart.

Either way, I didn't have time for her anger. I was leaving before Noor could command someone to make me stay. Some*one*... or some *mutt*. I refused to be locked in any room again. I'd be gone before they knew it, and I would be smart enough not to leave a trail for Beron to pick up.

I ignored her and continued to rummage through my things, plucking out what I would need and what I might be able to sell. I piled some gold jewelry on the bed, then turned to gather more from my chest of drawers, built specifically to hold my garish baubles. The stand on top for my aureole lay empty. I'd abandoned it, and my past, in Lumina, and though it was frightening changing my trajectory, I knew it was the right decision.

I'd trusted my youngest sister – who should never have given me the opportunity since I didn't deserve it –I stood with her against our tyrannical father. Finally. And now he lay dead.

I wondered if the priests had dragged him into the sand where every inch of him would rot. Where he would never reach the hereafter, and the ravages of the desert and scavengers would share his corpse until nothing but bone remained. Eventually, the sand would take even them. I smiled.

"You traitor!" Zarina spat as she stopped an arm's length away, the ragged edges of her tone pausing my hands. She clenched her fists at her sides.

I narrowed my eyes. *Did she come here to fight?* Slowly, carefully, I informed her, "I am no such thing."

"Noor is *not* the heir of Sol," she said so resolutely, I wondered if she might actually believe it.

"You saw her. You know that she is."

From atop the temple, Sol's light poured from Noor. There was no doubt that she had descended directly from the sun goddess. None of the prior Atens' skin, or very soul, glowed. Noor still had a golden, sunny corona outlining her shape long after she killed our father and I slipped away.

That aura sometimes leaked into her eyes, making them glow warm and golden, too.

As if those indications weren't enough, Noor was endowed with a trove of sun diamonds, so hot only she could bear to wear them – again, because of her lineage. Because of her mother: Sol.

Sadly, Zarina had been groomed by our father since birth to trust only him. Perhaps she doubted her own mind because of his poisonous teachings. He'd promised her more times than I could count that she would succeed him as Aten. He told her that Sol would listen when he recommended his eldest daughter. That he would pass me and Noor over.

He lied.

He knew who and what Noor was. He always had.

And like every other lie he'd concocted, it led to hurt and pain. This time they were Zarina's, and she was unaccustomed to such feelings. He had never coddled her, but he'd made it abundantly clear who she must become if he was to recommend her as the next Aten. As a result, she'd fought, stretched, and crammed herself to fit the mold he'd described. She'd cut away the pieces of herself he found invaluable to earn his favor, his praise, his occasional manipulative kindness.

Hadn't all of us, his daughters, done the same at least a thousand times?

Zarina pointed a trembling, accusatory finger at me. "Father told me what she, and you, have done. I cannot allow it. I cannot let her become Aten and steal this kingdom away."

I tilted my head to the side. "This kingdom was never yours." It was never Father's, truth be told. He only held it in trust for a time until Noor came of age and her body matured enough to contain the power her mother would endow. "Father was a liar, Zarina. A divider. I'm not sure what he told you, but you can be assured it was untrue."

She seemed to weigh my words, standing quietly for a long moment. "He said that in Lumina, you not only convinced Lumos to help you, but that the two of you made a darker bargain. One with Anubis." She hissed the 's' of his name, drawing out the sound to a whisper. She took a step closer as if we were confiding in one another. So close, she bent to place her mouth at my ear. "It was he on the temple steps, wasn't it? You can tell me the truth, Citali. You don't have to fear her, or him."

My bones went hollow. I pushed her away. "Don't speak his name in this House! Don't even speak it in this kingdom."

No one uttered the name of the banished god of the dead without consequences. When the Sculptor sealed him into the fire in the middle of the earth to punish him for trying to kill Lumos and Sol so he could take their powers, it was decreed that even uttering his name was forbidden. His history was given only as a warning to us all to be on guard against any dark magic that might escape the depths and spew like lava onto the land, and so that if anyone dared dabble, they knew what fate lay ahead.

Anyone who dealt with the banished god invited a curse upon herself and her family.

"Think about it. The dark one can make *anything* appear real with his magic. He could make Noor *look* like Sol had poured through her!" Zarina breathed, her eyes wild. "He spins illusions like twisted storms of sand."

I wished she would stop talking about him. I took a steadying breath, hoping she might see reason. If she refused, I hoped to at least shift the conversation into safer territory. "Father was desperate to cling to power, Zarina, and to keep Noor from ascending to Aten. He lied to you in a final attempt to turn you against everything he hated – Sol and Noor."

She flung a hand in the direction of the temple. "Explain the jackal on the temple roof, then!"

"That wasn't a jackal; it was a wolf," I explained. "The Wolven is the Luminan equivalent to our great Sphinx."

She shook her head. "Father told me that in the darkness of the moon's kingdom, your mind would be twisted. He warned you would come back changed. That was no lie."

I shook my head. "Zarina... have you forgotten how Father tried to use you to shield *himself* when Noor came? Or how he tried to run away, leaving you atop the temple alone to face her wrath? Father was a coward until his dying breath. He was a liar and a murderer. You *know* that. How can you possibly trust his word?"

"What did Noor do in Lumina to provoke such a strange change in her, when we had no indication of it here in Helios – her home – the land of the sun and Sol herself?"

"Noor came of age," I explained. That was the long and short of it.

Zarina shook her head, giving a mirthless laugh. She wasn't listening.

I tried again. "The Sphinx even *told* Father that Sol would reveal her heir when Noor came of age. Zarina, the goddess was waiting for Noor. Noor did nothing in Lumina other than attempt to find the crown. Instead, she found she didn't need it in the end because of who she is. *She is Sol's heir.*"

Zarina went still, her elegant frame straightening. She brushed a hair back from where it hung in her eye. "I thought you would stand with me, no matter what."

"I don't stand against you now, sister. But I do know the truth, and I won't stand against Sol."

She shook her head, her eyes catching on the small pile of clothing and treasures amassed on my bed. "You're leaving? If Noor is so wonderful all of a sudden, why do you flee your own home?" she challenged.

"I have no reason to stay."

A slow, vicious smile spread over her lips. My fists curled at the sight, as she looked just like Father in that moment before he was about to do something malicious. "I know where you're going. Father told me of your great secret, too." As if he'd sliced me from the grave, her words cut across my chest. Directly over my heart. No… No more. Never again would someone threaten him.

"I should pay him a visit. Introduce myself," she threatened.

"I'll kill you if you go near him," I quietly vowed.

She slid her hand into her pocket. Instinctively, I took a step back. When she withdrew her hand, she brought something with it: an obsidian dagger. Zarina bared her teeth. "You say you will kill me, Citali? What if I kill you first?"

She lunged, slashing at my side. I sucked in my stomach and jumped back, barely missing the bite of her blade. "You're insane!"

"You have been corrupted," she carefully punctuated, each word another jab, stab, slash. "Anubis has his claws in you. I can feel him within you, writhing. I can smell his burn on your skin."

Wild but fluid, she sliced the air between us. Fever turned her eyes to glass, her skin pale and ashen.

"The only one possessed by the dark one is *you*," I shrieked. "You and our wretched father!" I blocked a slice with my forearm, sucking in a breath when her blade zipped through my skin. A guttural cry clawed from my throat. "You cut me!"

I didn't have time to evaluate the wound, because Zarina kept jabbing, stabbing, slicing. I ran to a small table along the wall and slid it out between us to impede her path. Zarina gave a push and it teetered, then toppled, crashing onto the floor with a splintering crack. A spindly leg broke off and skittered toward me on the floor. I grabbed it and attempted to fend her off, bludgeoning as much as I could.

My confidence grew as I managed to land several hits. I bloodied her knuckles, cracked her brow, and split the tender skin there so blood pooled in her eye. She blinked and wiped furiously to stanch the flow and clear her vision as I prepared for her next attack... or to see if she was finished and her anger quenched.

Zarina's feet slipped over the blood she'd spilled from me as she lunged again. Now hers was mixed with it. "This is madness, Zarina!" I told her.

She answered with a roar and another slash.

Her knife caught in the wood of my table leg. She ripped it out, splinters and dust falling to the bloody floor.

I took a risk and snatched her wrist, stopping the dagger. She tugged and pulled to free herself, gritting her teeth and growling.

"Where did you get this? What sort of blade is this, Zarina?"

She gnashed her teeth at me, then slipped in the sticky blood and lost her footing, landing on the unyielding stone floor with a gasp. I kept hold of her to stop her blade and keep her close, all the while striking her with the wooden leg. She covered her head and face, screaming for me to stop. Her forehead was bruising, her lip swelling and bleeding. After a thunderous blow to her chest, the red beads layered around her neck, now soaked with my blood, broke and scattered over the floor, some landing in the crimson smears and puddles underfoot.

"Stop, Citali. Please!" she cried, panting, her teeth coated in blood. Her free hand braced in the air between us to block my next strike

I pointed the spindly table leg at her throat. "Threaten him again, and I will end you. I took Father's abuse for years. I will *not* take it from you. I will never endure such threats again and will eliminate the source of them without hesitating. This is your only warning. Blade or no blade, I will best you. I swear… I'll kill you and drag you into the dunes. I'll lay you right beside him."

I squeezed her wrist for good measure.

She relaxed. Her breathing slowed and she looked spent. "Please. I'll leave you alone. I'll leave the palace," she vowed.

"I don't care what you do or where you go now. Just stay far, far away from me and mine. If I free you and you try to cut me again, I won't stop the next time I raise this stick. I'll beat you into the stone itself," I panted, my chest heaving from the effort to keep her contained.

I couldn't let her know it, but I was weakened and my vision was swimming. I'd lost a lot of blood. It spattered onto the floor at our feet, constant as a fountain.

How could an arm bleed so much?

I let go of her wrist, flinging a finger toward the door. "Get out," I gritted.

She nodded and her feet slipped in a crimson puddle as she stood. I raised my arm to see how bad the cut was when I felt a sharp prick on my left side. Zarina's fist was against my skin.

No… not her fist. The handle of her dagger was pressed against my stomach, the blade sunk in as far as it could. A wave of warmth crashed over me.

Zarina's face was contorted in rage as she pushed the knife in further and twisted the blade. I pushed her away as hot water flooded my mouth.

"What did you do?"

She jerked the dagger from my body, sending a white-hot, searing pain through my stomach.

I couldn't hiss.

Was afraid to move.

Could barely breathe.

Dark blood oozed from the wound. It didn't seem that bad at first. Then it flowed, pouring like the river that ran south from Helios into Lumina. If I thought my arm bled a lot, it was nothing compared to this wound.

Zarina's dark eyes were now wide. Tears welled. Her chest heaved and her hands shook with a trembling force. Her fist opened and the glass-like dagger clattered to the floor. She pressed blood-coated fingers to her mouth as if unable to believe what she'd done. The obsidian turned to gold from blade tip to pommel when my blood swelled over it, the crimson puddle pushing it a few inches toward her, almost as if Sol wanted her to take it back up and finish what she'd started. To deliver a nobler, quicker death than the one she'd begun. Or perhaps it was a trick. If she touched it, perhaps she would perish for what she had done.

"Sol claims your blade. Touch it now, Zarina. Please," I gritted. "See what punishment the goddess will mete out. She saw... everything."

"Sol isn't here," she asserted, her voice quivering.

"Sol is everywhere, as is Lumos. And beyond the sun and moon gods, the Sculptor watches."

I kept my breaths shallow, but deep hatred welled in my chest, mixing with disbelief and fear. And most potent of all, agony. I'd come so close to leaving this place and finally going to him, finally able to be what he needed me to be.

I looked at my eldest sister, who watched keenly to see if I would lash out or keel over, and despite my weakening voice and the fact that every word felt like she'd stabbed me all over again, I promised her one thing. "Until my last breath, in this life, or in the hereafter, I will not rest... until you are dead."

Zarina hesitated for only a moment. She did not apologize or cry for help for me as she sloppily fled the room, a trail of sticky, crimson footprints evidence of her escape.

I didn't know what to do.

There wasn't much I *could* do now. My hands shook and my arms were leaden weights, but my legs felt like the spindly table legs, too weak and frail to hold me up any longer.

A cold sweat beaded on my forehead and spread down my neck and arms.

I fell to my knees. All I could think of was him. How to save myself. How I couldn't bear to leave this world without seeing him one more time. I wasn't ready to die. Didn't want to leave him.

*Noor...*

Noor would help me, but she wasn't there.

Frantic, desperate thoughts rushed through my mind. There was only *one* who might hear me. And with the commotion outside, I wasn't sure even his senses would be able to cut through to find me.

Still, I had to try.

I pressed my wound tighter, hot crimson bubbling around my fingers despite my efforts, took a deep breath and screamed his name as loud as I could. "Beron!"

My voice tore at my wound.

Sliding onto my side, I braced my weight on my elbow, holding myself up as long as I could. Then my elbow buckled and slipped forward, cracking my temple against the stones.

Suddenly he was there, standing at the doorway. "Citali?" his worried voice cried.

A slow blink.

He was on his knees, cradling my head. My hair was wet and cold now.

His hands were so hot. And strong.

I didn't feel strong anymore. Feeling bled from my fingers and feet, leaching from my arms and legs.

"Look at me. Stay with me," he begged. "Caelum!" he growled.

My vision swam, focusing on his sharp cheekbones and jaw. I thought of Beron's usual smirk. His teasing laugh. Even his frustrated growls. The way he chased me and told me I was a nuisance, spoiled, a ridiculous, petulant girl.

He hated me. But he was here now. He came when I needed him most.

Tears pricked at my eyes. I couldn't hold them back. They slipped onto the floor and on his skin, mixing with my blood.

I knew I wouldn't survive this but needed Noor to know… so she could protect my greatest secret, my greatest weakness. My greatest love. My lips and mouth were as dry as the desert. They were numb and didn't feel like mine, but tingled when I whispered, "Tell Noor…"

He stopped, brought his face closer. "I'm here, Citali. Noor is on the way."

A tear fell from my eyes, trailing down my cheeks. We both knew there was nothing to do for me now. "Tell Noor to take care of him," I pushed out weakly, wincing when a sharp stab of pain rushed through my wound.

"*You* can tell her. Caelum heard me. She'll be here in a second."

"Tell her to take care of him," I slurred.

A loud buzzing filled my ears, but the pain slowly began to release its grip on me.

"Who?"

A shake.

"Who, Citali? Who should Noor take care of? Talk to me."

A vision came to mind of a tiny hand curled around my finger, dark hair and skin that matched mine, so, so soft. Perfect little bowed lips. Toddling steps… He had grown so tall last I saw him. "He's so smart," I tried to say, but my words were slurred and disjointed.

He called me Cit-i. If things had been as they should, he would have called me mother. "My son," I managed. My voice sounded distant, drowned in a deep, dark sea.

Strong fingers stiffened on the back of my neck. "You have a son?"

"Beron?" I breathed, finally focusing on him. We locked eyes. "Protect him."

"I will. By my life and last breath, I swear it. But you must stay with me so you can protect him, too. Who did this, Citali?"

"Zarina…"

Could he hear me through the roar?

Could he see me through the bright white light that appeared as a glimmer but grew and blossomed in its intensity? Did he feel her heat?

*Sol …*

Sol was here for me. My spirit cried. I'd done such wretched things to her daughter, but here she was.

A terrible howl resonated through me, rattling my bones. The sand itself trembled. But it couldn't put out Sol's fire now that she'd kindled me.

# ACKNOWLEDGEMENTS

I'm ever thankful to God for his mercy and blessings in my life. I have to thank my family for their constant encouragement, my friends for their support, and fans for loving my characters and stories as much as I do.

A special thanks to Melissa Stevens for designing the perfect book cover, interior, trailer, tarot card and every other thing related to bringing this book to life visually. You are absolute magic and I adore you and am thankful for your friendship and presence in my life.

Thanks to Stacy Sanford for waving her magic red pen over my manuscript and polishing it until it shines brighter than Sol's sunny aura.

Thanks to Steffani Christensen for illustrating the gorgeous eclipse/dune scene featuring Caelum and Noor, along with our terrible, beautiful Sphinx and sly, handsome Wolven. I love your creativity and working with you is effortless.

Thanks to @NessiArts for illustrating a portrait of our favorite Lumin and Aten. You captured them beautifully and I'm so excited to finally share your work with the world.

Thanks to Cristie Alleman, Stephanie Christensen and Amber Garcia for reading this book before anyone else and helping me make the story better. I appreciate your time and keen eyes.

Thanks to my peers for reading House of Eclipses and providing endorsements. I know time is precious and I appreciate you taking time out of your busy schedules for this story, and for me.

Lastly, thanks to you, the reader. Whether you're a member of the Bondtourage Reader Group, social media stalker – er, follower – or this is your first Bond book, I appreciate you reading the story that bled from my soul.

# ABOUT THE AUTHOR

Casey Bond lives in West Virginia with her husband and their two beautiful daughters. She likes goats and yoga, but hasn't tried goat yoga because the family goat is so big he might break her back. Seriously, he's the size of a pony. Her favorite books are the ones that contain magical worlds and flawed characters she would want to hang out with. Most days of the week, she writes young adult fantasy books, letting her imaginary friends spill onto the blank page.

Casey is the award-winning author of When Wishes Bleed, The Omen of Stones, Things That Should Stay Buried, With Shield and Ink and Bone, Gravebriar, and more. Learn more about her work at www.authorcaseybond.com.

Find her online @authorcaseybond.